The Sounding Brass

The Sounding Brass

by EDYTHE LATHAM

Little, Brown and Company · Boston

LIBRARY OF CONGRESS CATALOG CARD NO. 53-7297

FIRST EDITION

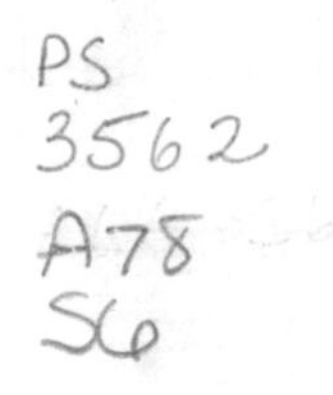

Published simultaneously
in Canada by McClelland and Stewart Limited

PRINTED IN THE UNITED STATES OF AMERICA

This book
is dedicated to the memory
of my father,
John Leslie Latham

Though I speak with the tongues of men and of angels, and have not charity, I am become as sounding brass, or a tinkling cymbal.

I CORINTHIANS, XIII: I

The Sounding Brass

EVEN from the beginning, Newtown was never anything but a city. It did not begin as a clearing, and grow to a village, and then to a town, and at last to a city. It began as a city.

Its streets were never paths through the forest, never wagon trails, never the one cross of clay-packed road before a general store. They were avenues even years before they were paved. For Newtown was something decided upon and carried out.

All through a winter, seven sensible men rode about the county, looking. They were commissioned to buy a town site and begin a city, which would be the county seat, and they considered carefully. Then, on a raw March day, all seven were agreed and of one mind. So they executed a deed and paid ninety-eight dollars cash to a young farmer named Nathan Sorrell for forty-two acres of red frost-bitten land. And even before sundown they had driven stakes, marked off forty lots and sold them all, except for four left clear at the square. There they began their courthouse on the cash taken in.

The lots northeast brought most. The sale of the smallest one paid for the brass angel to adorn the courthouse fountain, the angel to be cast by special order in the North.

So Newtown began as a city and the county seat. It had no past – nothing to live up to and nothing to live down. It went in a miraculously unmolested solitary way through the South's hard years of war. Some were ashamed before their kinsmen from other parts. Others, most, were only thankful that they had to erect no monuments and no memorials; for no battles were ever fought there, no such sacrifices made. Due mourning was done for its absent dead and due comfort given the bereaved; but its outskirt red productive fields never had a cruel spring of sparse uncertain corn, as frail and strange as fringes of grave grass; for in them slept no priceless unmentionable seed. Newtown strained only in the strife of business with the living. Its fallen were numbered there, not among the dead.

In fifty years, Newtown was large and rich. Its quickly spreading limits were a thing of pride to some. But others, a few, were apprehensive; for it was not boundaries which told the story and made Newtown a city. It was something else, something which is the good or evil of any city – the quality and direction of its growth, what it contributes and what it shares. Newtown lay unfriendly among its neighbors, like a cold and gaudy heart on the surface of the plateau, about it rolling belts of forest broken by spans of clay-banked fields. Quakers lived to the south, neat and passive and industrious. And near them, even less a distance from Newtown, on a slope of peaceful valley, were Baptists, busy and fruitful with common things. But neither ever drew any nearer to the city, or tried to. Newtown went alone toward the north and east as it had started that raw March day. And then, just before the century had turned, a strange and powerful man came to Newtown.

The man's name was Marcus Chadley, and in Newtown's mind it was a name synonymous with wealth and enviable success. Mr. Chadley had inherited a small fortune from his English-born father, who, during the War between the States, had secured his dollars by converting them into pounds and banking in Liverpool. In addition to this capital which had been left him early in his life, Mr. Chadley's mind was fortified by calculating shrewdness. At thirty-seven, his holdings had been sufficient to bring him respectful notice in the important financial circles of the state.

Then he suffered his one reversal – the loss of his wife.

Following her death, in those eight years which just preceded his removal to Newtown he was thought to be living in strict privacy and retirement; but he was, instead, developing a coastal pine wasteland into a heavy producer of raw turpentine. In his long period of mourning, he trebled his worth!

Since he was a widower, it was inevitable that his arrival in Newtown would excite obvious hopes in the breasts of Newtown's unmarried ladies. He was of an uncommonly romantic appearance, emphasized by an aloofness imagined to be from grief.

Newtown conspired to make Marcus Chadley its own. It displayed its industries, its assets and potentialities. It endured his cool, appraising, calculating eyes, which examined without respect. And when he made his one offer, it sold – at his figure. For little profit to its old stockholders, Marcus Chadley owned the Bank of Newtown.

Then he bought the mansion Dunmeade and the city knew he had come to stay.

He bought Dunmeade as he had bought the bank. He stood one morning with the agent just inside the high stucco walls which half hid Dunmeade from the street and gazed at the snarled growth of vines matted on the spraddling wings of the house. It was a curious house for that section of the country. It was old, the first mansion in Newtown. It was neglected, but not in any way crumbling or apologetic, perhaps because it was not traditional, not white frame with a veranda and stalklike columns. It was not Southern. It was Spanish. And it was not an inland house. It seemed to belong near the sea, for its rooms were unorthodox and of different levels as if it needed to be against a cliff. Its door was iron lace, and its color was quite Spanish – a pinkish tint in the sandy stucco. In the cold morning sun, the missionlike windows on the second floor had purple shadows from the roof.

The house faced the east. At the back was a low-walled patio where its first master was said to have walked restlessly back and forth, back and forth, over the flag terrace every evening during the hour of sunset. The old folks of Newtown claimed to have heard him from the street, which was separated from the house by a grove of sycamores. Newtown had long since ceased to speculate upon the unknown history of the Spaniard who had been Dunmeade's first mysterious master; but with the sale of his house to Marcus Chadley, some of the old romantic notions about him were revived.

To Newtown's mind, the Sorrells who bought it from the Spaniard had never been proper tenants for Dunmeade. They were too plain. They had neither mystery nor splendor to bring to any residence. Dunmeade required a master proper to it, a man like Marcus Chadley.

"You know, Mr. Chadley," said the agent as they started up the drive, "Dunmeade wasn't really its name. It had a foreign name. But nobody in Newtown can remember what it was. There was a kind of motto up over the doorway too. But old Miss Tessie Sorrell had it taken down right off. She didn't have any use for foreigners. She was the one that named it Dunmeade, after two generals. She's dead now."

Mr. Chadley said nothing to encourage him.

"They say it was built by a Spanish man, but that he only lived in it three years before he sold out to the Sorrells and went away. No one ever knew where he went. He wasn't lacking for money. He had plenty of that. Never worked a day in his life. That is, not while he was in Newtown. Funny thing was his name. Called himself Roland, but couldn't speak a word of English. There's a widow lady here remembers him. Says he was not much more than a boy honestly, and he had a little girl. There was another man living with them who did all the talking in English for them. He was a foreigner too though, and both the men wore silk pants. When Mr. Roland sold out to the Sorrells and left, the other man went with him. But he came back in a few years and settled out here in the county amongst the Quakers."

They were on the wide flags of the front terrace. Their feet clacked against the tiles.

"What is Mr. Sorrell's price?" asked Mr. Chadley. He held

out his hand for the heavy brass key the agent was flipping up and down in his palm.

"Twenty thousand."

Marcus Chadley turned and pitched the full force of his incredulous laughter in the man's face.

"*What* is Mr. Sorrell selling?"

"His family home, Mr. Chadley," snapped the agent. He was angry. His guileless gossiping voice was gone. All his soft Southernism dropped. He was smarting under the laughter.

"That's rather a mark-up for sentiment, isn't it?" The question was soft with the residue of amusement. It was not scornful. It was worse. It was indulgent.

The agent's short teeth were working against his lip. He was bothered with pride and the unexpected necessity of defending something of conspicuous value to Newtown, in fact, of singular value – its only romantic landmark.

"Jefferson Davis found it comfortable and to his taste," he said. It was a mutter more than speech.

"Perhaps because Mr. Sorrell quoted him no price for occupancy, as he is now quoting me. And perhaps because Mr. Davis spent only one night – if that." He walked around the side of the house and looked over the patio, across the weedy garden beyond and through the stiff sycamores hedging it from the street. Then he came back and opened the heavy Spanish door and entered the house, saying:

"I think the story goes that Mr. Davis slept in a boxcar on one of your railroad sidings rather than risk Mr. Sorrell's arrest for harboring a traitor. That was the truth of it, wasn't it? – with all respect to Mr. Sorrell's hospitality."

Inside, the sun through the little grilles in the far door leading to the patio glittered on the spider skeins across the iron banisters of the stair. It lit the growing stain of red along the agent's jaw. It lit the soft purple eyes of Marcus Chadley deep in the bony arches of his brow. Without fabric or ornament or any furnishings to absorb the sound, his whispering voice against the walls was sharp, almost as sharp as his offer.

"Tell Mr. Sorrell that my offer is twelve thousand cash." He was on the stair halfway to the gallery and still moving. The agent stared up at him and did not follow. Mr. Chadley paused and leaned over the delicate black rail.

"And tell Mr. Sorrell," he continued, "that you can't put history up for sale. You can only buy it, a little at a time, with blood."

Then he did what kept Newtown babbling for days, and yet taught no one anything about him.

He removed from his wallet a check which he read slowly while the agent watched below. Then he wound it about the key to the house and pitched it suddenly over the black iron banister. The agent's hands flew up and caught the insulting package.

The check was drawn to the order of Preston Sorrell in the amount of twelve thousand dollars, and it was four days old.

There was a warning to Newtown in the way Marcus Chadley bought the bank and then Dunmeade; but the city did not heed it. Newtown worshiped a cold trader, even a ruthless one. Mr. Chadley had only exploited his advantages, as the city saw it. Too, Newtown believed that it stood to gain by the Chadleys' residence. To Dunmeade would come the known and the rich of the state, the cultured and the sought-after. All who drove through Dunmeade's gates and dined at Marcus Chadley's table would belong to Newtown to woo and exploit; for to Dunmeade they too, the important citizens, would also be invited. And those concerned rejoiced at their foresight in letting him have the bank at his price. They were certain they would be rewarded each night the banquet tapers from Dunmeade's windows broke up the shadows of the sycamores hiding the house from the common street.

In the end, Preston Sorrell was urged to believe that selling his home for a poor price had been something of a stroke. And for cash, too! Dunmeade had stood boarded-up since the decline of 1893, when he had been obliged to move himself and his spinster sister, Lydia, into "rooms" and accept a salaried position in the little Exchange Bank. Meeting his taxes had become an increasing hardship; and, with the years, his hope of ever returning to Dunmeade and keeping it in its proper style vanished.

"It was good riddance," the wise business heads consoled Preston, "and you've established a valuable business relationship. You'll profit later. You'll see. Marcus Chadley's obligated to cut you in, now and then, here and there."

But ambition had deceived the city into seeing Mr. Chadley as it wished to see him, not as he was.

In the year that he came he was forty-five, large, long-boned, and so tall that the habit of leaning to listen had left him with an oddly attractive stoop to his shoulders. It gave a deceiving appeal to his appearance. It made him seem to be forever inclining his head in an attitude of sympathetic patient attention. But in truth he invited no confidences from anyone. He withdrew behind a condescending politeness. He wanted no intruders upon his privacy and he intended to cultivate no friendships.

By one of fate's ironic turns, upon his arrival with his family to take up residence, an incident occurred which Mr. Chadley seized upon to drive into the quick of the city's ambitious heart the angry realization that Dunmeade was not for it, and never would be.

It was near sunset on a chilly Election Day. There was a frost sky, heralding an early winter. All day the Democrats had been busy voting the Republicans out of the county offices. Even before dawn, the farm wagons had been massed about the courthouse and it was not until noon before a thin line of them began drifting back out the country roads to leave the voting boxes free for the Newtown crowd. A Lodge meeting had been taking place in its rooms over the lobby of Briggs Arcade and a knot of members was clustered on the sidewalk when the hack stopped and the Chadleys climbed out and followed Claude, the porter, with their traveling bags into the hotel.

Wilbur Briggs was at the desk – which, everyone said afterward, was certainly a good thing; for Mr. Chadley's suite had been reserved and if only Ralph Dobson, the clerk, had been on duty, he might have been afraid to object to putting up the Chadley Negro. But with Wilbur Briggs there, it had been a different story. Wilbur owned the hotel.

What happened was over so quickly that the Lodge members were still gabbing at the curb when the Chadleys marched back out of the hotel, piled into the hack and drove off. The Chadley Negro carried out their traveling bags instead of Claude, the porter. One of the little boys, the larger of the two, had his arm around his brother and seemed to be helping him. Old Judge Willetts, standing near them waiting for his carriage, reached out and helped to lift the sick-looking child up the high step into the hack. "Up you go, son," he said. The older boy hesitated a moment, took off his cap and said gravely, "Thank you very much, sir." And then he got in behind his brother. Mr. Chadley nodded to Judge Willetts and bowed slightly. It was not a friendly gesture, but the Judge recalled later that Mr. Chadley had had a certain smile about his face. The Chadley Negro put the traveling bags on the rack and then, with everyone on the sidewalk watching, the Chadleys moved about inside to make room for him. He got in and took the sick boy on his lap. The child's face, heavy-eyed and flushed, had been framed by the curtain as they drove away.

Wilbur Briggs's version of the incident was as follows:

Mr. Chadley came to the desk to register, and the other three (his little boys and the Negro) waited by the palms where Claude, the porter, had set the bags.

Wilbur said, "Glad to see you again, Mr. Chadley. There's some mail for you. I took the liberty of holding it instead of sending it over to the bank, since we were expecting you here today."

Mr. Chadley thanked him and took the letters which Ralph Dobson handed him from the pigeonhole. Then he leaned over the register and began to write his name, saying, "I'm afraid we'll be on your hands the better part of the week. Mr. York informs me that our house will not be ready quite as soon as he expected. I hope there won't be any difficulty about our keeping the rooms that long. I notice there's quite a crowd on the streets. Some sort of convention, is it?"

"Oh no," Wilbur replied quickly, "County elections – but most of the voters will get back home tonight." As he answered Mr. Chadley, he read what Mr. Chadley was writing – upside down. "Maybe you mean that bunch just outside the door. They've been to the Lodge meeting upstairs." He read on the register: *Marcus Chadley*, *Fenton Chadley*, *Lesley Chadley*, *Isaiah Craig*. Then he looked up and slowly took in the group waiting by the palms. The Negro had picked up one little boy and was holding him in his arms. He was a tall dignified-looking Negro who returned Wilbur's examining glance with a calm stare.

Wilbur coughed then and Mr. Chadley looked at him inquiringly.

"We don't have accommodations for servants, Mr. Chadley," Wilbur finally managed to say, almost in a whisper; but even so, he saw the Negro man raise his head a little. "I'll be glad to make arrangements for your man down in the colored section." And then, before the strange cold expression in Mr. Chadley's eyes, he had apologized: "It's only a few blocks from here. You see, Mr. Chadley, we have a number of maiden ladies who room and board here permanent and it just wouldn't – well . . ." He raised his hands eloquently as a finish.

Mr. Chadley had turned then and looked at his sons and Isaiah Craig. When he had turned back to Wilbur, the expression in his eyes had changed to one of mingled amusement and scorn.

"Wouldn't it seem reasonable to suppose, Mr. Briggs, that the maiden ladies might consider themselves threatened by the presence of *any* strange gentlemen in their midst – regardless of color?" he asked.

He picked up the pen and slowly crossed out the four names he had written on the register.

"Mr. York will have to make whatever arrangements he can for us at Dunmeade. Good night, Mr. Briggs," he said.

And then he went to where his family waited, and said distinctly, in his curiously high voice, "Mr. Briggs doesn't allow Negroes in his hotel, Isaiah. We'll have to drive out to Dunmeade. Bring the bags. Help Lesley to the hack, Fenton." And he had marshaled them out the door before him.

Wilbur's version of the incident was never contested, for Mr. Chadley never heard it and would not have changed the outline of the facts if he had. The Chadleys had not reached Dunmeade in the hack before the story was being related in Riley's Cigar Store at the south end of Willow Avenue, at the polls in the center of town, and to all who passed by the Lodge members still lingering in front of the Arcade.

Comments and reactions were of a marked sameness. The least Mr. Chadley could have done, folks said, was to explain that there was a particular attachment between his little boys and their colored man. After all, there were a few old-timey darkies in Newtown who had the run of the family – such as the Lyndons' Annie, who got out of place every Christmas when she was tipsy on eggnog. Mr. Chadley could have asked Wilbur, *as a special favor*, to allow his colored man to sleep on a pallet between the little boys' beds and Wilbur would have had something to go on. He could have explained to the maiden ladies and other guests that the Chadleys had the family darky with them and to please help him out by just noticing nothing. But Mr. Chadley hadn't given Wilbur a chance. Mr. Chadley respected that black man just like a white man. He had written for a suite and the suite, it turned out, was to include a room for the Negro. He wasn't interested in having a pallet for him made up on the floor. He was going to make Wilbur *register* him! In the Briggs Arcade!

So the talk went, for quite a time. Everyone was agreed that Wilbur had done the only thing he could have done under the circumstances. Those who were customers of the little Exchange

Bank said so out loud. Those contemplating loans from the Chadley bank allowed that there were two sides to every argument and that Mr. Chadley must have had his good reasons for his attitude.

The old men who spent a lot of time around the courthouse observing human nature said they didn't believe he had any reasons – that is, reasons concerning race and equality. They said there was no point in reading more into the mess than was really there. In their opinion Mr. Chadley was just being contrary. He was riding in the catbird seat and he could afford to act in a shocking fashion. He was that kind of high-handed man. The thing to do, they said, was to ignore the whole business and not let it start talk and trouble amongst the humble colored folks in town.

The old men's advice was good, but unfortunately certain individuals were not inclined to follow it. Gaither Lyndon, the mayor of Newtown, was one.

Gaither had missed the scene at the Briggs Arcade because he had left the Lodge meeting early to get home to his wife, Ada, who was expecting their fourth child and was still vomiting even in her seventh month. Gaither said that, as the mayor of Newtown, he felt he should pay a call at Dunmeade to hear any complaint Mr. Chadley wished to make about the Briggs Arcade incident. His real motive was his curiosity to see the Negro man Mr. Chadley treated as his equal. He did not really expect Mr. Chadley to say anything at all about Wilbur Briggs.

The brothers in the Lodge who had seen Isaiah had described him accurately. Even so, Gaither, who was short and heavy, with a face as florid as the profitable kilns in his brickyard, was startled at the size and presence of the Negro man who bowed slightly and ushered him to the drawing room. Gaither was well-off, according to Newtown's standards. He lived in a sprawling house and prided himself on the abandon with which he allowed Ada to spend his dollars on anything he could sit in or eat from. Yet he became awkward and ill at ease instantly in the atmosphere of formality which pervaded the room, half bare of ornament as it was. He wished for a moment that he had not come, or at least that he had underwritten his own importance by bringing an unimpressive fellow citizen with him. Gaither was a firm believer in elevation by comparison.

He was looking cautiously about, to see where Isaiah had carried his hat and coat, when Mr. Chadley himself arose from the wing chair in which he had been seated with his back to Gaither the whole time and said:

"Good evening, Mr. Lyndon, I hope you won't consider it rude if I have Isaiah return your coat to you. You'll be uncomfortable in here without it, I'm afraid." He reached for a bell cord as he spoke and then continued, "There is no means of heating Dunmeade until Mr. York has finished his repairs. I had expected to spend this interval at the Briggs Arcade." He instructed Isaiah to fetch the coat and then provide them a bottle of port. "Or perhaps Mr. Lyndon would prefer a hard liquor?" he questioned.

Gaither spoke out loudly against the naked walls: "One is as good as another with me." He marched closer to Mr. Chadley. "I had hoped Mrs. Lyndon would be able to call with me this evening," he blurted, as if he had rehearsed it, "but she is indisposed – temporarily. We are expecting. That is, Mrs. Lyndon is expecting." He flushed along his jowls like a strutting schoolboy confessing his first act of manhood.

"Oh?" murmured Mr. Chadley. "Is there a Mrs. Lyndon? I would have reckoned you a bachelor." He examined Gaither's bulk slowly and a smile spread his mouth so that his fine teeth showed. "Yes," he repeated, "I'd have reckoned you a man most properly cut out for a single life."

A little chill went through Gaither. The truth was that Ada had not been at all well during this pregnancy and every other day Gaither had come home to find her in a low-voiced conference with the Reverend Smoote. It had begun to get on his nerves.

"I have three daughters, sir," he said with a lift of his head and an effort to show tremendous pride in the fact. Then, remembering that Mr. Chadley had motherless boys to care for alone, he asked after them. At that moment Isaiah placed the wine and glasses on a great Georgian table stretching along the windows, loaded with small cases and cartons.

"My younger son is ill of the chill in your climate here, I regret to say," Mr. Chadley replied. "Being in unheated rooms has not improved his condition. I hope that I shall not have to fix blame upon anyone for any serious development in his condition."

Gaither could feel the moisture beginning to gather in the creases of his chin. He took the port Mr. Chadley proffered and stood waiting to see what he was to do next, sit down or drink it standing. But Mr. Chadley did not invite him to take a chair.

"To a son," Mr. Chadley said abruptly and held his glass to tip Gaither's at the rim. It was so unexpected a toast that it brought a heat to Gaither's face.

"Thank you, sir, thank you," he muttered and swallowed down half the wine in his agitation. He wanted a son desperately. He loved his daughters, especially Gussie, the eldest, who resembled his departed mother; but a daughter could never be the same as a son. Gaither wanted a son. He sighed and let the wine puddle in his tongue properly and slip down his throat. The threat Mr. Chadley had made concerning his own little boy faded for a moment from his mind. Then he looked at Mr. Chadley. Mr. Chadley's eyes were direct and cold upon him. He was not sipping his wine. He was waiting for Gaither to finish and go. The real meaning of Mr. Chadley's toast came to Gaither! Mr. Chadley had been raising his glass to his *own* son, his son who lay ill upstairs in a cold house.

"I am going into town before I return home," Gaither began nervously, "and I would be pleased to send Dr. Pickett this way to have a look at your boy." He wanted to do something. There had been enough talk about the matter. The time had come to act – or, as Mr. Chadley had suggested, there might be trouble. "Dr. Pickett has a special treatment for colds and such things. He pulled our Gussie through a terrible . . ." But he was not allowed to finish. Mr. Chadley waved off the end of his sentence with an impatient hand.

"I hope that we shall not need a doctor, Mr. Lyndon," he said softly, taking Gaither's glass to replace it by the bottle on the table. He began to walk Gaither toward the foyer and the door. "Isaiah is applying some particular poultice we use in the East for such complaints. I am trying not to think that my son's health has been so threatened by the stupid conduct of a hotelkeeper that he needs the services of a physician." Then he lifted Gaither's hat from a crate in the foyer and finished, "We are indebted to you for your graciousness in calling to inquire after our condition. Good night, Mr. Lyndon." He opened the iron lace door.

As Gaither stumbled down through the untrimmed drive he hoped Lydia Sorrell would be sitting with Ada when he got home so that he could stir her into calling at Dunmeade to help Mr. Chadley tidy up the place and nurse that little boy. Surely Mr. Chadley wouldn't resent good old-fashioned neighborliness. Lord! what a situation Wilbur Briggs had got them into!

When Mr. Chadley had bolted the door after Gaither, he found vellum and a pen to write to the university about a tutor for Fenton and Lesley.

On the gallery, on the way to his bedroom, he paused a moment to look toward his sons' apartment. It was quiet and he could see no light seeping beneath the door. Then, as he was about to go on without disturbing them, the iron handle of the door turned slowly and noiselessly and Isaiah came out.

He was as large as Marcus Chadley, but younger, with a proud gaunt face, a little stern and cold for his race. His eyes were anxious and disturbed. He was carrying a small basin with stained flannel rags wadded in it. A heavy resinous odor came from them.

"That gentleman was the mayor of Newtown, Isaiah," Mr. Chadley said. "Would you have suspected him of being a dignitary?" He smiled and shook his head slightly as if amazed as well as amused by the phenomenon. Then with malice he added, "He's afraid he's about to be father to a fourth daughter. I'm sure he takes up the subject nightly in his prayers to the Almighty."

But the Negro man did not smile. If anything, a certain resentment sobered his features still further at the bold reference to the Almighty. About his whole person was the sobriety of the deeply religious. And in his manner was suggested the text of his life, the tree upon which he was willing that a jealous white world hang him – "There shall be no other Gods before Me."

At this moment he was concerned with a trust his Lord had seen fit to place in his hands and when Mr. Chadley had finished his remarks, Isaiah said to him, "Lesley don't seem to be doing any better, sir. I put the poultice on him most an hour ago. He can't hardly get his breath. Mister Fenton is sittin' with him." Over this strong face there was an incongruous working of the flesh, as if he were about to weep helplessly. "Don't you think we ought to get somebody, Mr. Chadley?"

The two men stood there in the gallery, considering, with the sound of fear in Isaiah's voice still working in the air about them. Then – desperate to take some action, when Mr. Chadley hesitated still – Isaiah said, "You come on down here with me to the kitchen, Mr. Chadley, and get a steam kettle again. Mister Fenton knows how to fume him. Now don't you worry, Mr. Chadley. He's going to get all right. No need in us taking liberties, though. I'll go find us a doctor. Now you come on, Mr. Chadley." And gently he pushed Mr. Chadley back down the stair before him toward the kitchen, and the master of Dunmeade docilely allowed him.

Then, abruptly, before they reached the pantry, Mr. Chadley assumed authority. "That's the thing to do, Isaiah," he said firmly, the air of indecision and vagueness which had been about him gone now. "There's a doctor by the name of Pickett. Bring him back with you." He took the basin of soiled rags from Isaiah and pushed open the door to the kitchen.

"Yes sir, Mr. Chadley," agreed Isaiah, reassured. "Yes, sir. I'll do just that. I won't be gone any time at all."

The Dr. Pickett Isaiah was sent to find was not a doctor. He was a pharmacist. His name was not Pickett. He was a foreigner. But when he had learned to speak English and mix drugs, he had married Lucy Lee Pickett, his employer's daughter, and people who could not pronounce his name had called him "Lucy Lee Pickett's husband." Then he bought into Pickett's Pharmacy, and after ten years of being called "Mr. Pickett" while he ran the business during the real Mr. Pickett's slow drift to death, he found a poultice formula in the safe where the dangerous prescriptions for Dr. Willis Aberdeen's patients had been carefully locked away. He made it up and began selling the mixture over the counter under handwritten labels. He called it PICKETT'S POULTICE MIXTURE FOR ACHING JOINTS AND CHEST COMPLAINTS. He personally described its proper use to each customer and soon his customers became his "patients" and were listening and answering solemnly, "Yes. Yes. I see. Thank you, Doctor. Thank you." And then he got to be called "Dr. Pickett."

Most of Newtown had forgotten now that he wasn't really a doctor. His accent suggested learning. He was large and gentle and he moved heavily, with the dignity of the great dumb beasts. Newtown had great confidence in him. The poultice mixture was selling well, even out in the county where it was in competition with good home remedies. He'd make a fortune one day, Newtown predicted.

And he did – with Marcus Chadley.

Isaiah found him locking up his drugstore. It was still gassily lit-up for so late at night. It was in a good location. It fronted the street beside the Briggs Arcade. Traveling men either arrived with colds or caught them in Newtown. So Dr. Pickett's formula was being carried for him into all the states of the Union, slowly.

Dr. Pickett replied at once that he would be happy to go to

Dunmeade. His manner did not suggest any concern that the boy might have something he could not treat. He did not inquire as to the symptoms of the illness. He finished closing up. Then at the door he stopped. He left Isaiah and went behind the counter. When he returned he had a small jar in his hand and was polishing off the dust which had gathered on its tin top.

As he was setting the lock to leave, there was a knock on the inside door which opened into the hotel lobby. Dr. Pickett listened. When the knock was repeated, he turned up the night lamp which hung over the counter and then he opened the inside door.

Isaiah watched him anxiously. Almost an hour would have passed by the time he returned with the doctor to Dunmeade.

"Good evening, Doc, I was afraid I wouldn't catch you," a woman said and came in under the light. She was a nurse. She handed him a prescription. He read it, nodded, and then went into the pharmacy. The nurse followed him.

Isaiah waited for ten minutes at the door. Then he went to the counter and rapped. He could hear Dr. Pickett and the nurse conversing.

"Begging your pardon, Doctor," he said when they came out, "but Mr. Chadley is waiting."

"I'm awfully sorry," the nurse apologized in a murmur to Dr. Pickett. "I didn't see anyone waiting for you. I came in the front too." Then, directly to Isaiah, she said, "Tell the gentlemen that Dr. Pickett will be right out."

"Mr. Chadley's son is sick. Mr. Chadley sent me to bring the doctor to Dunmeade right away, ma'am," Isaiah explained.

It was not an explanation. It was the announcement of his intention. He looked at Dr. Pickett and insisted with his gaze that they delay no longer.

"I'll come back, Ida," Dr. Pickett said to the nurse reassuringly, "and leave the powders for you at the desk with Ralph Dobson. You'll have them for the morning dose."

"Oh, no," the nurse protested, pushing him a little toward Isaiah, "you can finish making them up tomorrow. I can start them on the afternoon dose." Then suddenly she added, after a glance at Isaiah's face, "Here, let me go with you. Is it something serious?"

"No, no, no, Ida. You go to bed," Dr. Pickett objected. He dimmed the counter light again and started forward, leaving the nurse to let herself out the inside door into the hotel lobby. He seemed confused about something. He fumbled setting the front lock. The nurse remained where she was, watching him, and then, looking down at the counter, saw the jar of poultice mixture he had forgotten. She picked up the jar and followed Dr. Pickett out of the drugstore and gave it to him when they got to Dunmeade.

Fortunately for young Lesley Chadley, Ida Starr was not only a good nurse and conscious of her limitations, she was conscious of the limitations of Dr. Pickett. With no apology, she pushed him aside when she saw Lesley and said sharply to Mr. Chadley, "Your son needed a physician hours ago." At the surprise and instant resentment on Mr. Chadley's face, she lifted her head higher and her accusing gaze did not change. "I am going to send your man for Dr. Langley," she said, "and I hope we will not be too late."

Mr. Chadley made no reply. With neither hostility nor condescension, but only relief at her decisiveness, he watched her order Isaiah. There were times when he felt quite alone, and had about him only the manner of a master, not the means. Such a time was now, with his boy ill and the city strange.

He drew Fenton away from Lesley. "We'll wait downstairs," he said and did not come nearer the bed.

"I'll need the boy with me," objected Miss Starr before they reached the door, "to show me where things are." And then she hurried to relieve the spasm of coughing which racked Lesley.

In all the haste and change, no thought had been given Dr. Pickett, who stood unnoticed by the window, watching wordlessly. But there was no embarrassment evident on his face. A broad layer of peasant humility before authority reinforced the thickness of his skin and saved him many destructive pricks to his feelings. His primary interest in coming to Dunmeade had not been to treat the sick child; therefore, he was content to wait as long as necessary for an opportunity to speak to Mr. Chadley alone. There was an abandoned tobacco prizery just outside the city limits to the south, along the tracks half a mile from the freight station. He needed a little over nine thousand dollars' capital, including what he would have to pay for the first lots of jars and screw-caps, to begin manufacturing Converted, the prizery would be large enough for the first five years of business – and then . . . !

He followed Mr. Chadley out of Lesley's room, down the graceful stair and into the cold drawing room where Dr. Langley would be received. His thick hand was around the small jar in his pocket. He took it out and held it forward on his palm so that the one bit of lamplight would catch on the tin cap. He held it until Mr. Chadley had turned and seen him, until Mr. Chadley's eyes had fallen to the jar. Then he spoke.

If Miss Starr and Fenton had not been so rapt in building up the grate fire in Lesley's room, they would have heard the long accented rumble of Dr. Pickett's voice, and after it the sudden explosion of Mr. Chadley's laughter and his exclamation:

"Lord! What a land I've come to!"

On the following morning, at half past eleven, Lydia Sorrell called at Dunmeade. The one good turn which Gaither Lyndon had done her, since trifling with her affections and then marrying her friend Ada Gudger, was to inform her that there was a place for a woman's sympathetic hand in Mr. Chadley's distraught household. He provided her an excuse to ignore the proprieties and call without the chaperonage of her brother Preston. Lydia did not share her brother Preston's disappointment over the small sum realized from the sale of Dunmeade, for there were reasons for Lydia thinking that her chances of residing once more in her old home were greater with Mr. Chadley its master than with her brother its absentee owner. Lydia was an old maid of thirty — that is, forty — and had been insecure in every phase of her life since the shocking moment when Preston, drunk one New Year's Eve, had said, wagging his finger at her accusingly, "You're an old maid. And I'd better stay a bachelor. Who's going to support you?"

Now had come Lydia's opportunity to remedy her condition. Mr. Chadley was a widower with two small sons — one of ten years and one of eight. He had no female relative to manage his household and be his hostess. Lydia was a settled girl — or rather, woman — of refined tastes and good upbringing and Dunmeade had once been her own home. Her family had had some importance in Newtown even if Preston now was only a small department head in the little Exchange Bank. Her father had owned the ground upon which Newtown had been built. He had sold it to the County Commissioners to found Newtown. There had been a time after her shock at having to move from Dunmeade when Lydia had gone about hysterically saying that Newtown had been built on what had been "practically papa's pigsty!" It seemed to dull her deep frustration to say such a thing. She had said it until Gaither Lyndon heard her repeat it to an actor from the North who was rehearsing with them for *The Fireman's Heart* at the Opera House. Gaither leaned over the footlights and wheezed quite clearly, "That's right, Lydia. It was built on your pa's pigsty — except for the part at the end of the trough he kept to bring you and Preston up in!" And that stopped Lydia.

Marriage to Marcus Chadley was her way of escape from proud poverty, her brother Preston and the stigma of reluctant maidenhood; so giddily Lydia washed her hair in vinegar to bring up the fading red, sat all night drying it in kid curlers and in the morning found her mother's cameo to fasten a ribbon tightly about her neck to bring blood to her pale face. When Preston had left for the bank, she walked to Dunmeade.

But she did not see Mr. Chadley, nor did she so much as enter the foyer.

"Mr. Chadley is not receiving callers this morning, ma'am," Isaiah said to her politely but firmly, blocking the door so that she could not see around him.

"Mayor Lyndon, who called last evening, told me that Mr. Chadley's younger boy is ill of a cold. I'm Miss Sorrell from whom Mr. Chadley bought this house. I thought I might be able to help in some way?" She said it with great appeal.

But Isaiah repeated, "I'm sorry, ma'am, Mr. Chadley is not receiving callers." Then hesitantly, as if he were not certain it was his place to comment, he added, "It was mighty nice of you to come, ma'am. I'll tell Mr. Chadley."

Lydia turned to leave. Then she asked, "Is the little boy very sick? I should like to send you a doctor."

"Well, he's feeling a good deal better today, ma'am. We got Dr. Langley last night. He's going to have him up on his feet in no time, ma'am," Isaiah answered simply.

In a sudden confidence, because she was lonely and had so little in her life to talk about, she said to the strange houseman, "I nursed my mother through her last illness right here in this house. We had Dr. Langley, too." She looked away in a sudden welling of emotion which arose as much from her disappointment at not seeing Mr. Chadley as from the memory of her mother's death. Then, with mustered brightness, she concluded, "You're in good hands," and started down the drive.

"Yes ma'am. Thank you, ma'am," Isaiah murmured, closing the door behind her softly.

When she reached the street, Lydia peeked cautiously from the gates. She wished to leave the grounds unnoticed. If her trip had been successful she would have sallied forth and hoped for a witness. But if she were to call again at Dunmeade, she would have to persuade Preston to take her, and if he learned she had already been turned away, he would refuse.

As it turned out, however, Gaither Lyndon aided her a second time by suggesting to Preston that it would be politic if *he* called on Mr. Chadley to dispel any notion Mr. Chadley might have that Preston was displeased with the sale. So, on Sunday, fortified with a few nips of corn from the fruit jar in his room, Preston escorted Lydia to Dunmeade.

It was a short and unsatisfying visit. And in less than an hour after it, Lydia, having picked at Sunday's cold joint in a fuming rage, had hurried to evening church services, to the ears of *important* Newtown, *female* Newtown – the caretakers, the watchmen of the city, their brothers' keepers. By the time Agnes McQuirter had stood up to sing "Fairest Lord Jesus," word had reached the contralto section of the choir that Marcus Chadley was letting his "independent, highfalutin nigger" look after his orphaned sons while he carried on with the first woman who had crossed his path, namely, Ida Starr! His sick child was sitting up (wrapped warmly in a blanket, of course, but sitting up!) and no trained nurse was needed at Dunmeade on his account. The eldest boy, Fenton, had told Lydia himself that Miss Starr remained only because his father wished it. He had been in the library showing her his departed mother's portrait. The painting still leaned against its crating, unhung, neglected.

"Mr. Aurelio painted it," he had said soberly, standing aside politely out of her light. "Father had him come from Italy."

"She was a beautiful lady, wasn't she?" Lydia had said admiringly and meant it. (Dead beauty constituted no threat.)

"Father says she was. I don't remember her."

And just as they had reached the door and Fenton had put out his arm to help her down the little step to the hall, Ida Starr had passed.

"Good afternoon, Miss Sorrell. Is Lesley all right, Fenton?" She had not waited for Lydia to reply. "We mustn't let him sit up too long."

The boy had looked up, his round grave eyes full of adoration. At the sudden opportunity to serve her, he almost started off and left Lydia standing. "I'll see, Miss Starr. He's in the drawing room with father." And then he had recalled his situation and blushed miserably and Ida Starr had quickly helped him with, "Just see him back to his room when you return. I'm going to give him his beef tea."

She had nodded to Lydia and smiled and gone on.

"Is your brother still so ill?" Lydia had asked even before the nurse was out of sight. "I thought he looked quite well – hardly in need of a trained nurse."

"Oh, he's been up two days," the boy had assured her. "But Father wants Miss Starr to stay until he can go out. She can make him take things better than we can." He had seemed then to be anxious to return to his brother and had looked toward the door, but as they had started into the hall, he had hesitated and then admitted with confusion and childish candor, "Lesley and I want her to stay too."

The mingled rage and despair which had burned through Lydia then had nearly sickened her and the bubble of anger which had swelled in her like a physical thing expanded to include the boy Fenton with his father.

In the drawing room, as they approached it, she could hear Preston saying, "Why, it's been in the last two years, Mr. Chadley, that Lucius Starburg's mills have leaped from a paid-in capital of three hundred thousand to a capital stock of nearly three quarters of a million." And then as she entered the room and the men arose to seat her, Preston concluded, "Mr. Starburg has been a happy and profitable addition to our census. He combines the best of the Jew and the best of the Southerner."

Lydia had turned to Preston in surprise and nodded. He was quite right. Even isolated, in a sense, by her emotion of the moment, she could yet appreciate Preston's brilliance in this unexpected observation. It was the first time she had ever thought of Lucius Starburg so. Suddenly, all her injury accumulated into one pain in her heart. "We have an aristocracy here too, you know, Mr. Chadley," she said and her head drew itself up and up as if it would leave her neck and the tears suppressed in her eyes were like gelatin through which she saw, softened, the oval of Mr. Chadley's fine long head. "We have an aristocracy of achievement."

For an instant, there was a motion in the silence which followed, as if Lydia's pain and pride and defeat were moving like detached parts of her among them.

Then Mr. Chadley said, almost with kindness, ignoring her

remark, "I hope you will do me the honor of presiding at the tea table this afternoon, Miss Sorrell." He paused and seemed to look past her as he finished, "It isn't often we are able to enjoy the spectacle of womanly grace in this household." He smiled thoughtfully and offered her the chair nearest his. For the instant of her walk toward him, she caught at his compliment to ease her. Then the little boys went out to meet Ida Starr at the door and she knew his appeal had not been to her. Isaiah came with the tray and she watched him lay the cloth on the spider-legged table set up beside her and arrange the Worcester service and shift the hot water within her reach. And then, when he had gone, she began mechanically to pour and inquire, first of Preston, then of Mr. Chadley (though she knew Preston's preference well), "What strength? And do you take milk or lemon?" Only at the last, when she had finished her plain cake, and the deep, deep anger was not weakened nor washed out with the ritual of tea and Mr. Chadley's courtesy, was she obliged to ask, insistently, "Was your man brought up in your family's service, Mr. Chadley? He has such a manner." She moved her fingers over the delicate handle of the cup. It was Isaiah who had most meanly used her, cheated her, really. He had declined her aid and said never a word about Ida Starr being in Dunmeade.

"Isaiah?" Mr. Chadley repeated as if faintly surprised and then he laughed gently and answered her in a tender grateful way as if he thanked her for asking him such a question. "Gracious, Miss Sorrell," he said, "I met Isaiah when we were having our yearly trouble with the squatters on my wife's old property off Prince River Inlet." He had a remarkable voice, so soft as to be almost feathery and without edge. "You've never had any experience with squatters, have you, Mr. Sorrell?" he turned to Preston and inquired, not meaning for Preston to answer. "Isaiah petitioned with such persuasion in behalf of the squatters on my property that afterward I offered him a position – to bring up my orphaned sons. Six days a week he labors in the care of our bodies – on the seventh, our souls. He's a minister." He sipped his tea for a moment, looking pensively across the cup rim into space.

Then he concluded quite suddenly, in a sharp, cold voice, "I'd as soon countenance injury to one of my sons as insult to Isaiah, Miss Sorrell."

And the call was ended and with it Lydia's vision of restored station. At the end of the drive, she looked back, searching along the upper missionlike windows, now black, with the sun behind them, and said to Preston, hardly, "Ida Starr is *living* at Dunmeade. I wonder what the Reverend Smoote will say to that!"

Preston did not answer. Instead he began to walk faster. He wanted to get home to his own room where he could shut out Lydia and the Chadleys and everything else that was troublesome in his life. He wanted to get out the fruit jar of corn liquor he kept hooked inside Lydia's dressmaking dummy. He wanted to lie down on his bed and tipple until he was drunk and had escaped them all.

Lydia's tale of the interesting household arrangements at Dunmeade lost a considerable portion of its appeal when Ida Starr took an emergency case of Dr. Langley's the day after the Sorrells' visit. Such a practical move refuted the report of a romance. Too, the men were more interested in Lydia's disclosures about Isaiah than those about Ida Starr. When a man's butler was revealed as his preacher (or his preacher his butler) – and that individual was known to be a Negro – it was news worth giving attention. And for reasons of his own the Reverend Smoote preferred shifting the emphasis of Lydia's complaint to suggest the need for spiritual rather than moral investigation at Dunmeade. Gaither Lyndon had confidentially estimated the size of Mr. Chadley's fortune to him when Gaither was helping him work out the pledge campaign to raise funds to equip the Sunday School room in the new church. It had occurred to the Reverend Smoote then that it would be friendly to invite Mr. Chadley to the special service on the last Sunday of the month when he intended to ask blessings upon the ground they were about to break. However, before he could get out to Dunmeade, he had recalled that Mr. Chadley was of English descent and that his native section had never freed itself of certain influences in faith and custom traceable to the rule of the English governors under the Crown. But then Father Slabcote had said nothing to him about gaining a new lamb in his flock. Lydia Sorrell's shocking recital provided just the necessary excuse to sally forth to Dunmeade, mission-bent and with a clear conscience. Even Mr. Chadley should not be allowed to bring up two innocent little boys like heathens without any interference.

So on the Sunday following the Sorrells' call, a day as chill and bright as a postcard, the Reverend Smoote ate a good breakfast of scrambled brains, put on his new heavy frock, and drove sedately to Dunmeade.

He found Mr. Chadley eating his Sunday breakfast too – fried country ham and popovers, split open and bobbing about in a deep dish of red gravy.

"I don't believe you have honored any pulpit in Newtown, have you, Mr. Chadley?" the Reverend Smoote inquired immediately, a certain residue of his old caution evident in the tone of his nasal whinny.

"I was not aware that my presence would have been considered an honor, Mr. Smoote," Mr. Chadley said, leisurely finishing the last square of ham on his plate. "Or should I address you as *Dr.* Smoote?"

The veins speckling the clergyman's jowls enlarged conspicuously. "*Mr.* is correct," he confessed, so inaudibly as for it to seem only a whishing sound of breath obstructed by his teeth.

"My wife's father was a bishop – Bishop Francis Prince Wortham," said Mr. Chadley, looking over the table. There was a dish of persimmons on the far side. "Will you bring a small plate for Mr. Smoote, Isaiah? I think he'd enjoy a persimmon," he ordered, and then he faced the minister and continued mildly: "The fruit is from the property my wife inherited from the bishop. It's the first of the season. My son Fenton is very fond of persimmons." He watched Isaiah serve the preacher; then he asked, "Perhaps you knew Bishop Wortham, Mr. Smoote?" – and smiled a strangely knowing smile. "He enjoyed a rather widespread reputation."

The Reverend Smoote put a persimmon between his teeth. At that moment a mighty indignation worked in him toward Father Slabcote for his treachery. While he chewed, he nervously dabbed at the sticky pulp on his fat fingers. "I regret to say that I never had the honor of meeting Bishop Wortham, though not for the reason of denominational differences," he murmured, removing a seed from his mouth. "He met his heroic end before I had had the opportunity. But there is hardly a minister in this region who has not used as a text Bishop Wortham's heroism and trusting faith in the Almighty to deliver him safely from the rising floods if such was the will of God." He looked heavenward as he finished, and escaped observing Mr. Chadley's glance of mingled incredulity and amusement.

"I'm afraid, Mr. Smoote, that I can hardly accept that compliment to Bishop Wortham's memory," Mr. Chadley said. "As he drowned, with that unfortunate child dragging him under, his cries heard on shore were clearly for Knute Ransun." He sighed slightly as if he regretted the obligation to make such a disclosure. "Knute Ransun was a man of trusted strength if not of trusted character. About the Inlet he had gained quite a reputation for bringing in shipwrecks. In his youth he followed the profession of Mr. Teach, the pirate." Mr. Chadley rose then from the table. "And I'm afraid I may have misled you regarding our church affiliation – with this conversation about the bishop, Mr. Smoote. We are not members of any church." He smiled in a generous, patronizing way, as if he were conscious of being engaged in a serious but futile conversation with the local idiot. Then he said to Isaiah, suddenly, interrupting his own discourse, "Will you have Fenton and Lesley come immediately to the library, Isaiah?" And when he had escorted the minister to that room, he continued, "I hope I haven't frightened you, Mr. Smoote. You do not find yourself among infidels, as you may be supposing at this moment. Wasn't it the Sermon on the Mount – 'And when thou prayest, thou shalt not be as the hypocrites are; for they love to pray standing in the synagogues and in the corners of the streets, that they may be seen of men'? My sons' religious education is carefully minded. It is simply that we hold our spiritual discussions in the natural privacy of our home."

Mr. Smoote looked at the bracket clock over Mr. Chadley's desk, a deep and saddening rage working in him and his mind searching wildly for a Biblical memory-verse which would assure him that the insolent as well as the evildoers would be punished on The Day. The clock hands stood at ten. It was time for him to go.

"I suppose that it is futile for me to invite you to stay for services with us, Mr. Smoote," Mr. Chadley said, in a tone of earnest regret. And then, as if to persuade the minister, he added, "It would be a rich religious experience. Our servant, Isaiah, is going to relate the trying of Job this morning." He appealed to Mr. Smoote with a half-hopeful gaze. "Isaiah is peculiarly fitted to relate this Old Testament story, I think. Have you ever heard a Negro describe the struggle of Job's spirit to endure, without blame?"

Mr. Smoote squeezed his face into an expression of great forbearing before the temptation to make a devastating retort and muttered mildly instead, "I don't believe I have, now that you question me." And he looked again at the clock hands and then at the door just as the two boys stood in the frame.

"These are my sons, Fenton and Lesley," said Mr. Chadley. He motioned them to enter and went on, "I have been telling Mr. Smoote about our lesson for this morning. Mr. Smoote is a minister, too." He smiled nicely and waited until the minister had acknowledged the identification with a nod. "Mr. Smoote is building a new church which will cost half a million dollars when it is done. He has a great deal of business to conduct from his pulpit and won't be able to stay for services with us. We are disappointed. Aren't we?" He made a gesture toward Fenton who answered promptly, "Yes sir, we are," and then dutifully came forward to shake hands in farewell and push Lesley toward the minister also.

Mr. Chadley walked his visitor to the drive. Then, when the Reverend Smoote had entwined his fingers firmly in the reins and was ready to flick the whip to his horse and bolt from the grounds at last, Mr. Chadley declared directly, "I have never believed that church attendance would underwrite any insurance against the triumph of evil in the human heart, Mr. Smoote. I intend to persuade my sons toward no creed or doctrine. I will tell them each Sunday what one of the great thinkers has had to say about Good and Evil, and I will allow our servant, Isaiah, to entertain them with a Bible story and teach them a hymn or two. But their petitions and apostrophes to God will be made privately and silently within themselves. Good day, Mr. Smoote."

So Mr. Chadley declared himself, and his life in Newtown was begun. In the first day he went down to his bank, he called for the file of his depositors and quickly went through the index until he came to the name LUCIUS STARBURG. Then he rang for his office boy.

"What is your name?" he asked.

"Estes," the young man said carefully, as if to make Mr. Chadley hear even the spelling of it, "William Estes, sir."

Mr. Chadley observed him with interest.

"Have you been in the bank long, Estes?"

"No, sir," was the direct reply, accompanied by an equally direct gaze. "I'm due for first promotion next month, sir."

Mr. Chadley nodded. Then, after a silence, he said, very seriously without a trace of mockery in his voice, "Do you think you could still manage errands for me until next month? I'd be very grateful."

"Oh, yes sir," replied Estes, "I'm sure I could, sir."

"Thank you," said Mr. Chadley. Then he moved his finger down the index of accounts on his desk and asked, "Do you know Mr. Lucius Starburg by sight?"

Estes nodded and discreetly moved closer to the desk. With this question he had subtly taken on the air of a confidential agent about to be given confidential orders.

"I want you to notify me when he comes into the bank next," said Mr. Chadley.

"Yes, sir," Estes murmured. Then he hesitated, stepped back from Mr. Chadley and said suddenly with an expression of complete approval and satisfaction on his face, "He has the biggest account we carry, sir."

Mr. Chadley smiled. "Yes, Mr. Estes. But we mustn't let that blind us to the possibility of engaging in further business with Mr. Starburg. Must we?"

"No sir," said Estes, more in a whisper of wonder than in speech. He backed out of Mr. Chadley's presence then, nodding his head up and down, up and down, as he contemplated what had been said to him and felt the power of the man who had said it.

At noon, Estes returned to tap on Mr. Chadley's door. "Mr. Starburg is being admitted below," he said, with his brows raised. He meant that Mr. Starburg was going into that department of the bank which guarded important private papers of its customers.

Mr. Chadley nodded. Then when Estes was gone, he looked carefully at his nails and then at the rose in his lapel. It was the Chadley rose, his own, for whose cultivation York and Amos had built a special greenhouse at Dunmeade. He adjusted the stem. Then he stood up and found his reflection in the windows looking on Willow Avenue. Satisfied, he walked to his door. Estes, across the corridor, nodded suggestively, as if to say, "That's him," and Mr. Chadley looked at the man approaching. He was fair with the fine delicate facial bones and bright coloring of a Biblical print. He was the only Jew in Newtown. Mr. Chadley stepped out to meet him and smiled.

"How do you do, Mr. Starburg," he said cordially. "My name is Chadley – Marcus Chadley. Won't you come in?" And he stood aside to invite Mr. Starburg to pass before him into his office.

Lucius Starburg was as secure in his world as Marcus Chadley, and as wise in his appraisal of his relationship to all other men. He had made for himself a decent place and he lived a good life. He had no quarrels and no festering envies to cripple him. He had married Margaret Willetts, a gentile, and the daughter of a free-thinking judge. Margaret was a church member, so Lucius had allowed himself to be baptized and taken into the church to please her. The Starburgs had three children, who passed usually for Christian. But it would not have mattered to Lucius whether they had or not. He was a highly civilized man; he ignored his Christianity just as he ignored his Judaism. And he had been in Newtown long enough to know that there were no Jews and non-Jews, no Christians and non-Christians – only rich and not-rich.

"I understand you were put to some discomfort on your arrival in Newtown, Mr. Chadley," he said candidly, looking across Mr. Chadley's desk. He was referring to the Briggs Arcade incident – and there was a certain admiration in the arch smile he gave his host. "I'm sorry Mrs. Starburg and I didn't know about it. We would have been honored to have opened our house to you and your family – all of it."

"Thank you, Mr. Starburg. I would have accepted," replied Mr. Chadley with equal candor. Then he added, "I suppose it's Mr. Briggs's privilege to determine what lodgers he shall have, and even what they shall bring into his hotel in the way of luggage."

Mr. Starburg nodded appreciatively. Then he said dryly, "My wife writes the management in advance when I travel – to spare the innkeepers possible embarrassment when I arrive." For a moment, there was a quiver in the sensitive Semitic nostrils. Then he finished, "I'm afraid strangers do not recognize my church affiliation here."

There was a silence. And then the talk suddenly went to marketing and stocks. At last Mr. Chadley said, "I hope it is neither premature nor inappropriate to suggest that I would be interested in discussing the financing of a bleaching and dyeing works with you, Mr. Starburg. I am interested in the manufacturing of cotton cloth and I have observed the singular advance of your mills. It seems to me you would profit by keeping your goods here for final processing, instead of shipping North."

Mr. Starburg smiled and stood up, "Your interest is neither premature nor inappropriate, Mr. Chadley," he said. "I would have called upon you soon in this office, even had you not invited me in today."

So the century turned and Newtown swelled and grew more golden. Mr. Starburg put up a bleaching and dyeing works to color his own cloth and stopped sending it North. Marcus Chadley was his silent partner. Mr. Briggs built a new hotel a block from the station to catch the salesmen going deeper and deeper into the South on the patent-medicine routes. Marcus Chadley made the loan. Dr. Pickett retired from his "counter practice" and took in Preston Sorrell as a manager and set up his poultice factory in the abandoned tobacco prizery. Marcus Chadley financed him. Gaither Lyndon added another big furnace to the yards and named it after his wife, who had died giving birth to his fourth daughter. In the spring, he was voted out of office and Charles Willetts, Margaret Starburg's brother, became mayor of Newtown on a skimpy majority. But he was quickly reduced to civic impotency for advancing a plan for a Citizens' Savings Bank in which depositors' accounts would be credited with any and all profits.

Often Mr. Chadley drew the blinds to his office and watched the silent electric busses going up and down Willow Avenue and estimated that Newtown would extend another twenty blocks north and east because of them. The city had a swollen feeling, like a heavy plant about to bud from a burst in the stalk. He was standing at the window the afternoon the Gilliam brothers fell from the scaffold over the new Ionic front of the courthouse. Their bodies hit the watering trough and Hazel's – he was the young dark one – was torn almost in half by the pump.

The whole spring was full of hammering. York and Amos

began on their contract to build a public grade school on the corner of Henderson Street and Custer Avenue, far out, on the west end of Newtown. And on a rise to the north, on upper Willow Avenue, with Hampton Park swirling out in wooded pockets around it, the Reverend Smoote's flock got on with their cathedral. It was nearly a block in size and its towers and turrets were higher than any building in Newtown. Everyone in the county had come at one time or another on a Sunday afternoon to gape or frown or sniggle at it. It would have cost close to half a million, but Gaither Lyndon sold the church members the brick at half price in memory of his dead wife.

And there was other building going on, and other structures were rising. On the outskirts of Newtown, parallel to Mr. Starburg's mills, near enough for the scent of the honeysuckle high on his fences to wave across it, was the dirt campus of the Negro college. Late in May it was filled for a day and night with wagons and buggies and long tables of country food. Crowds had come to welcome a thickset, gentle-voiced man with dreamy opaque eyes, the first Negro president of the college – Walter Craven Henshaw. Isaiah heard him speak and wrote down some of what he said.

On a Sunday morning before their service, he read it to Marcus Chadley:

"Now we are lawful citizens, with rights. We have the right to be paid for our daily labor, for the sweat of our brow. We have the right to make our labor profitable, to improve ourselves. We have the right to own a house and to inherit a house if it is willed to us. We have the right to go to school and be taught, and to send our children to school. We have the right to do for ourselves whatever we can, so long as it does not harm anyone else on this free land which protects us and gives us these rights."

When he had finished, Mr. Chadley reached over his desk to the five books he kept there.

"At the same time that traders were bringing Negroes to America and selling them into slavery, Isaiah, there was a man in England writing those thoughts which inspired Henshaw's speech," he said. "He was writing about white men who were slaves in their own country. And yet he opposed them when they arose to violently overthrow the tyranny which enslaved them."

He wrote Isaiah's name above his own on the flyleaf of the book. It was bound in leather and the title was pressed in gold: *Reflections on the French Revolution*, by Edmund Burke.

Isaiah held it in his hands a moment looking at it. Then he put it back on the desk where it had been.

"I'll leave it here so we can all read it," he said.

The lives of Fenton and Lesley Chadley began to be shaped into a pattern by that spring. A kind of sober, tender paternity toward his brother developed in Fenton, for Lesley had a curious frailty about him which disturbed the older boy. Lesley often sat in the patio, watching the shadows in the grove between him and the street, his strangely large fingers moving sensuously about the objects near him, feeling them as if he were able to see them better that way.

With their father, the boys were formal and kindly, seeming to understand that he was unable to furnish them any proper companionship. In the evening, after dining, the three sat in the library, while Mr. Chadley had his smoke and discussed business at the bank. Lesley only half listened, but Fenton was obediently attentive and expressed a kind of literal curiosity about money which obviously impressed his father. He was not afraid to ask questions, over and over if necessary, when he did not understand a reference to a transaction. He did it with a peculiar aggressiveness, as if it were his father who was at fault for having been unclear. Mr. Chadley liked him for it. But with Lesley — well, Lesley's quiet lack of interest in family discussions irritated him unreasonably. Mr. Chadley even courted impudence from him on occasion, so that he might reprimand him and relieve his odd but unmistakable animosity toward the boy.

Dunmeade was a curiously proper asylum for such a man as Marcus Chadley. Its isolation was not peaceful. It was a house full of unfinished struggles and secrets. Built to harbor a mysterious exile, its very foreignness of dark beams and iron lace put a suggestive forlornness about it. It was a dangerous and romantic place for brooding imaginative natures. It seemed at times to belong nowhere in the world and to owe responsibility for the acts within its confines to no authority. It wore a deceitful façade of calm retiring elegance which Marcus Chadley wore himself. As the first years passed in Newtown and Mr. Chadley lived removed from the city, connected with its life only in the conduct of business, he seemed more and more to resemble those certain other Southerners — last survivors of a romantic and graceful generation bred from the root of a culture frail even in its prime. Near-destroyed by war and soon to become mythical, they bled out the juice of their spirits in compromise — trading and bartering and assaulting their decent natures daily in the vulgar market places until at last the decent and unconquerable in them revolted and without warning they turned inward into the deep reaches of their own minds, or else escaped to die in the passed-up sleeping towns or moldering manors hidden behind squatters' swamps. They were of a kind, almost a race alone and fast dying, who were dreamers even with the stones of cities in their hands, and who at length sought out the dreamy places to dwell; who took their Homers and Livys and Henry Clays and Gradys and were gone.

But Marcus Chadley was not as these men truly. He would never put away worldly things. There was neither gentleness nor forgiveness nor humility in him.

Behind its façade of elegance and peaceful retirement, a conflict began at Dunmeade — a conflict which changed all the lives there.

As they grew older, Lesley and Fenton became even less alike than they had been as children. The difference between them lay deep in the internal springs of their natures.

Lesley was physically demonstrative, when he chose to be. He expressed affection for Isaiah openly, scuffling about in the kitchen and pantry with him and stealing things meant to be served Mr. Chadley at table. He was self-expressive in an almost militant fashion. He was interested only in activities prompted by his own imagination and would never join Fenton in a game only to please Fenton. Either he played at what excited him, or he went alone to a place he liked in the patio where he could sit and dream in the sun.

Fenton was quite dignified and restrained. He had a kind of nervous watchfulness about his expression as if he were expecting something serious and troubling to happen. He seemed to be hampered by an anxiety, so that he could not freely throw himself into any game. He reacted keenly to his father's evident resentment of Lesley's indifference to family interests; when the three were together, Fenton was more self-conscious and formal than he was at any other time. From the touching and tender paternity he had shown toward Lesley when they were small, he developed a protector's attitude. This guardianship was made conspicuous by the fact that their physical appearances belied the necessity of such a relationship. Fenton was short and thick-chested, whereas Lesley was large and tall with the masterful figure of Marcus Chadley.

Lesley understood Fenton's air of guardianship and accepted it. He thought that it was Fenton's way of indicating that he was next in line, regardless of size. He respected Fenton for keeping them all mindful of his place, and saw nothing but a proper development (which had nothing to do with him) in Fenton's beginning to go with Mr. Chadley to the bank occasionally. He did not even notice his father's annoyance that he did not also accompany them. He did not observe the additional curiosity and enthusiasm Fenton showed about business matters to overcome his absence and appease Mr. Chadley. He would not have altered his behavior even if he had seen Fenton's effort.

Fenton's going to the bank also made a good impression on the older men of Newtown. Fenton had a good memory and he remembered names and spoke first without waiting to be spoken to because he was Marcus Chadley's son. He was tactful and respectful. He always had questions to ask the older men, serious and worth-while questions, and he stood looking gratefully into their faces while they explained to him the workings of the poultice business or the sewer-pipe business. Lucius Starburg and Dr. Pickett grew quite fond of Fenton and when they would inquire about him and compliment him, Mr. Chadley would color slightly with pleasure and toss off the praise with some slightly disparaging comment upon Fenton's literal-mindedness.

So, even before they were out of their teens, the lines of their lives were laid down. It was not difficult to see who would be running the Chadley Bank one day. It was difficult to see certain other things at Dunmeade, but not that.

From their first winter in Newtown, Fenton and Lesley had a tutor who lived with them at Dunmeade, except for two months each summer when he returned to the university for his own study. He was a special tutor. During his ten years at Dunmeade he completed work for his doctorate and published regularly in the philosophy journals. His name was Hanley, and he was a mentally energetic man whose reasoning, unfortunately, was not as judicious when he considered present and immediate matters as when he vigorously analyzed in retrospection. This, along with other admirable liabilities he possessed – honesty and good intention – proved his undoing. From the first Sunday when Hanley observed the family service at Dunmeade and heard Isaiah relate the Biblical story of Joseph and then Mr. Chadley devilishly contrast Joseph the redeemer with Joseph the opportunist, Hanley was fascinated by Marcus Chadley. He came to the erroneous conclusion that Mr. Chadley treated Isaiah as he did out of a deep philosophic conviction concerning the dignity of man. Mr. Chadley's increasing domination of Newtown's commercial trading fascinated and awed him. He grew used to the luxury and comfort of life with him; and the hour of dinner and the hour after, when he sat with Mr. Chadley on the patio, or in the library, and argued ethics, or the philosophy of religion, or anything else Mr. Chadley wished, were moments of intense enjoyment for him. He wrote of them to one of his colleagues at the university and when he went for his summer study the two would speculate endlessly upon the enigma that was Marcus Chadley.

As for Mr. Chadley, he was interested in Professor Hanley only as a teacher. He had engaged him to teach his sons in a certain way, to help them obtain a certain education. Literacy did not mean the ability to read and write. He knew the sort of learning and acquaintance with the records of other men's thought that true freedom of the mind requires. Professor Hanley's energy was in his teaching. His zest for the classics made them of the moment and exciting to boyish minds which otherwise might have been distracted by the motion of the vigorous immediate world about them. So Mr. Chadley was satisfied with the professor and they got on. However, close as was his relationship to Marcus Chadley's sons, and equipped as he was to comment upon their needs and leanings, Hanley's advice on matters concerning their personal lives was never invited.

As the boys grew older, Hanley might have become the friend and confidant of one of them – of Fenton, most likely. But he made a blunder which ended that possibility, instantly and finally.

One noon, coming from his apartment, he saw Fenton enter his father's little morning room, leaving the door ajar. Fenton seemed in some haste and had apparently been sent there on an errand. Hanley hurried to meet him before he came out. He had never seen the inside of the room and he was curious. The room was not shut off; but, somewhat pointedly, he had never been invited into it. Its door was always closed. Now he stood boldly looking in. Fenton was leaning over the raised top of a glass curio cabinet, carefully lifting out a tray of enameled boxes to reach a display of porcelain figures. Until Fenton straightened up and turned around, Hanley could examine the room before him. And he did, wide-eyed.

There was no trace of its ever having been Spanish. The interior architecture had been altered and the ceiling brought lower. The mantel was classic Adam. The furniture seemed almost miniature, it was so graceful. A matching pair of settees, upholstered in a dainty-patterned brocade, stood on finely turned cabriole legs. It seemed impossible to Hanley that they could support a man's weight. Suddenly, he became conscious of the unusual fact of the room. It was not a man's, it was a woman's. And its mantel and delicate pieces had once been together somewhere else. The curtains of biscuit-colored silk were not new. Closer (for Hanley had unconsciously stepped forward), he could see their faded hems. Losing all caution, he moved to examine the sharp fine details of carving which decorated the mantel.

And then, with a start, he looked up into the eyes of the woman to whom, he knew, this place belonged! She stared out at him from the gilded frame of her portrait above. Hanley stood there, entranced, looking into the painted face. It was the beautiful woman of the formal Aurelio portrait which hung in the drawing room. It was Mrs. Chadley. But here she was not the same. This portrait was not the likeness of a face, of a figure, of a person. It was the likeness of a spirit, a turbulent, defiant, disturbed and bitterly unhappy spirit. Either the artist had known her intimately, or not at all. If his portrait revealed the true nature of the woman, then this room could not possibly have been of her taste! Hanley moved closer to the painting and searched for the artist's signature. He was excited. The painting would have excited anyone who saw it.

But there was no name anywhere on the canvas.

"My father is waiting for me in the library, Professor, if you've finished," Fenton said quietly from behind him.

Startled, Hanley turned around. He had forgotten Fenton. The boy was standing at the door, waiting for the professor to pass before him into the hall. His face was completely disapproving. For an instant Hanley was about to comment upon the beauty of the room; but Fenton's expression forbade his even offering an apology. By his unseemly intrusion into Mr. Chadley's most private room, Hanley thus lost whatever chances he had had to develop a friendship with Fenton.

Hanley walked with him down the stair and to the library, where Lesley and Mr. Chadley were talking. Whatever the conversation, it stopped when he appeared in the door. But in the instant he nodded to Mr. Chadley, he saw Lesley's face as he looked up from the chair he lounged in near the grate, and Hanley saw it as he had never seen it before. Though Lesley's features and tall figure strikingly resembled his father's, his face at that moment was the face of the woman in the portrait upstairs. It had the same brooding, volatile, charged expression of a spirit driven counter to its needs.

The portrait upstairs was the true likeness of Mrs. Chadley, Hanley knew, as he escaped from the house. And an odd little shiver went through him as he realized it.

It was a strange household, five men together alone.

Then one day Marcus Chadley went to the kitchen to call on Isaiah. Isaiah was boning a chicken for Sunday's cold supper and Mr. Chadley took a seat at the kitchen table.

"Isaiah," he said, "there are too many men at Dunmeade."

Isaiah did not look up from his delicate operation. It required all his attention.

"I have come to persuade you to do a little serious courting, Isaiah," Mr. Chadley went on. "I have decided that it is too much on you to do all the housekeeping. I have given the matter serious thought, and I am agreeable to remodeling the summerhouse to accommodate you and a wife."

At that Isaiah looked up and the little boning knife slid out of his hands on the floor. There was a solemn sheepish look on his face.

"Mr. Chadley, have you got anyone in mind, sir?" he asked.

"Yes," answered Mr. Chadley seriously, "since you ask me, I

have. I was thinking that Maude Tackett, whose sister cooks for Mr. Starburg, might be as good a selection as any."

He waited for some reaction from Isaiah. But Isaiah suddenly turned in a fidgety fashion and went off to the ice box with the chicken. When he came back, he was completely impassive.

"Thank you, sir," he said. "I'll try to oblige you, sir."

At the pantry door, Mr. Chadley turned around and said, "If I may make a suggestion, Isaiah, it might be wise if you turned up in the carriage. It's never harmed a man to put up a good outside front; it forestalls a lot of talking and persuading." He paused and looked straight at Isaiah. "However," he continued, "I have complete confidence in your oratory. I was just mindful that we ought to get it done and over before the cold weather sets in. It's October now."

"That's right," agreed Isaiah seriously.

In the drawing room, Mr. Chadley carefully closed the doors and faced Lucius Starburg, who until then had been peeping out the window giving on the kitchen wing. He had not come to stay long; he still held his hat and cane.

"Well?" he asked and then at the ludicrousness of their positions, they laughed aloud.

"I think we'll see action," said Mr. Chadley.

"That's encouraging," Mr. Starburg nodded. "Maude says that Isaiah is 'the fastest talker on the fancy-talk and the slowest talker on the preacher-talk' of any man she's ever seen. Maude is discouraged."

"Maude is a little harsh in that comment," Mr. Chadley said, smiling. His tone suggested that there was some explanation for Isaiah's reluctance to marry; but he did not say anything further, and soon Mr. Starburg, having succeeded in the purpose of his call, left.

When Mr. Chadley left him in the kitchen, Isaiah stood for a long time in the middle of the floor staring at the pantry door through which Mr. Chadley had disappeared. He had got used to the idea of never marrying. He meant to keep his promise, his bargain with Mr. Chadley. He had told Mr. Chadley he would raise his boys and take care of all of them until Fenton and Lesley were grown. And he had intended to keep his word. He had never told Maude Tackett of his bond. He had not wanted her to have any feeling against Mr. Chadley. But now he was free. He was going to have a family.

He went out and sat down on the kitchen step. He had to get himself together. It was time for him to take some sweets and coffee up to the professor's room. Lesley would be getting hungry, too, in a little while. Isaiah sat there staring at the hedges. The leaves were fading. Then he looked up and saw Mr. Starburg easing stealthily around the drive to the street. At first he only watched, without wondering why Mr. Starburg had not driven to the door, properly. Then he straightened up. The truth came to him slowly. Mr. Chadley had already made the arrangements; he simply hadn't wanted him to know.

Folks don't know Mr. Chadley, Isaiah thought, compassionately. Mr. Chadley is just as kindhearted as he can be. He's got the real religion. He's not ever going to be sorry for all he's done for me.

In a month Maude Craig, née Maude Tackett, moved to Dunmeade to the little summerhouse. And Lesley had a new place to lie dreaming, stretched by Maude's stove, studying her dark face as she mended his socks and hand-tucked his shirts. Quickly he adjusted to Isaiah's absence from the little room next to his own where for years he had whispered to him through the wall at night.

Lesley was growing – not only in his body but in his mind and senses, where a subtle and particular development was beginning, a development of which no one at Dunmeade was aware for quite a time, for its only obvious symptom was a preoccupation not unlike his usual inattentiveness and indifference to family concerns. For hour upon hour he sat in one place examining with a kind of special curiosity and satisfaction the quiet and changing world of forms about him – the vertical curls of dying leaves suspended from their bars of twig or the low exact triangle of an eave across the tip point of a cedar tree. With his study of these sights and shapes, and others more complex, he was inordinately engrossed.

And then, suddenly, Mr. Chadley noticed Lesley's new and pronounced preoccupation, and perceived the distinction between it and his previous self-immersion!

One evening, descending the stair, Fenton turned to address Mr. Hanley beside him, and caught sight of his father standing silently below in the drawing room door, gazing toward the gallery with a strange concentration. Mr. Chadley's eyes were on Lesley, who followed behind, and the thing which showed in them so startled Fenton that he left off speaking and stared down at his father until Mr. Hanley turned too and followed his gaze. But by then there was no one there. Mr. Chadley had stepped back into the drawing room.

Later at dinner, Hanley and Mr. Chadley were discussing money and its effectiveness or ineffectiveness as a medium of exchange. Hanley remarked, "Decidedly aesthetic natures, as well as ascetics who 'put away worldly things,' are often entirely indifferent to the value of money. With them, money has no buying power."

"Perhaps it has no buying power," Mr. Chadley observed, sharply, "because the aesthetic nature has nothing to sell – for money." Hanley was about to laugh, when he looked up and saw Mr. Chadley's face. It was full of emotion.

Neither Lesley nor Fenton had been listening and for that reason Mr. Chadley's sudden attack upon Lesley alone was all the more noticeable. "Lesley would understand that, if he were listening. Lesley hasn't much use for money, Mr. Hanley. . . ." By then the boy was looking at his father with a mixture of surprise and curiously mature composure.

"I don't know yet whether Lesley can be classed as ascetic or aesthetic – but I wouldn't trust him to run the bank a month. We'd be bankrupt." He was not laughing when he said it; but when he looked at Hanley, he caught himself, smiled suddenly, and commented on Fenton. "There's our literal businessman, Mr. Hanley," he said, approvingly. "No imagination at all – which is probably fortunate for him. Wouldn't you say?" And his eyes opened innocently as he asked Hanley, as if what he had said had had the most obvious meaning.

Hanley answered briskly, "I most certainly would." He would have agreed with anything Mr. Chadley had said; he was anxious to get away from the table. For the first time since he had been at Dunmeade his first real knowledge of Marcus Chadley was beginning to etch out in his mind. He begged off cigars and coffee and went to his room.

I don't know why it should have such an effect upon me, he thought, except that I have never before seen Mr. Chadley lose his equanimity. There was no provocation for his attack upon Lesley – and that is what it was, an attack!

Hanley was frightened by what he had seen, and he could not stop reviewing the scene in his mind. Sometime in the night he awoke suddenly as if from disturbing dreams, though he could recollect no exact dream images. He lay in his bed, listening, as if he expected to hear strange movements or sounds in the quiet house.

I am acting like a romantic idiot, he accused himself. Then with deliberate effort he turned on his face and smothered with that physical gesture any further temptation to speculate again upon the meaning of what had happened at dinner.

But when morning came, insight and a surprising resolution in his own mind came with it.

I am going to help Lesley Chadley to preserve whatever it is in him that his father so fears, he determined. Working behind that resolve was the understanding, at last grounded in a conclusion, that Marcus Chadley desired to destroy his own son!

On his way to the dining room for breakfast, he passed the closed door of Mr. Chadley's morning room. He was conscious of taking more rapid steps to get beyond it. Since the day of his intrusion and discovery of the mysterious portrait of Mrs. Chadley, he had never been free of a discomforting and yet undefinable feeling about that private place. Now, he saw again in his memory the beautiful face and again he asked himself the question he had asked over and over since that day: I wonder why there is such a final silence about her?

There was someone else in Dunmeade who slept fitfully and was disturbed by his speculations after that strange conversation between Hanley and Mr. Chadley. It was Fenton.

Soon after breakfast, when Isaiah was busy polishing plate, the boy went to the kitchen.

"Do you remember my mother?" he asked Isaiah, directly. He was particularly driven to ask the question. He had been trying to remember his life before his father brought them to Newtown. He had been trying to remember his mother. His father never referred to her or her family, except occasionally to make a derisive comment upon the "eccentricities" of old Bishop Wortham.

"Your dear mother was dead when I came to work for Mr. Chadley," answered Isaiah. He put down his polishing rag and looked inquiringly into Fenton's serious face.

"I know," said Fenton; "but you come from Prince River Inlet, where my mother's family lived. They were very prominent there. Don't you remember ever seeing her?"

"No, Mr. Fenton," said Isaiah, shaking his head.

Fenton was disappointed. He considered a moment and then asked, "Were there any servants in our house when you came, Isaiah? A woman my mother might have brought from her old home to care for Lesley, perhaps? He was less than a year old when Father found you. Someone must have been looking after him. Try to remember."

"Yes," Isaiah admitted, nodding, "there was Lilla. But she did not come from your mother's people. She was from Campton. And she had only been there since Mr. Lesley was born."

Fenton turned to go. Isaiah had supplied no information about the mother who was beyond recollection in Fenton's memory. The thought which had urged Fenton to question him was that somewhere in the past – *somewhere*, perhaps in some knowledge of his mother – there was a clue to the frightening riddle of his father's unchanging and increasing antagonism toward Lesley. Like Professor Hanley, Fenton had seen that the sudden strange anger which had come over his father at dinner was not provoked by anything which Lesley had said or done. More and more often lately, he had seen his father actually nag Lesley to show him disrespect, to contradict him. There was something very wrong. And Fenton had become desperate to learn what it was and to prevent, if he could, its growing to cause a final and irreparable breach between the two persons he loved most in the world.

He suffered in his awareness of the threat of destruction which, noticeably now, characterized his father's attacks upon Lesley. It was painful for him to examine his father critically in his own mind, to be tempted to attribute meanness to him. Mr. Chadley was not a lovable man, but he was a good man (or so Fenton believed) with a brilliant mind which Fenton had come to appreciate and admire as he had grown older and could understand the mental fencing between his father and Professor Hanley.

He respected his father. And he knew that Mr. Chadley, in turn, respected him, and that one day, not too far in the future, his father would turn over to him some of the responsibilities with which Mr. Chadley was now burdened.

The decision Fenton had come to, after his distressing night, was one which he knew carried a particular danger with it. He was going to question his father in a way which he hoped would surprise from him a clue to Mr. Chadley's deep animosity toward Lesley. On the pretext of discussing his own business future, and the preparation he might make to equip himself to administer the properties he would inherit, he was going to lead his father to discuss their Wortham holdings on Prince River. It had come to his troubled mind that perhaps there had been an unfortunate happening in the past – a dispute over a will, perhaps – the revelation of which might point him toward the answer he was so driven to seek. But he knew also that in pressing such an inquiry he was in danger of possibly having to forfeit some of his own cherished regard for his parent to pay for the knowledge he might obtain.

Mr. Chadley was dressing for dinner when Fenton stopped by his apartment to ask for an appointment to consult him on a personal matter.

"Is it something urgent, Fenton?" his father asked, surprised.

"Oh no, sir. It isn't urgent at all," Fenton quickly assured him. "It's something I've been thinking about for some time and I'd like to talk to you about it soon."

"You may drive with me to the bank tomorrow morning, then," Mr. Chadley said. "We can begin our conference on the way."

"That would be fine, sir. Thank you," said Fenton, and gently closed his father's door. Halfway down the hall he had a feeling that his father had not moved away from the door to go on with his toilet, but was standing there watching him through the paneling.

As he passed Professor Hanley's room, he heard Lesley's voice. He listened a moment and then knocked.

They were leaning over Mr. Hanley's big table desk, looking at some open velvet-lined cases.

"Oh," said the professor, startled. "Are we late? I don't think I heard Isaiah announce dinner." He was flustered and began quickly closing the cases and straightening himself. Lesley was holding in his hands a small plaster head of the Piltdown man, and he was examining it with a particular curiosity and excitement with which Fenton had never before seen him investigate anything.

"Dinner hasn't been called," Fenton said. His curiosity brought him closer to the desk to see the contents of the last case before Hanley snapped it shut. "I was just going to change and I heard your voices." He looked down at the modeled head of the Cro-Magnon man.

"These are new, Professor Hanley?" he asked.

"Well, no, they aren't. They were a gift from Professor Risdam for the little assistance I gave him on his book several years ago. I don't know why I didn't have them sent up from the university last winter when we were discussing prehistoric man." He spoke in an odd embarrassed way. "Lesley happened to remark this afternoon that Maude's head seemed to resemble the cranial structure of the Neanderthal man, whereas Isaiah's resembled the Cro-Magnon."

He made the explanation as if, conscious of being in a not-quite-approved situation, he hoped to supply an acceptable excuse. Neither Fenton nor Lesley ever visited Professor Hanley in his room, and he was never invited to visit them in theirs. Fenton felt the awkwardness of the situation, and blushed. He felt unwelcome, too. He was already tense and it seemed to him that his unexpected entrance had surprised Mr. Hanley and Lesley at an interest they had not meant to share with him.

"We'd better let Professor Hanley change now, Lesley," said Fenton with greater politeness than usual. And Lesley thanked the professor and followed Fenton out the door.

Before he retired that night, Professor Hanley came to a conclusion which bore out Fenton's suspicion that he had intruded upon a particular private discussion.

Why I have been so blind I don't know! the professor thought. What aggravates Mr. Chadley about his son is that Lesley can be a real scholar, not just a rich patron of learning as he is. I have made a really exciting discovery this afternoon. Lesley leans toward pursuits which his father does not follow and *could* not, no doubt. Lesley has the makings of a serious scientist. And I think his field is physical anthropology. I intend to encourage and instruct him all I can. Then, when I have something to go on, I'll discuss his prospects with Professor Risdam so that I may use his advice when I speak to Mr. Chadley.

There Hanley stopped thinking and refused to admit into his mind a certain realization which was degrading to him as a scholar. Although Mr. Chadley had never been rude to him in any way, he had, occasionally, had the feeling that Mr. Chadley regarded him somewhat as the Roman master regarded his educated Greek slave: not *quite* a servant. So of course it would be difficult to urge Mr. Chadley to encourage his own son to become a scholar – and perhaps a teacher.

But Hanley had become Lesley's sponsor, his rescuer. He was going to deliver him from his oppressor. He had embraced a cause, and he went to bed to sleep a dreamless sleep on the pillow of his innocence and good intention.

On their way to the bank, Fenton rode along beside his father with an air of agreeable patience, obedient to the code which dictated that only Mr. Chadley could open the discussion.

As they turned into Willow Avenue his father said, "Well, Fenton? We have some business together?"

They were eight blocks from the bank on one of the stretches of new paving with which the city was having trouble. It had sunk unevenly so that jagged seams cut the vehicle wheels. A great deal of complaint was being leveled at the City Council, which had given out the contract.

"Yes, sir," said Fenton, immediately. "Before Professor Hanley speaks to you about the possibility of sending me to the university, I wanted to speak to you first."

Mr. Chadley turned from nodding to businessmen and depositors along the sidewalk and observed Fenton with interest and approval. Fenton could feel his father's approval and he shrank away from it with guilt.

"Well, well," said Mr. Chadley, "I'm afraid I've lost track of the time these last few months. You are being prepared now for college, are you? You – and Lesley?"

At the hesitation before Lesley's name, Fenton felt again his fear come over him.

"Well sir," he answered quickly, "by next term, we will have a general preparation to enter almost any reputable school; but lately, sir, I have wondered if you might not intend me to be responsible for some portion of our interests for which I could begin preparing myself now." He could feel his heart enlarge and press painfully against his ribs. "I don't know exactly what our holdings and obligations are. I mean that besides your business as a banker, sir, you must have many more serious considerations to harass you than you have ever mentioned." Mr. Chadley waited for him to finish. "Well, sir, I am old enough . . ." he began, and then hesitated, and then went on, "I am old enough to be of some support to you." There was a terrible emotion in Fenton which made it impossible for him to face his father. He turned away. They were in front of the bank. "If I am to be a landlord, perhaps there are matters of property rights and suits and the like which I might begin to study. I don't know what burdens you carry, sir, in Lesley's and my behalf, but you have said frequently that Grandfather Wortham was not as shrewd in business as he was in the pulpit. It may be that the property my mother left on Prince River Inlet has been a liability to you – I mean for you to protect for us, sir. I should like to help now, if I am needed and if you will allow me."

When he had finished, Fenton felt a weakness travel all through his limbs. He had said all he could. If his father did not respond, he would not be able to question him again.

Mr. Chadley was silent. Then he put his hand awkwardly over Fenton's. At last he said, "Thank you, Fenton. Your consideration is very gratifying." He sat a moment longer before getting out to enter the bank. Then he said, "Yes, I think there are some confidential matters we might take up at this time."

By noon, when he returned to Dunmeade for lunch with Lesley and Professor Hanley, Fenton knew that he had inherited from his mother a certain tract of pineland running completely around the horseshoe of Prince River Inlet, a rich turpentine forest on the Eastern Seaboard. He knew that it had been a fruitless land upon which squatters had settled for years until his father had cleaned them out, opening the tract for turpentine. He knew that he was the sole owner and that no part belonged to Lesley, that his mother had made her will two years before Lesley's birth and never changed it. He knew that he employed his father by a lifetime contract to exploit the product of his land.

He knew much more than that – figures of gross and net returns and even his total independent worth. But the one thing that stuck in his mind, sharp and fast as a needle, was another curious piece of information against which the figures of his wealth and even the surprising source of it were insignificant. He knew that a person whom he did not remember ever having heard of before, a person he should naturally have known all his life but whom he had never seen, had a peculiarly knotted control over his activities on Prince River Inlet. That person owned a thread of pine woods one acre wide which completely encircled his land like a noose. He had no entry into the Inlet or back country except by crossing that belt of pine. That person was his mother's aunt, his Grandfather Wortham's sister, his Great-aunt Jessie. And to her each month he paid an astonishing fee to transport turpentine across her one acre's width in either direction. *That* person his father was sending him east to meet, with an offer to buy her out at any price she asked – the same offer his father had made each year in his name and which, each year, she had refused. Now she was old and ill with malaria. Their situation was critical. If she died and left her strip to some unscrupulous stranger . . . ! "Well," his father had said, in discussing their predicament, "There *are* means of protecting ourselves. But you resemble your Grandfather Wortham. You have his set about you. She might be disposed to sell to you, Fenton."

So, when Fenton returned to Dunmeade from the bank that noon and sat down with Professor Hanley and Lesley to his broth and corn dumplings, he was nearly weeping with confusion and shock. His new knowledge had increased the burden of questions which had already begun to torment him regarding Lesley and his father. He had been right. There was something he did not know which he needed to know, something about his mother. Most shocking of all to him was the knowledge that Lesley was penniless, while he was rich; that Lesley was entirely dependent upon his father, while his father, for some reason Fenton did not yet know, was growing to hate his own son.

Within a week, Fenton began his journey three hundred miles east. Along one local railroad after another he finally reached the flat sandy region where his Great-aunt Jessie lived.

Though he had been born in that country and had lived there until he was ten, when his father had moved them to Newtown, he felt no nostalgic excitement in returning and he recognized no landmarks. His mind was soberly absorbed in how he should accomplish his mission – his *dual* mission; for in the days which had passed since his talk with his father at the bank, he had decided upon his course and his role.

"Come in, Fenton," his Aunt Jessie said, when he had been announced and shown to her sitting room. She was in a large chair with the front windows beside her so that she could get the light on her petit point. She leaned forward to watch him cross the room. She was over eighty – his father had told him that. But even with her netted yellow skin she had such a bright illuminated look from constant fever that she seemed no older to Fenton than his father. Even her voice was not old. It was neither high nor wispy, as the voices of old ladies often are.

"Well," she said, "I can see why he sent you." She nodded to the portrait hung directly over the two rows of thick ragged ecclesiastical books in a wall case. It was of his grandfather. "You look like him all right. We'll see if you act like him."

"Thank you, Aunt Jessie," Fenton answered simply, "and I think you look like my mother. Or rather the painting of her in our drawing room looks like you." It was true. Fenton decided she might have been quite handsome before she became old. She was not ugly now.

The compliment had its effect. Aunt Jessie studied him a

moment with a softer eye. Then she went back again to her first challenging tone.

"It doesn't require any meditation to guess why he sent you."

"No," agreed Fenton. He was still standing. "But that isn't only why I came."

She stopped working her needle and set her eyes suspiciously on his face.

"What did you say?"

"I said that is not only why I came, Aunt Jessie."

"Sit down. Pull that rocker to the light. I want to get a good look at you. Sit so I can see your face." Her thread hung limp through her fingers. "Now explain," she said, "and don't lie."

The moment had come. Over and over on his journey he had rehearsed what he would say. "Sell me the land now, Aunt Jessie – but not for me." That was how he would begin. And then he would tell her about Lesley. She would understand and be charitable, he knew. She was his kin. The moment for him to ask had come. He looked into her face and suddenly his eyes filled with tears. He sat there silent, silent and lost. And what he said at last, when he was able to speak, was something that he had not rehearsed on his journey and that did not come from his mind or any plan. It came from the dark of his heart.

"Tell me about my mother," he said. "There's something terribly wrong."

For a long moment, she examined him – his face, the fine tucked shirt he wore, the cloth of his suit, the wonderful garnet pin which held his tie, and the look of bewildered sadness about him in spite of his elegance and youth. Then she said, apparently with no feeling about the fact of it at all, but only surprise at his ignorance, "She killed herself. Hasn't your father ever told you that?" After she said it, there was not a sound in the room. Fenton's breath was held in his throat, while his shocked heart took in the words. Slowly the words were absorbed. Then he closed his eyes and leaned over his hands and hid his face until his little sickness had passed.

"Why?" he asked softly.

"Why do you want to know?" she answered. She had begun to work her needle through the petit point. "It was a long time ago."

He raised his head from his hands and a strange little sigh passed from his lips. His thoughts had no order. In him his anxiety for Lesley moved him to ask for the land. But now his motive had been intruded upon by a new and more terrifying revelation than the animosity of his father toward Lesley. He could not hold both, or relate them.

At last he said helplessly, "I don't know, Aunt Jessie. I came to ask you to help me. I came to ask you to sell your strip of pine to me – for Lesley. He . . ." And then his voice wavered and he finished suddenly with all the unexplainable fright in his heart, "My father hates him, and he is penniless." He could say no more. It seemed to him in that moment that he reached into darkness for direction. His mind could not sort his knowledge from his fear. He did not know which supported the other. What he fought against and why, he did not know.

If he had been anything but the strangely matured and already saddened boy that he was, the account of his mother's suffering and death, as he heard it that afternoon, would have destroyed his devotion to his father forever. But in Fenton was a weakness, a resignation, an inability to act except to repair or defend. Though he had betrayed his father in asking for the land for Lesley, his purpose was honorable, he knew. He wished only to endow his brother and protect him from dependence, not to injure his father in any way. And when he heard out his mother's story, though he listened with distress and confusion and even shame, he made no judgment against his father and attached to him no blame.

"Your mother was an artist, Fenton," his Great-aunt Jessie said. "She was a painter. Didn't you ever know?" She looked with wonder as he shook his head; then she went on: "When you were old enough to be cared for without her, she asked to go abroad to study – not for a lifetime, but for a year."

Fenton nodded and sat quietly waiting, while she changed her thread. She talked softly, with the softness one uses in speaking of the dead.

"Your father struggled to defeat her desire. He belittled her talent and hung her paintings only to criticize them and wound her — even the one portrait she painted of herself as a gift for him. But she suffered his cruelty and continued her effort to persuade him to let her go abroad, even asking him to accompany her, agreeing that her talent might be slight and that he would be indulging her only because he loved her. Then he turned on her with his cruelest anger. He forbade her mentioning it again and threatened her with shame and divorce if she left his house without his permission."

As she said the last, she put down her petit point and looked into Fenton's eyes. For a moment, her own shone into his with a cold scorn as she finished, "Your brother was conceived in that hour of defeat and despair for your mother — and she never forgot her humiliation or forgave your father the infliction of his will upon her."

Fenton dropped his head and stared miserably at his hands. His face burned, and he drew his handkerchief from his pocket to wipe at the moisture he felt along his forehead.

"In time, she grew ill with unhappiness," his great-aunt's voice went on above his bowed head, "and after Lesley was born, one morning while your father slept, she leaped in her nightdress from the stair."

The tears dropped into Fenton's hands. An unutterable sadness and pity filled him.

"Didn't she love my father?" he asked, pleading with her in some confused way to further explain what seemed so incomprehensible to him.

"Your father did not love her," was the answer. "He cannot love anything or anyone he cannot master."

The room had begun to color with the glow of the lowland twilight. His aunt stirred and shivered.

"Help me," Fenton implored, suddenly — "help me. Sell your land to Lesley, Aunt Jessie. I will pay whatever you ask."

But his aunt did not answer him. She squeezed her shawl about her against the feverish chills which had begun to rack her. The sundown came and the last light reddened their faces opposite each other. Then the room grayed and shadowed for nightfall.

"Send your brother to me, Fenton," she said, at last. "Let him ask for the land himself. I can promise you nothing."

Fenton gazed at her in despair. He had made his plea and she had denied him. Her request had even complicated his concerns. How could he send Lesley east to Prince River? How could he tell him anything – ever?

So Fenton began his journey home to Dunmeade, traveling the tedious hours with a kind of numbness in him, thinking of nothing, neither remembering nor forgetting.

Only when he approached the outskirts of Newtown and saw the Starburg Mills, did he think of his father and of Lesley. He sighed and his mind stirred with the one permissible resolution he could make. He would watch Lesley for the indifference and unconcern which aggravated and wounded his father. He would try to detract from Lesley's self-absorption with closer attention and devotion himself. Out of all he had been told, the sad account of his mother's life, only one conclusive thought remained – his father was alone and his was the tragedy before them all. His mother remained for Fenton a figure about which his mind had accustomed itself to no history, a figure hopelessly remote in a past he had never known. He knew now his father's fear. He hoped that in time the breach which seemed to be widening between him and Lesley would close. He believed, because he could not endure to think otherwise, that Lesley would never, as his mother had, put forth a talent in rivalry to the devotion his father required. But for such devotion, his father was alone, alone; and Fenton pitied him.

He had failed in his mission, but he returned to Dunmeade with a relieving and self-induced hope in his heart. At least he would not be faced with having to tell Mr. Chadley that Aunt Jessie, out of some perversity he could not persuade her against, had agreed only to sell her strip to Lesley. That would have been his lie, if he had succeeded in gaining it for his brother.

And he would not have to report on his journey at all that very evening, for he was arriving on Mr. Chadley's birthday, his fifty-fifth, and the house would be involved in the festivity.

Fenton could not have been more innocent or more pathetic in his false hope; for scarcely had his train left Newtown Station carrying him east to find his Aunt Jessie, when Professor Hanley proposed that Lesley try his hand at reproducing the prehistoric heads which had seemed to so fascinate him. With a kind of shy confidence and pleasure at Mr. Hanley's flattery and constant persuasion, Lesley took the velvet-lined cases to his room and studied the execution of the models for a day and a night, and then began on the Pithecanthropus man, working on Maude's porch in the wet clay with a curious happy attention to his task.

Occasionally Isaiah would come and happily observe the ruination of his dough board and his kitchen silver which Lesley was using, and once he brought a wedge of beeswax. "Old Negroes the devil got hold of used to make voodoo out of it," he explained solemnly, offering it to Lesley. Maude would smile and rock heavily in her chair. Her time was on her and she could not move comfortably, so that Isaiah came from the kitchen often to reassure her in his dignified indirect way, with little offerings of sourdough hoecake or glacé for her sweet tooth.

One afternoon, Lesley looked up at Isaiah leaning against the porch post with a plate of caraway biscuits and said, "Turn your head toward the sun, Isaiah." He studied the dark long head in the light and then he lifted himself gently from the table on which he worked and went to where Isaiah stood. He put his hands on Isaiah's head and traced out the shape of it along the sunken temples and high hollowed cheeks, and back beside the thin close-set ears. Professor Hanley watched him with intense interest. Isaiah submitted to Lesley's examination passively and patiently.

Then Lesley said, "I think I am going to model Isaiah's head, Professor, if you don't mind." It was a decisive statement. As calmly as he could, Professor Hanley replied, "That should be very interesting. Go ahead." Inside him a tremendous excitement was working. He had been right. Lesley was exhibiting a true scholarly curiosity. He watched Lesley examine the commercially prepared gray clay he had been working in. Isaiah was watching Lesley too, with a happy absent smile on his face. He was pleased that he was going to pose. Already in his mind he was arranging his cooking schedule to allow for it. If Lesley needed him mornings he would have to switch around and do the mopping and dusting just after lunch.

"This isn't . . ." Lesley said and then he did not finish but instead stretched his hands out and twisted them in a gesture of dissatisfaction. He had the keyed-up look of a nervous runner about to dart prematurely down the track. He could only express his rejection of the medium, he could not furnish a substitute. Professor Hanley tried to help him. "The wax?" he suggested. But Lesley was not listening. He was looking at the fern pots of Wandering Jew which Maude had hung by a chain from the porch ceiling. The pots were native red clay. Mr. Gaither Lyndon made them as a side line, in his brick kilns.

"Wonderful!" agreed Mr. Hanley, following Lesley's eyes and anticipating his thought. "If you bake it, it will be permanent. That's a wonderful solution."

Lesley smiled. Then he said, looking at the mess he had already made on the table, "It'll probably be worse than this, Maude. I might get it all over everything on your porch." But Maude only nodded and grinned. "That's all right, Mr. Lesley," she said, glancing at Isaiah with pride. "You just do any way you want to."

Lesley made several unsuccessful attempts to build up the basic form of the head and mold it into shape before he began to space the features. He let the clay dry out too much and had to work a new batch. But he was absorbed in a way no one had ever seen him. He was patient with his own problems with the clay but he grew unreasonably irritated at any slight interruption. He was unreasonable too about the posing, and twice caused Isaiah to be late with dinner.

"I know you are concerned about Maude, Isaiah," said Mr. Chadley, the second time, "but there are obligations here in the house, you know. Maude is having the best of care. And Dr. Langley is quite satisfied with her condition, so there can hardly be such distress as warrants neglect of the household."

It was the first time Mr. Chadley had ever spoken so to Isaiah. Professor Hanley was distressed, and Lesley went to the kitchen immediately afterward to apologize. "I'm sorry, Isaiah," he said, putting his hand affectionately against Isaiah's back as Isaiah leaned over the sink washing his dishes. "I should have owned up that it was my fault, but the professor doesn't want Father to know anything until I get the head finished. It doesn't look like much right now."

Isaiah reached for a dish towel and snapped it playfully against Lesley's legs. "Get out of my kitchen," he said – "you're just a troublemaker."

"All right, all right," agreed Lesley, skipping away from the swinging dish towel in Isaiah's hand, "but if it turns out, I'll give it to Father for his birthday and then you'll sing a different tune. The professor says we can get Mr. Lyndon to bake it just like one of his pots. Won't that make you look pretty?" Lesley danced into the pantry and teased Isaiah from the swing door.

"Hush up now," Isaiah said; "you're going to get Mr. Chadley out here behind both of us if you don't be careful." And Lesley laughed and pushed through the door.

But the next day came and Lesley, with his fingers in the big lumps of sticky red clay, became as tyrannical as before, compelled by an ardor for what he was doing which completely freed him from any feeling of obligation to others. From the time the features began to form under his hand, he ceased to grope. He worked hour by hour with an intent and calculating expression as he brought forth the large fine nose and broad heavy chin of his model. He began each day with a peculiarly sure attack as if he had been modeling faces in clay for years. In his mind, before he began the first indentation or overlay, he had already decided his technique and prepared for his problems. He was becoming an artist, there under the blindness of Isaiah and Maude and Professor Hanley. As the wonderful crude head of Isaiah emerged in its final form from his hands, only stupidity and happy conceit in his belief that he had discovered a future anthropologist could have kept Professor Hanley from recognizing the truth – that Lesley was a sculptor, not a scientist!

Fenton would have seen, would have known in a glance that Lesley was not coldly duplicating protuberances and cavities. He would have known when Lesley indented the clay beneath the unusually stern straight lips and gave to the face Isaiah's beseeching sobriety. He would have known, without waiting to see the complete romanticized head, more heroic than Isaiah's and displaying Lesley's love. Fenton would have known. But Fenton was not there.

Excited almost beyond endurance, Professor Hanley carried out his good intentions and wrote to Professor Risdam at the university.

When Fenton entered the house he noticed at once the curious air of excitement about it. The preparations were going on for the birthday dinner. His father had not yet come in from the bank and there was a feeling of great scurrying-about in the back to get little things done before he arrived. Fenton went to the kitchen to speak to Isaiah. Maude was there, sitting at a table polishing the wine goblets and sherbets. She had a bright strained look on her face, trying to reassure Isaiah and relieve his mind until the birthday dinner was served and done. Her time was due.

"Welcome home, Mr. Fenton," Isaiah said, pausing a moment from basting the pheasants. He was busy, but he wanted to greet Fenton properly. "I knew you wouldn't disappoint Mr. Chadley," he smiled, and then excused himself and lowered the oven heat.

Fenton sniffed the birds and nodded to Maude. "I hope I'll have time to rest before dressing," he said. "I'd like to have a special appetite tonight, Isaiah."

Isaiah ducked his head with pride. "*Everything's* got to be special this night, Mr. Fenton. This is a big night. Just you wait and see."

Fenton left his grip of soiled clothes and went back through the house.

Upstairs, Professor Hanley was standing in his room with the door open. He was prying open the buttonholes of a stiff-bosomed shirt with a shoe hook. He seemed to be listening for something. Fenton rapped and spoke to him. Then he asked, "Where is Lesley?"

"Lesley?" Mr. Hanley repeated. "Oh, Lesley went into town, I think. He had to fetch something." He said it in an odd way, as if he were being offhand about something very mysterious. It irritated Fenton.

And then the front door opened below and Mr. Chadley stood in the downstairs hall. Professor Hanley discreetly closed his door and Fenton hurried down to his father.

"Well, Fenton, I see you are back," he said. He meant "back in time." He was pleased. He shook Fenton's hand and patted at his son's shoulder awkwardly.

"Yes sir, I hope you are well—especially well today, sir," Fenton smiled. Then he added, "I thought at first the drawing room was decorated in honor of my return, sir," he said, and blushed, making his little joke. He indicated the floral arrangements Maude and Isaiah had managed.

"You were quite right, Fenton," Mr. Chadley said. "It's all to welcome you home." Fenton's gentle teasing pleased him. Then he added, "Shall we have our talk directly after dinner?" He gave the impression that there was nothing important planned for the evening, that business might go on as usual, certainly *this* business.

"Well, sir, I don't want to deprive Lesley and Professor Hanley of your company this evening," Fenton demurred. "I imagine they rather expect we'll all retire to the drawing room afterward." He meant, of course, that they'd all retire to see the presents opened. Then Isaiah came to the arch of the back hall.

"Good evening, Mr. Chadley," he said, "this is a happy occasion."

"Yes, it is, Isaiah," agreed Mr. Chadley. "Mr. Fenton is back and in good health."

"Oh yes, sir," Isaiah followed the lead. "That's just what I meant. That's just what I meant, sir." He joined in the little joke to ignore the birthday occasion. Each one smiled happily at the other. Then Mr. Chadley and Fenton went up the stair and Isaiah returned to his kitchen.

It was while Fenton was at his bath that Lesley returned, carrying a large heavy block-shaped bundle. He went into the drawing room and carefully placed it on the table between the long east windows. Then he twisted it in a particular direction and stood off, studying the effect of the lamplight on it. When he was satisfied, he placed a card against the corner of it, which read, *For Father, with best wishes and also apologies, Lesley*.

Then he went out to the kitchen to speak to Maude.

"I saw Dr. Langley, Maude," he said, "and he told me to tell you there's plenty of time yet. He said it was going to pain you a good deal for several hours first. That's the normal course, he said." Lesley paused. "It hasn't begun to pain you yet – since I've been gone, has it, Maude?"

"No sir, Mr. Lesley," she smiled. "I'll be sure and tell you when."

"That's right," Lesley nodded solemnly. "You be sure and do that. Father will call up Dr. Langley right away." He looked down at her very sympathetically. Then he said, a little awkwardly, "It certainly is a lot of trouble for you, isn't it? But it will all be over soon now."

Maude smiled up at him gratefully. "That's right," she said, "it's all in the will of the good Lord, Mr. Lesley." And then suddenly there were tears in her eyes, the first fear she had shown.

Lesley lingered by the door. He wanted to leave her more

cheerful. "I put it on the big table right under the lamp," he said, brightening as he changed the subject. "It just came out of the kiln. Wait until you see it. You won't even recognize it. It looks — " And then he hesitated in a kind of embarrassment, and finished weakly: "It looks nice."

"I know it does, Mr. Lesley," Maude reassured him. "It's going to be the best present of all. You just wait and see." Then she added, lowering her eyes, "Isaiah's mighty proud."

Lesley pushed at the door once and then let it swing back. "Well," he said, "I'd better go and change now." Maude nodded.

He hesitated a moment and then, abruptly, he pushed open the door again and left.

Although every preparation had been made to insure the birthday dinner a spirit of real celebration, still it seemed to Fenton, even as the toasts were made and the glasses raised to his father's health, that the atmosphere was one of uneasy excitement rather than of conviviality. At first, being conscious of the approaching hour when he would be obliged to report to his father his failure to buy the land, he attributed the curious tension he felt around him to his own inner anxiety. But then, as the dinner progressed and the silences between bits of conversation became more noticeable, he observed between Lesley and Professor Hanley a curious interplay of glances and smiles, and suddenly he felt again as he had felt upon entering the house in the afternoon — as if he were intruding upon some secret activity which he could perceive but not identify. He had first sensibly attributed the undercurrent of excitement then to the commotion in the kitchen. But now the unusual and particularly obvious preoccupation of Professor Hanley, upon an occasion when more than ordinary attention was due his father, seemed to him more than rude — it alarmed him. Worse still, there seemed to be an impatience about Lesley to finish dining and move to the drawing room. He ate rapidly and then sat back after each course and twiddled the remaining silver by his plate as if he were hard put to contain himself until the others had caught up and they could get on to the conclusion of the dinner.

With relief, Fenton rose when his father indicated that they would take coffee and cordials in the drawing room while he opened his presents. Nothing unpleasant had happened despite the rudeness of Lesley and the peculiar behavior of Mr. Hanley.

"I'm going to save your gift for last, Lesley," Mr. Chadley said, examining the card against the big bundle under the lamp. "The card is quite original. I don't think I can guess what the object is." He glanced at Lesley and then observed to the professor, "Anticipating the selections is rather intriguing for me, Mr. Hanley. Gifts seldom reveal as much about the recipient as they do about the donor. When I open your own package here," – and his hand moved to the sedate plain bookbinder's card on Hanley's gift – "I know I shall find an expression of that exceptionally cultivated mental taste of yours – something someone should give to you."

Mr. Hanley's mouth opened and he blushed, but Mr. Chadley went on without waiting for him to answer: "And when I open this carefully tied box from Fenton, I shall find something personal and yet proper – something Fenton would allow me but not himself. Fenton always makes a gift of what he would consider an extravagance for him." Mr. Chadley smiled approvingly and regarded Fenton for a moment with an affectionate eye. Then he turned his head deliberately to contemplate the large bulky package which was his gift from Lesley. And as he examined its mysterious shape, his eyes narrowed and his expression changed suddenly from one of scrutiny to one of peculiar suspicion.

Unreasonably, Fenton began to be afraid of his opening the wrappings. He did not know what was in the package. There was no way to find out. He began to be fearful of the contents. He began to imagine that his father knew what Lesley had selected and that he was displeased. But then Mr. Chadley moved abruptly to pick up the present from Isaiah and Maude, and Fenton stared appealingly at Lesley, asking for some sign that the gift was innocent and ordinary. But Lesley was neither listening to his father nor noticing anyone else in the room. And in his aggravating old way he gave the impression of not being with them at all, for he sat in an absorbed contemplation of his gift, with a slight smile about his lips and his eyes distant and involved with sights he could not share.

"You see," Mr. Chadley was saying, "Isaiah thinks of the simple comforts of the flesh. To ease the flesh in this world, which provides him no luxuries and few necessities, is his concern." He had opened the hand-knit hose from Maude and Isaiah and was holding them in his hand, examining the fine stitch Maude had used to keep them light.

"Thank you, Isaiah," he said. "These are a further proof of our wise selection of a wife for you. Aren't they?" He smiled gracefully at Isaiah, who stood in the arch with the decanter and small cordials, but in some way, with his compliment, he had reminded Isaiah of his debt, as if he had said, "I see that I did not make a mistake in allowing you to marry." There was a puzzled look on Isaiah's face as he set down his tray and went back for the coffee.

"And now we shall see if I am right about you, Mr. Hanley," and he opened the edition of Pindar – in the original Greek. "You compliment me, indeed, Mr. Hanley. I shall be able to enjoy it only because your constant quotations in the years we have talked have stored numerous passages in my memory. I can quote where I cannot read." He bowed slightly to Hanley, and then suddenly, as he lifted his head, he caught sight of Lesley and the old unpleasantness which Fenton so dreaded to see came over his face.

"Do you notice, Professor?" said Mr. Chadley, in a hard voice. "Lesley takes a greater interest in his gift than I do. He is enjoying it vicariously, though it is no longer in his possession. It must have given him great pleasure to select it for me. I cannot wait to see what it is!"

Fenton could have cried out in frustration, "Oh, Lesley, Lesley! Pay attention to *him,* Lesley! On this one night. For all our sakes!"

"That's very shrewd of you," barked Mr. Hanley, unexpectedly, and he jumped up from his chair and came to join Mr. Chadley by the table.

"*Is* it?" snapped Mr. Chadley, startled. His face was like stone. "Then you must know what it is." He reached out for Lesley's square package under the lamp and his fingers played over the wrapping, searching for the opening fold.

"Just open it there, sir," cried Lesley without warning, and he stood up, his face vivid and alight with a wonderful excitement, as he put out his hands to show his father. "Right there!" – he pointed eagerly. And then, almost laughing, "I'll do it for you," he said, and he stepped in front of Mr. Chadley and took hold of the cords.

In all the room there was no sound but the sudden rip of the tissue. Mr. Chadley stood rigid, staring at his son's back. Mr. Hanley waited with a bright bursting smile on his face. Fenton sat frozen in fear, his eyes wide and fastened on his father's angry face. Lesley stepped out of the way with the torn paper in his hands – and there, with the lamplight crossing and high-lighting the glazed surface of the features, was his sculpture of Isaiah's head: Isaiah's sad, stern, haughty head, accentuated in its startling likeness by the color of the russet clay.

"Isn't it remarkable, Mr. Chadley?" Mr. Hanley shouted at once, and then subdued his tone in instant embarrassment. "Did you ever expect Lesley to produce anything like that? I must confess that I didn't. But there it is – and a first try! It's quite wonderful!"

He felt about in his pockets excitedly, going through the same ones twice, until he found what he wanted and withdrew a letter.

"I took the liberty of writing to Professor Risdam at the university about Lesley. This is his answer." He held the letter toward Mr. Chadley, going on breathlessly; "He is willing to take Lesley now, at eighteen. Think of it, Mr. Chadley. The finest physical anthropologist in this country – what a distinction! This is an occasion for *real* celebration, Mr. Chadley. I congratulate you." He took a glass of liqueur from the tray and raised it to Mr. Chadley. "I congratulate you upon your gifted son." Then he turned happily to Lesley, who was gazing at him in red-faced astonishment, and said, "To Lesley Chadley." Then he drank the thimble of liquid in the glass.

Over the room, when he had finished, there was a silence. As Mr. Hanley had spoken, Fenton had arisen from his chair.

"Anthropologist?" Mr. Chadley whispered. "Anthropologist, Mr. Hanley? Lesley, an anthropologist?" And then the most dreadful sound came from him. It was laughter, but it rolled out coarsely and cruelly from his throat in an angry mockery which set Fenton's flesh in chill. Louder and louder he laughed until he rocked against the table to stop and draw his breath.

"Anthropologist!" he gasped in derision, pointing his finger at Lesley. "Let *me* congratulate *you*, Professor!"

And then the most terrible moment of all came. All the wound and surprise which had come on Lesley's face at his father's ridicule left it. He trembled like an animal. And then, before anyone could surmise his intention, he sprang at his father with his fingers open to silence the laughter and the mocking voice. Together they fell across the table, pitching the clay head of Isaiah onto the floor. As it broke beneath them, Mr. Chadley cried out, "Isaiah!" And then again, "Isaiah!"

For a moment, Isaiah stood rooted in the arch, stupefied at the scene before him. Then he leaped to draw Lesley off and defend the master of Dunmeade, even against his boy. "Oh, Lord," he called softly. "Lord, help us!"

⁂

At the end of a long night of labor, Maude had her child and at sunup, Isaiah looked down upon his son. But there was little happiness in him in spite of his new pride. He had laid his hand against Lesley and he had lost the affection of his boy. His eyes were sorrowful as he looked upon Maude and their child. He knelt beside them to pray.

Fenton, lying awake through the night, arose when it was light and wrote briefly, with decision:

> Dear Aunt Jessie,
> I cannot send Lesley. If I ever thought I could, I know now it is impossible. He must never know what I know. Something very sad and terrible has happened here. I beg you again to help him.

Then he dressed himself to go downstairs to await his father. The time had come to tell him that he had failed in his mission to buy the strip of land. He looked at himself in the glass. "I am my brother's keeper," he said, and the burden of his understanding and the secret he must keep brought an almost unendurable pain into his heart.

At noon Mr. Chadley sent for Professor Hanley. He was seated at his desk in his study when the professor came in, and he did not arise or invite Mr. Hanley to sit down.

"Mr. Hanley," he said coldly, looking directly into the professor's eyes, "some months ago, you entrusted certain of your funds to me for investment. At the time, a particular opportunity for profitable speculation had been brought to my attention and though the amount you had made available to me was insufficient for the purpose, I nevertheless made the investment for you by augmenting your funds with a personal loan. In this way, I was able to avail you of the opportunity to realize a very substantial return upon your money."

Mr. Chadley paused and then pushed toward Mr. Hanley a check which had been lying beside the letter opener. He kept his eyes upon Mr. Hanley's face as the professor looked down at the figure. It was three times the amount given Mr. Chadley for investment.

"No doubt you will now consider doing further study in your subject, Mr. Hanley? Perhaps abroad?" Mr. Chadley suggested easily, and yet with a noticeable firmness in his tone. Then, when the professor did not pick up the check, but only raised his bewildered face to stare at Mr. Chadley, he added, "I should imagine that travel abroad would be a welcomed prospect for you at this time, Mr. Hanley. Ten years' tutoring in the restful confines of Dunmeade cannot have been very stimulating to your scholarly mind."

Professor Hanley did not answer. He looked again at the figure on the check. Then Mr. Chadley reached out and picked it up and handed it to him.

Professor Hanley left Newtown on the three o'clock, the train he always took to the university, the only one there was. He arrived early at the station. He had been packed, really, before Mr. Chadley had called him to his study at noon. He had been ready to leave Dunmeade. There had been no need to dismiss him. Through the night he had thought of all that had happened in the years he had been there. Then he had thought of Lesley.

He bitterly regretted the role he had taken upon himself to liberate the boy from his father's domination. He had done Lesley a disservice he could never hope to repair. And yet, even after such a cruel experience, perhaps in time, Lesley might turn again to the serious work he had encouraged him to try and all Hanley's effort and faith and good intention would serve him at last. For however Mr. Chadley had ridiculed the proposal that Lesley study anthropology, Mr. Hanley remained unshaken in his belief that the boy was capable of real scholarly endeavor. But he could not remain at Dunmeade to help him further. After the shocking event of the previous evening, only resignation was open to him.

On his way down the gallery with his hand luggage, Mr. Hanley passed the door to Mr. Chadley's strange little morning room. He stopped suddenly and stood in the hall and listened for movement inside. Then he approached the door and set down his bag. He was about to put his hand on the knob to turn it when some sort of caution took him and he knocked softly first instead. Then he waited. There was no answer. There was no sound at all from within. And then, as he waited, he began to feel the presence of someone on the opposite side of the door. The feeling was so strong that he took his hand away and did not try the knob after all. For no reason a sadness came over him, replacing his curiosity and desire to see the room once more. The whole house was still – almost without life, it seemed suddenly to him. He was glad that he was leaving, glad that he was leaving his years there behind him. He reached for his bag.

And then the door opened.

"You're going now, Professor?" asked Mr. Chadley. "Your train doesn't come into the shed until 2:40." He took out his watch and observed the positions of the flat platinum hands. There was no surprise on his face at seeing Mr. Hanley before the door.

"I thought I would go down early," the professor began to explain, "and see Mr. Riley in the freight office about picking up my trunk." Until that moment Mr. Hanley had not thought of such a thing. Isaiah would have attended to his trunk for him. But he was agitated and it gave him something to say. "I did not want to leave Dunmeade without telling you good-by, sir," he went on suddenly, and at the time he said it he meant it, "and I wanted to thank you for your many kindnesses to me. It has been a privilege . . ."

He could not finish. In spite of all that had happened, all the indignation, the regret, the bewilderment, the frustration, and the sense of helplessness that he had experienced, what he said was true and emotion filled him. It *had* been a privilege – Mr. Chadley was a strange, great man, a giant of his time. Professor Hanley believed that.

"Thank you," said Mr. Chadley quietly. "Thank you for taking the trouble to knock." He was looking steadily at Hanley. He held out his hand. The garnet links on his cuffs shone in the light. He had immaculate strong hands. "I wish you good fortune, Mr. Hanley."

At the foot of the stair Mr. Hanley paused and looked back up along the black iron banister. He wanted to remember the house. He had lived in it nearly ten years. It might even have been called his home. Certainly he had known real luxury and freedom in it, and written his best work, and obtained his doctorate. His eyes moved up the graceful curve of the stair. It was a beautiful house – beautiful. For a moment he was almost stifled with feeling for it. And then he saw Mr. Chadley watching him silently from the depth of the gallery. Mr. Chadley had followed him and now was watching him go. He stood there with a queer smile on his face, almost a grin, as if he were about to laugh unpleasantly at something low and contemptible. Mr. Hanley was sorry that he had lingered. He hurried to the door.

All the way through the city to the station he could feel Mr. Chadley's smile at his back. He shivered and looked out the window to fill himself with a last look at Newtown. He wanted to see it with the sharp eyes of departure, which to him were always clearer and fresher than the eyes of first arrival in a strange place. It was one of the moments he savored when traveling – the experience of seeing things really for the first time at the hour of departure. A kind of excitement began to take him. Now he would be able to indulge himself a little. He had money. He could go to Europe. It made a difference, having a little money to spend. He could give things away, make presents. That was the trouble really between Lesley and Mr. Chadley. Money had no effect – but then he stopped his thoughts before they went back into a futile reiteration of the unpleasant time just passed.

All through the warehouse district he was conscious of Mr. Chadley's presence just as if he had been beside him. Newtown was Mr. Chadley's just as much as Dunmeade. His will had shaped the organs of Newtown's commercial body and made it a rich and impressive sight. And Mr. Hanley had been privileged to see his will done. He had had Mr. Chadley talk about method with him and forecast the futures of certain of his interests. That had fascinated Mr. Hanley, hearing Mr. Chadley objectively discuss and argue method, and then later witnessing the practical result of Mr. Chadley's theorizing.

Suddenly Mr. Hanley had a shocking and wonderful thought. "He has benefited from his talks with me!" He had never thought before that he might have contributed to Mr. Chadley's wealth and influence. Now he saw in the mills and warehouses an application of the principles of logic they had argued and discussed so many nights over cigars. He felt a tremendous elation. He understood, now, why Mr. Chadley had made such profitable investments for him. Mr. Chadley had wanted to repay him. It was Mr. Chadley's way of thanking him for his subtle service! Mr. Hanley swelled inside and looked at the last building before he reached the depot. It was the storage house for Dr. Pickett's poultice supplies. "I had a hand in that," he thought proudly.

By the time he boarded his train, Mr. Hanley no longer felt Mr. Chadley's strange insulting smile at his back. He knew that it was gratitude which had prompted Mr. Chadley's generosity. He had *not* accepted a bribe to depart and remain silent.

As for Lesley, he became, after that night, still more solitary. He dined occasionally with his father and Fenton, but since Mr. Chadley did not insist upon his presence at table, he more often took a tray early in his room. He was polite to Isaiah, thanking him for the extra service, and daily asking after Maude and the child Ralph; but his trust in Isaiah was gone and with it his devotion.

What he thought of what had happened, no one knew. He did not make any comment upon Professor Hanley's departure from Dunmeade. He did not describe to Fenton the interest Professor Hanley had promoted in him to try reproducing the prehistoric heads. He did not question Fenton as to why Mr. Chadley had so ridiculed Mr. Hanley's suggestion that he study anthropology, nor did he remark upon his own astonishment at the suggestion when it was made.

And Fenton, for his part, did not inquire as to how he had come to do the head of Isaiah. Burdened as he was with a knowledge and understanding of the tragic situation which involved them all, he prayed only that it would not engulf them, that time would pass and Lesley's unexpected expression of an interest which so offended his father would prove sporadic. He saw with deep distress the look of grave puzzle which clouded Lesley's face at times and he knew the character of the thoughts which must be troubling Lesley then. But he remained silent, feeling a helplessness to enlighten his brother – and consoling himself, whenever guilt threatened him, with the rationalization that if Lesley were to be an artist, he would be, despite confusion and opposition; for true gift survived and proclaimed itself.

And then at last, before the lost look which finally settled upon Lesley's face and the depressing atmosphere which persisted in the house, Fenton went to Lesley and pleaded simply, "Come into the bank with me."

And to his surprise, Lesley looked at him gratefully and nodded his head.

Then to Mr. Chadley, Fenton pleaded, "I know he's ashamed of himself, sir. Give him some occupation with us. Forgive him, sir."

He received a curious reply.

"Have I ever given you reason to believe that I would not forgive him, indeed that I would not always endure my own blood – whatever its tempers?"

Mr. Chadley's face was chill and ungenerous. "Bring Lesley to the bank when he's ready," he said.

And Fenton took Lesley the next day.

For a time, matters seemed to be relieved. Lesley was successful with his figures and books. He showed up well, and Fenton was quick to praise him in a carefully grateful way. Even Mr. Chadley seemed pleased and directed conversation about the day's transactions to Lesley when they sat together in the evening.

Then one evening Isaiah met the three of them at the door.

"There's a Mr. Spencer in the drawing room, sir," he said to Mr. Chadley.

Mr. Chadley's brows went up in surprise and an unconcealed displeasure came over his face. He walked to the drawing room.

"Good evening, Marcus," his visitor greeted him first. He was already standing and he looked at the three of them with a kind of grin about his mouth.

"Good evening, Harry," Mr. Chadley replied, but did not offer his hand.

"Which of the young gentlemen is Mr. Lesley Chadley, Marcus?" the visitor asked, still smiling. His eyes went to Fenton.

Mr. Chadley shook his head. "This one." He indicated Lesley.

"Really? The one who looks like you, Marcus?" he asked, seemingly further amused. He examined Lesley with interest. No one spoke. Then he said, addressing Lesley only, "Mr. Chadley, I represent the estate of your recently deceased relative, Miss Jessie Prince Wortham." He paused and glanced easily at Marcus Chadley, and then went on, "I shan't intrude upon you this evening, but if you will be good enough to take luncheon with me tomorrow at the Briggs Arcade, I shall apprise you of certain information which I believe you will be pleased to learn."

As he said it, Mr. Chadley's manner changed completely.

"Indeed!" he said. "Lesley, show Mr. Spencer up to the West Room. And will you inform Isaiah, Fenton, that we have a guest and ask him to unpack Mr. Spencer?" He pointed to the light traveling bag beside the lawyer. "Mr. Spencer and I are old friends," he explained, smiling and urging Fenton and Lesley to action. "Your mother was once engaged to him – before I had the pleasure of persuading her to change her mind. Isn't that so, Harry?"

Mr. Spencer only smiled and let Lesley lead him out of the room.

When they had followed the curving black stair to the gallery and were alone, Mr. Spencer said to Lesley, "Tell me, son – is the portrait your mother painted of herself here?"

Lesley stopped. He turned slowly and stared into Mr. Spencer's face. Behind his motionless eyes was the feeling of great movement, violent movement, in his mind. The grave puzzled expression Fenton had seen came to him again for one moment and then was gone. His eyes became bright and grim with sudden anger. He turned abruptly and went down the gallery to his father's little morning room. He opened the door and stood waiting for Mr. Spencer. "It's in here, sir," he called back with such a strange urgent heat in his voice that Harry Spencer hurried to enter the room with him. Lesley pointed to the painting above the mantel. "That's it. Isn't it?" he asked, almost defiantly. And Mr. Spencer turned from Lesley's intense face to gaze at the handsome, driven one of the boy's mother and answer "Yes," with a kind of shock – "Yes. That's it."

When Lesley returned from his trip east with Harry Spencer to claim his inheritance from his great-aunt Jessie, he was noticeably changed. He would not come into his property – the fine old house and the pine strip encircling the turpentine tract – until he was twenty-one. But income derived from it would be deposited in trust for him. In a measure, he was independent. But he did not indicate that he considered himself so. He continued to work diligently in his position at the bank. And he remained much the same in his habits at Dunmeade. The change in him was revealed in the way he took to observing Mr. Chadley with a detached and slightly scornful amusement, listening to his father attentively and even encouraging him to talk more intimately of his part, past and present, in the business enterprises which consumed Newtown. He would nod and raise his brows and smile constantly and never take his eyes from Mr. Chadley's face. At times, his concentration was almost rude. Mr. Chadley seemed strained under the constant, mildly amused scrutiny. But there was nothing about which he could complain.

One day, Mr. Chadley said to Fenton, "I think the superior attitude your brother has developed since being apprised of his inheritance, is, to say the least, disappointing and even vulgar." They were standing by the windows of Mr. Chadley's office looking out Willow Avenue. Lesley had crossed the traffic before them, on the way to the courthouse with a folio.

Fenton watched until he was out of sight. Then he said irrelevantly, "Not that it matters, sir, I consider myself most fortunate – but I cannot think what I did to Miss Wortham . . ." He looked down at his fingers, twirling the drapery tassels, and avoided his father's eyes. "I must have made a poor impression indeed. She didn't even know Lesley."

This pleased Mr. Chadley.

"I would be entirely confident of your gracious behavior under any circumstances, Fenton," he consoled his son. "It was Miss Wortham's conduct which was erratic – and I might say spiteful. It was quite pointed in the fact that she altered her will on her deathbed." He made one of his awkward pats at Fenton's shoulder. "There's no reason for you to reproach yourself. Even the finest intelligence is often useless against a fool. You may observe that here each hour we are open for business." He smiled. Then a grim pleasure came into his voice. "Miss Wortham was the last of that name."

Involuntarily, Fenton shivered. "Perhaps I should be getting back with these, sir," he said, excusing himself and picking up a sheaf of newly signed papers. He wanted to leave his father's presence. Then, at the threshold, he hesitated and turned back. "You are always very generous to me, sir," he said. Then he closed his father's door behind him.

Newtown never knew of the breach between Marcus Chadley and his son Lesley. The city was busy dabbling in tobacco and making a killing at it, which was very gratifying since there hadn't been any tobacco trading since the Continental Tobacco Company had built its big plants thirty miles north in little Huntsville. But when the prices of tobacco began to soar, some of the smarter, or rather the richer – it did not matter how smart one was if one hadn't the money – reconstructed the old warehouses down on Donaldson Street and added a few new ones and started marketing the weed. It was a temporary enterprise, a speculation kept in the financial family so to speak – little arrangements between Starburg and Lyndon, Chadley and Lyndon, Chadley and Starburg, each separately and then all jointly with Dr. Pickett and young Amos, who had taken over York and Amos Construction when old Mr. Amos died.

There were other things going on around town, too, in that carefree period. Gaither Lyndon broke down and married Lydia Sorrell. She was wonderful with his Gussie, who was always ailing, and she was a good woman, his first wife Ada's best friend. There were many good reasons to support the action. There were always good and obvious reasons for supporting the actions of anyone in Newtown.

Lucius Starburg, with Marcus Chadley again as his silent partner, put up a print works next to the dye works. They bought up a carpet mill which had stood in the site and enlarged it. Then they secured a load of New England machinery and began printing designs on cotton dress goods. Keep the manufacturing close to the cotton field and market in the North – or abroad, they maintained, and it was quickly to come to that, later, in the 1920's.

World War I gave Newtown a serious scare. When America became involved, some emotional sneak got up to Washington and suggested the cock-eyed notion of building a big army training camp just outside the city on the Quakertown road. The idea outraged the businessmen. Things were bad enough with all the young men being shipped overseas and labor shortages in the mills without having the city swarming with irresponsible strangers, in uniform or out. An army camp would cause cheap concessions and boardinghouses and camp followers and all the rest to appear. Newtown would be full of cafés and dancing places and big-mouthed Northerners causing trouble among the nice working folks of Newtown. It was just no good, all the way down the line. No one could even find out who had got the army surveyors down from Washington to look for the camp site. It couldn't have been a prominent person, with the city's real interest at heart. But things looked serious for a few days while the surveyors were put up in the Briggs Arcade, figuring. And then, suddenly, they moved on from Newtown and put the site just outside Huntsville not five miles from the Continental Tobacco plants. It was such a relief that everyone in Newtown got drunk. Word went around that Mr. Chadley and Mr. Starburg and Mr. Lyndon and some of the other big men had "slipped a little inducement" to the army men to keep out of Newtown. But of course the rumor was quickly scotched, for it was common knowledge that government officials could not be bribed.

After that, the war wasn't so troublesome to Newtown. There were casualties in the afternoon paper once in a while, when some local boy no one knew was killed in France. But on the whole, things were not unbearable.

Then something happened. Influenza. It raced up and down the avenues and back roads, through the mill villages and the city square, with a wild abandon and impartiality that was wondrous to see. It altered and shriveled in fear the bold brassy countenance of the city. It was dreadful.

And Newtown had no coin to buy it off.

In 1917 Lesley Chadley died in the new army camp at Huntsville. He was twenty-five years old. He was not an officer. He could scarcely have been called a soldier. He had had six weeks of drill, and then a pleurisy, then pneumonia, and then had died. And even the notification of his death did not come to Dunmeade from the War Department. It came on thin ladylike vellum, written in a broad ungoverned hand, and postmarked QUAKERTOWN. It came from his *nearest of kin — Gilberta de Ventura Chadley, his wife!*

> *Dear Sir* [it was addressed to Marcus]:
>
> I enclose the telegram which I received this morning informing me of the death of my husband, your son, Lesley Chadley.
>
> My family and I will receive you and his brother Fenton tomorrow evening after seven.
>
> Very truly yours,
>
> GILBERTA DE V. CHADLEY

Lesley's death notice alone would have profoundly shocked Dunmeade. But this was not alone the notice of his death. The incredible letter, terse and unemotional, contained the notice of his life, his true, his actual, his secret life, away from Dunmeade. And the immediate effect of it was to bolt his mourners each into his own privacy, too stunned to question or console each other.

Isaiah simply grieved, and as simply acted. He went to the station to wait for the train from Huntsville bearing Lesley's body home, though not to Dunmeade. He would bow down as it passed. He would honor his boy. He was not concerned with what secrets Lesley had lived with and left behind now, approved by Dunmeade or not. He was concerned only with Lesley's soul, for which he prayed. He left the house with no explanation to Mr. Chadley or Fenton. His little boy Ralph, who was seven, ran to him across the crackled leaves of the yard, then stopped at his father's weeping face and fled. When the train came in, near four, Isaiah stood under the freight shed of the old station and prayed for the young child he had loved, the boy who had turned from him in bitterness before his unexplainable disloyalty, the man he had hardly known, the husband and the soldier, the stranger to Dunmeade, though he had kept his room and gone to table through the seven strained years since that birthday night long ago. Isaiah's grief was pure and of the heart only. He wept that he would not see the loved face again, however turned from him. He mourned that his service was ended, however unused it had been. He felt his loss, and no propriety restrained his tears.

Fenton went immediately to the bank. He closed his father's office and his own and declared his family's bereavement. A wreath was fetched immediately and hung across the ring of the etched brass doors of the building. The tellers and clerks and even the girls in accounting came to the front one at a time to speak to Fenton. Then when they had all gone home and only Briney Morgan, the watchman, was left, Fenton went down to the vaults and opened his personal safe. From it he took a key and opened his brother Lesley's strongbox. He sat down on the marble floor with the sealed papers beside him and slowly and carefully read through each one. This was what Lesley had told him to do. It took him two hours, and when he was done it was twilight outside and time for him to return to Dunmeade for his father. It was time for them both, Marcus and him, to go to Quakertown for Lesley's wife. It was time for them to bring home Lesley's child, his daughter, to Dunmeade – where she belonged.

> DEAR FENTON, MY DEAR BROTHER [he had read in the long letter addressed to him and dated April 1917. The ink was clear and fresh, only six weeks old]:
>
> I am looking down on your head as you sit in the sun in the patio with father. I have watched you many times below me sitting with father. He is talking to you. You seem to be listening. But I think you are not. This is a serious day for you. You were turned down this morning when you volunteered for service at the courthouse. You must have been the first. On your way to the bank, weren't you? I was an hour behind you. That's how I know. Captain Stark mistook me for you, back again to make trouble for him. He didn't know your character, of course. Even when I tell you and Father tonight at dinner, as I intend to, that I am leaving early in the morning for the camp at Huntsville, you will congratulate me; but you will say nothing

about yourself. And there will be nothing for Father to see on your face. But I will see it; for I know your face very well, Fenton. For seven years I have been looking at it and studying it – ever since I came back from the east with Mr. Spencer after Aunt Jessie's death. I have been waiting for you to tell me that you went to Aunt Jessie and asked her to sell you the Prince River strip for me. I have been waiting for you to tell me that Mother herself painted the portrait over the grate in Father's morning room. I have been waiting for you to tell me that Father drove her to her death and that now he hates me, because I am like her, because I am an artist. But I know that our only communication will be through this letter, after I am dead. We will never talk together about any of this. You must have settled your mind upon silence after the night I attacked Father. Or was it Father who attacked me? Do you know, Fenton – that terrible night has never faded in my memory? It is fresh in my mind now as I write this letter – fresh as if it were only last night.

If I return, I will have the moment I have savored so long in my mind and put off only to have more facts to torment him – that moment when I can watch his face and the misery which will come over it when I tell him how peacefully I have worked at my sculptures, not ten miles away from him, at the farmhouse where I have lived with my wife and child! Yes, Fenton, I have wanted to tell you, often. I am married and I have a little girl. And I have wanted to show you my room and my work that he meant to kill in me unborn. But caution for your sake, since I was not ready for him to know, has kept me silent. Often I have wanted to show you the heads I have done. The lot of them are yours if you want them.

Before you opened this letter, you no doubt glanced at my policies and the deeds to the Prince River strip and Aunt Jessie's old house. Then you know how I have left things for Gilberta, my wife – and August. August is not yet two. She is named for the month of her birth, since we could not agree on any other name for her. Gilberta is Spanish. You will see her one day. Either I will live to present you, or you will go alone and offer her your kindness and consolation. But let me tell you now, Fenton, briefly and honestly, since whatever of my life I leave behind becomes your burden, my wife will not grieve deeply.

Do you remember the story the agent told father when he bought Dunmeade? He said that a Spaniard had built it and lived in it only a few years with his little girl and another Spaniard who seemed to be his advisor. And then all three had moved away and the house was sold to Sorrell. People thought the Spaniard died getting back to Spain. At any rate the advisor returned later with the little girl and settled out in the county – among the Quakers, he thought. He said that there had been a motto over Dunmeade's door, carved in Spanish into the stone, but that the Sorrells had had it chiseled down. I know what the motto said, Fenton. It was PIETY AND GOD. And I know about the Spaniard and his friend and the little girl. The little girl married her protector when she was seventeen and bore him two children, a son – Rafael, named for her lost father, and a daughter – Gilberta. You will meet Gilberta's mother, Fenton; but Señor de Ventura is dead. You will meet Rafael too. His land adjoins theirs.

When you see Gilberta, Fenton, you will better understand what I shall say next. I hope that she and Señora de Ventura will be standing together, as they were when I first saw them. They are beautiful, Fenton, with white untinted skin and eyes of stone blue. And their long necks stem up from small sloping Spanish shoulders. They look so strange in their farmhouse in Quakertown. And they are so unhappy there. Understand my pity for them, Fenton. And understand my love for Gilberta and my guilt, which makes me forgive her the bitterness which tries her love for me. She believed me the elder brother. She believed that Dunmeade would one day come to me. And I deceived her, Fenton. Look at her – and blame me, if you can. All her life she has been prepared for the day when she will live in El Refugio. (That is the name they call Dunmeade.) Señor de Ventura brought her mother back to be near it, to watch over it. He meant to buy it back for her. All his days in Quakertown he schemed. Gilberta and Rafael know each flag of the patio and each twist of iron in the banisters, though neither has ever entered the door. But Señor de Ventura was not a farmer, and all his schemes failed. Nor is Rafael a farmer, Fenton. You will see. Sometimes his plows rust in the fields while he sits under his trees with a guitar and sings. He is wonderful to see, Fenton. He will not do what it is against his nature and his lineage to do. And Gilberta never forgets the role she was meant to play – mistress of El Refugio. If she did, her mother would quickly remind her. Her marriage is a terrible error to her. She is chained to a man who not only cannot avail her of her birthright, but who will forever prevent her from gaining it any other way. No, Fenton, my wife, my love – to whom I am such a slave that I have not even the nobility to free her – will not deeply grieve when I am dead. My death will free her. She can try again to gain her castle. Do you see, Fenton? Pity her.

See to my little girl, Fenton. That is my one fear in dying. I have an almost unnatural concern deep in my heart for August. There is a feeling there, Fenton, a feeling that warns me there is danger to August from Father. I shudder to think that he may one day control her life. Gilberta is so *driven,* Fenton. If I am gone, she will turn again toward Dunmeade – and to whom? – unless, by some mercy, to you. Now her name is Chadley and her child's name is Chadley. She will feel that she is doubly entitled to her place there. August is Father's grandchild. Gilberta will secure her place, if she can, through August. Watch over my child, Fenton! But I know you will. Father will not allow my death to cheat him of me. August is my continuation. She may have inherited my talents. Then heaven spare her! He will punish her, if he can. The world is a harsh insensitive place for artists – for any decent heart, Fenton. It is not hard to break a spirit.

If I live, I may return without the anger which eats away at me for the wrong Father inflicted upon me. I am gifted, I know. And I have taken that gift seriously, I assure you. But now, somewhere inside me, I am undone, unsettled.

When I began this letter, I thought that it would be hard for me to write these things to you. So much time has passed and we have lived so differently for so long – all of us in this house. But instead, I feel a great freedom. Perhaps it is because I am safe from your eyes afterward. Then let me tell you, my brother – if I have suffered a deep hatred for the man who is my father, I have held a deep love for you. I have known your sacrifice for me – at what final cost to you no one will ever know, for there is no way of knowing what you might have made of your life had things been otherwise. But let me say that I am grateful to you, and that I shall be as long as I live, Fenton.

I can see you and Father rising now to go in. Isaiah will come to call me in a moment. I shall put this letter in my box and give you the key later tonight.

Pray for me, Fenton. God bless and keep you for what you do.

Good night.

Lesley left his insurance to Gilberta, about thirty thousand dollars in small policies. He deeded Aunt Jessie's old house in Prince River to August, along with title to the strip of land surrounding Fenton's and Marcus's turpentine tract on the river. The toll he had collected from them over seven years for the right to cross it had been deposited in a savings account. It was to be paid his wife, upon his death. There were no other assets and there were no debts. He had lived on the rent collected from the lease of Aunt Jessie's house, along with his salary from the bank.

Fenton rearranged his papers and the will, put them back into the box and into his own safe again. Then he methodically and slowly destroyed the letter he had just read. When he was done he went upstairs and Briney Morgan let him out of the bank and locked the doors behind him.

He walked home toward Dunmeade. He replied to an occasional sympathetic nod from someone he passed. But he was absorbed in a merciful thought which spared him the consciousness of his grief. Lesley had not left him alone. He had left him a rare legacy, a care, a charge. And Fenton had a lifetime before him to mind her welfare. He walked faster, the sooner to reach Dunmeade and go to Quakertown to claim his inheritance and begin his happy and unexpected parenthood, to see his child, August de Ventura Chadley.

Beyond him the gates to Dunmeade were closing slowly. Someone was calling to express sympathy. Mr. Starburg, perhaps?

It was nearly six o'clock. Fenton hurried to overtake the caller. He was not certain his father wished to receive condolences yet. They had not decided upon the announcement to make concerning Lesley. He wanted to spare his father any awkwardness. They must arrange to bring Lesley's body home – to Dunmeade. They must receive sympathy together, all of them who had been in Lesley's life.

The front door closed ahead of him. He was certain that it was Mr. Starburg. It might even be wise to confide their curious predicament. Mr. Starburg might be proper to circulate some tactful announcement of the existence of Lesley's wife and suggest that the marriage had been known all along to Dunmeade. Fenton took heart. Then he remembered August. No one knew about August yet, not even his father. He must manage in some way to speak to his father immediately, privately. Perhaps Mr. Starburg was still waiting in the drawing room to be received, and there would be time.

He put his key into the lock. And then before he could turn it, the door opened and his father stood there, holding it back. Fenton looked quickly toward the drawing room, but Mr. Starburg was not there. No one was there.

"I thought I saw someone ahead of me, sir," he said, puzzled and embarrassed. "I imagined it was Mr. Starburg calling."

Mr. Chadley smiled oddly and then began to lead Fenton down the hall to his study – without saying anything at all. At the study door, he paused and put his hand on Fenton's shoulder. Then he urged him in, still smiling.

There was a last spring fire glowing in the grate and a lamp was lit near the window. Mr. Chadley moved him toward the young woman standing by the mantel with a child in her arms. She was wearing her hat still.

"Gilberta," Mr. Chadley presented him in his fine high voice, – "this is Fenton, Lesley's brother."

He waited until Fenton had bowed and then he finished quietly, "And Fenton, this is your niece, August de Ventura Chadley – my granddaughter."

Fenton looked into the face of Lesley's wife and held out his arms to take the little girl from her.

"I'm glad you have come to Dunmeade, Gilberta," he said kindly. "I hope you will want to stay."

And that was all.

Mr. Chadley had seen to his affairs. Fenton had had to do nothing for him. His house was whole and together. He was indeed the master – the lord and the master of Dunmeade.

The service for Lesley Chadley was a private one; only the two families, strange to each other, and a few old friends were present. Gilberta was dignified and did not weep. And Isaiah, who had loved Lesley with such unquestioning devotion, spoke the only prayer, mentioning with humble dignity the loss to earth of Lesley's soul, and the gain to Heaven. Then Mr. Chadley unexpectedly concluded the service by reciting the first lines of Donne's apostrophe to Death.

> Death, be not proud, though some have called thee
> Mighty and dreadful, for thou art not so;
> For those thou think'st thou dost overthrow
> Die not, poor Death; nor yet canst thou kill me.

Only Fenton saw Mr. Chadley's face. His father's eyes were open and distant, purple as ever, with no change from the years. And his head was forward in the thrust from his shoulders which Fenton had seen so often in battle. It was a challenge he spoke. No, his father was not done! Lesley's death had not defeated or released him!

Fenton hurried from the room when it was over, quickly, with

August in his arms. He went up the black iron stair to the room at the far end of the gallery where Maude would come to keep her. He murmured to her, while she stared into his face, smiling and examining the working of his mouth with her fingers: "It's all going to be all right. You're safe and sound, safe and sound." And he was not conscious that he spoke to a child who knew no alarms and no reasons to have any.

Newtown was shocked that no ordained white minister had held the service. The city declared that Lesley Chadley had been buried in the earth like a heathen with no real blessing upon him, and that Mr. Chadley had been out of his mind to let a Negro servant preach his own son's funeral! There was even talk of getting up a petition and making a protest. But then Newtown's mind was taken off the subject very suddenly. A case of contagious influenza broke out in one of the schoolhouses down in colored town, and the threat of the epidemic took the city's attention. The talk died down, then, and families stopped riding out to the cemetery on Sunday afternoons to gape at Lesley's grave.

In time, Fenton succeeded in erasing the whole memory of Lesley's funeral service from his mind; for in that sad hour he had unexpectedly accomplished the solution to his dilemma—that dilemma in which Lesley's instruction, to father and guard his child August, had placed Fenton.

He had been watching Gilberta during the service, anxious for her under the strain. She seemed to him so delicate, and she looked so lost among her new strange kin. Then, as he watched her, she turned her head suddenly and her eyes gazed into his. The unexpected quality and emotion of her expression struck Fenton like a missile. Her glance was something another person, less sensitive, would scarcely have noticed. Isaiah had bent his head to pray, and Gilberta's eyes went slowly down from Fenton's. The moment was done; but a shameful, almost indecent, thrill shook Fenton beneath all his grief for his brother.

I am the answer, his heart pressed him, in its instant of longing. *And it is the right way*, his conscience consoled him. *Gilberta will have Dunmeade, which she covets, and in return I shall have the child, as Lesley devoutly desired.*

It had been a harsh year and even Newtown was sobered and spent. There had been the autumn of the Armistice and by late winter the first returning soldiers and the beginning of not enough jobs. And still the spreading of the great influenza epidemic over the country.

Newtown had had an early start in losses. Gaither Lyndon's sickly Gussie died, and Lucius Starburg's wife, who had been Margaret Willetts. The Reverend Smoote had keeled over at the York boy's funeral – and passed on, himself, four nights later. Preston Sorrell had come home one afternoon with a chill and tanked up to sweat it off and never rallied from the fever. And old Doc Pickett, worn out with running all over Newtown from morn till night making Pickett's Plasters, crawled into his bed one early dawn, too tired to apply his own remedy and never arose again. With Preston Sorrell, his limited partner, not cold in the sod when he was laid to rest nearby, there was then a crisis in the business. Orders were pouring in from the North, national distribution was being offered in the national epidemic – and who was left behind to meet the challenge? Doc's slow, conservative son, George!

But the orders were filled. Doc's brother-in-law, Hartley Pickett, came to Newtown for his funeral and thereafter took hold of everything. In the confusion, it never occurred to anyone to question his doing so, though Hartley Pickett had never had an interest in the firm before, and might never have had, if Doc's death hadn't given him a chance to grab.

Time passed violently with dying and building that year in Newtown – 1918. There were changes, but not in the outward shape of life there, of course.

Mr. Chadley was not well. First he, and then Fenton, and then Gilberta suffered attacks of influenza. Mr. Chadley had never been ill before and he was impatient of his weakness – contemptuous, in fact. He got up from his bed and went to the bank to help Lawyer Ramsey settle some estates and last wills, and that effort ended his active life. He developed a heart condition. He was sixty-three years old, as big-framed as ever, the flesh of his face stretched without a wrinkle over the structure of bone beneath, his purple eyes unfaded in their hollows under his brows and his hair still thick. But even so, he was not the man who had come to Newtown eighteen years before.

The morning Fenton chose to speak to his father about marrying Gilberta, he found Mr. Chadley sitting before his grate fire with a light rug over his knees. It was spring; but in Newtown, even late in March the storms and sudden sleets of winter were not done. It was Saturday – and a fortunate thing, Fenton thought, looking at his father's bluish face. (It was bluish more often than not, lately.) On Saturday at least he would rest, for the bank was closed at noon.

"Could I have a word with you, sir?" Fenton asked him. "There is something I've been wanting to discuss with you." He had decided to be direct and put the proposition before his father as he would a business matter.

Mr. Chadley looked up slowly. His movements had always been studied, purposefully studied. Now for the first time they were artlessly so and, in a curious way, seemed unnatural.

"Yes?" he responded, and then gazed into Fenton's face and repeated, "Yes?"

Apparently Fenton had interrupted him in some reverie. He could sense a distance between them.

"I wanted to speak to you, sir, about marriage," Fenton began. "I feel I should be thinking of marriage."

He paused then, hoping for some reaction from his father, a nod or a sympathetic expression to help him on. He had prepared his speech but the exact words as he had rehearsed them were slipping irretrievably out of his memory. It seemed to him suddenly an ignominy to have to ask permission to marry.

Then Mr. Chadley moved forward in his chair and looked up at Fenton and said, "It's Gilberta, isn't it?"

It seemed to Fenton that his blood emptied out of his heart and left him without strength. All the reasons he had found to persuade his father to the match were now without purpose, a limp string he grasped to support him.

"Yes, sir," he said, "I think it will be a solution for us all. I have given it a great deal of thought."

He expected his father to agree or to say something, but Mr. Chadley only smiled and waited.

"If I brought a wife into this house – a proper wife, of course – she would expect to assume the responsibilities of mistress here," Fenton began to argue. "But in the year since Lesley's passing, Gilberta has filled that position – and with great charm and manner, I think you must agree, sir."

It was true. Gilberta had managed Dunmeade with a devotion and care almost touching to see.

"She has a small child, and she is very proud," Fenton went on. "I don't think her nature has provided her with the patience to live in a secondary position among us. She would imagine herself to be insecure among her husband's own kin. That would be an intolerable burden upon her spirit."

Still Mr. Chadley said nothing. He was hearing Fenton out – whether sympathetically or not, Fenton could not tell. On his face was a strange expression, as if he were listening to some naive, ambitious child recite a poem, the meaning of which he had neither the experience nor the perception to understand.

"And then, there is little August," Fenton finished, with what composure he could manage. "She needs a father – something more than an uncle and a grandfather. She's a dear, sensitive child. She deserves great care. And I should like to provide it."

At this point, Fenton became aware that his father's attention had suddenly gone to something above and behind Fenton's head. Mr. Chadley's eyes had softened with a moisture not unlike tears, as if they were watering in defense against his stare into too-brilliant light. Fenton turned around to find the object which drew such a gaze.

It was the portrait of his mother.

Without sun on it from the windows, it was even more brooding in expression, with a strange and inescapable accusation in the eyes.

"Do you love Gilberta, Fenton?" his father asked him suddenly, to his back.

"Yes sir," Fenton answered.

"Then ask her to marry you," his father said. "That is the only reason you require."

Fenton and Gilberta were married in the garden. The young minister who had been sent to fill the Reverend Smoote's pulpit temporarily, nearly two years before, performed the ceremony. He had vigor and pep and was a good fund raiser, but it was not these qualities which caused him to be selected to perform the Chadley ceremony. He was merely the least objectionable cleric to Mr. Chadley.

Gilberta, like the Chadleys, belonged to no church, though she was soon observed to read the Bible in a strange, almost violent habit, as if she were a devout member of some distinctly absorbing and clearly defined faith. Often when she came in from reading on a garden seat by the front wall, far from the house, she would have an unearthly distance in her eyes as if she were calmly following some star unseen by anyone else. And then again, she would appear at luncheon, agitated and impatient, as if the pages she had sought in her Testament were missing — torn out to thwart her by some irreligious tease.

Gilberta troubled Fenton. His sensitive heart, long ago prepared by Lesley's revelations, struggled to provide for her a garment of devotion and sympathy to wear against her anxieties. For him, there was mystery in Gilberta, not mystery of person, or the strange female nature, but another mystery, more sad and more warlike, hinting a harsh history and its wound. He loved her, and on the afternoon soon after their marriage, when he was summoned to his father's apartment, he was thinking of her.

Mr. Chadley was standing at the windows of his sitting room when Fenton entered. He joined his father and with him looked down the drive to the gates at the street. Gilberta was walking out. When she had passed from sight, Mr. Chadley turned to him and abruptly began the business for which he had called him. He was thin and his illness was beginning to glitter unmistakably in his eyes. He went to the door and locked it quietly. Then he brought a small mahogany document box from the closet concealed behind the drapery of the tall-post bed.

"I am thinking of returning to our home in the East," he said, "and I am about to burden you with the responsibility of our affairs here." He smiled then and some of the old mastery came into his voice. "I want to go over some confidential details."

That was all. It was his farewell to Newtown. And Fenton knew it. His father was going home to die. The actual day of his departure was months off. But Fenton knew that he had left Dunmeade as of that moment, just as Gilberta had passed beyond the gates. His father had taken his leave of the business world in which his enormous energy and brilliance had functioned. He was going home, to the place from which he had come. What peace he longed for or what rest he hoped to find there, Fenton did not know. But this Fenton did know – the charge for life which had been so bright an illumination in his father's face was going, dimming out. Fenton sat down beside him to see his record and accept successorship.

"As to this house," Mr. Chadley began, "I think that I shall deed Dunmeade to August. She will take title when she comes of age." He took some papers from the box and began to arrange them before Fenton.

Fenton did not speak. An enormous and uncontainable guilt was swelling in him, numbing his mind. He could not nod that he had heard and understood. He could not spur himself to make one protest against such a destruction of Gilberta's hopes. He could only sit silent, resigned before his father's stronger will.

In time, he promised himself – desperate and wordless, as Mr. Chadley's recital of business began – I'll find a way to make it up to her. I'll make the bargain . . . And then his pride refused the word and he substituted: I'll make the marriage good.

Often in the next years Fenton went to the flat pine region of Prince River for long visits with his father. He first went alone. On the last trip, he took August, who was nearing six.

They drove the big sedan, through the fruit plains, east beyond the swamps of cypresses, to the pines and sand and sea. They traveled the last afternoon along a narrow road parallel to the inland waterway, coursing south. Sand blowing across the bluff of dunes beside them seeped into the engine and the car wheels raced and struggled to pull. They were ferried by hand-ropes afloat a barge across a narrow neck of Prince River. Then on the new shore they followed a private road until they came to fields and at last a long moss-shaded yard, beyond which stood the house, remote and shuttered. By day it was shuttered against the heat; by night, against the dark.

A Negro boy came down the walk to meet them. He was Ralph, Isaiah's son. He was tall and overgrown, with a stoop to his bony shoulders. He waited for Fenton to speak, his face sober and respectful, yet showing a shy excitement. And then to Fenton's greeting, he answered softly, "How do, Mr. Fenton, sir," in the typical dropped flat vowels of the coast region. Then he reached to carry August's little patent leather box, in which she kept her "hair things," her ribbons and barrettes.

"This is little August, isn't it?" he asked, looking at her admiringly. Fenton smiled and nodded, about to answer yes, when in an instant August drew up stiffly. "You call me *Miss* Chadley!" she said, her child's voice atremble with indignation, and she jerked her box from his dark thin hands.

Stung, Ralph met her hostile eyes staring up into his face and then he turned his head. "Yes, ma'am," he murmured, "*Miss* Chadley, ma'am," and stepped aside dumbly for Fenton and August to walk ahead of him.

The three went in silence up the path.

At the steps to the porch Fenton took August's hand and gently eased her up to the top. The chairs had been turned down against a sudden dawn shower. It was warm and close and the twilight lingered yellow and eerie through the hanging moss. Maude and Isaiah stood in the door, the big screens flung back against their arms.

"You remember Maude and Isaiah, don't you, dear?" Fenton coached her quickly, even before he nodded himself. He looked down at August beseechingly and urged her forward a little. Then Maude came out, reaching to take August in her arms.

"Dear Father, she's a grown lady!" she cried, her face alight with affection and welcome. "She most surely is! Aren't you proud, Mr. Fenton? Will you just look at that child, Isaiah?"

But August did not move. She looked straight into Maude's face with not a flicker of recognition in the stare of her terrified eyes. Maude might have been from another world. August turned to Fenton, but Fenton had gone, was in the house shaking Isaiah's hands in his own, talking to Isaiah in self-conscious, almost unmanly emotion. August was forgotten, left outside the screens, alone with Maude. She looked into the bold dark face smiling coaxingly, trying to lure her into the reaching arms, and her little body quivered and drew back in fright before the unexplained familiarity. "No!" she cried out suddenly, snatching at the screens to get into the house, "No!" They swung back and she scrambled into the hall after Fenton. "Uncle Chad!" she screamed, then stopped in panic to decide the way he had gone. And then a firm hand fastened on her shoulder.

"Good evening, young lady," a quiet high voice said. "He hasn't deserted you." For a moment August did not move. Cautiously, she observed the hand on her shoulder. Then she raised her head. The man who had spoken was tall and pale in the shadow of the doorframe. He was wearing a fringed shawl about his shoulders and he rested on a whittled cane. She looked up to his great height above her and then carefully moved out from under his fingers. "I am your grandfather," he said, dryly, "aren't you glad to see me?" For a moment August contemplated the strange amused face without replying. Then, very deliberately, she reached up to put her arms around his neck and the tall figure carefully bent over to oblige her. "Good evening, Grandfather," she said very sweetly, with her face beside his ear. She hesitated ever so slightly and then she kissed the waxy bone of his cheek.

For the first few days of the visit, Mr. Chadley was spared one of his attacks. The excitement of guests in the house seemed to stimulate him and a little color, not entirely healthy, came into his face. He was gaunt with scarcely any flesh seeming to cover his large frame. He had lost no weight; but with age his bones had grown thicker so that his flesh was drawn tighter over the fine structure of skull and limb which made him so handsome a figure. At times his old amused expression came back into his eyes, which, instead of dimming with disease, had grown brighter and more purple than ever. In the mornings, after his breakfast, he sat on the small back square of garden and listened to Fenton recount the business transactions which had spellbound Newtown since their last meeting. He enjoyed particularly Fenton's account of Hartley Pickett's failure to outsmart two Yankee "scientists" he had hired to convert the poultice plaster ointment into throat pellets. Hartley had tried to pay them only for the time they had worked; but the two men claimed he had offered them a percentage of the product's sale and they kept the new formula secret and sued. The whole business had been aired in court and Hartley had had to make certain guarantees. So now there was a strange bookkeeper sitting beside old Willy Simpson, who had had free reign over the red-and-blue columns of the Pickett Poultice Company's ledgers ever since Marcus Chadley had financed Doc's conversion of the tobacco prizery into a poultice works. The Yankees insisted upon strict accountings. It was the first time anyone had got the best of Hartley Pickett since he had seized the company from old Doc's son, George.

"But there's another Pickett coming along," Fenton imparted hopefully, "and from all I've observed he resembles neither his father nor his great-uncle." And then Fenton described the shock-haired little boy who had climbed over the gate at Dunmeade one winter afternoon and seriously asked Fenton for August's hand in marriage. He had been dressed in an Indian suit complete with feathers, and he had brought offerings including the stiff skin of a black snake and his own recently lost front baby teeth on a watch chain. They had seemed to Fenton gruesome tributes to August's charm; but August had accepted them without a shudder. Indeed, Fenton had learned upon investigation that the young ladies of August's set at Miss Lena Nyrick's School at the Country Club were accustomed to receiving anything from live frogs to tin can collections and that Mr. Billy Pickett was not without a rival in the field. One of Uncle Hartley's "scientists" had moved just down the street from Dunmeade, and there seemed to be an aggressive young bachelor in that household too. He was in the habit of whistling to August across the side yard of Dunmeade and inviting himself in to show her how to explode Christmas Stars — a fireworks concoction his father had made up for him. At the present time, the rockets and fizz powders of little Mr. Barron were making a more favorable impression upon August than the regular flow of bird's wings, shellacked beetles, and live toads which Billy Pickett brought to Dunmeade every Sunday morning at 9:30, in time for cocoa and sugared German doughnuts.

Marcus Chadley looked around at his granddaughter rocking gently alone on the screened-in back veranda. She was busily drawing a needle and thread in and out of a piece of cloth stretched across a ring. She was embroidering a tea napkin with a simple stenciled jonquil design. She might have been fifty years old, from the patient diligence she exhibited.

"That's her project," Fenton said. "She goes to Miss Nyrick's School."

"Is she always so self-contained?" asked Mr. Chadley. "She hasn't shown the curiosity one would expect from a child in a strange place."

There was a criticism of August in his question. Fenton felt it in his father's voice even before he noticed Mr. Chadley's particular expression. Long ago, when Lesley had sat dreaming in the patio with his mind far away, with Mr. Chadley helpless to gain his attention except with a sharp demand, Fenton had seen his father's face as it was now.

"Oh no," Fenton hastily reassured him, "she's trying not to intrude or cause you to change your habits to accommodate her. Gilberta has instructed her not to make herself conspicuous and not to enter her elders' conversation unless invited. She's very obedient. In fact, she's inclined to be rather literal-minded, with not a great deal of imagination." He paused and then finished, "I suppose that's an attribute in a woman."

As he said it, the slow warmth of guilt began to spread over Fenton. What he had said was not true. August was not without imagination. The particular embroidery upon which she was now working with such absorption attested to it. And Fenton did not believe his aspersion concerning women. He had said it to take his father's attention from August, to lure him into a general and safer discussion. But more shamelessly, he had discredited August to deceive Mr. Chadley. He was anxious for August—afraid for her, really.

"It's an attribute in anyone unless he has the gift and insight of genius to use it," Mr. Chadley observed dryly in response. "Imagination in a fool is a dangerous weapon." But he turned his head only momentarily from studying August. Fenton had failed.

At last, when August apparently was not going to look up at all from her embroidery so that he might beckon to her discreetly, Fenton sighed, acknowledged defeat, and said to Mr. Chadley directly, "I think I shall ask you to help me with August in a certain particular, sir."

He waited until his father had assumed that pose of attention he had always given any request for advice.

"There was a little incident upon our arrival last night which has given me a great deal of concern," Fenton went on. "Unfortunately August's behavior was entirely correct according to her viewpoint, or rather, her viewpoint was proper in general; but, as is so often the case, her elders — and I take the blame upon myself mainly — had not prepared her to meet the exception to the rule." It moved him to remember the little scene, and he paused a moment and cleared his throat. "I'm afraid August has unconsciously wounded and shamed Isaiah's nice little lad. . . ." He moved a little in his chair to see if anyone were overhearing. Then he said, "I don't quite know how to make her understand. I remember how easily you steered our relationship at Dunmeade — Lesley's and mine to Isaiah and his family. I wonder if perhaps some idea occurs to you here. You see, there are only Susie and Addie in our present household — August no longer requires a nurse, and the situation there is rather more formal." Then he related August's hostile rebuke to Ralph — "You call me *Miss* Chadley!"

Mr. Chadley listened with great interest.

"I don't know how to make her understand that there are differences in colored folks — " Fenton finished in a lame floundering.

"You don't know how to teach her to use generosity with her inferiors without inviting impudence. Is that it?" Mr. Chadley replied, and he turned to watch his little granddaughter, who had moved now and seemed to be lingering on the stoop without knowing whether to join them or not. He appraised her now with a different eye. In a curious way he seemed pleased with what he had heard.

"Would you care to sit here in the sun with us, little lady?" he called in his soft high voice, and further invited her by holding out his hand. She smiled.

Then she came down toward them, folding her hoop and needles in a piece of muslin to keep her work clean. The gesture

would have been almost prim had she not had a childish physical unbalance to her body. The little-girl awkwardness saved her from prissiness.

Fenton pulled up a cypress lawn chair and helped her to get in it. Her legs did not touch the grass, and she spread her starched pink pinafore neatly over her knees and felt with her heels for the chair rung to anchor herself. She was quite sturdy, not in the least delicate and helpless as a girl is expected to be. Oddly, sitting in the mid-morning sunlight, she seemed quite gold-blond in complexion and hair, whereas truthfully she was dark, after the coloring of her mother. Her facial features were Chadley features; but in general appearance she was unmistakably Spanish. Both Mr. Chadley and Fenton sat in silence a moment admiring her. She was a handsome child, with too matured a beauty to be called pretty. All the structure of her face was clearly defined. She had none of the soft merging of feature and coloring characteristic of mere baby prettiness.

"Would you like to live here with me, Miss August, instead of in Newtown with your – " and almost imperceptibly her grandfather hesitated, about to say "father," and then quickly finished – "your Uncle Fenton?" It was almost a flirtatious invitation. Mr. Chadley smiled in a wooing sort of way. August looked down at her hands, resting quiet on her lap. She thought a moment. Then very politely, she said, "I would rather live with my Uncle Rafael if I didn't live at Dunmeade." She raised her eyes very seriously to her grandfather's.

The unexpected answer with its affront to his vanity startled Mr. Chadley. He glanced sharply at Fenton. He was angry with her; but he smiled quickly and said with underscored amusement, "She's rather let both of us out of the running, hasn't she?" A moment before, asking August, he had been courting preference over his son. Now he included Fenton in his rejection.

"Her Uncle Rafael plays the Spanish guitar," Fenton supplied in a desperate explanation of August's attraction to Rafael de Ventura. "He also tells her stories in Spanish, which of course she cannot understand; but it makes her laugh to see him act out bullfights and all that, you know. Rafael is something of a clown."

"And little else, isn't he?" retorted Mr. Chadley sharply.

Fenton flushed. He envied Rafael. And he knew why August would have liked living with him. She longed to participate in the unabashed exhibitions of affection between Rafael and his children. Even when he punished one with a hickory switch, Rafael would cry out, loudly and brazenly, along with the culprit, and bemoan, in Spanish, the terrible acts of children against their fathers. Such occasions were mighty catharses, purges, which left both participants and onlookers a little drunkenly happy and relieved after. Such seemingly unreasonable scenes were quite necessary to the happiness of the de Venturas, Fenton had decided, and he sorrowed for August, who was a de Ventura also, and filled with hilarity and strange silences and quick angers like them. She would alternate between moods of sweet gay childishness and a kind of sober rage as if she felt herself wronged or misunderstood in some way. Fenton wished that he were able to shout and run with her about the grounds of Dunmeade and tumble her roughly on the lawns to help her at times. But such a thing could never be. Fenton did not know how to ignore decorum. He had never run in his life. But he knew why little Earl Barron with his rough Yankee-boy ways and shooting firecrackers excited August. And he knew, with sadness and humiliation at the thought, why Gilberta, his wife, would never be happy with him.

"Perhaps she has some inclination for music," Mr. Chadley suggested to Fenton, in his distant objective voice, most cold of all when he was wounded. "I am surprised you hadn't considered that. There must be some acceptable teacher in Newtown who could sound the child out. You should see to it when you return," and he suddenly stirred to get up. "I'm going to show you a rare fine instrument, not a Spanish guitar, my little lady," he said to August, shuffling to free his feet of the light afghan which had been across his knees. Then he clapped his hands twice for Ralph to come and escort him to the house.

"Allow me, sir," Fenton hastily offered his arm.

"No, thank you," declined Mr. Chadley, and he looked pointedly at August while he continued. She had slid down from her chair and was waiting either to lead or to follow. "Being my support is one of Ralph's many kind services in our house." He looked about. "There you are. That's the boy." And he raised his arm to rest heavily on Ralph's slightly lowered shoulders.

Along the path to the front of the house, he continued addressing August, who walked beside him. "Ralph is going to be leaving me soon," he said mildly, as if he were remarking upon the inevitable harvest of crops in the fall after the previous planting of seed in the spring. "He's going to come to live with you in Newtown." He paused a moment. His breath was quicker and a little noisy. "Ralph is going to be *your* friend, Miss August. Isn't that right, Ralph?" He moved a little slower and seemed to rest an instant before each step. "Yes, sir, Mr. Chadley," the boy replied courteously. He was busy balancing the weight of his charge so that no strain fell to the man. Fenton noticed the stoop to the young shoulders.

"Ralph is going to study at the fine Negro college in Newtown," went on Mr. Chadley; "he's going to be a teacher. We've already seen to the tuition. We have a splendid letter here from Walter Craven Henshaw, haven't we, Ralph?" He turned his face slightly to the side to add to Fenton, "Isaiah attended the inaugural address on the campus when Henshaw became president of the college." They were at the front steps. "He must be on in years by now, wouldn't you say? You must keep the letter he wrote you, Ralph. It will be something of value to your children. Walter Henshaw is one of the great leaders of your race." They stopped to rest.

"Papa," Ralph called suddenly through the vined lattice which filled the space from the ground to the high veranda on either side of the steps. Isaiah answered from under the porch where he kept his flower pots and tools. He was mending the sprinkler hose.

To Fenton, watching Isaiah emerge from under the steps, Isaiah seemed quite unchanged from his boyhood memory of him. And indeed, there had been little change. Isaiah was ten years younger than Mr. Chadley, and though he had been only in his thirties when he had come with the Chadleys to Newtown, he had seemed as middle-aged to the boy Fenton as he was in reality now. He was still strong and still as tenderly resourceful.

Isaiah wiped his hands again on his duck apron and reached to lift Mr. Chadley firmly under the arms. And as he did so, Ralph stooped down and put his shoulder against Mr. Chadley's back and his hands forward under Mr. Chadley's bent knees; together they quickly lifted the man up the steps in a human chair of their own bodies. Tears sprang into Fenton's eyes at the touching spectacle of care. He took August's hand and nodded to her to see it too. The little girl was already watching the two Negroes quite seriously.

"There you go, Mr. Chadley, sir!" said Isaiah at the top, and gently he let down his burden on the porch.

"Now," asked Mr. Chadley, smiling at August in triumph, "wasn't that extraordinary? I weigh a hundred and sixty pounds, my lady!" He demanded her admiration and applause. He was like an impresario calling for bravos for his performers and then somehow stealing them for himself. Isaiah and Ralph hovered about him until he designated the next direction, and then the three began their trip down the hall in front of Fenton, who followed with August.

It was a spacious house with hundreds of footsteps between one high-ceilinged room and another, upstairs and down. Their footsteps echoed in the hall where two pier mirrors and two small settees were all that broke the bareness of the walls. Dunmeade was formal and distant by its luxury; but this house, which had been Marcus Chadley's father's home, and the place where Fenton and then Lesley had been born, was austere and almost naked in feeling in spite of the lush landscape about it. Dunmeade had been furnished from it, and though what was left in it was as fine as any of its parts which had gone to Newtown, the robbery had given the house a stiff, depleted look, as if its blood had been let too long and it stood erect only out of great will and spirit.

The house had a depressing effect upon Fenton each time he visited it. It seemed to disturb his memory and yet to forward to his mind no clear and positive scene from his life there as a child. He could remember no object or happening to associate with any room, or the view outside any window. There should have been something he recognized with his emotions, not alone his eye.

The room they entered was dim behind shuttered windows, and though it was immaculately clean there was about it that musty feeling which is in the closed front parlors of farmhouses, where nothing takes place except the periodic formal resumés of living — weddings and funerals.

Isaiah opened the blinds, but no stream of sunlight relieved the dimness. The windows faced the east, where the broadest shade of the yard trees fell across the roof. It was a beautiful room — unviolated as the others had been by the theft of parts to Dunmeade. Here the sashes of satin which tied back the draperies fell in perfect pleats to the floor, and the graceful looking-glasses on opposite walls reflected each other's crest of carved and gilded flowers across the top. The polished knees of the chairs were highlit against the dull pile of carpet supporting them. And at the far end, with two great hurricane lamps placed to light the music rack, was the instrument Mr. Chadley had brought August to see.

"Come here," he said and walked her forward with him to the velvet stool.

Fenton was too absorbed and too astonished at what was going on suddenly in the middle of that quiet morning to search his memory for any incident which might have prepared him for what he witnessed. His father with August's hand in his led her to stand beside him at his left while he sat down before the closed keyboard and rubbed his fingers before he began. Then he opened the harpsichord, shifted the stool, and placed his hands to begin. Isaiah and Ralph stood quietly at the back of the room, as if they were awaiting the organ prelude in church. There was no surprise on their features. It seemed to be a performance they had witnessed frequently and were prepared to enjoy again.

The shock of being in a room which had always been in the house and familiar to him before, but which was made strange now by the sight of the instrument and his father playing it, unnerved Fenton and he sank trembling into a chair to listen.

With ease, and an obvious love for what he was doing, Mr. Chadley began Bach's *Komm' Süsser Tod*. His touch was sure and firm. He had played it many times – and well. His age and the weakness characteristic of his illness was nowhere evident in his performance. August stood beside him, absorbed for the first time in what her grandfather was doing. Mr. Chadley responded to her as a concert artist when he feels the fascination of his audience. The music moved out from him and his instrument to hold them all in one listening attention. And when he finished the final bell-like precise tones of the last measures, he said quietly without turning his head, "Isaiah?" And Isaiah began simply, from the back of the room, "Come gentle death . . ." in his rich untutored voice. The whole was repeated again.

"Thank you, Isaiah," Mr. Chadley murmured when it was done. Then he turned to August. "There is not another one in the whole of this country," he said softly, taking her child's hand and running the tips of her fingers sensuously back and forth to feel the wood of the case. "It's rosewood. Your great-grandfather brought it from France long, long ago. He gave it to your great-grandmother on her wedding day. And I gave it to your grandmother on hers." He paused. He had taken his hand from August's fingers, but the little girl still searched the satiny grain of the wood.

Suddenly she leaned her cheek to further caress the cool, dark surface and looked up into his face. "I want the piano," she said. She looked steadily into her grandfather's eyes, her head tilted to rest against the case, a coquettish plea on her face.

Fenton started up. The sound of August's voice came through the dreamy aftermath of the music with shocking curtness. He had forgotten August. He jumped up and hurried to take her. He was frightened for a moment – Mr. Chadley was not accustomed to bold demands, certainly not from a child. "Now, now, dear," Fenton began to August; but no one heard him.

Mr. Chadley was laughing. He was amused. He was more than amused. He was delighted with her. She wanted something which belonged to him, something he could give her or not – as his fancy chose. He had reached her. She could be bought! "It's a *harpsichord*, Miss August, not a piano," he teased. "Can you say that? *Harpsichord*." He repeated it and coaxed her to say it after him.

"Yes, sir," she answered, unperturbed. His amusement had not for a moment swerved her attention from the instrument. "*Harpsichord*," she pronounced perfectly. She mashed on the keys happily, trying to play it.

"Here, here," Mr. Chadley restrained her, his voice still light with laughter, "this way. Now – " And he began to press her fingers one at a time through the theme of Bach.

Fenton stared at the unbelievable sight, man and child engrossed in a peculiar courting play, shutting them off together away from the others in the room. Fenton could not understand. No preparation had ever been made for the revelation of music in that house, or in any other Mr. Chadley dwelled in. He felt suddenly that his father, whom he had always approached with the greatest respect and attempt at understanding, even in the terrible days with Lesley, had played some ridiculous joke upon him. He could see Mr. Chadley's sly smile of pleasure, as if he were saying, "No man will ever plumb my mystery. There are depths and depths, places and places you can never fathom. Not even you, Fenton!" It was almost antagonistic – as if he meant to hurt Fenton. Where had the harpsichord been before? Fenton had never heard it! He could not remember Mr. Chadley's ever referring to it. If his mother had ever played it, he could not remember. In the years he had lived in this house, before they had moved to Newtown, he had never heard its sound. More than that, Fenton could not recall even a conversation in which Mr. Chadley had remarked upon music in a way to indicate his ever having studied any instrument! Occasionally, when Professor

Hanley had been holding forth in some discussion of aesthetics, Mr. Chadley had drawn parallels between the mathematical patterns of certain musical forms and the similar progression of solutions in logic. . . . But these opinions had been academic. There had been no hint of a love for music in them. . . . Or perhaps there had been? At that moment Fenton doubted all his past judgments and recollections.

But it was not really astonishment that his father could play the harpsichord which troubled Fenton most. It was something more personal – and a little shameful. He was jealous. Isaiah had sung, and Ralph had listened with familiar admiration on his face. Such occasions, obviously, were an ordinary recreation here – and Fenton had not known about them, or been allowed to share in them ever before. It was a discrimination he did not deserve; and ignoble or not, he took out his indignation brooding and reading in his room throughout the remainder of the day, leaving August to Maude's care.

Then, just before dinner, Isaiah came to knock with a message from Mr. Chadley.

"Your father isn't up to coming to the table, Mr. Fenton," Isaiah said. "He's going to take a little something in his apartment. But he wants you to take your coffee with him." Then, at the surprise and start of alarm on Fenton's face, Isaiah added, "It's nothing out of the ordinary, Mr. Fenton, to be truthful. It's been some months since Mr. Chadley went to the table. I was aiming to have a word with you the last time you came to visit us; but it seemed like Mr. Chadley had a notion what I was going to say and he never let me get alone with you."

Isaiah wanted to talk to Fenton and Fenton was anxious to have him; but there were only minutes before Maude would have the tray ready and Isaiah would have to go to Mr. Chadley.

"Tell me, Isaiah," Fenton asked abruptly, "did you ever know my father could play the harpsichord?"

Isaiah came farther into the room and lowered his voice. "That's just what I wanted to speak to you about, 'mong other things, Mr. Fenton. That's what's wearing out his strength. Sometimes Mr.

Chadley isn't just himself – " Then, suddenly realizing the boldness of his suggestion, Isaiah was quick to amend it. "I mean, when Mr. Chadley is coming down with one of his spells," he said, "he ought to coddle himself and take it easy as possible, but instead it seems like he can't bear to lie down. Sometimes he plays for half the night before I can coax him to bed." He looked away. "I know you are depending on me to look after Mr. Chadley." He had borne a responsibility Fenton had not been aware of, and he was distressed at having to report it.

A kind of shame filled Fenton at the sight of Isaiah. "I'm very grateful, Isaiah," he murmured stiffly. Fenton was rarely able to express his feelings in any way except formally. And he grew more distant with emotion. "I am sure that when my father is at his best he thanks you too." It was not at all what he really wanted to say. He cleared his throat and fumbled about his toiletries for a comb and brush. Isaiah turned reluctantly to the door. He was disappointed. Fenton had not relieved his burden.

"Before I retire tonight, Isaiah," Fenton said, in a kind of desperation, "I wonder if I could trouble you to fix me a hot toddy. I haven't been resting so well." When the house was quiet, they could talk again. He wanted Isaiah to understand that he was not abandoning him. He looked at Isaiah appealingly, not able to say any more.

"Yes, sir, Mr. Fenton, certainly sir," Isaiah answered. Then his face brightened. He understood. At the threshold, he paused a moment; then he said happily, "Miss August takes after Mr. Lesley considerable, doesn't she, Mr. Fenton?"

Fenton blushed with gratitude. "Yes," he agreed. "She's very much like him. I'm glad you noticed."

When Isaiah was gone, Fenton arranged his handkerchief methodically and went quickly to August's room to escort the little girl downstairs to table. He did not want to think any more of Mr. Chadley.

At dinner, Ralph served. August sat at one end of the long stretch of faded mahogany table and Fenton at the other. With the cold cucumber soup, Ralph hesitated, not knowing which person to serve first. Fenton smiled at him and nodded ever so slightly toward August. She was following Ralph with her eyes, which were still a little unfriendly and suspicious. She could not accord Ralph an exact place in her mind, not yet, in spite of her grandfather's open intimate behavior toward him that morning. But she was trying to understand what he was, servant or friend. She did not like him. Somewhere inside her, there was a fear of him. She was conscious of her fear. She would have struck him quickly if he had come too close or pushed against her or not done as she had told him instantly. It would have been a reflex. But if she had stopped to think, she might not have struck him. She would have been too frightened.

She watched Ralph now with the platter. He never smiled. He was not like the colored boys she watched through the gate at Dunmeade on their way home from the Starburg mills. They went in droves and shouted and catcalled and swiped each other's empty lunch tins and made a great racket. They laughed and talked loudly so that one could tell where they were and what they were doing. But Ralph was quiet. From the way he looked at her, when he thought she didn't see him, he seemed to be saying, "Uh-huh, just wait!" – threatening her.

When he came to lower the platter of shrimp for her, holding it steady until she served herself, there was a strong odor of soap from his hands over the spice of the sauce. It stayed in her nose even after he had gone through the pantry.

At Dunmeade, her mother cautioned her often to stay inside the gates when millworkers were passing after work; there were so many Negroes, she said. August could be kidnaped and hurt, even if Uncle Chad paid a lot of money to get her back. Addie and Susie were different, of course, her mother said. They were nice colored people who knew their place. Susie undressed August and bathed her, cared for her clothes and brushed her long straight hair and tied the ends, and came whenever August called. August liked Susie. Occasionally, when Uncle Chad and her mother went out, Susie sat by her bed and told her stories about the Indians. She told her one particular story of the cruelty of the White Man to his brother the Indian, of how the White Man had stolen the Indian's land, and driven the Indian into captivity and broken his great free heart. She had told it to August over and over again, and always August had wanted to cry at the end.

Once she had asked Susie to tell her about Br'er Rabbit and slave times; but Susie had said she didn't know anything about slave times, and she had declared it so firmly that August had not asked her again. The little girl had been disappointed. At Miss Nyrick's School, they told Br'er Rabbit stories at recess; but August had never been able to volunteer. Vincent Starburg had told four stories. The funniest had been about a little slave boy who had stolen some biscuits and fried sidemeat off the white master's oven when the mammy cook wasn't looking, and, when he had been summoned for a whipping, had hid in the flour bin. He almost suffocated, and, obliged at last to jump out, he had been as white as the white master! It was a story which had come from old Aunt Sudie, who had been born a slave in the Willetts family.

"Was Isaiah a slave, Uncle Chad?" August blurted suddenly down across the glass and tapers to Fenton.

The question so shocked Fenton that he put down his light-roll halfway to his mouth. As softly and yet as firmly as he could, hoping to prevent further questions until they were away from table, he replied:

"Isaiah and Maude and Ralph work for us because they want to, dear. We are their friends. We pay them for their service, just as the bank pays me." He paused to listen for a sudden swing of the pantry door behind him before he went on. Then he finished: "We owe a great deal more than money to Isaiah and Ralph and Maude. Your grandfather is very ill and he requires their constant care. I don't know what we should do without them." There was an unmistakable indication in Fenton's tone that he did not wish her to pursue the subject further.

August sat straight in her chair, staring at the pantry door, humiliation bright on her face.

"I was just going to ask Isaiah to tell me a story about slave times," she murmured. "Susie doesn't know any." Tears came up in her eyes and she buttered her light-roll over and over again and tried to push it into her mouth. She felt rebuked, and she had said nothing to deserve rebuke. She struggled to swallow the unchewed lump of roll. Fenton looked at her with great distress in his eyes. He wanted to say something quickly to erase the injury but Ralph was bringing in the pears to slice over the salad, and he could say nothing. He tried to smile at August but she looked away and would not accept the gesture.

"I don't care for pears," she said bluntly.

Ralph looked down at the salad bowl in dismay. He could not decide whether August was complaining of the whole salad or whether she merely meant him to leave the fruit out. He looked at Fenton.

"The pear is a little too rich for Miss August, tell Maude, please," Fenton said quietly to Ralph. "Perhaps she has some grated egg – "

"I don't care for any salad at all," August said firmly. She addressed Ralph. "I would like to have my dessert served now, please."

For a moment, Ralph wavered in complete confusion, and a kind of desperation came over his face. He did not know whether to abandon serving the salad and do as August ordered him or wait upon Fenton first and go for August's dessert after.

"Ask Maude to send in Miss August's cobbler now, Ralph, please," Fenton said, resignedly, "and I'll finish with salad – no dessert. Perhaps I'll take it later – if Maude will be good enough to save it for me, please." Fenton sighed. He was tired and he felt the longing of the emotionally exhausted for peace, even if for only a moment.

They finished dinner in silence. Then Fenton helped August from her chair. He did not know what to say to her. She was wounded and unforgiving.

"Come and tell your grandfather good night," he said, sadly, "he retires early." Then he stood aside for her to lead him out of the dining room.

When August had said her good night to him and closed the door, Mr. Chadley remarked quietly, with a pleased expression, "I have noticed that our little lady has some of the avariciousness which makes her mother so charming." He looked at Fenton with a cocked brow. "Greediness is somewhat becoming to the female nature, I think. It shows an incapacity for satiation – not because there are depths in the female nature which cannot be reached – but rather because there are no depths at all." He was quite pleased with the slander. "Great wars have been waged for greedy queens who could not be satisfied with treasure. Great discoveries have come out of conquests in their names – this nation, for example."

Fenton nodded. He meant not to answer at all, but to smile the applause his father expected. Then he said suddenly, in indignation at such a harsh conclusion drawn from a child's spontaneous demand for a present: "I think that's probably true. But wouldn't one have to have some knowledge of values to be completely devoted to greedy acquisition?" Then he completed this with the worst possible defense: "I don't think August's childish requests are prompted by more than random wishes from moment to moment. I was hard put to persuade her to keep a doll her mother had gone to great trouble to obtain for her Christmas gift last year. She was ready to give it to a little girl in her school not a fortnight after the holidays. And yet she had pleaded for it from the moment she saw it in *Dooley's Toy Catalogue*."

Fenton might have stopped there, but a stubborn insistence had grown in him to render innocent August's demand for the harpsichord. "I want to apologize for her unmannerly behavior this morning," he said. "I can assure you that by now she has entirely forgotten the harpsichord, and I hope that you are not entertaining any serious notion of giving it to her. She was obviously carried away for the moment. Its sound was new to her and she merely expressed a childish whim when she asked you to give her the instrument."

Mr. Chadley's face sobered into a cold stare. There was a silence. Mr. Chadley continued to look at Fenton without answering. At last Fenton moved uncomfortably as if he were about to get up and were searching for something to say to conclude the visit and take his leave. Then, in a kind of despair, he sighed slightly and said, with real sincerity: "You play with great understanding and command, sir. I'm sorry I have not enjoyed hearing you before. I am so inarticulate myself, my sole artistic experience is in my appreciation of other's talents." He colored at the confession and then excused himself, "That is not a complaint, sir."

"Thank you," Mr. Chadley said cruelly. "I enjoyed some study of music in my youth; but it never unhinged me, as an artistic pursuit distracted certain weaker natures I have had the misfortune to observe in the past. I managed to conduct my life and my business career with success in spite of being able to play Bach's *Komm, Süsser Tod*."

He gazed steadily at Fenton. His eyes had become opaque and distant. Then he said, "I want you to go into Campton in the morning and drive Lawyer Glover out in time for luncheon."

Fenton nodded.

"You should breakfast by eight," Mr. Chadley instructed; "advise Maude before you retire."

And then, before Fenton could offer to assist him in any way with his toilet, Mr. Chadley rang unexpectedly for Isaiah and dismissed Fenton with only a gesture of his hand.

"Good night, sir," Fenton murmured from the door, "I hope you rest well." He was depressed and somewhat angry. His father had used him rudely, and yet he struggled against holding any real indignation against a man so ill, for whom he had come to feel such pity.

From the hall, Fenton could not hear what Maude was saying; but he could recognize the murmur of long discourse and guess that she was telling August a story. He moved to August's door to listen. Then August broke into laughter. Fenton smiled. Then he almost laughed too, though he had caught not even an amusing phrase. He was relieved. He was not going to have to say anything to August, after all, about the misunderstanding at table. He waited until she had become quiet, then he knocked and opened the door.

August was propped on pillows and Maude had drawn a chair to her bedside. They turned when Fenton entered and Maude stood up quickly.

"Don't get up," he said, "don't let me interrupt." He wanted them to go on and to let him join them. "I'd like to hear the story too."

"Oh, that was all, Mister Fenton," Maude said, "I must be tucking Miss August in now, anyway." She was embarrassed. She began to fuss with the coverlid and put down the pillows behind August's head.

"You may come tomorrow night, Uncle Chad," offered August. She was still smiling and laugh-tears were in the corners of her eyes. "Maude is going to tell me another story tomorrow night."

"That's right," agreed Maude, easing August down flat; "but that's tomorrow night. Right now, you've got to coax that old Sandman, hasn't she, Mister Fenton? Mr. Chadley will be having us all put out of here if this house doesn't quiet down." She finished and took the soiled petticoat and socks lying on the blanket chest at the foot of the bed and bunched them together under her arm.

"Sleep tight," she said to August. "Good night, Mister Fenton." Maude left the door ajar for Fenton and went softly down the hall.

Fenton leaned over to kiss August on the forehead. She reached up out of the spread and put her arms around his neck and kissed his cheek. Suddenly she had about her that curious charm of a woman caught in uninhibited excitement, generous with some secret joy inside herself.

"Good night, Uncle Chad," she murmured and scrooched down to go to sleep. He turned out her lamp. At the door, he looked back a last time to her bed. The hall light lit a strip of floor and crossed her pillows. August was smiling at him, one eye exposed and the other concealed in her arm. The eye had the bright shiny look of a little bird. "Maude knows lots of slave stories," she said slyly. Fenton made no reply. He hesitated, then he put his hand on the doorknob to draw it after him. "Good night," he said and closed the door between them.

The clock chimed at the end of the hall. Fenton wound and set his wrist watch. He was tired. At that moment he wished Isaiah were not coming to talk to him. He had allowed himself to become unduly emotional over the musical event of the morning, and he was beginning to feel ashamed of the heat with which, later, he had defended August against his father's really unintentional criticism.

Then Isaiah knocked and brought in a tray.

"How is Miss Gilberta?" Isaiah asked right away. He was so pleased to be alone with Fenton that he spilled a little hot water from the jug.

"She's very well, I'm glad to say, Isaiah," Fenton answered. "She keeps quite occupied with her charities and her flowers."

"That's fine. That's just fine," Isaiah smiled, dipping out the sugar into the toddy cup. "We were mighty disappointed she didn't get down this time. Mr. Chadley was saying it had been a long time – "

"Yes, I know," murmured Fenton, embarrassed. He had tried to suggest to Gilberta that this visit might be the last to his father, but she had somehow refused to understand.

Isaiah waited until Fenton had tried the hot drink.

"Just right," Fenton nodded.

"Miss Gilberta always had a way of cheering Mr. Chadley up, didn't she?" Isaiah continued, with a faintly regretful, faintly reproaching tone. "Mr. Chadley was real fond of Miss Gilberta. She knew more about flowers than old Willie-Pete did. Nobody had ever been in the greenhouse but Mr. Chadley, and Willie-Pete, until Miss Gilberta came. I never even knew what went with all those flowers we didn't use in the house, did you, Mr. Fenton? But Miss Gilberta knew. She knew long before she came to live with us. She said they went to Dr. Langley's hospital. The nurse that tended to her papa out in Quakertown when he passed away told her every room had fresh flowers every morning. Miss Gilberta had a rose the nurse brought her pressed in her Testament – and Mr. Fenton, it was Mr. Chadley's rose." Isaiah was so touched by the mere recounting of this revelation of Mr. Chadley's goodness that his voice broke. "Wasn't that just like Mr. Chadley – not to say a word? Willie-Pete used to take the flowers away in his cart every morning. And I thought he was going off to sell them. Didn't you?"

The story was not new to Fenton. He had heard it from Gilberta also, when she had suggested they continue the service. It had given him quite a turn.

"I suppose Father was grateful for Dr. Langley's pulling Lesley through pneumonia when we first came to Newtown," he had said to Gilberta, in the only explanation he had been able to offer. And he had suffered with embarrassment before her shocked expression.

"He's a fine man, Isaiah," Fenton said now, "no one will ever fill his place."

"No sir, Mr. Fenton."

They were silent. Then Isaiah said quietly, "I don't think there's much more time to go, Mr. Fenton. Doctor comes once a week now – pretends like he wants some advice about his investments. But he gave me some medicine the last time and told me to give it to Mr. Chadley quick and put the hot bottle to his feet and ice to his head if he was taken bad all of a sudden. I've got the bottle right here, Mr. Fenton." Isaiah drew out the vial and held it in his palm for Fenton to see. His eyes were big with pleading for some reassurance from Fenton. "That's what I've been wanting to tell you, Mr. Fenton. I think Mr. Chadley knows I've got it. He treats me so kind-like." Isaiah's voice was soft and whispering. "I get such a fright, Mr. Fenton, when Mr. Chadley goes in that room at night to play music. Doctor don't want Mr. Chadley to get himself worked up. And he does get himself so worked up. He acts just like in the days when I first came here to look after you all." Isaiah groped to explain. "Mr. Chadley wasn't himself then – not when I first came. I never saw a man like him. Why, he used to play music and talk out loud to your mama in his mind just like he talks to her now. That's what he does, Mr. Fenton. He talks out loud to your mama. He calls her name. He goes on all night, Mr. Fenton, if I don't coax him out. That's how come I can sing like this morning. I tricked Mr. Chadley. I had to do something to make him take me in there to be with him when his spirit moves him so. I begged him to teach me to sing a beautiful hymn." Isaiah closed his hand over the little vial. "I don't hardly shut my eyes at night, Mr. Fenton. I have to listen out for him. We've got to *do* something, Mr. Fenton! What can we *do*, Mr. Fenton?" The frantic plea was nearly soundless and in anguish he stared into Fenton's face.

Fenton could feel himself nodding his head up and down, up and down, to show Isaiah that he had understood, that he had been listening, even though he did not answer. "You aren't going to go back and leave us here all by ourselves again, are you, Mr. Fenton?" Isaiah asked softly.

Fenton looked away. He could feel himself pushing against the appeal, trying to force it back to its unspoken state. He wanted not to have heard it, not to have to reply to it. He wanted not to believe the truth of what Isaiah had told him. He wanted not to plan any defenses, any courses to protect anyone – only to let what must happen, happen, as it would, and let him sink as he would against its inevitability and finality and then recover. He wanted not to wait for Death, or be warned of its near approach. His strength for all of them would come after the fact, when his duties were left for him and their performance formed his solace and his certainty.

"Father would not let me stay here – " he faltered, groping for escape, speaking almost to himself. "This is Father's home. He left me in charge in Newtown." Then, slowly grasping the way, the way of evasion, his necessity, he reached out and put his hand across Isaiah's. "Father isn't alone, Isaiah. None of us is ever alone. You haven't forgotten that, have you?" He smiled reassuringly. His tone was that of a minister, all soothing compassion for Isaiah. "I could not do for Father any of the things you do. In many ways you know him better than I know him. In many ways you are his closer friend. He relies upon you, Isaiah. Take comfort in that. If I were here, he would shut me out. He would not let me be of service as he lets you. I would be helpless to help him. You see? Even tonight, he would have come to table as he came last night, wasting his strength. It was you who kept him to his room resting." He paused, and looked earnestly into Isaiah's face. He was speaking the truth. He had found it, the comforting truth to believe. "You have been with him so many years. He wants you in your old place to the last. He wants to finish out his days where they began. It suits him to be here now. I don't think he would allow me to interfere with his way. Do you, Isaiah?"

As Fenton finished, Isaiah's face lost its suffering, sad expression. His attention changed. A subtle transfer was made. That unassailable blind faith of the dependent in his champion, which for thirty years had qualified Isaiah's tie to Marcus Chadley, moved to Fenton suddenly, without a waver.

In that old familiar yet deferential tone he had always used to Mr. Chadley when they stood together before calamity (as on the night when Lesley had been ill and they were strange in Newtown, long ago) Isaiah said, "Excuse me, Mr. Fenton, I know you have everything in hand. I had no business to trouble you about Mr. Chadley. Don't you have a worry in the world about it now, sir. You get a good night's rest." He felt the water jug to see whether it was still hot. "Do you think that's going to do the trick, Mr. Fenton?" He nodded to Fenton's half-empty cup. It had cooled in Fenton's hand. "I think so, thank you, Isaiah," Fenton smiled. He put the cup back on the tray. "I hope you'll have a restful night too, tonight."

When Isaiah was at the door, Fenton added, "Do you remember what you used to say to Lesley and me, when we were small and filled with childish questions and doubts? You said that if something were going to be, it would be; that we mustn't question the ways of the Lord."

"That's right, Mr. Fenton," Isaiah answered with something of shame in the nod of his head, "that's right."

Halfway to Campton the sun was still fresh upon the ocean beside him and the sand was not yet hot.

Fenton had thought of taking August with him to show her the beautiful slowly moldering town with its ruined mansion of the old governors still standing haughtily behind worn fences; but then it had occurred to him that if left alone, she might make friends with Ralph, as she had with Maude. She was such an intense child. All her responses were made with the same degree of energy. In a way, August had the forcefulness of his father, the same sort of pronounced ego. He thought of his father playing the harpsichord alone at night with his mind gone back to the days when his mother had been alive. He began to understand that, in himself, his father loved music or the expression of any art. Whatever gift *he* possessed, he did not despise; but when his wife had wanted to become a painter, then art had become his enemy. Her love of her talent had seemed to exceed her love for him. She had wanted to paint, not for amusement but as a serious artist. And she had been willing to leave him, indeed she had been anxious to go. That had been the wound deep in his ego, the insupportable injury.

Driving now in the warm morning, with the waves of cool sea-damp crossing the road at intervals, Fenton shuddered. So much of his life had been influenced by that old struggle between his parents. The pain and anger in his father would never die, he knew. The surface of the sore had healed, but the place itself had never ceased to bleed and ache; for his father had never ceased to probe it, his mind sometimes curiously courting its pain. Still he nursed his old grievance without even mercy for himself.

Suddenly, sweat steamed out over Fenton's face. What in heaven's name had made him leave August there alone! He pulled to the side of the road and looked up and down the highway before swinging the big car around to return. Then he stopped short with the wheels twisted to turn. He could not go back. What ever had made him think he could? What was the matter with him? What did he think his father would try to do to Lesley's little girl? He sat there with his hands gripping the steering wheel and his legs straining simultaneously against the brake and the accelerator, while the engine raced furiously. Then he relaxed and cut off the ignition and leaned back against the seat with his eyes closed. All about him the air was quiet and restful. He must stop thinking about his father. He straightened, turned on the engine and started along the sandy road again, watching the flat land about him, with its unexpected swamps and then dunes and then stretches of sea. He could feel his heart beating rapidly and a nervous chill had begun to sting the flesh of his throat and face. He had such fear for August. Her safety was almost an obsession with him. And yet, his fear was not without reason. He had to say that, in his own defense. But there was nothing he could do now except hurry Lawyer Glover and return to his father's house and hope there'd been no upset. Surely nothing — well, surely nothing unpleasant could happen in the short time he would be gone.

When Fenton was halfway to Campton, it was nine o'clock in the house and August was coming down the stairs to have her breakfast. She had put on her best socks, pale blue with dark blue cuffs. And she was wearing her best day dress, a blue piqué with cross-stitched yoke. The ruffles of her petticoat ballooned her skirt hem in a circle around her sturdy knees and she had tucked her initialed white batiste handkerchief in her watch strap, for a little touch. There was going to be a guest for luncheon and she had dressed for the guest.

She walked carefully down the polished hall to the dining room. She had worn her pumps only twice, and the soles were slick and stiff. As she passed the last pier glass, she stopped and observed her image. Her hair hung straight and silky in an even cut below her shoulders. The two gold barrettes which held it back from the center part caught the light and shone at her temples. She was engrossed in her examination for a few moments and then she walked on, looking back over her shoulder to catch the reflection of her dress. She was looking back when she walked through the dining room doors and collided with Ralph, coming out. "Excuse me," he murmured, and shuffled to right himself and hold out his hand to steady her. But she teetered against the wall and regained her own balance and would not accept his hand. Surprise and fury blazed in her face. Savagely she examined her dress and snatched at imagined wrinkles to smooth them.

"I didn't hurt it, did I, Miss August?" Ralph pleaded, the quaver of terror in his voice. "Did I, Miss August?" He stared in fright at her, unable to move his eyes from her angry face. He wanted to weep and run and hide.

Everything had gone wrong. Before she had come, his mother had told him how kind and friendly she would be. And he had believed she would be, because he could remember her himself. He had been seven when Mr. Lesley had died in the camp, and they had brought her to live at Dunmeade. He had taught her to walk, holding her up, firmly and gently, and never dropping her once. She had let him mind her without ever crying or being afraid. He had been waiting two weeks for her to come east to visit, to fetch and carry for her and show hospitality. He had meant to take her crabbing on the sound and he had planned to row her in his boat up and down the inland waterway so that she could see the swamp flowers.

Now she was going to go and tell Mr. Chadley he had knocked

her down and mussed her dress. She hadn't even answered him. She hadn't even said a kind word to ease his misery. Vainly, he fought against the self-pity rising in his heart.

"Breakfast is being served on the veranda, Miss August," he said, swallowing. "Mr. Chadley is out there. I was coming to tell you . . ."

August nodded; then she turned and walked away from him, back down the polished hall.

For a moment, as he watched her go, Ralph hated her with the mute, sorrowful hatred of the helpless and abused. Mr. Chadley was going to send him away one day to Dunmeade to go to school. Mr. Chadley had told him that Miss August and Mr. Fenton would be his good friends. But he knew it would not be so. And if he had to go to Dunmeade where he wasn't wanted and just be humbled, he did not want to go. He sagged against the wall with his face half hidden in the doorframe. Then, suddenly, he twisted himself up and lunged back toward the kitchen with a single whimpering cry and the tears filling his old unchildish eyes.

"Good morning, young lady," said Mr. Chadley to August. He was eating wild blackberries.

"Good morning, sir," August replied politely. She stood at a chair, making no move to draw it out and sit down.

Mr. Chadley poured more cream over the last of his berries and ate them. Then he became conscious of the little girl still standing and looked at her quizzically.

"Is this my place, Grandfather?" she asked. It was the only other chair at table.

For an instant, he was about to nod impatiently. Then he understood. He put his napkin beside his plate and prepared to rise and help August into her chair. It took an elaborate effort. He was leaning over to reach for his cane when Maude came onto the porch with a hot dish.

Mr. Chadley straightened up and said to her, "Will you kindly help Miss August into her place, please, Maude? I'm sure she'll overlook my infirmity. Won't you, my dear?" There was faint self-pity in the way he said it; but he glanced at his granddaughter with certain approval. He watched her as she carefully arranged her napkin to cover as much as possible of the smocking on her dress. Then slowly his face hardened and a strange expression came over it, an expression which might have been terror, had terror not been an emotion so unlikely in a man of his character. But it was a fear of some sort, and it brightened his eyes coldly as he observed the self-contained little girl before him. This child, this little girl, would one day have the power, if some whim possessed her, to waste like ash her portion of the careful accumulation of his life; for she was his heir, with Fenton. She was the last bloom of his flesh, his proud strain. But she was not exclusively of his blood. He watched her, displaying unconsciously at that moment a forceful independence. She was absorbed in attending to her own needs and was completely indifferent to his presence beside her. She was descended from Elizabeth, his wife, too. She was the daughter of his son, Lesley. And his fear of her shone in his purple eyes, intent upon her child's face as she ate her fruit. Fenton had not reassured him. She would give away her own toys without thought or discrimination, Fenton had said. And in time the rich place on earth, which he had inherited and further secured and passed on to her, might be wasted or abandoned—without thought or discrimination. She could betray him as her father had tried to do! Suddenly he stretched up in his chair, gulping painfully at the air to stop the spasm strangling his heart.

"Maude!" the child screamed at the sight of his face. Her voice ran like a blade through the house. "Come back! Come back!" she cried out, watching her grandfather's struggle, her fingers glued to the berry bowl, paralyzed at the spectacle of his pain.

Then Isaiah ran to the porch. "Oh Lord!" he prayed. "Help me, Lord. Oh, Lord, help me!" He rummaged frantically for the little vial of medicine. He did as the doctor had told him.

Then he waited and prayed, with Mr. Chadley leaning against his side, his ashen face wet from the moisture of pain.

"Do you feel better now, Grandfather?" August asked timidly, edging close enough to him to whisper. She looked down at his closed eyes, a kind of mustered bravery in her deliberate examination of him.

Mr. Chadley did not respond; but his mouth seemed to hang open a little and his eyes moved under his veined lids. He had heard her.

Isaiah stood still, not touching Mr. Chadley with his hands, but curved against Mr. Chadley's weight so that he seemed to be cradling the shaken man so dependent upon him. His eyes left the perspiring head against his side only once to look at August and smile reassuringly at the little girl when she spoke.

"You go ahead now and finish your breakfast, Miss August," Isaiah said softly without turning his head. "Everything's going to be just fine. Get Miss August some fresh cakes, Maude, and some of that New Orleans sugar we had melted down specially to put on them." He talked along to them all, calming them and restoring the life of the house to normal. "Mr. Fenton will be coming on any minute now and look at us. . . ."

He waited a few moments more, then moved slightly to stir Mr. Chadley. "You just rest easy now, Mr. Chadley, while I get your cushion to prop you up. I won't be gone a minute. It looks like we're going to have a specially fine morning. You ought to stay right out here on the porch and take it in." Very gently, he tilted Mr. Chadley's weight to the chair back and went quickly into the house.

August sat quietly in her place, looking purposefully out into the stretch of yard to the road. She tried to fix her attention upon some object until Maude or Isaiah returned. Beside her, Mr. Chadley breathed slowly and noisily. Unconsciously she counted as he inhaled and exhaled. She felt a little as if she were going to be sick. She did not think she could eat her hot cakes when they came; but she was going to try. She took a deep breath. In her mind she repeated over and over, "He's just fine now. Everything is just fine now. Uncle Chad will be back any minute. Everything is just fine. Isaiah is here and everything is just fine."

She began listening for the sound of someone returning. She wanted Isaiah to come first, before Maude with the cakes. Isaiah knew what to do for her grandfather. Even her Uncle Chad stood back for Isaiah. Alone on the porch with the ill old man, she dignified Isaiah with her dependence upon him. She accorded him ability and power beyond the ability and power of Fenton. Growing anxious, she longed for him to return so that she would be safe again. She sat rigidly staring ahead counting her grandfather's breathing. And then, with the cushion for Mr. Chadley's back under his arm, Isaiah tipped softly through the screens, Maude following. Gone was the moment when he had been special and necessary to her life. Relieved, she looked down at the hot plate Maude put before her. Calmly she took the lustre jug and poured a stream of sirup over the cakes. Isaiah was busy arranging Mr. Chadley in his chair and propping his feet up on a little stool. The excitement was over. Only the hovering-about went on. August looked toward the road and chewed her breakfast politely.

"I think I'll just let you help me to my sitting room, Isaiah," Mr. Chadley said quietly. He hadn't seemed to get comfortable even with the added cushion.

"You don't think the air would do you more good out here, Mr. Chadley?" Isaiah argued gently. He wanted to help the man to breathe less painfully.

But Mr. Chadley was already moving to get up and there was nothing to do but help him walk the few steps to his room.

When the screens sucked softly shut behind them, August decided to leave the table and let Maude find her plate as it was, her breakfast half uneaten. She edged to the door and peeked into the shaded hall. Carefully she eased the screen doors open. Then she walked quietly to the stair, past Mr. Chadley's half-closed door, and began the steps up, taking two together. She skidded on the slick new soles of her pumps and had to pull on the banister to keep from falling. Then she stopped hurrying. After all, she was only going to her room to work on her napkin. She wanted to be away from her grandfather while he was ill. He frightened her. He might die. She wished her Uncle Clad would come soon.

When she was at the first landing, Isaiah came out of Mr. Chadley's apartment and met Maude coming from the dining room. They stood just beneath the stair. August stopped and waited, hoping they would not look up and see her.

"How is he?" Maude whispered.

Lowering his voice, Isaiah said, "He seems to be relieved. I wish Mr. Fenton would get on home. Somebody ought to get hold of Doctor. He won't let – "

And then Mr. Chadley called Isaiah and, without finishing, Isaiah went back to him. "Yes sir, Mr. Chadley. I'm coming sir," he answered.

August hurried up the rest of the stair. She stepped into her room, closed the door quietly and stood against it, listening for Maude's footsteps. But there was no sound. She sighed with relief and went to the window to hold back the curtains and look through the trees for a car on the road. But the foliage was too thick and she could see nothing. Then she turned a little to the left and, startled, caught sight of the figure by her bed. It was Ralph. He was standing at one of the posts with an oily polishing rag in his hand. He had been standing there silently waiting for her to see him and do something, or scream. His eyes were large with terror.

"Go downstairs," August said. Her voice trembled and she backed against the window frame. Ralph fled from the room, leaving his tin of wax and polish and dropping his rags along the floor. August went to the door crack and watched him run down the hall. Then she shivered and began to cry. She wanted to go home.

Mr. Chadley was lying on his couch by the window when August came downstairs and peeped in his door. He held some of the curtain lace in his fingers and twisted the scalloped hem back and forth, back and forth. August stood outside watching him. Then she asked wistfully, "Is it all right if I come in, Grandfather? And sit with you?" Fenton had not returned. She was alone and driven to shelter with him after her greater fright upstairs.

"There's a little rocker just across from the highboy," Mr. Chadley said politely.

August came in and looked around the room. She saw the little rocker. She hesitated and then drew it over by his couch. She examined it with interest before she sat down. It looked like a doll's chair with a pretty velvet seat. "This must have been your chair when you were a little boy, Grandfather," she observed, settling herself into it to get her back straight. Then she opened her napkin, which she carried folded in her hand, and fitted it into the embroidery hoops.

"It belonged to your grandmother," was the quietly spoken answer. Mr. Chadley turned his face away to look out the window. The narrow knobs of his knuckles were circled in blue veins and his long finger tips moved restlessly over the pattern of the white curtain.

For a few minutes, August was occupied with changing her embroidery thread. She made a catch knot in the linen and caught it into the green leaf of her flower. Mr. Chadley watched her, a slight frown between his eyes.

"Would you like to see the place-mat I've already finished, Grandfather?" she pursued. She spread out the hoop toward him and smoothed the jonquil design with her finger. "This is the napkin but you can't tell much from this. My place-mat is prettier. All the other girls are making napkins too, but Miss Nyrick makes the tracings on theirs."

"It seems to take a great deal of time," Mr. Chadley murmured, trying to be courteous and to conceal his disinterest.

"It does," August said proudly, "especially when you do the tracings all by yourself. I do the tracings by myself." She wanted him to see that she was different from the other little girls, admittedly superior in common competition with them. She jumped up and put her embroidery ring on the velvet chair cushion and went hurriedly out of the room. Her Uncle Chad would be arriving at any moment with the guest and she wanted to show her grandfather the place-mat while she could. Half an hour earlier she had longed to see the car roll into the drive, but now, excited and anxious for her grandfather's almost certain praise, she ran happily up the steps, slipping and sliding in her new shoes, and dug about in her allotted drawer for the mat. It was there in its tissue, brought along on the trip because somehow she had overlooked one yellow bud and had wanted to finish it. She carefully carried it down in its paper to keep from rumpling it.

When she came back to his side, Mr. Chadley seemed to be sleeping. August sat down with her linens in her lap and waited for him to open his eyes. Though she wanted him to awaken, she made no movement which might disturb him. She listened apprehensively for the sound of Fenton's car approaching.

Then as the minutes passed and Mr. Chadley did not stir, she began to prepare her mind for not being able to show her place-mat to him at all. She was disappointed. She could wait only a few moments more and then, if he did not turn, she would have to slip out of the room and back upstairs. Her grandfather would have no time to examine her design and discuss it with her. It would be better to pretend she had never brought it to him in the first place.

She decided to go. Mr. Chadley had not moved. Then she lingered one moment longer. He might still open his eyes in time. She wanted him to so much! Then, as she hesitated, she heard a sound beyond the windows. It seemed to be voices, but when she strained to hear, all was quiet again. Isaiah passed the door toward the porch. Then Mr. Chadley moved and turned his face to look at her sitting there. She did not stir or speak to him and he did not speak to her. Mr. Chadley seemed to have forgotten that she had gone to fetch him something. August was patient, awaiting the moment to unwrap the tissue. Then Mr. Chadley looked down at the fragile bundle in her hands. He seemed to be making some effort to remember, for his glance at her face was inquiring.

"Here it is," she said with relief and slipped the linen mat out of its wrapping. She spread it out across her knees and stretched the ends between her hands so that the full pattern was clear to him.

"I see," he said, and he began to examine the design politely. Then, as August pointed out the details, his attention narrowed to the figures around the border and he frowned.

"I wanted to put them like ladies in the garden," she explained, "and Miss Nyrick couldn't draw them like I meant so I made them like this." She traced her index finger over the shape of a dryad-like figure peeping around the stem of a robust jonquil to the back of another dryad-like figure doing the same thing, to complete a chain of shapes and flowers around the edges of the oblong linen. It was an odd and yet inoffensive mixture of literal reproduction and delicate imaginative drawing; and Mr. Chadley stared at it while she waited for him to raise his head and smile and compliment her, as everyone had done who had seen it. She waited for him to say something nice. Her heart beat rapidly with anticipation of praise. "I'm the best in our class," she urged him.

But Mr. Chadley said nothing. He did not speak at all. Outside, voices moved nearer the house and at last were clearly Fenton's and Lawyer Glover's on the porch. The linen mat lay between them and still Mr. Chadley said nothing. August fingered her embroidery, her eyes wide with disappointment and pleading. Then, suddenly, she dropped her head and struggled to hold back the tears. Mr. Chadley observed her coldly, on his face a look of deep and unforgiving anger.

To this scene Fenton brought Lawyer Glover, following Isaiah in without waiting to be announced. "Here we are, dear," he said anxiously to August. "You haven't tired your grandfather, have you?" Then in his nervousness he rushed on to present the guest to her before Mr. Chadley could greet the lawyer. "This is Mr. Glover, dear," he said. He put his hand to August's back to help her rise and speak to the slight dried man who stooped smugly to speak to her as if he were acknowledging a dwarf. But August did not stand up. She ducked suddenly past Fenton, under his arm almost, and scurried from the room, dropping her hoop and needle and yellow thread behind her on the floor and pitching her place-mat into a corner.

Fenton watched her dart through the door with shock, but Mr. Chadley did not even turn his head.

"What could have frightened her so? Something must have frightened the child," he asked his father. His question was accusing. He looked down at the needlework on the floor and then reached to smooth it out and collect it for her. The tenderest area in Fenton had been struck, a surface already irritated by his imagination on his drive to town. This antennaed place in his heart fathomed more quickly than any informer could have told him that some damage had been done his child. "What made her run from us like that? Here's her jonquil thrown on the floor!"

"Did the little girl do this?" Lawyer Glover tried tactfully to reroute the unpleasant currents in the room. "May I look at it closer? May I?" He fingered in his vest for his glasses to concentrate on the colored threads worked around the border of the cloth. "She seems a remarkable child, doesn't she?"

Fenton looked to his father to respond to the compliment. But Mr. Chadley said nothing. He lay on his side as he had been when they came into the room. Lawyer Glover kept his eyes on the embroidery.

"Yes," murmured Fenton at last when the wait became too long, "she *is* remarkable." Fenton's chin went up and he strained for height as he always did when he was conscious of being in an undignified position.

"She is fortunate, if I may say so," added Mr. Glover, "in having such a discerning and appreciative guardian. A stepparent, we have observed in the law, is not always so eager to discover ability in children not his own. Little Miss August will not have to fear lack of recognition."

Fenton blushed. He was about to thank Mr. Glover when that

quiet high voice which always, in whatever room it spoke, commanded all the ears, said slowly, "I believe, if this interesting discussion of children by two virtual bachelors is concluded, we'll have some refreshment before luncheon. Will you see to it, please, Fenton." And then having dismissed his son, Mr. Chadley said to Lawyer Glover, "Yes, Mr. Glover, my granddaughter has some rather marked characteristics and leanings, not the least of which is jealousy of attention and a desire for praise. I don't think we need concern ourselves with the possibility of her living with her light, whatever it may be, hidden under a bushel. She herself will bring it to notice, though she burn down the bushel to do it."

Mr. Glover cleared his throat and cocked his head slightly to wink at Mr. Chadley. Frail as he seemed on his couch, this man was still master of the house and it behooved his servants, legal as well as domestic, to agree with him and approve his wit, cruel as it might be.

Some of Fenton's indignation was assuaged by the news Isaiah gave him of Mr. Chadley's severe attack of the morning.

"I shall be going back to Campton to drive Mr. Glover just after luncheon, Isaiah," he said, "I can report to the doctor then. Or do you feel I should telephone him now to call this afternoon?"

Isaiah was assembling glasses and decanters on a tray to carry in to Mr. Chadley.

"I don't know, Mr. Fenton," he replied, shaking his head, "I just don't know. He seems to be resting tolerably easy now, but . . ." He did not finish. He wiped the silver head of a decanter cork, improving its gleam.

"Well, do you think he will be annoyed if we send for the doctor without his permission?" Fenton asked.

"Well," Isaiah admitted, hesitantly, "he doesn't like to be fretted over. That's mighty aggravating to him."

Fenton thought for a moment. Isaiah lifted the tray and stood waiting.

"Perhaps it would be better if I spoke to the doctor while I'm in Campton," Fenton decided. He looked at Isaiah for approval. But Isaiah only murmured, "Yes sir," and kept his eyes down on the tray of glasses as he started from the pantry.

Fenton left him at the stair and went quickly to find August. When she did not answer his knock, he opened her bedroom door. Water was running in her bathroom. Fenton waited. Then he tapped gently. "Are you there, dear?" he asked. She came out drying her face. Another towel was tucked about the neck of her dress to keep it dry. Her cheeks were puffed.

"I have your napkin and mat," Fenton began, holding them up for her to see. "Mr. Glover was very impressed with your work. He said he thought you were unusually talented."

August made no reply.

She hung her towel and then took her embroidery out of his hands and neatly put it in her chest of drawers.

"Is there something you would like to tell me, dear?" Fenton asked awkwardly.

She shook her head. Then she selected a hair ribbon from her box on top of the chest and held it up to her cheek. It did not seem agreeable. She selected another. Then she ran it under her hair in the back and drew it up along her ears to the top of her head. "Would you put your finger on the knot and hold it for me, please?" she said.

When the bow was made, she stretched open the loops. Then she smoothed herself once more. "I don't think Grandfather ought to come to table with us. He was sick this morning while you were gone," she said, suddenly.

"Yes, I know," Fenton replied, "but you mustn't worry about it, now. He's all well now."

"I'm not worried," she said. They started down the hall together.

In the middle of the stair, August stopped. "Grandfather doesn't know very much about linens. Does he?" she asked.

Then, before Fenton could answer, she added, "He didn't have any little girls." Her tone was half critical, half tolerant.

"No, dear, he didn't," Fenton said, "and I'm sure it was a great disappointment to him." He held her hand firmly and they went on.

At last he knew what had disturbed her, what had sent her in tears from his father's sitting room. He looked down at the top of her head with admiration for her. She had managed her inward repairs privately, with dignity and tact.

It was midafternoon when Fenton drove Mr. Glover back to Campton. Luncheon had been short, but Mr. Chadley's conference with the lawyer, from which Fenton was pointedly excluded, had lasted an hour and at times the voices of the two men had become disturbingly audible. Once Mr. Glover had clearly protested: "I shall do what I can, Mr. Chadley; but it is impossible to write in such a restriction. There is no precedent for such an arrangement." Now, Mr. Glover sat beside Fenton in front with his briefcase perched upright on his knees while August rode in back on one of the little seats which raised to make the car a seven-passenger. There was no conversation. Mr. Glover seemed disinclined to attempt even general talk as he had done on the way out. And Fenton was experiencing a kind of resentment and embarrassment at having been left out of the business discussion, so he drove in silence.

As they neared the center of Campton, Mr. Glover pulled himself together and shifted his briefcase and shook his head from side to side with his upper teeth stretched down to pinch at his lower lip in an expression of bewildered resignation. Then they drove up before his house.

"Thank you, sir, for your trouble," said Fenton to the lawyer, as Mr. Glover scrambled to the sand walk. "I hope you won't find that anything dire has taken place in your absence." He held out his hand. He tried to sound amusing.

Mr. Glover put down the briefcase and shook Fenton's hand. "Oh no," he protested heartily, "I'm sure nothing has happened."

Behind him, standing at the little door of the doll-like house which stood in the front yard and was used as Mr. Glover's law office, was a young Negro boy. He came out on the sand walk. "Excuse me, Lawyer Glover, please sir," he said and halted behind the lawyer until he was acknowledged.

Mr. Glover stopped smiling and turned around, "Yes, Horace," he answered. "What is it?"

"There's a message come for you over the telephone just this very minute."

"Well? Am I to go to the phone or has the party hung up?" the lawyer asked, a little impatient with the boy.

"No sir," replied Horace, "I've got what it was, written down right here." And he stepped forward and handed the penciled note to Mr. Glover. He was very proud of his usefulness, very proud that he could write a message down. He bobbed his head respectfully to Fenton and shuffled back a step. "How'd do, ma'am?" he murmured to little August standing up in the back seat of the car watching him. He lowered his eyes and waited for Mr. Glover to speak.

Mr. Glover read the scrawl. Then he seemed to read it again. His head was lowered but his eyes did not move back and forth across the two lines of writing. He swallowed, then he opened his mouth and looked at Fenton.

"It is something for me, Mr. Glover?" Fenton asked. He knew that it was.

"Yes, Mr. Chadley—yes, my boy—yes," said the lawyer, suddenly dignified and sympathetic and kind-intentioned and hard-put to tell the news. "Yes, it's for you and I am so sorry to give it to you." And he put the memorandum across the seat into Fenton's fingers.

Mr. Chadley was taken bad just after you all drove off and passed away without coming to, it said.

Fenton never ceased to sorrow that he had not been with his father on that afternoon when Mr. Chadley's life was wrenched away, so violently and with such pain. He was the only son, the only kin. He should have been present to hold his father as Isaiah had done, higher and higher for the last little air. It seemed to Fenton that his father's death, unattended except for his servant, was an ignominious end for such a man.

When the funeral hour came, he took August by the hand and stood sedately beside Gilberta, who had come on the late morning train from Newtown, and proudly observed the small group who came to accompany the family to the hedged-in private burial ground a mile away. And he did not forget Isaiah in the moment of his own solemn grief; Isaiah stood with them, next to August, at the grave. Fenton received the condolences and accepted the hands offered in sympathy almost as if he were tabulating the scene to describe to his father, when they should meet again and he could say, "It was a fine day, Father, warm and clear. Governor Brockhurst brought up the others just after Gilberta and August and Isaiah and me. Do you remember a Mr. Anderton, sir? I don't believe he was a person of these parts, but he came to the service and spoke to me afterward. He said that you had once done him a great turn when he was in bad circumstances and that he appeared in behalf of his grateful family. He followed our little service with some disappointment, I'm afraid. I observed him for the first time just after Judge Lynberry spoke and he had a curious questioning expression on his face as if he thought we had not half praised you for the man he had known you to be. But he was mistaken, Father. Even the day blessed you, and the place where we left you beside Mother was quiet and sheltered and peaceful, and nearer to the sea than I had remembered as a child."

And there Fenton's mind always stopped when he recalled his father's funeral.

Mr. Chadley's last wishes were directly and simply set forth. And contrary to the usual sound of such documents, his will seemed to record his own voice in its clauses. Fenton caught himself listening with a feeling of reassurance as Lawyer Glover read it, as if suddenly he had heard his father speak to him again. What he understood was: I have left you in charge, Fenton. August will come into her share of my estate when she is eighteen, including Dunmeade, which I deeded to her before leaving Newtown, you recall. You will see that Isaiah receives the cash amount I have set down and that income from my Prince River house and property and proceeds from its sale, if you should dispose of it, are credited to him faithfully. You will see to the boy Ralph's education as always planned and provided for here. You will present, for me, the casket of small jeweled pieces to your wife Gilberta. The pearls were my father's last gift to my mother. You have now the responsibility of maintaining our holdings, which are yours — except for August's portion. You will protect her interests for her, naturally, since she is a woman. . . .

Fenton removed from his memory entirely the shocking disclosure Mr. Glover had felt an obligation to make before the formal reading of Mr. Chadley's last will.

"On the very day of your father's untimely death," the lawyer had said, noisily unlatching the brass clasp of his briefcase, "he discussed with me an alteration he wished to make in his will." He looked up at Fenton as he pulled out two identically folded documents. Then he set aside one and kept the other in his hand. "I penciled in that change — at his dictation — on his own copy, which he provided." He opened the document in his hand and spread back the long legal pages one at a time.

Fenton said nothing. His face was impassive, his eyes were lifted deliberately above the pages Mr. Glover turned.

"Mr. Chadley was most positive in expressing his wishes," the lawyer said, locating the newly written-in lines. He indicated them for Fenton's inspection. "In simple terms, your father wished you to inherit his entire estate. Upon your death, he wished any and all parts remaining to be inherited by your *direct* descendants. If executed, this would have been a considerable change from the provisions as they now stand."

Fenton made no reply. In his ears were the words, but his mind resisted their meaning.

My father was ill, he said to himself. I must remember that. He was very ill.

To Mr. Glover, he had said finally when the lawyer stood there without putting the revised will away, "I think that we should have the reading now, sir" – and he put out his hand to invite Mr. Glover to pass before him.

When the painful absorption of the provisions of Mr. Chadley's will was finished in Gilberta's heart – and it was in her heart and not her mind that the loss of Dunmeade was truly catalogued – she resigned herself to final defeat. Somewhere during her struggle with disappointment she came to the realization that she was dependent upon the unreliable grace of man in man's world and as a woman could make no protest against any theft, for there was nothing which was ever hers which could not be, in a moment, taken away. Therefore, she resolved in defense to invite no attachment to any possession, and thus to guard herself against loss. Little by little, she gave over August into Fenton's care and lived apart yet with them, absorbed with her flowers and the pleasurable task of running Dunmeade, for as long as she would live there.

As for Fenton, he could make no explanation to her and he could guarantee no repair beyond that which time makes upon a wound. In their increasing estrangement, he drew August even closer into his attention as if he feared in some way that Gilberta would punish him by taking away his charge.

But of course Gilberta did not; and August accepted her adoption with a curious unconsciousness of her mother's abstinence from ordinary motherly concerns. It was due in part to her own inability to think of Gilberta as her mother in the way other children identified a parent through their needs or fears. August could not use Gilberta. She could not cling to her or weep into her skirt. She was put off by a naïve and passionate worship of Gilberta's beauty. No one so beautiful could be serviceable, and all mothers were serviceable.

Without knowing it, August wanted to look like Gilberta. She was dark, but not so dark as Gilberta. Her eyes were blue, but they were not de Ventura blue, like stones. And she was tall, while Gilberta was dainty and small with soft flesh rounding her figure. August's structure of face and figure was pronounced beneath her skin, and she observed her child's world from eyes set unmistakably in the arched brow which had characterized the foreheads of her father and Mr. Chadley.

Occasionally when Miss Glenn, the seamstress, came to camp for two weeks in the sewing room to strain over patterns for Gilberta's summer sheers, August would sit quietly in the window seat, arranging colored scraps into designs on a piece of cardboard. And she would watch with intense enjoyment when her mother stood for a fitting and Miss Glenn, bit by bit, with pins, outlined Gilberta's figure until the garment was whole before them.

But, other than shopping together and conferring over her own school skirts and jackets, August knew few activities which included her mother. Indeed she knew few activities which included anyone, and for that reason her experience with Earl Barron that summer after her grandfather's death was all the more poignant.

The Chadleys returned from the East to a quiet neighborhood. There were no droves of boys roaming up and down the street smashing cans with sticks and screaming. Only Earl Barron was nearby in the funny house at the other side of Dunmeade which his father had rented already furnished. All the other families had toured off to either the ocean or the mountains. The department stores had done a two weeks' frenzied business in black-and-red-striped bathing suits, "thermos" lunch-cases, and bolts of mosquito netting. It would be after Labor Day before the procession of T-models and newer seven-passenger touring models with the convertible isinglass curtains would come rolling home from the damp cots and sandy bread of the elaborately named boardinghouses which drew them both east and west to the state's natural scenic beauties. So August had been the only companion for the little Yankee stranger with his sophisticated toys and no decent male audience.

For the first time, August escaped through the gates to walk sedately with Earl to where the city was swinging a bungalow and two willow trees from one side of the street to the other to clear the ground for a new park.

In the early summer mornings she had been able to catch the distant sound of the churning revolutions of the cement mixer and by noon she was standing with Earl at a respectful distance under the maple trees of the Boltons' deserted side yard watching the denimed workmen eat their fried meat and biscuits with their backs against the clodded roots of the excavated willows. All about her, lining the street itself, was a world quite new and magic since she had never trafficked in its parts before. The houses were large frame ones with big tree-shaded lawns and iron fences around them — almost identical, just as their owners were identical. Indeed, some were related to each other and their jobs were the same. The Bolton twins, Mr. R. C. Bolton and Mr. Alfred Bolton, lived across from each other on opposite corners and one was the head bookkeeper for the Starburg Print Works and the other was the head bookkeeper for the Starburg Spinning Mill. Their houses were partly open, because each was staying behind until the last week of the summer before he joined his family at the seashore. It never occurred to them to close one house completely and live together in the other. They met instead each morning at their joint bicycle shed with their trouser-legs wrapped tightly about their ankles and fastened with metal clamps to keep them free of the pedal chain. Then they would tour off together to the mills looking for all the world like tightly wound umbrellas neatly snapped to the shaft. August had often watched their progress up the slight hill behind Dunmeade when she was dressing. They wore hard straw hats and gray-and-white seersucker suits and their bicycles were high and professional-looking with thin-rimmed wheels. They were a curious sight to her and she could never understand why they were twins. They did not look in the least alike. They had other differences, too, but she would not have known about that.

Mr. R. C. Bolton had a bushy mustache and some gold in his front teeth which flashed in a sinister manner when he smiled and tipped his hat when he met August and Fenton turning into the back drive. His wife was a large gray-haired woman with light brown eyes, who on a winter's evening could be heard calling in her two sons, Pinkie and R. C. Jr., in the same powerful high C she used to paralyze the congregation of her church on Sunday. Mrs. Bolton's high C had become a curfew for all the other children in their neighborhood. Fenton had rammed down on the brakes the first time he had come in contact with it and stopped the car with a jolt. He was terrified that he had struck down a passer-by though there had been no thud against the fenders. It was a shrieking wail of a sound that would have done justice to the bloodiest collision.

Mr. Alfred Bolton was quite different. He was thin-haired with cold blue eyes too light for his skin. His own wife, except on Sunday when she wore her flowered chiffon, was rarely seen without her orchid boudoir cap over her kid curlers and her black-checked gingham house dress, washing the bird droppings off the front porch with the hose. She would run at the screech of her vigorous sister-in-law's voice to pile into the R. C. Boltons' round-snooted sedan, and chug to the market they patronized—just out of the city, where the veal and chicken was always two cents less per pound than in Newtown proper. For this favor she would gratefully reimburse Mrs. R. C. half the gallon of gas consumed for the ride. They were good, upright citizens, whose vices outside of piousness and pinching pennies lay in a once-a-week game of Rook. They were inhabitants of a strange world to August, who enjoyed staring rudely at their dwellings that summer when they were away. They never came to Dunmeade.

That is, they had never come but once. When they had called briefly on Gilberta, their call was never returned.

When Earl Barron that summer questioned August lonesomely about the other children in the neighborhood, the ones so conspicuously absent—the boys—August had no information to give. At the same time, she resented his questions because she felt his dissatisfaction with her company only, though she was attentive and complimentary to his show-off tricks and listened patiently to his long technical explanations of the art of road building in New Jersey where he came from, and where he mightily wished to return. He was nearly nine and she was only six, but her dignity and intelligence helped to bridge the gap. She was very serious in her responsible position of the newcomer's only friend. She was very hospitable. She lent Earl several of O'Smyre the gardener's tools from the greenhouse when Earl was converting a piano crate into a pirate's den in his back yard. She had allowed a great commotion to take place at Dunmeade over the disappearance of a trowel O'Smyre set great store by and she said not a word to betray Earl. The trowel was bent out of any possible use when Earl struck a rock digging the subterranean entrance to the piano crate. Together they had taken it to the pit where the workmen on the park job were using the steam shovel, and just at the precise moment when the teeth of the shovel were opening, they had thrown it into the steel jaws and seen it mashed with the red clay. So the damaged trowel was never found and O'Smyre did not dare accuse Mrs. Chadley of messing about alone in the greenhouse and mislaying the tools.

August had acquired the happy habit of listening for Earl's raucous secret signal to come out of the house and play, when suddenly all was changed. The summer ended. Somewhere in the night, the first of September, both families of Boltons and the Gladsons and two others of the street's inhabitants had rolled home from mountains and shore. Dunmeade in its shroud of trees and wall heard nothing of the bustle and commotion accompanying the return of the natives.

The next morning August thought Earl had a cold or that his

mother had sent him into Newtown to fetch something for her, for there was no whistle or call. She went out into the patio and sat quietly working on the last of her jonquil embroidery and waited for him to come. At eleven o'clock she asked Addie for some milk with chocolate sirup in it. Then she took a long time drinking it. She thought it would be better when Earl finally came if he found her busily going on with her own business. Then at twelve o'clock noon when she could hear, faintly, the mill whistle beginning, she walked down the side path beside her mother's little rock garden and went out the gate at the back of Dunmeade. The sidewalk along the sycamore grove would lead her within sight of Earl's back yard and she could see him without his knowing it.

She looked over his yard carefully. There was no one in sight. The piano crate sat against his side fence nakedly in the noon sun. She thought a moment and then decided to go in and ask Mrs. Barron if Earl were home. Mrs. Barron was a very nice lady, August thought. She didn't bother Earl much, he said. She was busy with her work. She was writing a book of poetry. She answered August's knock on the screen door of the side porch.

"I don't know just where Earl is, dear," she said nicely, "he was going down the street the last time I saw him."

August drew back from the door.

"No, thank you," she said when Mrs. Barron held it open and invited her with a gesture to come in. "It's time for my luncheon."

She went back down the steps, then stopped on the bottom and looked up at Mrs. Barron, "I didn't want anything. I thought maybe he had a cold."

"It was awfully sweet of you to come and ask," Earl's mother replied and looked down at her tenderly.

Crossing the yard to get away August knew Mrs. Barron had not gone back into the house. She could feel the eyes on her back all the way.

Then, just before she got to the sycamore grove, safe from sight, *they* came charging down the street, whooping and hollering and kicking each other off the sidewalk into the street – Pinkie and "R. C. Jr." Bolton and Harvey Gladson and Price Phillips and Mr. Alfred Bolton's great tomcat of a son, Creedmore, and right in the middle, Earl! He could not have been more changed if suddenly his skin had turned red and blue and his hair orange. He was transformed suddenly into a wild jumping and snarling creature not even a boy – and August shrank back from him in a shyness so extreme it amounted almost to fear. In an instant, even before he ignored her and jostled along into his yard leading his new cronies to the piano crate, she knew that she was deserted forever, that her friend had not been her friend and that he did not even wish to remember that she had been his only company during the two months until his natural companions returned from afield to claim him as one of their own.

She let the last of them brush past her and then she hurried through the sycamore grove, fastened her gate and eased back to the patio she had left ten minutes before. Addie and Susie had not missed her. She sat down quickly and picked up her embroidery and began making careful stitches with her needle while the tears welled in her eyes and anger all but burst her heart.

Earl doesn't like me, she understood in her heart, I'm a girl. And it might have been the same pain which Marcus Chadley had endured when Elizabeth Wortham rejected him: "I want to paint and study. I don't want to be here – with you."

Numb and quick by turns, that spirit in the child, from the fusion of proud Chadley and prouder de Ventura blood, swelled up – outraged, demanding revenge. "He'll be sorry some day," she said aloud, forgetting herself, and then she lifted her head high and leaned back against the chair slat to stop the tears sliding down her face. "He'll be sorry."

Summer was ended, and the new street in front of the new park was paved and closed off with lantern-lit barricades at night.

And from her window, August, straining her eyes, could see through the trees the erratic movements of the children playing kick-the-can on their skates over the velvety powdery surface of the paving. And sometimes in the patio she would look up at a shout from the street and see Earl and the Boltons swinging themselves up on the back of the icewagon to steal chips while Will the Negro driver pretended to rail at them and force them off, all the time slowing his horse to avoid hurting one. But she never again went out to the street herself and entered the life of the neighborhood that encircled Dunmeade like a noisy village about a castle. She watched the Rolling Grocery make its stops with interest, and she looked up a moment when some countryman tried to drive in the gates with chicken coops tied to the back of his Ford and his wife calling out lustily: "Fryers! On foot! Fryers!" but she did not go to watch the sale when Addie went down to look over the coops. The hucksters were no longer magic and foreign and inviting to her, since she was an audience alone to them. It had been different when she had sedately followed behind Earl as he ran to investigate a cart of black-eyed peas, roast'n ears, snaps, honeydews, butter beans, okra and sweet churned butter.

She took her own life back inside Dunmeade, and contented herself with following Brisloe, the polishing man, around from floor to floor, hearing him chuckle and tell her over and over again why he was bald-headed. ("The little birds come and eat the hair right off my head, Miss August. That's a fact.")

Billy Pickett came home from a boy's camp, and his first Sunday in Newtown skipped gaily across the back garden to where August was having her breakfast with Fenton and Gilberta.

"I brought you a hatchet case," he said, without any preliminary inquiries as to the health of anyone present, and plunked down a leather article he had tooled himself. He stood beaming at her, waiting for her to express her pleasure and surprise.

"I don't want it," she said rudely, not even looking at it and hardly raising her head from her eggcup. "It isn't for girls."

Billy Pickett reddened and twisted self-consciously. Some of his sturdy aggressive air left him as if he had collapsed inside.

Fenton put down his toast and wiped his fingers unnecessarily on his napkin. He was dumfounded. "Come and have some cherry jam, Billy," he said, "here's a chair between August and me." He pulled at one of the iron lace chairs but Billy did not respond. "I want to examine that case," he went on, reaching for the leather straps.

But Billy put his hand over it quickly and took it from the table. "I have to be going," he murmured; "my mother and father are waiting." He looked out toward the street hidden from them by the sycamores, as if to suggest the presence of the car there.

"Well, good-by," Billy said, throwing up his hand in a sudden awkward gesture as if he had been at the end of the yard and not directly in front of them. Then he turned and ran.

"Come to see us," Fenton called after him. He liked the gay little bristle-headed boy with his straightforward manly manner. He could not imagine what had come over August to treat him so.

"Did you have to hurt Billy's feelings?" he asked her sharply.

Gilberta had sat quite still throughout the scene. Now there was a strange smile on her face and there was no indication that she intended to correct her daughter. Fenton looked at her, puzzled. What could be wrong with everyone today? Gilberta was usually strict with August about the proprieties. He was about to ask for some explanation when Gilberta said, "He shouldn't have flung it at her as if she had to take it just because he gave it to her. He'll know better next time. He'll find out whether or not she wants a present from him." Then she rang for more coffee and went on with her kipper.

Suddenly, August got up and ran into the house without a word.

Upstairs, alone in her playroom, she leaned against the mantel and began her tears. She had struck her enemy a blow. She had witnessed the wound. The heart of Man was neither invulnerable nor inaccessible. But for all the comfort of this knowledge, she wept.

"Wouldn't you like to have a Christmas tree for your classmates?" Fenton asked August early in the first December she had gone to public school. "We could have a beautiful one in the foyer – large enough to hang presents for everyone right on the branches." At the prospect of Dunmeade full of laughter and avid little faces, Fenton's eyes shone with pleasure. There had never been a noise of any kind in Dunmeade, certainly no scuffling feet and scrambling after favors hid about (not too carefully) under chairs and lowboys. In Mr. Chadley's time Christmas had always been formal with the effort entirely upon *not* making a display of one's emotions.

Now, instead of opening the house and inviting in their only relatives, the de Venturas, Gilberta always managed to confine their celebrating to the opening of gifts at six o'clock in the morning, breakfasting from an exquisitely decorated table, then driving to the de Ventura farm with presents too expensive and too useless to be anything but embarrassing. Fenton longed to be a host and offer up his larder and cellar for the approval and enjoyment of his family and friends. He would have paid any price for feeling: *Here, now,* in this room full of holly and the scent of burning pine cones, *here* among these faces which belong to my life, I have brought happiness – and to myself, love and a place.

"Wouldn't you like giving a beautiful party for your classmates?" He repeated his request (and it *had* been a request, not a question): "There must be a number of the little children from the mills who won't have such a large Christmas as we will, you know. Wouldn't it be a dandy thing to give them a great big tree and presents to take home?" He was urging her and persuading himself that his desire to have her give a Christmas party was to benefit the little mill children and not to fill the emptiness in his own heart. He wanted the tree and candles and stockings that his boy's mind had conjured up in expectancy every Christmas – and which he had been denied all his life.

August looked up from his knee and closed her reader with one finger in her place to hold it. She was reading the story of Pinocchio and Fenton had disturbed her at the place where, as a result of his lying, Pinocchio's nose was assuming alarming proportions. She was irritated with the incredibles in the story. Pinocchio's very existence was incredible and she would never have read the book except that it was the second semester reader.

She listened to Fenton intently, trying to decide whether or not she wanted to have the class come to her house for a Christmas tree. She found it hard to carry her school and her associations there into her real life, which was inside her and which she merely suspended while she sat in a classroom with other children. She was obedient about involving herself with what was proper in school. Her real life was resumed again when, like Lesley, she sat in the patio dreaming and imagining until Susie called her to tea. In her fantasies she took no hero's part and conquered no unconquerable worlds. Such dreams were boys' dreams. Her mind was reshaping physical things. Her hands moved unconsciously in her lap making seemingly meaningless motions which sometimes caused Susie to ask if her fingers were cold or if she had caught something. And then, startled, August would sit on them in embarrassment. Only once had she ever answered Susie without thinking. She had said, "The umbrella tree is about to fall down. Look – it's falling down – " and the sense of what she meant was described by her hands.

She seemed never lonely. She managed never to invite a little girl to spend an afternoon with her, though Addie was willing to make beaten biscuits with slivers of ham and funny-men cookies for her to serve.

Now she carefully thought over what Fenton suggested. His mentioning the little mill boys and girls had been unfair. When she started public school, Fenton and Gilberta told her that she must be nice to the mill children and not let them feel that they were different from her or any of the other children who had come in at mid-term from Miss Nyrick's School at the Country Club. It was the first time she had been close to any mill children. Occasionally she had gone down to the gates at the drive and hid behind the wall and watched the millworkers coming home with their black tin lunch boxes and denim overalls and sweaty smell which whisked in her face as they passed. But she had never seen any mill children her own age until she went to Sycamore Primary. They looked quite different from Newtown children.

Newtown girls wore thin knit union suits in winter with brown stockings buttoned in front to the waist. Their shoes were brown kid with suede tops of fawn or grey and their dresses were wool with prints on them – or else they dotted up the playground in their bright plaid skirts and red or green velvet jackets. On Sunday they changed to white stockings and black patent leather shoes with white kid nine-button tops and crepe de chine dresses with heavy smocking across the front.

The mill girls' dresses were faded and starched coarse gingham or rejected flannel with round collarless necks and long sleeves with wrist bands pinned together by straight pins twisted under not to show. They wore black stockings which never met their bloomers and always showed a stretch of union suit behind the knee. Their hair was cut rawly in Dutch bobs crudely shingled up the back with their fathers' razors. And about them, ever and forever, was a smell of dye and waste.

Even more different in appearance were the little Yankee girls, whose fathers were chemists or plant managers in the mills. They braided their hair like older girls and wore dresses of hard serge or dark plain cotton, high above their knees. They wore heavy wool plaid socks and coarse blunt-toed brogans with no tops, and their legs were frostbitten and chapped all winter.

There was only one day when it was hard to tell the Yankees and the mill girls from the others – and that was on gym day when everyone wore a uniform.

August thought of Ruby Boyle, who sat in front of her – B before C. Ruby's dresses opened in a kind of tape down the back; and once, when the placket had gaped, August had reached over to button it and there hadn't been any button or any buttonho' either. Ruby had jumped at the touch of her finger and jer' around, eyes glaring and face red with anger. Then, becau

August's astonishment, Ruby had realized that she had meant only to make an obliging gesture such as she would have made to Jessie Willetts or any of the Newtown girls. Ruby had tried to smile then but she hadn't been able to, not so quickly. She had fished a straight pin from somewhere and had reached back and pinned the place together from underneath. It had been over in an instant, but it had frightened August, and always after that day August had been possessed by an odd feeling about Ruby. She had become not just one of the mill children but all of them, to August. In another second Ruby might have slapped her. At some unexpected moment the little shell of respect for her which protected her from all of them might break and she would be attacked. So she took care never to look directly at Ruby or to show any interest in her.

When Fenton had told her that in time the mill children would have a school of their own out in the village but that until that time she must do everything to make them feel at home in town, she knew that he had meant he wanted her to try to make friends with them, to try harder than she would try to make new friends among the Newtown children. But soon August learned that neither she nor they ever wanted to be friends.

"I don't know whether we should have a Christmas tree or not," she considered, seriously, glancing at Fenton from the corner of her eye. "It will be a great deal of trouble for Mother. Mother and I will have to buy all the presents and there are over forty not counting the teachers."

"I think your mother would like to do it," Fenton objected quickly to this argument. "Certainly I will be most happy to help if you will provide a shopping list."

August was about to say, "Well, it will be a big mess in the house and I think we ought to ask Mother first," when Fenton went on, "Why wouldn't it do for me to write Miss Horton a letter and ask her to give us the class roll with her gift suggestion beside each name?"

Perhaps if he had given in to her a little with her first objection she would have been more easily persuaded. But now her face was set and in her agitation August pulled her finger out of her place in *Pinocchio.*

"I don't know whether anybody will come or not," she said, suddenly.

Fenton was startled. "Why not, dear?"

"Well," she said, swallowing and dropping her eyes, "I don't think they'll want to. They don't like me." She picked at the pages of her reader. Fenton was speechless. He could not understand. He lifted her chin so that he could look directly into her eyes. Then he said slowly, "I don't think you're telling me the truth, dear. I'm sure you have no real reason to say your little friends don't like you. And I'm sure that they will come, if you invite them." He continued to hold her chin firmly in his hand so that she could not turn away. His disappointment in her darkened his eyes. "But if you are reluctant to ask them, then I will invite them for you." With that he suddenly got up from his chair. On the way to the door he stopped at the little Pembroke table to pick up his copy of *Three Soldiers.* He was angry.

"We won't talk about this any more tonight," he said from the door. "Finish your homework. I'll write the invitation to Miss Horton myself and we'll mail it on the way to school. I think that you are being a very selfish little girl."

When he had gone, August leaned slowly over her *Pinocchio* and pressed her face against the stiff cover. Shame and frustration filled her heart. He's wrong, she thought bitterly, he's wrong.

And then, the cruelest thought of all occurred to her. *He even does not trust me to take the letter to Miss Horton. He's going to mail it himself.*

❧

In the morning, August arose before there was any sound in the house. She ran her own tub and dressed quickly. Then she tiptoed down the gallery to her playroom to her desk and stationery. She took paper and an envelope from the portfolio he mother had given her on her birthday.

Dear Miss Horton [she wrote slowly, trying to keep the words from going downhill as she moved to the edge]:

I am going to have a Christmas party at my house and I would like to invite you and the whole first grade. I want Miss Applewhite and Miss Cooper and Miss Norman to come too. If you will help me make a list of the presents for everybody I will appreciate it very much. I can stay after school any day this week. I hope you and everybody will come.

Sincerely yours,
August Chadley

Inside her there was a deep swollen feeling, a physical pain, which was not relieved by writing the letter. She dreaded meeting Fenton and her mother. She knew how they would treat her — nicely and sadly. She could not bear to be "endured" and "treated."

She went down to breakfast as soon as she heard Addie and Susie stirring about. Then she started her cereal and waited for Fenton to come. At her first opportunity she scrutinized his face, trying to guess if he might have changed his mind about writing Miss Horton the letter. Faced with the prospect of having to sit all day in school in front of Miss Horton, after her own invitation had been given, and not knowing which mail would bring Fenton's or what it would say exactly and what impression it might give Miss Horton, made her a little sick. Fenton's letter could easily make everything look suspicious, unless by some mercy it only sounded as if he were writing so that Miss Horton would know that August's invitation came with proper permission. But August had no means of discovering what Fenton had written unless she asked him outright. And that was impossible. She looked at his face each time she could use her napkin and raise her eyes. But she discovered nothing. Fenton was attentive, as was usual, to Gilberta. At last, bitterly sure that the time was past for him to reveal some sign of forgiveness and assurance that the humiliating letter would never be posted, she set herself for the ride to the schoolhouse with him.

Fenton was silent until he had drawn up to the curb and August was ready to hurry up the wide concrete walk with its cracking sections, still chalked-up from yesterday afternoon's hopscotch. Then he cut off the ignition and locked the car and got out with her.

"I have decided against writing Miss Horton about your Christmas party," he said quite naturally to August, "I think it will be more cordial to go in with you now and invite your little friends."

He acted as if their dispute had been entirely over *how* the children were to be invited and not whether they were to be invited at all. He moved up the double walk with her, observing the frost on the branches of the willow trees on either side of the school lot.

They got to the steep concrete steps which led up to the porch and second floor of the building where the second and third grades were gathering; then August touched Fenton's elbow and indicated the little tributary of a walk leading around to the right beneath the steps to a basement door. She would have explained, "The first grade is down here," but she could not speak a word. She could not even look at anything fixedly. She moved by habit. Her eyes saw the general familiar surroundings of the school, the clanking arm swings slapping against their iron posts in the side yard, the colored cut-out paper Christmas trees in a chain pasted across the front windows of the second grade above, the whole square outward shape of the solid old brick building. And she walked steadily in the proper direction into the sudden steamy heat of the basement hall and along its wavering floor to her room marked 1A MISS HORTON. Then she stopped before the glass of the door and waited for Miss Horton to look up. Fenton held his hat lightly under his arm and pulled off his gloves.

Miss Horton was at her desk. She was grading papers. Her reddish brown eyes, which resembled the crust of cornbread, were half closed under the pucker of her lids now. Suddenly she marked vigorously with her red pencil all over the paper she was grading and smacked it shut, breaking her lead in a wicked D beside the name. August shivered. And in the same instant, Miss Horton jerked up her head to survey the room and gauge attendance and saw August and Fenton outside.

If she had been able to, Miss Horton would have slipped open the shallow center drawer of her desk and looked down into the little mirror lying face up there. But there wasn't time to pick at her hair. She arose, smoothing her dress with her hands as if she didn't know what her hands were doing and came out to the hall. She was smiling. At least her mouth was open and her teeth were showing. The veins popped in a string under the thin skin of her forehead. She walked as if she were bowlegged, but August, who had seen her in her gym bloomers, knew that she wasn't. It was just that her body was flat and long-waisted and her legs unexpectedly and wrongly short and stout. Her sandy red hair was ratted fluffily at the temples, then squeezed in a flat platter knot on the crown of her head. She was a uniquely homely woman.

"Good morning, Mr. Chadley," she said, reddening until her nutmeg freckles were solid over her face. She conspicuously closed the door behind her to prevent the pupils inside from eavesdropping. August clutched the strap of her book bag. She did not know whether Fenton meant her to be party to the invitation or not. She looked at Miss Horton smirking at Fenton, and she could have vomited nastily all over the floor. She hated every face her eyes could see at that moment. She was ill with violent unspecific threats against her whole world. She could have run down the hall screaming and swinging her book bag from side to side until all the glass doors were broken.

"Good morning, Miss Horton," replied Fenton, solicitously, "I hope I'm not upsetting your schedule with an unannounced visit like this."

Miss Horton protested vigorously.

August could stand the scene no longer.

"I have to go in now, Uncle Chad," she said suddenly in words so muted that neither Miss Horton nor Fenton heard her distinctly, "I have to do something before the bell." She ducked around Miss Horton at the door and escaped into the schoolroom. She walked swiftly down the aisle to the cloakroom and hung up her coat and tam and book bag. Then she looked up and down the length of the cloakroom to be certain she was alone, put her books and tablet on the floor and, crouching down, opened the binding of her reader. There was the letter addressed to Miss Horton. Very deliberately she tore it into perfect squares and then into smaller perfect squares until she could squeeze the little stack of fragments into the narrow pencil pocket of her book bag. Tearing it so coldly and systematically helped her. With the letter gone, it was as if she had never had the good intention. The bell was ringing and she had to go out and take her seat behind Ruby Boyle and smell the gingham dress and homemade soap again. Miss Horton would probably tell the class about the Christmas party just before they went home at two o'clock. It would cause too much commotion if she announced it now. August moved up the aisle and took her seat and carefully kept her eyes lowered until she had shoved her books under the desk top and arranged her pencils and taken her Palmer pen out and seen that the point was clean. Then she raised her head and saw all the class ducking and peering and smirking at each other.

Fenton was standing beside Miss Horton.

It was difficult for her, in the first moment she saw him there, to understand what was happening. But just as Miss Horton began to tap foolishly for attention (there was no one who was not paying attention) it came to her as one last appalling catastrophe that Fenton was going to invite the first grade to Dunmeade himself! August wanted to ease down in her seat and hide and not have to look at him. She felt an unbearable embarrassment for him. For a moment her other feelings toward Fenton were submerged in a defense of him; for she knew the children sitting beside her, up and down in rows, were hastily criticizing his every feature and movement. The boys in their ugly nose-picking attention were only waiting until Fenton was done to snicker and ape him, crooking their fingers around their eyes to mock his weak ones and talking *at* each other with their noses raised. And she knew that when they came to Dunmeade they would gobble down everything put before them and then sneak off in twos and threes to other rooms to whisper and giggle as they made fun of everything in the house. And no one liked her anyway. Oh, she cried out silently, why couldn't he have let *me!*

"August and Mrs. Chadley and I would like the pleasure of entertaining all of you at a Christmas party on the afternoon of the twentieth – which is the day you'll be leaving school for the holiday. We live at Dunmeade and August will tell you how to get there," Fenton was saying in the nice polite voice he used when he asked someone permission to let him do a favor. "If any of you wish to come in our car, I'll arrange to have it here at Miss Horton's convenience" – and he smiled at Miss Horton and stepped back and indicated that he was ready to go. "I hope you will all come."

That was all.

When he had gone August felt the wave of the children's reaction creep toward her like an invisible fence, moving her back from them. Now she was special to the teacher. She was alone up high and favored and they were down below her to receive what she had conspired with the teacher to give them without their consent. Miss Horton smiled at August and then suddenly in an afterthought got up from her desk and walked back to August and put a fifty-cent piece on her pen rack. "Your lunch money," she whispered as if it had to do with some plan for the party which the others must not hear. "Your father forgot to give it to you." And then Miss Horton went back and August moved uneasily and tried to thank her without attracting any more attention. Now that there was going to be the party, each time a teacher spoke to her and talked to her where the others couldn't hear, it would look as if it had something to do with the party. She would be tied in all their minds to the teachers and the teachers would be even nicer to her than before and her isolation, bad enough before, would now be complete.

On the next Saturday afternoon, Miss Horton and Miss Applewhite came to Dunmeade for tea. They brought with them the enrollment lists of the first grade of Sycamore Primary. The teachers had spent four evenings going over the names and noting beside each one the gift they thought would be most appreciated. Fenton had been careful to remind Miss Horton, on the day he had issued the invitation to the party, that the occasion would provide an opportunity to give to many of the children a present which their parents might not be able to afford. He particularly wanted to give to the mill children the warm sweaters and breeches and hose which he was sure they would not receive otherwise. So Miss Horton and Miss Applewhite, appreciating his thoughtfulness and kind intentions, had written beside certain names *Knit underwear*, or *Overshoes*, or *A flannel petticoat* or *Outing pajamas*. By the names of children of respectable but not well-to-do parents, they had written such things as *Book bag*, or *Pen-and-pencil case* or *Umbrella*. By the names of the rich Newtown children (Cora Simmons, Amos and Vincent Starburg and Sue Jessie Briggs and the others) they had left discreet blanks.

Miss Applewhite was the home room and spelling teacher for 1B, but she also supervised the Drawing and Crafts period for 1A and here she taught August.

At one point during tea, while August was still with her mother and Fenton and the teachers, Addie, serving a fresh muffin to Miss Horton, slyly asked, "Which one gets behind our baby when she don't do right?"

At this intrusion of the servant into the social conversation, everyone was startled and August blushed red and lifted her cup to hide her face.

"Well," laughed Miss Horton, nervously, her cornbread-crust eyes on Gilberta, "so far there hasn't been any cause to say a word to her. But of course Miss Applewhite and I never expect to have trouble with little girls from lovely homes like Dunmeade. Do we, Miss Applewhite?" She bit into her fresh muffin with a delicate crumb-shaking gesture.

Miss Applewhite smiled and looked over at August. "Do you think little girls like you ever cause us any trouble, August?" she asked, smiling, sniffing a spoon of hot tea.

Fenton beamed at what seemed to be obvious affectionate teasing. He was positive that August was a model of decorum.

Boldly August answered Miss Applewhite, "I'd rather not say until after I'm promoted."

Everyone laughed at August's little impudence and then suddenly the social occasion seemed to come to an end. August told her teachers good-by politely and went to her playroom.

Then Miss Horton moved to sit beside Gilberta with the class roll of 1A in her hand and Miss Applewhite was left to go over the roll of 1B with Fenton.

Fenton listened attentively as Miss Applewhite called out the suggested gifts, his eyes following her short finger as it moved down the list. He agreed, "Oh yes, I see," and commented, "I suppose the chap in the boys' department will know the sizes when we tell him the ages." And she assured him, "Oh yes, I'm sure so. And, of course, Mrs. Chadley will know right off anyway."

Then they were finished suddenly and Miss Applewhite drew her breath oddly, leaned closer to Fenton's ear and said, "I have been wanting to pay a call to Dunmeade for some time, Mr. Chadley. I was delighted when Miss Horton told me that we were coming here." She looked candidly into Fenton's face and he blushed at what seemed a blunt compliment to his home. But then he noticed that Miss Applewhite was not gazing admiringly about the room but was instead studying Gilberta and Miss Horton as if gauging the possibility of a sudden break in their conversation. But they were engrossed in flattering each other with attention first to Gilberta's ideas, then to Miss Horton's.

"I have had the privilege of supervising your little girl in Drawing and Crafts this semester, Mr. Chadley," Miss Applewhite said. "I wonder if you have noticed any of her projects – if she has shown any to you?"

Fenton felt a sudden warmth in him. He knew the teacher was going to say something good about August that she could not say about any other child.

"No," he said, "I don't believe she's brought anything home unless she's put it away in her playroom." And then, because he couldn't help himself, he said, laughing with inner pleasure, "She does quite well, doesn't she? It's because of her father. My brother was a sculptor." Then, to his embarrassment, he realized the teacher might not know his exact relationship to August and he added, "I am August's uncle and stepfather, you know. I haven't a shred of talent – but her real father, that is, my brother, was unusually gifted. He died in the last war." He was so excited he wanted to call out across the room to Gilberta, "You see, I was right. They have noticed her at school too." But he restrained himself, waiting to hear Miss Applewhite underscore in her own words the praise he had already given August.

But with a strange mixture of puzzlement and pity on her face, Miss Applewhite said, "I'm afraid I've misled you, Mr. Chadley. I wanted to talk to you about August because I'm afraid that unless we can help her, I won't be able to give her a passing grade. She seems to have a hopeless inability to reproduce anything – even the large simple patterns I give her."

Fenton's breath went back down into his chest and stayed there hard and unmanageable. He could not have been more shocked if the teacher had said that August was stupid and that it was useless to try to keep her in school. He gazed at the teacher's face, waiting for her to laugh and explain that she had only been joshing him.

But Miss Applewhite did not laugh and reassure him. She was so earnest that her flat face looked grotesque with the bright focus of her round eyes on Fenton, pleading with him to follow her and understand. In her mind she could see August clearly, just the way she sat in class, peeling dried paste off her fingers and sometimes tasting the stinging spicy flavor of it absent-mindedly as she mooned at the blackboard before her. In the beginning she had thought that August simply had difficulty managing the manual tools — the crayon or the scissors — but before very long she had been forced to the realization that August had no intention of following the assignment because she simply would not see a pattern literally. She drew on her paper what she saw in her own mind and she did not trouble to follow the suggestion of the teacher. Miss Applewhite had to make Mr. Chadley see what a serious situation this errant behavior could lead her to — this heartbreaking fault of not being able to go along with the crowd. And there were stupid children, *really* stupid children, in her class who were going to go home at mid-term with A's!

"You see," she said, "it isn't that she does not apply herself painstakingly; she is concentrating, even when she seems to be gazing into thin air. I have discovered that. Whatever she thinks out, she expresses on her paper, and she is very critical of whatever it is she draws. I have seen her tear up a whole period's work and start again just as the bell rings. But what she draws, even when it pleases her and she brings it to me, is so, so . . ." She floundered for words and then finished, "I simply cannot pin it up. If I did, it would be condoning her refusal to follow the assignment. And even if my conscience would let me call it a boat or a house according to the assignment, I would have to mark it down for being poor execution, you see. I have been terribly troubled about it. The semester will end soon and August should go to the second grade art program just as she'll be going up with her other studies."

Fenton looked over at Gilberta and Miss Horton. He had watched them from the corner of his eye all the time Miss Applewhite had been talking to him. He did not want Gilberta to hear what was being said.

"What *does* she draw when she's supposed to be making — what did you say it was? — a boat or a house?"

"There was one last week she called 'The Man at the Sheep House' but it was not a drawing of a man. It was a pink hillside under a pink sun and at the top of the hill she had made a little black roof and chimney," Miss Applewhite said seriously. Then she added sadly, "All the other children were copying 'The Bridge of the Trolls' from next semester's reader."

But Fenton was not concerned with the other children and what they were copying from next semester's reader. He lowered his voice and bent again over the class roll she had brought as if they were still discussing the presents for the children. Gilberta and Miss Horton were rising and going to the long table with the Bristol lamps at either end. "Oh, mercy," Miss Horton was saying on the way, "I wouldn't want to be responsible for anything happening to them, Mrs. Chadley. I don't think we can be too careful about moving all breakable pieces from the room. The little girls are fairly reliable but the boys. . . ." By then her back was to Fenton and her voice had died.

"I wonder if you would withhold your decision to give August a low mark until I can see her work and go over it with you, Miss Applewhite? I think I know what she was trying to show us with her 'Man at the Sheep House.' If it looks as I think it might look, then perhaps our trouble is not quite as serious as it seems."

Miss Applewhite agreed, but there was sorrow and doubt on her broad unpliant face.

"Once in a while when we have a pupil like August we recommend that she be taught privately or sent to a smaller school," she said hesitantly, then took a breath and finished out the thing she felt she was obliged to say. "For you see, Mr. Chadley, August isn't compatible with the life in a public school. She doesn't make friends. She's older than the others somewhere in her mind, and she can't join with them at any point."

She could not have said a more devastating thing to Fenton. Sending August to a public school had been a holy duty to him. He had been set aside from normal associations in his childhood and boyhood by simple isolation within Dunmeade. He had been starved and not known it until he had gone to work in the bank and had had the same persons say "Good morning" to him day after day. He had come to know their faces and to look forward to greeting them in a certain order as he entered the doors. He knew the absences even before a report was sent to his office because he knew the slightest variation in the order of his greetings. Such a trivial thing as nodding to each teller was as important a part of his business life as examining notes and loans and mortgages. He had even gone occasionally to fetch August from school just to sit in the car and enjoy the sight of August coming out of the building with other little girls and boys.

And, now, with the kindest of intentions (and courage too – for he was cognizant of the teacher's position and understood what she had taken upon herself without authority) this mild lady was telling him to remove August from association with other children and imprison her in an attentive circle of paid attendants. And she, as he had, would starve for companionship, in the midst of constant company!

"No," he asserted sharply, "I don't think it will be necessary to take such a step. I'm sure that with patience we can help August to adjust to your methods. Certainly I intend to try, Miss Applewhite."

His tone frightened the teacher. "I hope I haven't offended you, Mr. Chadley. I think a great deal of August. I want to see her grow up happily, to a satisfying position in her world." Her eyes were beseeching and earnest.

"And what do you think August will be when she grows up, Miss Applewhite?" Fenton asked, his voice now controlled and his manner calm.

"I don't know specifically, Mr. Chadley," she replied. "I'm only confident that she will develop into an exceptional person – given the proper opportunity." She could not help adding the last, though she knew it would aggravate him.

"I will tell you what I think August will be, Miss Applewhite," Fenton said, in a tone of quietest finality. "I think she will be an artist – perhaps a very great one."

"If that is what she wants to be, then I hope she will be, Mr. Chadley. No one could wish more for her than I do." And without meaning it to be the rude gesture it was, Miss Applewhite looked about suddenly for Miss Horton and the way of escape.

Once in a great while Miss Applewhite had helped a child struggling alone along some secret track of his own at odds with his group. She had protected him against coercion to press him into the mold of the crowd, until he could come in by himself. But she did not believe that August Chadley would ever come into any group desiring a place in it and suffering outside its company. And this parent, this most particular guardian, whom she had expected to thank her for urging him to give his unusual child the attention of private teachers, had instead grown angry and insisted that August would someday be a great artist — *of all things* — when she had been pained to tell him that she might not be able to pass her on Drawing and Crafts for the semester! Miss Applewhite was sorry that she had come to Dunmeade and she was sorry that she would have to come again for the party.

When the teachers had gone, Fenton reflected upon what Miss Applewhite had said about August. He wanted to be just in his consideration of her comments. After his first resentment had passed, he had recalled something odd which August herself had said, something to which he had objected at the time and put down as an effort on her part to deceive him and avoid bothering with the Christmas party. August had said, "No one will come even if I invite them. They don't like me." He wanted to speak to August now, about her schoolmates, about her teachers, about her particular interests among her subjects. He wanted especially to see the drawings to which Miss Applewhite had referred with such dissatisfaction. He had never heard August complain of any inability to get on in any of her courses. And he was certain that if it were true that she did not fit perfectly into her little group, it was due to her superiority and not to any perversity in her character. However, if he discovered that August were unhappy in a public school, he would, of course, take her out. But August herself would have to ask him.

When he had changed for dinner, he went down the gallery and knocked on August's door. But there was no answer. He waited, and then he decided to try her playroom. He heard her come across the floor after he tapped.

"I am studying for a test," she said, holding back the door for him to see the book and tablet open on her desk. "Did you want something?" She was polite but not very hospitable.

"I shan't disturb you," he assured her, standing there. "I only wanted to tell you that your teachers said very nice things about you and that I am very glad you are getting along so well." Then he added, "They think the party will be lovely and that you are very sweet to give it."

August did not answer. When she did not respond to the compliment from her teachers, Fenton went on, almost insistently, "Miss Applewhite told me about your drawings in her class." He looked about the walls of her playroom hoping to see them pinned about. "I was awkward, I'm afraid," he said, "for I wasn't able to make any comment at all. I don't believe you've ever shown them to me, have you?" He tried to keep reproach out of his voice. He wanted to sound as if he meant, "Have you shown them to me and I've forgotten them, perhaps?" But he did not achieve the tone.

August went to her desk, leaving Fenton at the door. Then she stooped carefully, avoiding strain on her silk socks, and opened the deep bottom drawers on either side. She took up a bundle rolled round and put it on the floor and began to smooth out the sheets in it.

"Come in," she said, remembering Fenton suddenly. "You can't see from out there." She removed one sheet from the rolled stack and stood up holding it. "This is the one I made last week. I like it best," she said, looking at it with approval.

She carried it to the wall and held it flat and waited for his reaction. Fenton came closer. He peered at the colored masses on the paper. Then he removed his glasses and took another pair from his pocket. Without the thick lenses over his eyes, his lids seemed pink and tired and his weak eyes pale and small. He put on his strong reading glasses. August smoothed the drawing again and held it by its opposite corners.

"Mother didn't even know what it was," she said, smiling, quite confident that Fenton would recognize the scene instantly. She waited, accepting his long appraisal as admiration.

"It's the little cabin at the de Venturas'," he said. He could not look at August with the guilt he felt for being so positive of giving the correct answer. It was indeed "The Man at the Sheep House" and it looked just as Miss Applewhite had described it, as strange and as dependent upon prior knowledge for recognition as she had claimed.

For a brief instant Fenton thanked Miss Applewhite for her literal and despairing eye; she had saved him. And then he raged against her shortsightedness for not grasping the struggle of the child to impress with a few bare crayon lines and waxy smears the image of something about which she felt deeply. Formless as it was, her scene suggested the forlornness of the actual place as it had always seemed to every child who had ever stared at it at sunset and strained to see the strange man returning to sleep until sunrise when he would go alone again with his sheep to a pasture too far for them to discover. August had never seen the sheepherder. All she had ever been able to see was the thin black smoke which would come from his chimney a few moments after he and his flock came into the dip of valley and home. On her drawing she had twirled in black crayon the smoke, which to her was the presence of the man.

"It's splendid," Fenton said, taking it from her hands and looking at it with a serious scrutiny. He wanted to hide the emotion working within him. He was both angry and relieved. He was angry at Miss Applewhite's stupid insistence on geometrical tracing-paper renditions when before her a wonderfully sensitive child was putting down the images of things of deep mystery which had awakened her child's imagination.

August went through the rest of the drawings, selecting the

ones she liked next-best and then next-best. Then she held up one in particular and waited, smiling, for Fenton to identify the figure. It was her cousin Pedro bleaching his hair behind the tobacco barn. She had stroked his hair in yellow crayon just the way it fell over his face as he sat with his head between his knees to catch the sun on his crown. And she had drawn his body as a long doubled-up knot as grotesque as he had appeared to her when she and María had peeped at him through the cracks in the barn boards. "What's he doing?" she had asked in a whisper. And María had answered, blushing, "He's making his hair light." "Why?" August had asked. "Because he doesn't like to be dark like us." And then she had pulled at August to leave before Pedro caught them there.

Now August observed her drawing, feeling again her disgust and resentment. The head was as yellow as the lemons he had rubbed on it. She could smell him just as she had never ceased to smell him since that afternoon, the acid fruit and tobacco dust and scalp oil all mixed together in her nostrils.

"It seems very familiar," Fenton groped.

"Oh yes, you've been there. . . ." She nodded encouragingly. It was like playing the party game – "You're warm . . . No, cold again . . . Now hot!" – and shrieking at last "That's right! You've got it!" At last she became impatient for his praise and exclaimed all in a breath, "It's Pedro hiding behind the barn in the sun with lemon on his hair to make it turn light." She tilted the drawing back and forth to keep the lamp reflection off it.

Fenton could not say a word. He was speechless with astonishment. He could not imagine why she had wanted to picture such a scene. The idea was almost shocking to him, almost indecent. He opened his mouth slightly in consternation and August accepted his expression as indicating great surprise and approval. "Miss Applewhite said it was different from anything that had ever been handed in," she declared proudly, "and she's never even seen Pedro."

She began to put away her drawings. At the bottom of the drawer was one which had come loose from the roll when she removed the others. She examined it a moment but decided against showing it to Fenton. It was the first drawing she had made when she began 1A and could take Drawing and Crafts. Miss Applewhite had asked them to make something they had seen on their summer vacations. Everyone had worked busily and then, one by one, pictures of cows, ocean waves, mountains, boats, haystacks (and even an alligator by one child who had been to Jacksonville, Florida) had been held up for inspection. August had drawn a large black moon-eyed face with little corkscrews of hair sticking up from the scalp and a mouth which was not a mouth but only a pucker. She had written in crayon under it, "Ralph Craig," and had handed it to Miss Applewhite.

"Was that a little friend you made on your vacation?" the teacher had asked her, appalled at the ugliness of the face. August had stared back in surprise an instant and had then answered, "Oh no, he's my grandfather Chadley's butler's little boy – before my grandfather Chadley died. I mean his father was my grandfather Chadley's butler."

Now she rolled the drawing in with the others and stuffed them all back into the drawer.

"We should be going down, shouldn't we?" she reminded Fenton, and, silent and filled with his tender thoughts of her, Fenton let her lead him out of the room and down the stair to where Gilberta was waiting.

Fenton lay awake long into the night thinking of August and the strange little scenes August had drawn. They were not pleasant. Yet he knew that August liked going to visit the de Venturas. She liked the country suppers under the big walnut trees in autumn, with all of them standing about while her Aunt Grace ladled the Brunswick stew from a great iron pot on the coals. Fenton himself liked these gatherings, except that he was often made nervous there by Gilberta's too frequent disputes with her brother. They spoke in Spanish so that Fenton did not understand what they said; but he could read an expression of pity and scorn for Gilberta on Rafael's face and it upset him. Often he tried to bring himself to ask Gilberta what it was they quarreled about, but he dared not. He was afraid it had something to do with him. Whenever Gilberta was angry, she left the supper and went across the meadow to her mother's house to stay the evening until Rafael sent their second son William for her with a lantern.

William was not like Pedro. His ways were sweet and gentle after the ways of his mother. August liked William best of her cousins. And knowing that, Fenton wondered why she had drawn Pedro and not William. It was William who always hid an extra fried pie behind the stove for August to take home. And it was William who went with her to the well house and dipped up her buttermilk from one of the brown crocks. If she had made a picture of William, she could have given it to him. William would have been pleased, however vague the likeness.

Certainly she could never show Pedro the curious unpleasant thing she had made of him. It was full of dislike, and Fenton was doubly conscious of the feeling in it because he himself felt a disapproval of Pedro. Indeed he felt more than a disapproval. He had felt a justifiable alarm concerning Pedro's character since the shocking incidents following the summer's fire which had destroyed Rafael's barn.

One afternoon just before closing, Pedro had come into the bank and had asked for Fenton. Stockard, his secretary, had obligingly offered to fetch him from across the square, where he was attending the weekly meeting of the Merchants' and Bankers' Club. But Pedro, laughing pleasantly, had said, "It isn't important. I only wanted to cash a check – which you can do for me as well as Uncle Fenton, can't you?"

Flattered by this attribution of authority to him, Stockard had introduced Pedro at the window of Estes, the bank's oldest teller.

"This is Mr. de Ventura, Mr. Chadley's nephew. He has a check to be cashed for . . ." And then he had waited.

"Seven hundred," Pedro supplied calmly, pushing the check under the grille to Estes. It was from the Tower Fire Insurance Company of Newtown and New York City.

The amount had startled Stockard for a moment, but he had no intention of wavering before Estes, who was staring coldly through his window at Pedro. Always anyone withdrawing money was suspect to Estes.

"Will you endorse it, please?" Estes had said matter-of-factly, and when Pedro had endorsed the check, not with his own name but with Rafael's, Estes, after a momentary hesitation, had counted out the money in fifty-dollar bills.

"I've given it to you in fifties. Is that satisfactory, Mr. de Ventura?" Estes had raised his eyes and looked straight into Pedro's when he said it. Fifties were hard to cash. For an instant, Pedro's annoyance had shown in the bulge of his cheek as he bit his teeth together. Then he had caught himself, smiled again, and reached for the stack of bills.

"Fine," he had said; "many thanks" – flicking them through his fingers to be certain that he had been given the right amount. It had been three o'clock exactly at that moment and Mr. Girk, the day officer, was already bending down over the door sill to set the bottom lock. Pedro had set off across the marble floor in a trot to reach him in time.

"Thanks very much," he had called back to Stockard from outside on the sidewalk. "Come out with Uncle Fenton sometime, won't you?"

A moment after he had disappeared, Fenton had walked up from the opposite direction.

"Wasn't that my nephew leaving just now?" he had asked. "What did he want?"

"He cashed a check."

"Whose check?" demanded Fenton. He had met Pedro on the street near the Briggs Arcade before going to the meeting and Pedro had said nothing about wanting to cash a check.

Visibly frightened by Fenton's tone, Stockard had replied, "Let me call Mr. Estes. He has it."

But Estes was already coming to meet them, the check in his hand.

"I gave him the marked fifties just to be on the safe side, Mr. Chadley, begging your pardon, sir. Your father always insisted on that in cases of doubt," Estes had said calmly to Fenton's astonished and miserable face. "If it's all right for him to have the money, then there's no harm done. If not, we can give out the numbers and stop him spending his papa's money before he goes through it all. He's just trying to act like a big man, Mr. Chadley." He had nodded consolingly but Fenton had dropped his eyes to scrutinize Pedro's forgery more closely but even more to hide his face.

"Thank you, Mr. Estes," Fenton had said at last, with pronounced formality. "I'll handle the matter from here on. I'm sure there is a satisfactory explanation." His hands had trembled so he had had to press them against the desk top. "Thank you so much. Don't let me keep you from your work." He had looked above Estes's head to the great brass clock suspended in the middle of the bank. "Will you locate Mr. Stockard for me, please, and ask him to have my car brought around?" Then he had slipped the check into an envelope and the envelope into his inside coat-pocket, and gone to the door to await his car.

At first he had thought that he might find Pedro in Newtown. Then he had realized that Pedro would keep out of sight to avoid having to give up the money. So he had decided to drive instead to Quakertown to see Rafael, never doubting that Rafael would be willing to take some action if Pedro did not return home by evening. And he had been prepared to offer suggestions for handling the matter discreetly so that all of them might be protected from injurious gossip.

But his interview with Rafael had been as shocking as the news he had brought with him. Rafael, leaning over the pigsty under the chestnut tree, doing no more than gazing at his wallowing hogs and humming, had resented Fenton's intrusion instantly. He had kept his eyes averted when Fenton had drawn the check from his pocket and held it out to exhibit the forged signature.

Finally when, after a silence prolonged to the point of rudeness, he had spoken, he had simply said, "He's my son. What difference does it make who takes the dollars? If he has use for them, well . . ." And, shrugging, he had left the sentence unfinished.

For a moment Fenton had not believed that Rafael could really mean to ignore Pedro's serious delinquency; but when Rafael had shielded his eyes to look out over the pasture toward the shepherd's cabin and had then moved away from Fenton to watch the wandering cows ready for home and milking, Fenton had known that Rafael's one remark upon the subject had been made and that there would be no punishment for Pedro. Anger had risen in him against this unapproachable man, who would live by and respect no laws but his own, and he had followed Rafael and said — before he could stop himself and prevent the damage he knew such criticism would do — "Pedro has broken the law. And now you wish me to break the law and honor his forgery. I insist that you give me your own signature."

But Rafael had neither turned his face nor spoken. Instead he had called out suddenly, "William . . ." and when William had emerged from the well house, he had waved his black, hair-thick arm toward the pasture commandingly, and then had stood watching with complete absorption his conscientious younger son driving in the cows.

And that had ended Fenton's interview with Rafael. Rafael had not endorsed the check, and Fenton had been obliged to honor a forgery! Bewildered, angry, and shocked, Fenton had returned to Dunmeade. He had had a rude tutoring in a sad lesson. He was, and always would be, a stranger to his wife's kin.

Now Fenton wanted to find out why August reacted so to Pedro. He was deeply disturbed by the scene she had drawn. It was not a happy observation upon a place and a person of her world. He wished that he might speak to Gilberta about the picture of Pedro but he knew that he never could. To Gilberta such a question about Pedro would signify, however irrationally, a criticism of her brother's whole family. There was little communication between Gilberta and him upon any subject. He was completely isolated in the part of a protector in which she had cast him at the beginning of their married life. And out of courtesy for her sensibilities as a woman, he had not demanded that she accord him any other consideration or privilege beyond that of allowing him to provide for her comfortable life. It was only at such times when he needed to feel a loyal being beside him who could hear him speak of the responsibilities which burdened him, and yet not judge him weak, that he resented Gilberta's unconcern and lack of interest. It was not that he wished her to understand the intricacies of the banking business. He neither wanted nor expected Gilberta to attempt to advise him. But he would have appreciated a discreet inquiry from time to time as to how things were at the bank and how the "business outlook" in general appeared. But she never mentioned the bank nor expressed any interest whatsoever in his career as a banker.

He missed his father and those perfectly formal and yet intimate conversations it had been their habit to have, even when he was a small boy and had sat with his father in the library after dinner while Mr. Chadley had his smoke. Out of his loneliness, he came to understand his father and the deep resentment Mr. Chadley had felt toward Lesley, who could sit in the room with him looking into his face but hearing nothing of what he said, and not caring.

Fenton knew that he could never attain any deep and true union with Gilberta and that he was as far removed from her intimate life as if he dwelled in another house and not merely in another room. And yet with this certain knowledge of no real marriage to her, he made himself believe that his devotion and wholly good unselfish love for her would be enough to sustain him through all the mature years of his life, and he would never regret taking the one way of binding Lesley's daughter into his indisputable care. He was wrong, of course. There were times, as on this night after the teachers' disturbing visit, when he was grateful for the dark which hid the unmanly emotion upon his face.

Driving her home from school one afternoon soon after, Fenton discovered one reason her cousin Pedro had become so vivid and so unpleasant a figure in August's mind. She was afraid of him.

"I was wondering if we oughtn't to ask your little cousins, the de Venturas, to the Christmas party," he fished. It really did not seem proper to him to invite them since it was a classroom affair, but he hoped that the suggestion might bring a revealing answer from August.

"Aunt Grace couldn't come," she said flatly, "she's busy all day."

"I wasn't thinking of Aunt Grace and Uncle Rafael. I meant Pedro and William and María."

August was silent a moment, then she murmured indifferently, "I don't mind, if Pedro doesn't hurt anyone."

She looked out the window of the car, waiting for the train to cross the intersection just down the grade below them. The gates were drawn and the watchman was waving his lantern back and forth though it was not yet dusk and the lantern was unlit.

"Good gracious," said Fenton, his tone purposely a little doubting, "that's not a nice thing to say of poor Pedro. I can't imagine he has done anything to deserve that." He waited, carefully keeping his eyes over the wheel.

"He does lots of things," August answered defensively. "He beats the hounds all the time."

"Well, of course that's very ugly of him," Fenton agreed, shifting the gears and moving the car on again, the brakeman in the caboose waving to August as they passed. "But I'm sure he won't behave that way when ladies and little girls are present."

"Yes, he will," August contradicted. "I saw him push Myrtle Finch down. María and I both saw him do it."

"Oh, but it must have been in play," Fenton insisted, glancing at her without taking his attention too long from the road.

"No, it wasn't," August declared emphatically; "he pushed her right down, hard, and mashed her. We saw him. They were smoking rabbit tobacco in the barn and María and I saw them through the loft window when we were on the haystack eating biscuits and brown sugar." That seemed to settle the matter and August turned once again to look out the window. They were only a block from Dunmeade and were passing Earl Barron's house.

"I'm afraid I don't understand," Fenton said. A shocking thought had come into his mind. He wanted to contradict it if he could. "Where did you say he pushed her?"

"When María and I climbed up on top of the haystack next to the barn," she said slowly and patiently as if she were spelling out the words for a dunce, "we looked in and saw him push her down and mash her."

Fenton was silent. He was afraid at last to pursue the subject further. Perhaps it had all been perfectly innocent. He hoped so. He turned into the gates of Dunmeade.

"They were smoking cigarettes and acting silly," August said, disgust clear in her tone. "Aunt Grace won't let him smoke rabbit tobacco when she can catch him, but she never used to go in the barn to look for him, so that's why he went in there before Uncle Rafael had the fire and it all burned down. I don't know where he goes now."

"I see," Fenton said. He drove into the garage. Then he said, patting her hand, "We mustn't have anyone at the party who is going to frighten the little girls. You are quite right. I had no idea Pedro was so rough." In addition to his shock from the image suggested by August's description of Pedro's behavior with Myrtle Finch he now suspected that Pedro had caused the fire which had burned Rafael's barn.

"He is not a nice boy," August concluded, scrambling to get her book bag pulled off the seat behind her.

"Yes," murmured Fenton, following her to the patio, "I can understand why you are reluctant to have him at the party."

❧

There was a member of the de Ventura family in Dunmeade for the Christmas party, however. She came early in the morning of the day before it and spent the night in the small back room down the gallery near the servants' stair. She was August's grandmother, who in her childhood had lived in Dunmeade — who, in fact, had seen it built and whose own bedroom had been the room she slept in now as a guest. Her father and young Señor de Ventura, his friend and companion, had occupied the front chambers, leaving the lonely timid child to the companionship of an old unhappy nurse, whining to return to Cádiz, and a coachman turned into a valet and housekeeper, who trotted ceaselessly up and down stairs keeping his eye on everything and doing nothing.

Señora de Ventura had paid few visits to Dunmeade since Gilberta's marriage to Fenton. It seemed to content her that her daughter was there in possession. She never called the house Dunmeade. It was always El Refugio, the name her father had given it.

She was a small person but she had such an air of elegance that she might have been caught in the labor of sweeping leaves from the patio and yet given the impression of being surprised pirouetting in practice for a ball. She was a beautiful woman, whom Gilberta resembled in features and coloring. But her face throughout the disappointments and denials of her life had taken on a calm patience which Gilberta's never would have and she reminded one of the primitive Madonnas, removed and wise in their niches, far from flesh and the world.

She restrained any show of affection she had for August. Occasionally she smiled approvingly at the adult dignity of the little girl. But she never kissed August, not even in greeting or departure as she did her daughter Gilberta. Gilberta was her youngest child, born fifteen years after her son Rafael. Two girls had been born lifeless between, and Señor de Ventura was aging and ill with not much of his strength or attention left for any of them, but she had been a strong mother for her daughter and Gilberta had not missed having a father. Sometimes she tried to talk to August directly when Gilberta brought the child to her house beyond Quakertown, the house in which August had been born. August could not understand, however she concentrated and watched her grandmother's gestures; so usually after an interval of embarrassing struggle their communications had to be transmitted through Gilberta. It would have been difficult to tell to what degree she favored her grandchild. She never discussed August, even in her long quiet conversations with Gilberta. Yet there was never a visit that she did not give August something beautiful and old and valuable. On this occasion, when she arrived to witness the tree trimming and the party for the school children, she brought her granddaughter a locket of gold in the shape of a delicate bell.

August reacted to her grandmother with neither great affection nor curiosity. She was a taken-for-granted appendage, like an arm or a foot, but not necessary at all. However, she was conscious of her grandmother's presence. There was an odor about her, an odor August had begun to identify with all old people, which reminded her when she walked along the gallery that her grandmother was not far away. It was the musky odor of dried aromatic leaves which have lost their oily pungency. And it was more noticeable in thin old people than in stout ones.

When the immense tree was brought in, all the household went to the patio to witness the unloading and to contribute grunts and warnings to the nurserymen who had been engaged to set it up in the large front foyer where it would tower past the height of the gallery. It was a magnificent blue spruce ordered from the North and shipped with great care and expense, arriving only three days after it had been cut from the forest.

With the others, August watched the nurserymen secure the tree with wires intricately woven in and out its branches all the way to the ceiling. Then she went up the stair to look down upon it. The fresh strong resinous scent traveled quickly through the house and suddenly the presence of the great tree charged the air with excitement.

It was not like any she had seen on the rolling landscape about Newtown, or even in the wide sandy stretches between Newtown and the sea where the famous pines with the foot-long needles grew. It seemed an indignity to hang the decorations all up and down the spruce tree. When she had looked down on it from the stair it had seemed to her not entirely the figure of a tree. It was more the tall body of a person, a man — a great and kingly man. And the tapered head of the spruce had worn a crown of bluish greenish frosting that was, of course, the closer clustering of the light-tipped needles. It had seemed very solemn and regal to August and she imagined its disapproval of the baubles and gilt with which they were about to make it ridiculous.

In a sudden impulse she wanted to call out to the others that the tree should be left as it was and not decorated. But the moment passed with her lips opened to cry out but not crying out, and then she ran silently up the stair and down the quiet hall to her room. She had not wanted to have any part in readying the house for the party. She did not think of the party as being in any part hers. Now with the great quiet tree in the house another emotion had come, an emotion welling up out of her imagination.

With no warning, she sat down in her little ruffled rocker and began to cry. She cried aloud, unconcerned for the disturbance she might cause in the house. She cried as she had not allowed herself to cry since she had begun going to Sycamore Primary. She wept at having to do something she did not want to do and which she was certain would turn out badly. She wept for the helplessness of the spruce tree, which she identified with herself, trapped and defenseless against the acts of its captors. As her feeling of frustration increased, her sobs changed from the sounds of grief to the near-screams of rage and resistance. She beat her fists into her knees while her tears dripped on her knuckles. Her door was opened and closed firmly and someone stood watching her until she felt the presence and looked. It was her grandmother, Señora de Ventura.

For an instant, August held her breath and jerked her head upward to tilt back the tears. But the instant of pride and shame passed and the strong emotion she attempted to curb rose up afresh and she bowed her head with a wail.

Señora de Ventura drew the dressing-table stool beside August and sat facing the weeping child. She was scarcely larger than August. She might have been a child-friend witnessing and sharing a fellow child's defeat, except that her face had none of the cruel unconscious curiosity of a child and her eyes were mournful and resigned before the spectacle of August's suffering. She did not touch her granddaughter or speak. She sat before her silently experiencing her sorrow with her, waiting for exhaustion to stop the tears. If she could have spoken, she would have said to August, "Even if I could help you, I would not so rob you. Learn to grieve without anger or promises to yourself to avenge the wounds in your heart." But she was silent. It did not matter what had brought the tears. When they were done, the experience would be over, whatever it was, and the young spirit would have aged a little toward its inevitable and necessary maturity. The quiet Spanish face waited patiently with that eternal air of cooperation with fate.

Once August flung out her arm in a protest against this witnessing. But her grandmother did not draw back. At last, August rested her head on the cushioned back of the chair and finished out the last hiccuping sounds. Señora de Ventura pulled the lace handkerchief from her cuff and put it on August's knee. It rested there unused while the last drops spilled from August's chin onto her collar.

They were a strange sight, sitting together in the winter daylight. The grandmother did nothing to comfort the child. The child made no appeal to the grandmother. There was no yielding and no tender sound between them.

At last August stood up and examined the mess of damp spots over her dress. She went to her closet and took a velvet jumper out of the linen sack which held her nicest clothes. She stretched to reach the hanger. The back muscles of her legs swelled and her small round ankles trembled at the strain and uncertain weight.

She went into her bathroom with the jumper over her arm. For a moment, she debated the question of closing the door while her grandmother still remained there watching her. Then she looked at Señora de Ventura and smiled and made a gesture indicating that she wished to refresh herself. "Excuse me please," she murmured and then, still awkward about it, she closed the door.

When she came out Señora de Ventura was gone. Her handkerchief lay on the floor where it had fallen from August's knee. Now she picked it up and smoothed its lace and sniffed the scent on it. It had a dry dead-petal odor. She blew the smell of it back out of her nostrils violently and held the handkerchief away from her. She would give it to Susie to return unless her grandmother remembered and came for it. She did not want to go to Señora de Ventura's room.

When she reached the foyer downstairs the spruce tree was alone. She glanced at it sharply to see if it stood secure. It was suddenly huge and independent. She shivered at its height and went to look for Susie.

But no one was in the pantry or kitchen. Outside, August heard a commotion and the clear formal voice of Fenton directing someone to "Just rest there, please, until I put down my own bundle and then I'll help you." She opened the kitchen door and looked across the garden. The December day was fading and she could see only the plants against the closest greenhouse windows. Fenton was putting down two wreaths of holly and tipping across them gently to rescue Gilberta, who was caught in the doorway with a ten-blossom pot of giant poinsettias about to be cut sharp through their stems by the low lintel. August watched them with great interest. Slowly a kind of anger began to grow in her and move out from her mind to encircle Gilberta and Fenton and convert them into hateful images. Here they were, totally enmeshed in their own schemes and arrangements for the party, *their* party, and all the rest of the house forgotten – specifically, August forgotten. It came to her that even Fenton had not come running at the sound of her crying an hour ago. He was occupied in the greenhouse. He would not have known it if she had been taken ill and had died in some terrible attack. Her Grandfather Chadley had died so, with only the colored man near him. But even Susie and Addie were nowhere in sight here.

She looked toward the greenhouse just in time to see Addie and Susie and O'Smyre, the gardener, come out behind Gilberta with their arms ringed with mistletoe and holly wreaths like doughnut sticks. Then she turned and ran quickly back through the house and upstairs to her room.

From her side window she watched the procession reach the kitchen door. Then she went to her bell pull and frantically rang and rang and rang. She stopped a few minutes to listen for steps coming up. Then she rang again faintly. She did not listen this time. Instead she hurried into the bathroom, looked at herself quickly in her glass, took a deep breath, leaned over the lavatory and stuck her finger far down her throat.

It was just as she had successfully gagged herself and managed to splatter the front of her velvet jumper that Susie came in. August sank gently to the floor grasping the edges of the basin.

"Oh, mercy Lord!" breathed Susie, running to lift the little girl off the cold tile. "Mrs. Chadley," she called, "Oh, Mrs. Chadley, ma'am!" and she half dragged and half carried the entirely conscious dead weight of August to the bed.

At seven o'clock that evening Fenton and Gilberta and Señora de Ventura sat down to a light supper. Dr. Keyes-Rudd, the new child specialist, had come and gone and August was asleep with a sedative. The doctor had sent everyone out of the room while he examined the little girl. "Children are self-conscious," he had said calmly and had closed August's door in the faces of Fenton and Gilberta. He was a dark man with rough black beard coming through the skin of his cheeks by the end of day. His eyes were deep under his brow with long lids and short, heavy lashes. He was handsome and strange to August with his mysterious doctor odor, and tubes, and pills.

Lying there looking up at him with his thermometer in her mouth, she felt a passionate longing to reach her arms out of her covers and put them about his neck and hold onto him. When he asked her to put out her hand so that he could count her pulse, she laid her fingers palm down in his as if she were giving them to him forever. He smiled and adjusted her hand to hold it at the wrist.

"Do you know what Santa Claus is going to bring you?" he asked her. "Just nod your head, yes or no."

August shook her head violently *no*. Her breath had shortened with irritation at the mention of Christmas and she drew a long sigh through her nose, her lips tightening over the thermometer. The doctor watched her with his fingers firmer on her pulse and a slight squint in his eyes. He put down her hand and withdrew the thermometer from her mouth and read it, expressionless. Methodically he parted the lace and tatting on her night gown to examine her chest with his stethoscope. A little shiver went through her which raised her flesh when he put the cold disc against her ribs near the armpit.

In a few moments she could have begun a chill from only the excitement of the whole adventure of making herself sick; but the doctor finished his thumping and listening quickly, took out a pill from his satchel, poured a glass of water from her night-table decanter and asked, "Will you take this for me, please?" August swallowed it in a gulp with her eyes on him over the rim of the glass.

"I'm afraid you won't be able to trim the tree with Mother and Daddy tonight," the doctor said. "In a little while you'll be sound asleep. I'm sorry."

He was observing her with an inquiring eye.

"I hope I won't have to keep you in bed all through the Christmas party tomorrow. Your father tells me nearly fifty little boys and girls are coming."

August slid sensuously down into the covers and peeped at him from over the sheet top.

"I don't want to go to the party," she said. "I don't mind being sick."

The doctor made no comment. He packed his little satchel and told her good night.

"Good night," she said, and let her head weigh back into her pillow.

"Are you certain there's nothing at all, Doctor?" asked Fenton incredulously, when Keyes-Rudd came down the stairs. "The little Starburg boy came down the same way with appendicitis." And then Fenton blushed. "I'm not doubting your diagnosis," he murmured, "it's just that Mrs. Chadley and I are anxious. August has never been sick a day."

"I'm sure it was a temporary upset," Dr. Keyes-Rudd assured him, "or at least I'm satisfied to put it down as such at this point. She seems a very spirited child." He began putting on his muffler. "Occasionally we find nothing more than an emotional excitement – anger, or resistance – behind such symptoms." Then he caught the frown on Fenton's face at this rather critical suggestion, and added, "It's common among very sensitive, responsive individuals. They seem to suffer occasional physical ills which have no discernible physical basis. Keep her on a simple diet – no Christmas cake or sweets, no baked ham and the like. If she develops a temperature, telephone me."

Then they said good night.

"She's going to be fine by the time for the party, dear," he boasted confidently to Gilberta, when he was serving Señora's plate. "It was just some digestive upset. There's been such a commotion going on . . ." and he trailed off. "Cranberry, Señora?"

Señora de Ventura nodded and accepted the plate. There was a certain thoughtfulness in her attention to Fenton. Throughout the disturbance with August she had carefully remained in the background offering no comment about anything. Now when it was all over, she pronounced quietly, "She is sick because she does not want the Christmas in her house."

Gilberta looked sharply at her mother, protesting, "*Every* child loves the Christmas. She will receive a beautiful piano – very expensive – made only for her." Each spoke in English with the stiff phrasing of a translation.

"No," said Fenton patiently to Señora de Ventura, "you misunderstood. She is ill in her stomach." And without meaning to, he placed his hand across his own.

Señora de Ventura shook her head sadly and reached to break her bread.

The Christmas party began at four o'clock. By four o'clock all the children were within the gates of Dunmeade. The fetching had begun at three with two trips in Fenton's car and one with Gilberta's to bring all who had met at the school with Miss Applewhite and Miss Horton. Fenton stayed personally at the door as the children of parents he knew began to arrive – Vincent Starburg, Cora Simmons Amos, the little York girl and so on. He waved a greeting to the fathers and mothers parked down the drive watching their dressed and curled and instructed little ones making for the beautiful iron lace Spanish doors where Fenton waited to shake hands.

Just inside, Susie showed the little girls to a guest room to put off their coats and caps. Her cousin, Smith, corraled for the occasion, took anything the shy little boys would part with and hung it in the downstairs closet, cleared of family clothes an hour before.

Gilberta and August stood at the drawing room, August first and her mother to her right.

"This is Agnes Simpson, mother," August would say as a little schoolmate dawdled and then finally plunged toward them.

"How do you do, Agnes," Gilberta would offer her hand, "we're so glad to have you."

And the child would murmur and take back her hand quickly and dodge awkwardly into the drawing room.

After a time, August whispered to Gilberta, "These are from the mills," and Gilberta turned to find Ruby Boyle stolidly apexing a wedge of mill children uncomfortably wavering between Fenton at the entrance and herself and August before them. They looked at once belligerent and awed, clustered at the base of the giant Christmas tree, as if in a moment they would split out of unity and escape wildly in all directions.

"My mother wants everybody to come in here first," August called to Ruby, holding her right hand back and out like a rudder to guide them past her, "before we serve the refreshments." She waited for them to understand and leave if they wished, when they learned the refreshments weren't to be served at once. Ruby looked over her shoulder at her flock, gathering them closer for the charge past Mrs. Chadley. Gilberta waited with a set smile on her face and a kind of fear and distaste in her eyes as she examined the strong hostile little girl confronting her across August. This was the one for whom she had bought the largest wool petticoat and longest stockings.

"This is Ruby Boyle, mother," August said.

For an instant, Gilberta almost withheld her hand. She could feel the chapped and soap-cracked skin of the girl's knuckles before she touched her. She could smell the homemade soap. Ruby marched toward her. Then Gilberta suppressed her shudder and reached out.

"Come right in, Ruby," she said, offering her hand for Ruby's firm spasmodic jerk, "take your little friends over to the Magic Stream. It's right across the drawing room. See? Over there . . ." And pleasantly directing their attention to prizes beyond her, Gilberta escaped the single introductions to Willy Quate, Leo Lakis, Marvin Murphy, Hazel Hull, Gladys Weaver, Mary Gertrude Ham and four others who eeled past her.

In the last load, which O'Smyre had sedately driven from the schoolhouse, were Miss Horton and Miss Applewhite. Miss Horton had really meant to be at Dunmeade from the beginning. But each time she had tried to squeeze in the car either the telephone in the office had rung or Lowdey the janitor had needed her or else Miss Applewhite had taken that moment to change her frock in the "Tidy Room."

With the arrival of the teachers the party officially began. Fenton escorted them into the drawing room and stood beaming at the clumps of children, rooted here and there about the walls waiting to do whatever they were going to have to do. Miss Applewhite looked at them kindly, conscious of their mixed timid and hostile groupings, not even united before their common suspect, the host. Miss Horton smiled waxily, hoping by concentrating upon one clot of children at a time to start some chain of activity going.

August went upstairs to her bathroom to put some powder under her arms. Susie had frowned and bobbed her head pointedly toward August's armpits until the little girl had understood and run quickly to her room to stop the circles of damp beginning under her sleeves. She was excited and tense.

Gilberta, when she had greeted Miss Horton and Miss Applewhite, slipped to the kitchen to see if Señora de Ventura were addling the caterers. She looked back once to be certain Fenton intended to start the games. Then she hurried on to the pantry.

Throughout the house there had been a feeling of excitement for hours. It had reached a climax when the men came to install the Wishing Pond and sink the prizes under the water of the Magic Stream.

Now with the children before them at last, *his* children for that afternoon, Fenton almost jumped at them in his eagerness to see them pleased and astonished. "Who's going to help me fish a treasure out of the Wishing Pond?" In his eagerness he laughed so that his challenging invitation was lost in a gurgle. Then unexpectedly, he bowed slightly to Miss Horton. "You?" he suggested, "will you?"

Miss Horton opened her mouth in surprise and sucked a full breath before her wits returned and she barked loudly in her gayest tone, "I should be delighted! But I promise you – I'm a poor fisherman!" She took Fenton's arm and swooped out her free hand to encircle the children and draw them along behind her.

Miss Applewhite herded up the rear and the children dutifully crowded about the intricate Wishing Pond and watched Miss Horton dangle her hook back and forth and around again until she snagged one of the rings at the bottom.

"Pull it toward the edge," Fenton said. "That's splendid –

now, let's see . . ." and he helped her pull the ring along its proper channel to the lock which released the prize.

"Oh! Oh quick," murmured Miss Applewhite as she watched a make-believe stone on the outside wall of the pond yawn open drawer-like and drop out a package.

When the miracle of the machinery was revealed, the little girls squealed and crowded closer to see and the little boys, bored until that moment, showed instant professional interest in the workings. Fenton caught up the package and held it out to Miss Horton.

"How exciting!" she laughed, tearing at the wrappings, blushing into one henna freckle. "Oh, how perfectly beautiful – Oh – Oh, how lovely!" She lifted up the bottle of perfume in the shape of a golden ballet dancer for all to see. And that was the magic word "Go!" for August's Christmas party. There was no need to coax the children after that.

August returned to the drawing room in time to see Miss Horton hook her prize in the Pond. She had watched for a moment through a slice of clearing between the elbows of James Duffy, the dairyman's son and Louise Byers, who was kin to Cora Simmons Amos on her mother's side. Then the elbows had come together and everyone had crowded forward and August could see nothing. She looked at the backs of her classmates. Then she looked down at her small wrist watch. It was 4:45. In another hour it would be over and they would all be gone.

She turned to survey the mock Post Office bulging with packages of all colors – blue, silver-and-blue, red, gold-and-red, plain silver, plain gold, some printed with Swedish scenes, or English carol singers, or German Santa Claus prints. After refreshments her Uncle Chad would play Postmaster and call out the names and it would all be over.

Smith, the extra man in to help Addie and Susie, came from the direction of the library carrying what appeared to be a sheet in a frame. It was a great drawing of a donkey minus his tail, ruefully looking backward.

"Just where did Mrs. Chadley want me to set this, Miss

August?" he paused to ask. Under his arm he was clutching the thin box of donkey tails of varying shapes, sizes and colors.

"Right over there," August pointed to a cleared space of wall where a large table customarily stood. The children had their backs to that end of the room and Smith quickly arranged the large cloth donkey shape a foot or so from the wall. August watched. Then she remembered and motioned Smith to move out the figure a little more and turn on the row of cylinder-shaped bulbs lying along the base molding. Instantly the donkey glowed in relief like the lady-head silhouettes on the lampshades in her mother's dressing room. August laughed. The place where the tail was to be pinned shone with a clear light of its own. Fenton had punctured the cloth practicing.

"Everybody who has finished fishing can line up over here by me," August called out suddenly. "We're going to play 'Pin on the Donkey's Tail' and the one that comes nearest gets a prize."

Vincent Starburg, who was on the fringe of the group and a little bored, turned happily and yanked at Jane York. "Come on," he said, "let's get first chance."

"I'll blindfold," August announced, taking a bright red kerchief and a fancy donkey tail with a wool tassel out of the box. "Who wants to go first?"

"Let Jane." Vincent shoved her toward August.

August stretched up a little to get the kerchief around Jane's eyes. "You'll have to stoop down," she complained. Then she knotted the kerchief so tight that Jane screeched, "You're mashing my eyeballs!" August loosened it a bit and then grabbed the little girl and twirled her about savagely, around and around, until she not only helped her to lose her direction but so dizzied her that Jane belched loudly with nausea.

"Now," said August happily, "pin it on!" And the random gropings and hysterical laughter began.

At a quarter-past five, the dining-room doors opened and the whole length of the miracle which had taken place on the banquet table was spread before the astonished eyes of the children. There, as if its being there were the most natural thing in the world, was the Castle of the Sleeping Beauty! – all in a hundred tints and colors of cream and cake and sherbet. Even its chimneys were smoking with frail wisps of cotton candy wafting north toward the lifted drawbridge of black currant cake. And around it flooded a moat of punch with whole cherries and yellow fruits bobbing along like refuse on its surface.

Into this room, to demolish the exquisite and delicious palace, the children were invited and given scoops and dishes and cups to accomplish the attack. They were not shy. The games had overcome their timidity. Quickly – all ringing the table, their scoops stretched toward the purple gables of the roof, the orange turrets, and the mint-green balustrades – the digging was done, the castle fouled and gobbled up. The melting ruins mingled with the punch of the moat and were dippered up like sea-foam in their cups. All the cake windows and doors were pushed in and shoveled onto their plates. Gone, all gone – the whole of it in ten minutes! Señora de Ventura, who, with Gilberta, had supervised the creation of the fairy place, sighed at its destruction and looked sadly at young Homer Travers, who, in one happy snap of his jaws, devoured the frosted watchman from the tower.

Their plates piled with colored globs of cake and cream, the guests settled in corners and window sills and on the floor behind furniture and gobbled as fast as they pleased. Then, when the silence of completed stuffing began to settle on the group, the children looked uneasily about at their neighbors, wondering what to do next. At that moment Fenton appeared in the door, dressed in a blue-grey postman's uniform complete with badge and visored cap. "I have a special delivery package here for . . ." – he looked down again at the red Santa Claus card pasted on the gold metallic paper – "Miss Adelaide Guthrie." He smiled and looked about eagerly for the owner of the package to come forth and claim it. The children looked around too, searching among themselves. Adelaide Guthrie was not in the room.

Miss Horton examined her brood sharply, face by face. "She came with you, Estelle," she addressed a short girl with a square calm face.

"No ma'am," Estelle contradicted in concise Yankee accents, "she came with Robert Carney and Mary Welsh."

Miss Horton colored at the refutation. Miss Applewhite hurried to her and quietly murmured, "Perhaps she had to go upstairs."

Then, in the awkward silence, as Fenton was about to withdraw and lead his little guests after him to the Post Office near the Christmas tree, the missing Adelaide came sidling down the curve of the stair and stopped at the bottom and peeped cautiously into the drawing room right into the faces of all her classmates.

"There she is!" every one squealed at once and pointed. Fenton reached out to give her the package. But in an instant, Adelaide's face whitened and, without a word, she turned and scurried back up the stair.

"Good heavens," gasped Miss Applewhite, "what in the world! We must have frightened her." She said it to Miss Horton, but Miss Horton was no longer beside her. She was half up the stair behind the fleeing child.

At the gallery Miss Horton met Señora de Ventura, returning from fetching her digestive tablets, now staring at the little girl running frantically in and out of first one bedroom and then another as if she were out of her head.

"Here! Adelaide!" cried Miss Horton, catching her breath after her gallop up the stair. "Stop that!"

Adelaide appeared at August's bedroom door, looked wildly up and down the gallery for another room to try, and broke into a sob of terror. In her hand she clutched a glass bottle. Its iridescent stopper sparkled under the sconce beside the doorframe. She clutched it half-tilted toward her feet upon which great drops of its contents were splashing. The strong exotic perfume rose quickly and spread along the gallery.

"Stand right there now, Adelaide," ordered Miss Horton, as if she were attempting to still a wild and bucking animal by the force of her voice, "just stay right there." She began to creep toward the child to capture her.

Adelaide's eyes were huge in her chinless face. She stood frozen. Then her head moved jerkily toward Señora de Ventura and in some way, with her terrified stare, she pleaded with the strange woman to help her. The cry for deliverance was as clear as if she had screamed it down the gallery. Señora de Ventura walked rapidly to overtake Miss Horton's ridiculous-looking figure inching along about to pounce on Adelaide. She put her hand on the teacher's shoulder.

"No," she said firmly.

Miss Horton did not understand. Then Señora de Ventura said impatiently, "Downstairs." And she pointed the way for Miss Horton to depart. Without waiting longer, she put her arm about Adelaide and pushed the little girl before her into Gilberta's room.

Downstairs, Fenton and Miss Applewhite had herded the other children to the presents waiting in the Post Office pigeonholes. Gilberta, with Susie, passed out the packages as Fenton called the names, for a curious shyness had come over the group and hardly a child would come forward to claim his gift.

"You're not to open these before Christmas, now," Fenton admonished over and over gently.

Then, as he reached the last letters in the alphabetically arranged pigeonholes, Miss Horton came down the stair. August, standing in the curve of the banister, asked nicely, "Is Adelaide going to be sick or something?"

Miss Horton's face worked to loosen the stony set of her jaw. She opened her lips and spread them back into a smile.

"I don't think so, dear," she said, patting August on the hand and then squeezing it curiously, almost painfully. "Your grandmother has her." Her head lifted against the glances and the questions insistent in them. "My goodness," she evaded brightly, "there's been enough excitement to last us all for another full year! Hasn't there, children?" But her voice cracked, struggling with frustration and anger. She wanted to promise, *I'll get little Miss Guthrie. Just you wait!*

"Martin Uddell," Fenton called out, "and Jane York." Jane

York came forward to take her present in its blue paper with silver shooting comets. Then Gilberta slipped to the rear of the house and upstairs.

August watched her mother leave. Then she carefully looked over the group. She wanted to go upstairs too, to find out if her grandmother were letting Adelaide Guthrie play with her things. She did not like the thought of a strange child rummaging about in her playroom, examining her personal toys. Adelaide was so funny-looking and she had such an odor. She was new in Newtown. Her father was an undertaker and Adelaide lived upstairs over the funeral parlor. Her family had bought an old house on a side street connecting Willow Avenue to Gerrard Place. It was faded and shabby, and people hurried to pass the "things going on" behind its shutters when they crossed the block to Willow Avenue. Adelaide's smell and the veins standing out like blue twine inside her elbows and under her knobby knees made the little boys in 1A say that she was ready for burying, herself. August wished her mother would come back and bring Adelaide with her. The presents were all given out and Susie was looking at her to start the little girls to the guest room for their coats. She moved up a step higher and caught Fenton's smile and nod.

"I'll help you find your coat, Cora Simmons," she said then to Cora Simmons Amos, who was nearest her. She started up and looked back for Cora Simmons to follow. But Cora Simmons was not interested in getting her wrap at that moment. She had just succeeded in gnawing through the little knot of gold cord which had been laced prettily around the unusual shape of her Christmas present. In a rip she had the paper off and the odd and delicate gift revealed.

"Oh lookee!" she squealed. "Doll skates!" And all the little girls crowded around her and squealed and plucked at them. For a moment it seemed as if an irresistible urge to unwrap their gifts instantly were going to take the whole crowd. But Miss Applewhite came forward with August and they said almost in chorus, "You weren't supposed to open your present, Cora Simmons!" And Miss Applewhite reached up and pulled down Cora

Simmons' hand from the air, where she dangled the miniature skates for everyone to see. The other children looked hungrily at their own packages, their anticipation of a like extravagant toy apparent in their eyes.

"The party is over now, girls and boys. We must be getting our wraps," Miss Applewhite urged them to move. "We've had a lovely time and we must all tell Mr. and Mrs. Chadley on our way out," she reminded them. The march upstairs began.

When she had helped to marshal the girls into the guest room to start digging and snatching for their coats, August slipped away and went to her playroom. She flung open the door to surprise the intruders she expected there. But the room was empty. Then she went to her mother's door and stood listening a moment. When she heard her mother's voice, she opened the door without knocking and entered. She walked to the dressing room and there Gilberta and Señora de Ventura and Adelaide Guthrie stood before Gilberta's mirror, sniffing all the crystal and silver stoppers on all the large and small bottles of perfume. August's heart moved jerkily in her breast and a curious sense of shock came over her. It seemed obscene to her for Adelaide Guthrie to be in her mother's most clean and beautiful room. All the mystery of that sweetly fragrant pastel place so associated with the care of her mother's beauty seemed violated by the presence of the strange ugly child.

Tears were close to her eyes when Gilberta turned to her and said, "Adelaide says her mother doesn't have any perfume and she wants to take her some of mine instead of taking a Christmas present for herself." She gazed seriously at August. "I told her you would have to give it to her, because it's the perfume you gave me for my birthday." She held up the particular bottle. "She's afraid Miss Horton is going to punish her for taking the perfume first without asking." Bewilderment and jealousy and pity moved painfully in conflict in August's breast. "She may have it, Mother," she said. She swallowed and then added, "She may have her present downstairs too. I'll get it for her." Then she rushed out to the gallery to join the chain of little girls threading down the stair and to the entrance to say their good-bys and be gone.

The Christmas party was over.

"It went off just fine, didn't it?" Fenton asked August when the door was closed on the teachers, last to leave. He wanted to be complimented. He wanted to be told that he had done all the right things and that she was proud of him. "They liked the refreshments, didn't they?" he insisted, wanting her to say that everything had been perfect and that she admitted it had been a success after all.

"Miss Horton will fix Adelaide Guthrie," August said solemnly, "even if I *did* give her Mother's birthday perfume." There was no desire in her tone to see punishment inflicted on the child who had stolen and been caught. She was simply stating a fatalistic attitude concerning crime and punishment.

"But it isn't necessary to punish the child," Fenton objected, shocked. His mind leaped to the vision of a cloakroom beating. "We'll go to see Miss Horton about it. Tomorrow."

"It's vacation," August reminded him.

"Then we'll telephone and ask to call on her." He appealed to August for support. "We can call at her . . ." He hesitated over the proper term for the teacher's living quarters ("boarding-house" was so undignified) and finally used "residence."

"She'll only take it out on Adelaide," insisted August quietly and stubbornly.

"I don't think so," said Fenton firmly, unnerved and aroused now both by the idea of Miss Horton punishing the pitiful child and also by August's maddening acceptance of it. "We'll see her immediately," he said, "and nothing will happen to the little Guthrie girl." His breath came short in his nostrils and his tone was threatening.

August did not dispute it. But she smiled in a slightly superior, knowing way. She had known from the beginning that something would happen to spoil the party. And something had. Miss Horton, she knew, would do as she pleased about punishing Adelaide Guthrie for stealing the perfume, no matter what protests Uncle Chad made. So she did not argue with Fenton further.

In the morning, just after breakfast, Fenton said to August, "We'll drive to your school before taking Señora de Ventura home. Both Miss Applewhite and Miss Horton are there. I have just telephoned their residence and their landlady has informed me that she expects neither home until the afternoon."

He wanted to get to Miss Horton immediately. He was afraid that the teachers might already have sent for the Guthrie child or her parents, that it was the reason for their being at the school. He hurried August into her coat and leggings and they drove to Sycamore Primary.

There was no answer to their knock at the big front door up the flight of concrete steps which formed the school's entrance, so August ran down the steps and under them to the basement door leading to the lower grades. Somewhere within she heard voices, then a truck motor starting violently behind the school drowned them out. When the truck was gone she knocked briskly. She could hear footsteps on the creaking floorboards inside. "They're down here, Uncle Chad," she called up to Fenton.

He was peering with August into the deserted school hall, when Miss Horton came into view inside. She strode to the door, unlocked it noisily and said, "Come in, Mr. Chadley." She expelled her breath. "I was just going to telephone you." Her face, bony as it was, was so bloated with anger as to seem full-cheeked and ruddy. "Come and look at this. It's outrageous." She marched forward to her office curtained off from the home room of 1B.

For a few minutes Fenton and August stood and watched Lowdey the janitor come in and go out without understanding what he was doing. Then, after his third trip, when he had deposited four more large packages on the stack already rising beside Miss Horton's desk, August said, "They're our Christmas presents!" in a hard, high, child's voice which hit against the slate blackboards like gunshot. She stooped down and rested on her heels and picked up the card from one of the torn packages. "*Merry Christmas to Willy Quate from August Chadley*," she read aloud. Then she held up a pair of coarse corduroy knickers.

"I don't know what to say to you, Mr. Chadley," Miss Horton began. "I have never seen such a display of ingratitude in all my experience. Believe me, I haven't. If it hadn't been a man they picked to return them – why I . . ." She fumed off without finishing her threat.

Fenton turned away, ill and shocked. He lifted his shoulders higher and held himself erect as if he feared he were about to crumble and sink to his knees. "Was any reason given?" he asked when he was able, at the same time reaching out his hand to find August's head. He patted her hair reassuringly.

Miss Horton began to repeat the message. "They said that if any of their children needed . . ." And then Miss Applewhite appeared and interrupted her.

"I think, Mr. Chadley," she said quickly, with her earnest flat face raised to his, "that if Cora Simmons Amos hadn't opened her present in front of the others at the party, we wouldn't have had this . . ." She hesitated for the exact words: ". . . regrettable misunderstanding."

Fenton did not understand what she meant.

"Cora Simmons received doll skates, and, well – " she explained – "there *is* a difference between doll skates and winter underwear and corduroy trousers." She let her flat, soft eyes dart for a moment to Miss Horton's face before she finished. "I'm afraid Miss Horton and I are to blame. We listed what we thought these children needed, and you and Mrs. Chadley followed our suggestions. We were all mistaken, Mr. Chadley. They needed luxuries, not necessities." A certain lift came over her own thin body when she said it and she seemed at that moment to be much larger than she was and full of dignity.

"It's very kind of you to claim responsibility, Miss Applewhite, but, of course, it wasn't your mistake at all." Fenton looked at the torn wrappings on his unwanted gifts, his feelings loose and unsettled inside him. "I spend a great part of my business life anticipating and measuring the financial requirements of others and arranging help in the most dignified manner I can. It apparently has taught me nothing if I have allowed you ladies and Mrs. Chadley and me to invite such a situation." He looked away toward the half of a window left in the office by the curtain partition and his hand trembled so that he lifted it from August's hair. "I would be very grateful if you would conspire with me to keep the knowledge of this from Mrs. Chadley." He looked from Miss Horton to Miss Applewhite appealingly. "She would never – well, she would be so distressed. She thinks her little guests enjoyed our tree and – " He could not finish.

For a moment Miss Horton lost her fractious expression and seemed about to touch Fenton's hand consolingly.

"I imagine you ladies belong to some charity or other, don't you?" he asked, nodding suggestively toward the presents beside the desk. "They often hold bazaars where merchandise is contributed for sale."

The teachers nodded and tried to help him by moving toward the door. The ugly instant of truth was over.

It was not until he had walked with August half to the street, holding her hand, that Fenton remembered Adelaide Guthrie.

"We must go back, dear," he said.

And in silence they returned and rapped again on the basement door.

Miss Applewhite answered.

Fenton held his hat and the bright noon winter light struck without reflection across his glasses' lens so that he turned his head nervously to see. "I called this morning to ask that you and Miss Horton let the matter of the little Guthrie girl rest as it was ended yesterday. I was about to leave without speaking to you about it."

Miss Applewhite smiled. "Merry Christmas, Mr. Chadley," she

said. She reached out and shook Fenton's hand. "Merry Christmas, August."

So Christmas came and went, with Newtown decorated, and sales good, and the streets noisy and some folks drunk. Then the cold short stretch of winter began and the children went back to school to half a grade higher than when they had been let out for the holiday.

August brought home her report card. Fenton looked quickly down the subjects, then turned his face away from his little girl and went to his study window and said from there, "It's just splendid, dear. It's splendid." He held the card at the subject listed "DRAWING AND CRAFTS. *Grade:* C." In the column for *Remarks* was written, "The pupil is highly imaginative."

"Would you like to go to a school where only little girls like you go, August?" Fenton asked August, his silent thanks said to the teacher who had had the courage to act on faith. "I've never asked whether you liked Sycamore Primary or not. Wouldn't you rather go to a school like Miss Lena Nyrick's—except for older little girls?" He turned around to watch her closely when she answered. He was going to leave the decision entirely to her. He was going to make private school sound attractive. He was going to be as courageous as Miss Applewhite.

August colored instantly and said in anger, "I'm not afraid of the mill children. I'm not afraid of Ruby Boyle." She curled her fingers under her wrists and pulled at her cuffs in agitation. "I don't care if they don't like me. I'm glad they sent back their presents." She gazed at Fenton, her mouth trembling and her body stiffening in defiance. "I can go to Sycamore Primary if I want to."

"Of course you may, dear," murmured Fenton, starting toward her. "Of course you may. That wasn't why I suggested . . ."

But he did not finish, for August had turned and run from him. He stepped quickly to the door and called out to her. She was half up the stair. He hurried to the well and beseeched her as she reached the gallery, "Don't be disturbed, dear. Please. You misunderstood."

She looked over the banister at him one instant, her face full of indignation. Then she ran down the gallery to her playroom.

For all the days since she had gone with Fenton to her school and seen the humiliating and shocking spectacle of her gifts returned, she had been pressing down her feeling of outrage, burying it deep, shrouding it comfortingly in pity for Fenton that he should have been so mistreated (though she had warned him, of course). Now he had suggested that it was *she* who was downed, defeated. He had offered her escape from Ruby Boyle, from all the others who were also Ruby Boyle. She blew her nose into the eyelet of her petticoat and soiled her hands. Savagely, she cried out "I hate them too!" and distractedly wiped her fingers along the tucked bodice of her favorite dress.

Certain progress was made in Newtown during the next seven years. Five new buildings were erected in the crowded center of town. And the fine shade trees along Willow Avenue were uprooted to widen the street and accommodate the increasing automobile traffic.

The courthouse with its classic Ionic front was torn down and a new one built only a block away, near Mr. Guthrie's funeral parlor. The ugly rubble on the old site on the square was curiously softened by weeds by the time the property was leased, a year later, to a gasoline dealer who put up a service station.

A Northern concern, with some local backing, put up a two-hundred-room hotel to catch the tourists and real estate speculators flocking to Florida. Gaudy road signs directed travelers to the garage of the Hotel Dixie Belle where luggage was hauled through a tunnel into the lobby while cars were checked for leaks, cracks, and broken axles – all free of charge.

Pickett's Poultice Plaster Company raised a nine-story office building coincident with the initial distribution of its product in two European countries. Before its completion, the ground floor was leased to the Property Owners' Loan Company, which conducted business there until 1929 when its assets ceased to exist. Then the space was leased to Wallow Drugstores, Inc., the first of the chain in Newtown. The small offices of the ninth floor, under the roof, were rented to the salesmen for various grocery products companies who were assigned to that territory and obliged to live in Newtown every other week.

Four doctors, including Keyes-Rudd, the child specialist, put up the Doctors' Clinic, complete with ambulance service for bringing in accident cases from the highways. In a short time, as old Doc Langley's interest in the practice of medicine waned in ratio to his increased interest in the bull markets of 1927–1928 and 1929, the new hospital was competing with his for "the better type" of private patients.

The Newtown Burial Insurance Company, formed in 1927, transacted a sufficient volume of business by 1928 to require the use of three floors in the old Lawyers' Building next to the Chadley bank. A carefully selected staff, trained to describe burial plots with tact and cheerfulness, handled the policies of the "insured," and the company feverishly bought up mortgages and cheap property as premium payments increased its funds for investment. Gaither Lyndon, who had originally owned the cornfield which became Rosefield, its cemetery, was one of the stockholders; but the president and important member of the firm was a newcomer to Newtown. He was a man named Rench who had left Virginia after certain reversals in his fire insurance business, and after certain strong opinions held about him had convinced him that he would be happier in a new place. He was a good cold businessman, well qualified to run the company. No restraining sympathy for any other individual hampered him in exercising his rights with respect to foreclosing mortgages or canceling policies. At first, the old boys sitting about in the back room of the Briggs Arcade made remarks about his name. "If anybody can Rench it loose, he can!" they would say, laughing coarsely; but very soon they developed toward him an attitude of uneasy respect, which began when he made a shocking deal with Mr. Guthrie, the undertaker, to embalm deceased policyholders and furnish them adequate coffins for a certain flat rate, an arrangement which resulted not only in profit for him but so increased Mr. Guthrie's business that in a year he was able to move his anemic Adelaide and Mrs. Guthrie out of the floor above the funeral parlor and into a house. Adelaide took up ballet dancing, and Mrs. Guthrie drove about Newtown in the big black limousine used on less happy occasions to convey the bereaved to Rosefield. So, very steadily, Mr. Rench achieved prominence and influence in Newtown, although Fenton Chadley voted against him when his name was proposed for the Newtown Merchants' and Bankers' Club. (Fenton could not see in which category Mr. Rench qualified for membership.) Nevertheless, Mr. Rench was taken into the Merchants' and Bankers' Club, and at his first opportunity made a statement to the *Newtown Record* reporters and had himself photographed at a county political rally congratulating the speaker.

A group of manufacturers from the North, foreseeing a reduction in their profits as a result of the organizing of labor, moved South, where they offered employment at attractive wages to young men and women of legal working age, whether out of public school or not, and with or without previous working experience. Many of their employees came from the surrounding farms and were surprised to find how easily they could earn enough in a mill to buy an automobile on the installment plan.

Property taxes were lowered by a new governor, who had a few business interests of his own and understood the businessman's viewpoint. And the city elected a mayor with a talent for keeping the city's books in the black. He was a plumber who had benefited from the installation of the Newtown sewerage system, and he knew how to cut corners. It rather shocked some of the old set when they awoke one morning to read in the newspaper that a plumber had been elected mayor of Newtown; but the membership committee of the Country Club quickly voted Mr. Jessie Oats an honorary card, and circulated the soothing story that plumbing companies in the North displayed their bathroom fixtures in their Main Street show windows.

So Newtown prospered those seven years, and no city in the country was more outraged or felt more tricked than Newtown when, on October 24, 1929, it began to question the quotations threading out of Gillie Davis's machine. Every one with a grain of sense hurried to a telephone to sell his stocks – quickly! But of course it was already a little late for that. The brokers' wastebaskets were crammed with orders to sell and there were no buyers, all of a sudden. In due time – approximately four days – quite a percentage of the small businessmen and private citizens of Newtown were without any assets at all.

Of course, there were some not affected financially by the collapse of the stock market, at least not directly and not immediately. They were the very, very rich and the very, very poor. Little short of revolution could have altered their respective conditions. Of the very, very rich Fenton Chadley, Vincent Starburg and George Pickett were the more noticeably unaffected in Newtown. Vincent Starburg was too timid to risk investing a nickel in anything he could not see before him, such as a bolt of cloth or a brick building. George Pickett died on October 15 and, before breathing his last, sold his stocks, leaving his profits safely in his estate. And Fenton – Well, in the months preceding the great financial collapse, certain dramatic events had altered the courses of the lives at Dunmeade, too.

On a cold night in March 1929 Pedro de Ventura came to fetch Gilberta to Quakertown. Señora de Ventura was dying. Fenton went with Gilberta and waited the night in the cold farmhouse parlor, hoping simply that the Señora would leave the world painlessly.

"She had been down only a few hours," the doctor from Quakertown reported belligerently when it was over and he was getting his coat in the first glare of day. "She put up no resistance at all. I've had elderly patients come through pneumonia." He was angry at his defeat, Señora de Ventura had betrayed them. She had helped the enemy. "I used to know the old lady. She helped me deliver one of her grandchildren on a hot summer's day. And I thought to myself at the time, 'Now there's a spunky little woman for all her little bit of weight!' Child must be a pretty good size by now — "

"Yes," Fenton answered, "she'll soon be fourteen." He was pleased that the doctor had remembered August's birth. "She will be with us at the . . ." He was about to say "the church" when he recalled that Señora de Ventura had belonged to no church, so he finished, ". . . the services." The doctor was ready to leave and only grunted, waving Fenton back from accompanying him to the door.

However, there was not even a service for Señora de Ventura, for she had directed in writing that she be buried without prayer.

She left her property to Rafael — her house and land, which adjoined his own. Her only bequests to Gilberta were contained in a small leather box, with two gold locks. The country lawyer, when he had collected his fee, gave over the keys.

In the box were a letter and two objects — a miniature painting on ivory of a young man in rich Spanish dress, and a crucifix of a particular character, which was wound carefully in a silk ribbon so that it would not rattle in the box. It too was made of ivory and was so old that it had turned a yellow brown. Translated from the Spanish the letter read as follows:

> DAUGHTER,
> Over El Refugio's door was a coat of arms which I have remembered and drawn for you. Here is my father, very young, before coming to America. The cross — I do not know. My father left these things when he did not return and Señor de Ventura brought me to be near El Refugio. I have no memory of any faith. Señor de Ventura never declared.

It was signed LUIS-ROLAND DE VENTURA and beneath the signature was a sketch of the coat of arms which old Miss Tessie

Sorrell had had chopped away from Dunmeade's entrance. Written beneath it in larger letters to be certain it was not missed on the shield, was the motto: PIETY AND GOD.

The immediate effect of viewing these objects was to further deepen the mournful mood which had settled upon Gilberta following the night at her mother's deathbed. She made no comment upon the articles but replaced them carefully in their box and then took them to her room.

"Wouldn't you prefer taking them to the bank and putting them in the vault?" Fenton asked solicitously. He was so shocked that he could only suggest the practical precaution he would have advised any client's taking, to safeguard personal valuables.

But Gilberta looked at him solemnly and shook her head. Then she left him to wonder what resolution would come out of her deliberation upon the contents of the little box. If she were to conclude that she had been born into the faith suggested by the crucifix, Fenton would not disapprove her taking up that faith if she chose. But upon one question, which would then arise certainly, he had come to a clear and firm decision. August was not to be denied the right to freely examine and choose for herself. She was not to be made to feel any obligation to follow her mother into the church.

His feelings were so strong when he anticipated the quarrel he might have over this that a sudden sickness came over him. When it did not pass he rang for Addie – or anyone who was up and could bring him a glass of cold water. He snapped off the lamp nearest him and sat there with his eyes closed.

"I'd like to have some water, please," he said, when he heard someone come into the room. He opened his eyes to see August standing there in her robe and slippers, her long hair wound on top of her head to keep its strands out of her mouth while she slept.

"Aren't you feeling well?" she asked, anxiously.

"It's nothing serious," he reassured her, "I have a little headache."

"I'll bring you a tablet," she said and hurried to get it.

When she returned, he reminded her, "It's past eleven o'clock."

"I know," she admitted. "I came down to find something to eat. There wasn't any dinner tonight; you and mother didn't come to table. And Addie thinks I can still eat mush like a baby." She observed him thoughtfully and then suggested, "A headache can come from not eating, you know. Why don't we have some chicken sandwiches – little ones, and some milk?"

Fenton was not hungry, but he was both amused and touched and so he agreed, "You're probably right. I'm glad you thought of it."

August brought a tray and sat on a stool beside him, munching her sandwiches happily, while Fenton sipped his milk, resting his head against the wing of the chair, and watching her nibble off the bread corners and gradually encroach upon the meaty centers. She looked up suddenly and caught him studying her and grinned self-consciously in an oddly boyish way. For an instant, her face was the image of Lesley's. Fenton closed his eyes and sank away from the memories it evoked.

"I guess we ought to do something to cheer up Mother," August said.

Fenton set his glass on the tray. "Yes," he said, "I've been thinking about what we might do. I've been wondering if we oughtn't to call the house El Refugio again and put the shield back over the door. I think the house means a great deal more to her than it does to either of us. It belonged to her people. It has memories for her, even though she never lived here until she brought you here as a baby."

August was silent. She looked slowly around the study, as if appraising it. Then she smiled again, in that oddly boyish way. "Mother may have this house," she said, "I don't want it." She lifted the tray abruptly and carried it out to the kitchen. When she returned, she said, "I wonder why Grandmother didn't leave her property to Mother? Uncle Rafael already has a farm."

Fenton did not reply at once. A painful throbbing had begun in his head.

"There are two de Ventura sons to inherit from your Uncle

Rafael," he answered when he was able. "Your grandmother was probably considering them when she drew her will."

"She needn't have considered anyone but William," August said. "Pedro won't stay in Quakertown and farm. He'll sell out and leave."

"Well, I'm afraid, dear, that that will be his privilege, if he inherits a farm," Fenton reminded her, "No one can compel him to stay if he feels he can earn a better living elsewhere."

August snorted. "He wouldn't sell out to go into something else. He's never going to do anything anywhere."

Fenton raised himself from his chair. He was ready to end the conversation and retire. His head and eyes ached almost unbearably. "Let's not condemn Pedro without provocation," he cautioned. "Perhaps, if he inherits his grandmother's land, he'll want to keep it. Let's have a little faith in him."

August grunted cynically.

At the stair Fenton wiped his hand across his eyes and stumbled taking the first step.

"Didn't the tablet help?" August asked.

He made an effort to start briskly up to the gallery with her. "Of course, dear," he reassured her, "I'm a little tired, that's all. It's been a trying day and I'm concerned about your mother."

"Oh, she'll be all right," August said, putting her arm about him and unconsciously trying to help him up the stair. "Don't worry about those old mementos grandmother left. Mother isn't going to do anything about them. She'll just brood over them and then go back to her flowers." At the top she put her face to Fenton's for her good-night kiss. "You go to sleep," she admonished, "and don't worry."

In the morning Fenton was not able to dress and come to the table. He lay face down against his pillow, further blotting the light from his eyes, though the blinds were drawn and his room in shadow. He had slept only the hours of early morning. During the night he had crept to and from his bathroom soaking towels in cold water and holding them across his forehead, aching in long sharp recurring pains which ended always in the balls of his eyes.

He pulled his bell cord and when Susie came and tapped discreetly, he spoke to her through the door.

"Is Mrs. Chadley down?" he asked.

"No sir, Mr. Chadley, she's going to take her tray in her room this morning. I was just telling Addie to hurry on with Miss August. Everybody seems all turned around this morning, it looks like." Susie was a little quarrelsome with extra service upon her.

"Would you be good enough to ask Mrs. Chadley if she will telephone for Dr. Langley?" The effort of instructing Susie increased the waves of pain through his head.

There was silence outside the door.

"Did you understand me, Susie?" Fenton asked wearily.

"Yes sir," Susie answered, her tone subdued, as if with his instruction she had suddenly imagined herself selected to carry a dying request. "I'm going right away, Mr. Chadley." Fenton felt the vibration of her heavy feet plunging down the hall to Gilberta's room.

He made no effort to tidy himself for the doctor's visit. Ordinarily, he would have been self-conscious and apologetic at having to ask for a doctor at all. But with such suffering, he lay in the dark, untidy, his shocked nervous system reducing him near to tears of despair. He was frightened at his pain. He prayed for the doctor to come quickly. At that moment he was not the owner of a rich, small bank, a substantial stockholder in the Starburg Mills, the major stockholder in the Wortham Turpentine and Lumber Companies of Prince River, the second largest stockholder in the Pickett Distributing Corporation and the possessor of one million dollars in Government bonds. He was, on that morning, a young man of thirty-nine who was going blind, and who, in his terrified heart, knew it.

Dr. Langley did not come. The hospital sent a young doctor

named Madison, who entered Dunmeade half impressed with his summons to attend such a prominent man and half determined not to be impressed. But as he walked across Fenton's rug and observed the effort of his patient to pull himself up on the pillows to receive him, he quickly became professional. His patient, he saw in an instant, could not determine which side of the bed he approached. Very quickly he slipped to the right and put his hand into Fenton's, already outstretched.

"How do you do, Mr. Chadley," he apologized, "I'm sorry you were kept waiting. I'm Dr. Madison. Dr. Langley is away and I was on rounds when your wife telephoned. Now what seems to be the trouble?" He set a chair beside Fenton and opened his satchel on it.

In half an hour he left Dunmeade.

He reported briefly to Gilberta who came out to the foyer from the drawing room as he was descending from Fenton's bedroom.

"I'm going to call in a specialist, with your permission, Mrs. Chadley," Dr. Madison said simply. He was sobered by the seriousness of his findings.

"Is he going to be ill?" she asked. "He was perfectly well last evening." Her eyes were circled and she stood in a fixed posture as if she were struggling against overwhelming fatigue.

Looking at her, Dr. Madison thought of Fenton's distress at his condition. "She has just lost her mother," he had said, "I hope I am not going to burden her with caring for me at this time."

"I'm afraid he is going to have to have an operation on his eyes, Mrs. Chadley," Dr. Madison said, not withholding the truth, "but his complaint is not what he feared it might be when you called the hospital." She frowned slightly and raised her brows in a visible effort to understand and he realized suddenly that Mr. Chadley had neither described his symptoms nor confided his fear. "Your husband was afraid the disturbance with his vision and the severe headache indicated some pressure on the brain," he explained kindly. Then he smiled reassuringly. "I've given him something to ease the discomfort and help him to sleep." He looked about for his hat and coat. At the door he said, "I'll call again in the late afternoon, Mrs. Chadley. If he should be hungry when he awakes, give him one of the foods ordinarily on a light diet." He walked down the drive to his car. As he unlocked it, he looked back at the house. The still bare tree branches were silhouetted in stiff webs across its strange and beautiful windows.

Just before teatime, Dr. Madison returned to Dunmeade with the specialist who had driven up to Newtown from the newly opened Doughtry Memorial Hospital, near the university.

Dr. Glasson gave a professional grunt in the direction of Dr. Madison and pronounced, "Acute glaucoma." His examination had been both quick and gentle and he stood back from his patient and said, "Mr. Chadley, I advise an iridectomy."

For a moment Fenton was silent. Then he asked, "Is it necessary immediately?"

Dr. Madison answered him. "I think Dr. Glasson would like you to come into the hospital tonight, Mr. Chadley."

Fenton was shocked. He squeezed the blanket border in his fingers and asked, "Is it an emergency operation?"

"Oh no, it's not an emergency operation," Dr. Glasson said in a hearty bluff voice he meant to be reassuring. "We have a few little tests and examinations to make." He began to drop his instruments back into his satchel and their clink was almost unendurable to Fenton.

"Is it possible to give me some indication of the time I shall have to be away from my office?" Fenton asked. "This is all very sudden. I don't know that I am really prepared to leave my business interests on such short notice." He was reluctant to agree instantly to the operation. At the moment his pain had been diminished by the drugs Dr. Madison had left for him.

There was a pause. Then Doctor Glasson evaded cheerfully, "You won't be away any longer than necessary, Mr. Chadley. I'm going to do my best for you. We've had very marked success with this. Your vision will be restored and except for slowing down a little here and there, you'll never know you've been sick a day." He reached down and gave Fenton's hand a manly brush across the knuckles.

"Thank you, Doctor," Fenton said stiffly. He was exasperated. He turned his head from side to side unconsciously trying to locate Dr. Madison and address him. He could hear the doctors readying to leave as if there were no more to be said and his entering the hospital that night were all settled. "I'm afraid I shall have to insist that you tell me the probable length of time I shall be in the hospital," he said, trying to keep the irritation out of his voice.

There was a silence. He could feel the doctors conferring silently, over his bed. Then Dr. Madison answered, "I think I would arrange to be away from my office for several weeks if I were you, Mr. Chadley. This condition quite often is brought on by great nervous and mental strain. You should have a long period of rest after the operation. It's essential to your complete recovery."

"I see," Fenton murmured. He thought for a moment and then said, "I gather then that you were suggesting I arrange my affairs to prevent such strain in the future. Is that correct, Dr. Glasson? I believe your phrase was 'to slow down a little here and a little there'?"

"Well, yes," Dr. Glasson admitted, "that would be advisable, Mr. Chadley. But let's not cross any bridges until we get to them." Again he lapsed into cheerful professional speech.

Dr. Madison moved a chair back to its place and then coming close to Fenton on one side he began, "Mr. Chadley, I looked into the possibility of ambulance service for you this evening. . . ." But Fenton interrupted him. "Thank you very much, Doctor. I prefer traveling in my own car, if I have your permission. I . . ." He hesitated and then explained, "I want to avoid shocking Mrs. Chadley if possible. The sight of an ambulance at this time . . ." He did not finish but only raised his hand expressively and then settled it back against the coverlid with the palm open.

"If it's easier for you that way, why then, of course, go in your own car," Dr. Madison replied.

"I'll have made all the arrangements for admittance, Mr. Chadley," Dr. Glasson assured him. His voice came from across the room at the door.

"Thank you very much," Fenton said. He pulled himself up a little on his pillows to say good-by to each of them. Then when he heard the door fasten softly, he sagged back. The footsteps went down the gallery. He was alone.

He lay still trying to rest and to keep the thought of the coming ordeal from rising in his mind. In a while he would speak to Gilberta and arrange for O'Smyre to drive him to the Doughtry Memorial Hospital. He sighed and plucked at the monogram on the pillowcase. He breathed slowly and regularly, occupying himself with the effort to drowse and avoid thinking of what the doctors had said. There was a light tap at his outer door. He waited a moment before answering to be certain he had heard. When it came again, he invited the person in.

Gilberta came to his bedside. "I'm sorry," she said kindly. She drew a chair nearer. Fenton heard her arranging it beside him.

"Thank you," he said, "I'm sorry too. I'm sorry it had to be just at this time." Then he stirred to face in her direction. "I don't want you to trouble. It won't be necessary. I have every confidence in the specialist who came this afternoon."

"Yes," she said, "Dr. Madison recommends him very highly." They were silent awhile. Then Gilberta said, "Dr. Madison will be here at eight o'clock to drive with you to the hospital. And you may have something light if you wish. Does anything appeal to you? Addie and Susie are both distressed. They want to make something special, I think . . ."

Fenton was so touched he could not reply. It had never occurred to him that the young doctor would return to take the long drive out of town to the Doughtry Memorial. And the concern of Addie and Susie surprised and embarrassed him. He was not hungry. He did not know that he could eat anything, even to please them.

"A little 'floating island,' perhaps?" Gilberta urged when he did not answer. And then he realized suddenly that she, too, was anxious to be of some special aid to him. His heart beat almost painfully inside him. He could feel her sitting there attempting in some way to comfort him and not knowing how. With his blindness between them, she was, at that moment, in a more tender and intimate union with him than she had ever seemed to be before in their years together. He wished he could speak out his gratitude and his shame to be lying so helpless and unattractive before her but he could say only, "Yes, that would be nice. I'm sure you know what would be best for me." He pressed his palms down beside him to conceal the trembling of his hands.

Then she stood up abruptly and carefully replaced the chair. She lingered a moment before she moved to the door, and he thought with an almost unbearable excitement that she was about to lean down and kiss him. But then he heard her step away and cross the rug as if she went on tiptoe.

"I'll speak to Susie now," she said at the door.

Suddenly he grasped at something to say to detain her. He half sat up in bed and the jar of the quick movement sent a nauseating throb through his head.

"Gilberta," he called out, a little loudly against his competing discomfort, "it is possible that when I recover from the operation, I will retire from active business." He waited for her to answer. In his throat was a swelling which almost suffocated him. Until that instant, when he said it aloud, he had not even considered taking such a drastic step. Nothing his physicians had said had suggested the necessity of so extreme an action. And yet when he made his shocking announcement, his mind had already accepted the possibility of retirement as an actuality he intended to bring about. "I will resign from the bank."

Gilberta came back into the room. "Well, of course," she said, "there's never been any reason for you to work." She spoke in a mild undisturbed voice. Fenton could not decide whether her unconcern was meant to soothe his agitation or to connote real disinterest.

"I felt you should know," he said, with disappointment, "I wanted to tell you."

"Thank you," she murmured, "it was very courteous of you." She stood politely waiting for him to say something more if he wished. But Fenton had no further comment to make.

Gilberta left his outer door ajar and went to instruct Addie and Susie about his tray.

Downstairs Fenton could hear August practicing her scales. He listened to her with deliberate interest. She attacked the instrument with vigor and determination. Even in the monotony of the successive notes played up and then down, he could feel her energy as she struck each key accurately and precisely, without variety. She was quite diligent. From the time he (or rather Santa Claus) had given her the piano, she had applied herself with enormous concentration to the task of learning to play it. Occasionally, when she played for him after dinner, she would turn at the end of the selection and dip her head in a bow and smile for his applause, and it would suggest in a discomforting way to Fenton that she worked at her music only to please him and was without any real interest in it herself. No matter how faithfully she followed the marks of expression, or how expertly she memorized so that her attention was not distracted following the notes, she played without feeling for the instrument and without any interest in it as a vehicle for her own interpretation of a theme. But he knew she would continue to take lessons until the happy day when he would release her.

Of late he had been going over in his mind the problem of ascertaining the extent of her interest in studying art. He had watched her attention to her drawing-class projects in school and tried to decide from her obviously developing ability when she might be ready to study. But she herself made no comment and some guiding sensitivity to her warned him that the request to study painting must come from her. He knew she would not learn to paint to please him as she had learned to play the piano.

From the time of her struggle against the assignments of Miss Applewhite, she had not changed in her self-assertiveness. Fortunately, as she had gone up the grades, the assignments had progressively allowed for more and more individual expression. Her creative impulses were in frequent agreement with the projects of the ninth grade whereas they had been at complete odds with the pattern-tracing of the second. So she came home now with A as often as any other mark on her report. But whatever her grade, there was one thing of which Fenton was certain: August was capable of becoming an artist; and her resistance to persuasion, in any direction but that dictated by her own necessity, simply underwrote his certainty.

The practicing below stopped and in the silence Fenton strained to detect footsteps upon the stairs. He hoped August would come to see him before going to change for dinner. He felt a great desire to talk to her, about her school, about her interests, about the things they might plan to do together, now that he would no longer be going to the bank. Suddenly he realized how much the care of her life possessed him. Realizing his devotion to her, his spirit experienced a sweet elation. He had been faithful to the task Lesley had left him. He had watched over her and protected her and insured her freedom to express herself in any way. He had loved her always. He would gladly have resigned from the bank without having had to suffer the calamity of blindness if ever she had required more constant attention.

He lay reflecting happily upon this when suddenly an accusing realization shattered his repose. He struggled to ignore it but it swelled in his consciousness until he was forced to admit its cold truth. He had *wanted* to sell the bank. He had *wanted* to resign. He had become frightened of his world, for he had begun to fail in it—and in his hidden heart he had desired a calamity which would honorably free him from his responsibilities.

The bank had grown large and rigid about him like a prison. He could no longer control its activities. It had become a risk and a charity to serve his old customers, those to whom the bank's funds should be accessible, for loans on crops and mortgages on modest property. His transactions with the large banks of the North had increased as the awesome rise of the stock market's power had created the multiple-functioning investment trusts. He had had to engage more tellers, more bookkeepers, more clerks, and to authorize night work in the mortgage and loan departments. The accounts of the most thrifty and conservative customers had recorded an astounding traffic in deposits and withdrawals from week to week. All Newtown had been buying lots, selling lots, speculating in stocks, opening new businesses on heavy loans backed by securities, selling businesses to each other at unhealthy profits, and behaving with a carelessness and irresponsibility shocking to him. The mushrooming of doubtful enterprises and the hysterical activity about him had terrified him and he had shrunk back from the race toward an end he could not see and dared not imagine.

He had wanted to escape. He had wanted to go back to a time he knew had slipped irretrievably into the past; for he belonged to that past, lost as it was. His illness had opened the way of retreat. He was saved. He could sell the bank with decency and face. It might even turn out a proper time for such a transaction. Certainly he would take every care to insure a profitable disposal of an interest which had been so personal a one of his father's and so serious a one of his own.

At his outer door, there was a soft tap and the sound of voices conferring and then a jarring rattle of silver against glass. But Fenton did not hear. The knock was sharply repeated and August called out, "I'm here with your dinner. Wake up." She did not wait for his permission to enter, but shoved the door with her foot and slipped into the room with his tray balanced carefully in her hands.

"Don't let me impress you with this fancy service," she said, "I didn't carry it up from the pantry by myself." Then she remembered, and added, quite without embarrassment, "Oh that's right – you can't see me, can you? Well, perhaps it's just as well. I don't think I could make a steady living doing this. Mother has Grandfather's sprig china on here full of little dabs. And she's got out the best water goblets and a lace cloth I'm supposed to spread over your lap – oh goodness, she got so mad when I told her it was just a nuisance because you couldn't see it anyway." Then she stopped talking and looked down at him in silence a moment. "You know," she said, "this is the chance of a lifetime. I'm going to get to feed you with a spoon. How Mother ever thought you were going to manage 'floating island' is a mystery to me. You'd have it everywhere but in your mouth. Now, let's see" – and she examined his pillows to determine the best arrangement to make – "are you too sick to sit up higher?" she asked.

Fenton shook his head and raised himself. Gratitude for her gallantry had painfully closed his throat.

August went often to see Fenton when the operation was done and he lay with his eyes bandaged, recovering, awaiting the day when the gauze would be unwound in a carefully dimmed room and he would know that he could see. Always, August brought him a gift, telling him what it was as she put it into his hands, describing its shape and color for him without hesitation or embarrassment.

One afternoon when she came, Fenton was not alone. As she tipped through the small sitting room of his suite to surprise him, she heard, not his day nurse Miss Clancy's habitually cheerful voice, but a man's voice, reading aloud. She stopped and listened. Then she stepped to the door of Fenton's bedroom.

The strange man was standing at the window with his back to her, and the *Wall Street Journal*, from which he was reading, was spread across one of his knees, raised to convenient height and braced against the window sill. When he finished the article, he began to turn the pages, calling out the headlines to Fenton so that Fenton might indicate his next choice of an article.

August hesitated a moment, and then, interrupting the stranger, she spoke out to Fenton and crossed the room to kiss him.

At the sound of her voice, the man straightened and turned around and stood facing her across Fenton's bed.

"This is Mr. Abbott, dear," Fenton presented him, when he had returned August's greeting. Fenton held her hand and turned his head awkwardly as he spoke. "And this young lady is my daughter, Mr. Abbott," he said.

And so August met Walter Abbott.

"How do you do," she murmured to him. And he responded, "How do you do." And then, after a silence, when Fenton did not ask him to go on with the reading, he mentioned the time and asked if he might be excused to catch the next bus back to the university. He put the *Wall Street Journal* on a table and said, after he had told Fenton good-by and nodded to August, "I hope the news when I come tomorrow will be very, very good." Then, without any instruction to do so, he closed the door behind him and left August to ask, when she heard his steps reach the corridor, "What did he mean by that? And who is he?"

Fenton's lips beneath his bandages trembled, and the corners twitched. Then he answered. "He shouldn't have said that. I intended to surprise you and your mother on your next visit. They're going to remove these tomorrow," he said, putting his hands up to his eyes and lightly feeling the bands of gauze with his fingers.

"Gee," said August, and she gently wiped the fine frost of perspiration from his forehead, "That's wonderful."

For an instant, she felt tears rising, but she hurried to talk about the happy day ahead to defeat them. "Mother is coming tomorrow and she's going to stay for dinner with you. She's already spoken to Dr. Glasson. She's bringing you a present, a special one."

"Is she?" Fenton asked softly and happily, not referring to the present.

But August thought he was, and she went on, "Oh, yes. She's gone to a lot of trouble about it and I think I should tell you what it is." She paused, and then explained, "You might not be able to see perfectly at first, you know."

"That's true," Fenton agreed, touched.

"It's a new smoking jacket which Mr. Garland has made like your old brown velvet one. It's blue and the material is silk with a kind of ribbon stripe of the same color, which looks lighter because of the satin finish. So when you see it, you might say something about the contrast. Mother thought the fabric was especially nice."

"Thank you," Fenton said, "I'll remember to comment as you've suggested." His hands worked the sheet hem until suddenly he became conscious of their twisting and then he held them still.

"Of course, if your bandages are on, she won't expect you to say anything except to guess what it is from feeling it," August said.

"Yes," said Fenton.

August leaned across his legs and found his feet. She pinched his toes and asked suddenly, as she held them, "You aren't afraid, are you?" And when he did not answer immediately, she said, "Anyone would be. I would be. All kinds of terrible thoughts would be going through my head. I probably wouldn't want to take off the bandages to find out whether I could see or not. Is that the way you feel, now that the time has come?"

"Yes," said Fenton quietly.

"Well, I'll be thinking of you tomorrow morning when I'm conjugating *je suis, tu es, il est,* for Miss Anderson." She gave his toes a final affectionate twist and went to sniff the gladiolas on the desk. They had no odor. Then she picked out the crusted filberts from a box of candy by them and returned to eat the handful, sitting beside Fenton.

"Who is Mr. Abbott?" she asked directly, working herself into the chair seat and stretching out her legs.

"Mr. Abbott? Why, Mr. Abbott is studying for his doctorate at the university and he earns a part of his expenses doing general secretarial work for any patient requiring it here in the hospital. Dr. Glasson recommended him."

August ate two nuts together after she had sucked off their

hard sugar coatings. Then she said, "I could read to you any time Miss Clancy is off."

Fenton smiled and unconsciously moved his hand to the edge of his bed near her, as if he were trying by the gesture to reassure her. "I know you could, dear. And I would not hesitate to ask that favor of you. But Mr. Abbott takes letters and attends to some other small business details for me and he's familiar with the stocks listed on the board and he reads me the quotations." Then after reflecting a moment, he added, "He has made some rather sharp observations pertinent to the trading of late. He seems to have some knowledge of finance."

August chewed the filberts and did not comment.

Then Fenton asked, after a silence, "How does Mr. Abbott look?" and as he asked it his cheeks below the white gauze colored, and he seemed to hold his breath in a kind of pain at his curiosity and the condition which forced him to expose it.

"Well," August said, "let me see if I can describe him." Then, very deliberately, pulling her feet back again and leaning forward, supporting her arms on her knees, she stared at the polished rubber tile floor under Fenton's bed and began; "He's taller than I am, but not much. He has hair that is about as dark as Mother's, and it's straight and grows in a point at his forehead." She reached her fingers to her own forehead. "His eyes are brown, I suppose, but not very, and he has perfectly straight eyebrows." She stopped and thought. Then she continued, "He was wearing a heavy tweed jacket and brown flannel trousers and very good shoes. They were polished and they had thick walking soles." She stopped again and thought. Then she concluded, "He looks like an Englishman." Then she sat back in her chair and stretched out her legs again and looked up to Fenton's face and waited.

Fenton cleared his throat. "Thank you, dear," he said.

"Is that the way you imagined he looked?" August asked.

"Well," Fenton hesitated, and then confessed, "No, it isn't. I had imagined him to be rather slight and perhaps fair and dressed more conventionally in the formal attire one associates with men of serious scholarly endeavor."

"He doesn't look anything like a professor, if that's what you mean," August said.

"I see," murmured Fenton. Then he sighed almost inaudibly and added, "It will be interesting for me to see him for myself."

They were silent. Then August suddenly asked, "Why have you always called me your daughter and I always called you my uncle?"

Fenton turned his head toward her and lay there as if he could see her face and were studying it before he answered. Then he said, "I suppose it has always been awkward for you at your school, hasn't it? I'm sorry you didn't tell me."

"Oh no," said August, "I haven't minded. I'm just curious. I hadn't thought about it really until you called me your daughter to Mr. Abbott. I just wondered why I never started calling you my father when I was little; you and Mother were married before I could talk, practically. I wouldn't have known the difference. And you really are my father, and I am very glad that you are. Can't we change now?"

"We would have to ask your mother, dear," he said, "and it might be painful for her to have to refuse. She feels, and properly, I think, that you should . . ." He faltered and was unable to finish and then began over, "We feel that I should not diminish in any way the recollection you have of your father. And I am happy to be called your uncle, so you must never think that I feel at all" – and he stopped and did not complete the sentence but turned his head back to the position of a stare into the room and pressed himself back into his pillows as if he were trying in some way to escape something he felt surrounding him in the room.

"I don't have any recollection," August said, but her tone was not argumentative. "All I know about my father is what you have told me. I don't have any feeling about him."

Fenton did not reply. He put his hands beneath the coverlid.

"You know," August observed, "Mother doesn't look like a mother. I don't feel as if she were my mother, sometimes. I think that Mother is very unusual."

"Do you?" Fenton murmured.

"Yes, I do," August said, "I think we are very different. Do you know, Mother really likes sitting in your chair at table? I think she is very childish about some things. There is something the matter with her tooth, too, and I can't make her go to the dentist. You had better mention it to her."

"All right," said Fenton, "I'll remember to do that."

August got up and went back to the box of candy. She picked two more filberts from the assortment. Then she returned and resumed the conversation.

"Mother and I don't look at all alike. Do we?" she asked. There was a faint wistfulness in her voice.

"You are both very beautiful," Fenton replied cautiously.

August did not reply at once. She ate her candy. Then she commented, "I knew you would say something like that."

"Did you?" Fenton said. He smiled.

"But we really don't look at all alike, do we?" August insisted.

"No," said Fenton, "you resemble your father."

"I suppose it really is best for me to call you my uncle, isn't it?" August concluded.

"I think so," said Fenton.

When she was ready to leave, August kissed him. And then she held his hands together in hers and said, "Don't be frightened and get your nerves all upset now. Dr. Glasson says that everything is going to be just fine."

Fenton nodded. He could not speak.

August hesitated and then she added, "There wouldn't be anything to worry about anyway, because you would always be with Mother and me and both of us love you very much."

She put her cheek down against his, still holding his hands firmly, and kissed him again. Then she walked quickly out of the room and left the door open behind her.

When the soft gauze was unwound and the shields removed from his eyes, Fenton could see. His lids dropped over the odd keyhole shapes of his pupils and his thick glasses further concealed the evidence of the change behind them. He learned quickly to turn his whole head to right or left in order to see a person or object beside him. And in a month from the night of his terrifying attack, he was home in Dunmeade to begin his convalescence — and his retirement.

He left the Doughtry Memorial Hospital as the warmth and rains of April began and the earth softened for the rise of pallid grass islands in the seas of rotted brown leaves. And just before the spring twilight, when he was led down the pyramid of entrance steps to his waiting car, almost on the day itself, unexpectedly, the accomplishment of the two undertakings upon which his mind had dwelled during his illness, was begun: the fulfillment of Mr. Chadley's wish that Ralph be educated in Newtown, and the final and profitable disposal of his interest in the bank.

There had been little for Fenton to do for Isaiah after Mr. Chadley's death, except to watch over the collection of rent from his father's old homestead and see that the money was properly paid to Isaiah and Maude. In time, if advantageous, he would sell the property and arrange for the proceeds to be credited to them. But at the moment the estate was profitably leased to a group of Coast merchants who used the house as a Club from which to fish the inlets and hunt the marshes.

Always, he had made a particular effort to see Isaiah when he had come to the East on business at the turpentine tract. Always he had visited awhile on the front porch of the plain, unpainted, sand-swept house which Isaiah had built out of his cash from Mr. Chadley. It was not far from the old homestead, perhaps ten miles to the south and nearer the ocean. It was where Mr. Chadley had seen Isaiah first, nearly thirty-seven years before, when Isaiah had stood on a cypress stump to plead for the right of the Negro squatters to keep the treacherous ground from which they had managed to eke an existence.

First with surprise and then with sadness, Fenton had begun to mark increasing age upon Isaiah, though his health was good and he seemed content with his life in that remote stretch of sandy land falling into the sea. He fished and hunted with Ralph and read aloud at night from the papers and books which Fenton sent regularly from Newtown. Peaceful secure retirement was what Mr. Chadley had wished for his old age, and certainly Isaiah had been provided it. But it had seemed to Fenton upon his last visit that, though Isaiah was happy to see him and exhibited an almost childlike reluctance to have him depart, there was noticeable about Isaiah a distinct air of sad resignation, as if inside him some deep disappointment for which there was no remedy had begun to spoil his proud spirit. Observing it had shocked and depressed Fenton and he had tried to draw some complaint from Isaiah to account for it. But Isaiah had reported to him nothing of a troubling nature. And, except that Ralph suffered with malaria off and on, there was no illness among them to distress him. At last, noticing a despondent tone in Isaiah's subsequent letters, as he recounted the unvarying activities of his household, it came to Fenton's mind that Isaiah feared his hope for Ralph's education was not to be realized, since Fenton had not begun preparations, and that he was too respectful of Fenton's guardianship to question him. It was then Fenton wrote that the time had come for Ralph to return to Newtown to begin his studies at the Negro college as Mr. Chadley had willed. And he was rewarded with an immediate reply of such unconcealed gratitude in the carefully composed sentences informing him of Ralph's record of marks in the county school, that Fenton reproached himself over and again for having caused Isaiah to suffer.

Resting in the hospital, Fenton carefully considered how he might best help Ralph prepare for college; for, even with the instruction Mr. Chadley had given him in Latin and composition and sums, his schooling was inadequate and he could not meet the requirements for entrance. The county school to which he had gone after Mr. Chadley's death operated upon an uncertain schedule conditioned by insufficient funds and a lack of teachers for Negro schools. Added to Ralph's academic unpreparedness was the fact that he was a timid boy, accustomed to living unto himself, and Fenton knew he must anticipate with some terror the prospect of being sent from home to live suddenly in an intimate fashion in a dormitory with perhaps a hundred strange classmates. So he decided that Ralph was to come to Dunmeade for the summer, where, at the same time he accustomed himself to life away from his parents, he would be tutored to stand the entrance examination required when insufficient credits were submitted. He was confident that Ralph would pass satisfactorily if given proper instruction. His father had assured him that Ralph was an apt and faithful pupil, "possessed of intelligence far above the usual observed in his race."

He dictated to Mr. Abbott a lengthy letter in which he outlined his plan to Isaiah and requested that Ralph be sent to Dunmeade at the end of May. He concluded with the news that the operation upon his eyes had been successful and that with a few weeks' rest he would be enjoying perfect health again, and that he was grateful to Isaiah for his letters and prayers during the anxious days. Then when Mr. Abbott had read it back to him and held it firmly for his signature, Fenton said, "Mr. Abbott, I realize that you would not presume to draw any conclusions as to the business referred to in this letter, but I noticed at moments an expression of serious interest on your face and it occurs to me that you might care to know the circumstances which led me to write it."

Mr. Abbott glanced at Fenton in surprise, and busied himself sealing and stamping the envelope.

"I'll admit my interest was aroused after a time," he confessed.

"At what point, Mr. Abbott?" Fenton asked pleasantly and studied him carefully through his dark lenses.

"When you observed that Ralph might find it difficult to move suddenly into a community of Negroes of his own age when he had lived only with his parents or in your father's household," Mr. Abbott answered.

"It was at that point that you realized my letter was being addressed to a colored person," Fenton stated for him simply.

"Yes," Mr. Abbott nodded.

"Isaiah is a person whom it would be impossible for me to regard with higher opinion or deeper devotion," Fenton said. "He has been a member of my family since I was a child of two and I am indebted to him for a kind of faithful service and loyalty which seems to have all but disappeared from our society these days. There is little I can do to reward him. Educating his boy to become a teacher is the effort I shall make, in my father's name, since it was my father who first expressed the wish for it to be done."

"I see," said Mr. Abbott. He made no comment. He began to put away his paper and pen and fasten his briefcase.

Fenton observed him in silence until he was finished and then he said, almost wistfully or regretfully, "I am about to ask you, Mr. Abbott, to come to my aid in this endeavor."

Mr. Abbott raised his brows and tilted his head and regarded Fenton with a faint frown of puzzle and inquiry.

"I am going to ask you to come to Dunmeade for the summer and undertake to prepare Ralph to meet his examinations," Fenton said and then he paused before he added, "provided, of course, you feel no reluctance to tutor a colored person." He looked steadily at Mr. Abbott and with the faintest lift of his head, concluded, "It was my father's habit to give him some instruction daily from the time he was of school age until my father died, at which time Ralph was eleven."

Mr. Abbott did not reply at once. He looked sharply at Fenton and then quickly away from him. Then he went to the window and stood looking out. At last he said, with his back to Fenton, "I work on a farm during the summer months, Mr. Chadley. I have arranged to work this summer."

Fenton did not know what to answer. He was surprised. It was difficult for him to imagine Mr. Abbott in a farmer's clothes working with his hands in a field or a vineyard. He knew that he would accept modest employment but it had never occurred to Fenton that he would seek it outside the world of teaching and study. And yet, now noticing, he could see that Mr. Abbott was accustomed to some sort of hard physical labor, for his physique was not that of a man used to life indoors at a desk. Mr. Abbott's back was broad and his legs long and muscular, outlined by the tightness of his trousers, which, along with their ill-fit, were noticeably worn.

"It means much more to me to have your help than I have indicated perhaps, Mr. Abbott," Fenton said. He paused, expecting for some reason to have Mr. Abbott turn around and come nearer again to resume the conversation. But when he did not, Fenton went on, "In business, one often pays a high figure to obtain a unique service and counts it well worth the investment. I am prepared to offer you twice what you had expected to realize from a summer's farm work."

Though Fenton's voice was soft and the formally phrased offer flattering to Mr. Abbott, there was yet beneath what he said a feeling of firmness and resolution suggesting that he did not intend to be disappointed.

Mr. Abbott put his hands in his pockets and visibly worked his shoulders inside his jacket as if trying to loose them from some invisible binding. Then he sighed in a kind of impatience.

"I shall be continuing some research I have already begun for my thesis, Mr. Chadley. My labor will not be entirely physical. To be truthful, only the smallest part of it will be."

Fenton closed his eyes and sagged deliberately against his pillows to thwart the faint dull ache of tension beginning across his forehead. He was worn still from the shock of the delicate operation and suddenly he was fatigued with his unexpected struggle against Mr. Abbott's determination to continue with his former plans. He began to prepare himself to accept failure.

Then Mr. Abbott said, "I am complimented that you consider me capable of successfully instructing a pupil so poorly prepared for college entrance. I should like to ask you why you do." And he turned to face Fenton, though he remained at the window away from him.

"I have not made any inquiries into your teaching ability, Mr. Abbott," Fenton answered, "and I do not know that you would be the best instructor I might engage. I had not thought of asking you to come to Dunmeade until I observed your particular interest in the contents of my letter to Isaiah. It was opportune for me to ask you. I knew only that you have taught in the past and that you expect to teach again next winter. This information you furnished me yourself in one of our pleasant social conversations."

Mr. Abbott rocked back and forth on his heels. Then he removed his hands from his pockets. He stretched his shoulders again inside his jacket. Then he said with a faint smile, "You have no conviction or evidence to persuade you that I am the proper tutor for this boy. You have suggested that I might even object to teaching a Negro. And yet you offer me twice the money I expect to earn farming to change my plans and undertake this project whose success means so much to you."

"That is substantially correct," agreed Fenton with a certain resignation.

Mr. Abbott walked to the foot of the bed. He studied Fenton with puzzled interest and a suggestion of admiration in his face. "I'm going to accept your offer, Mr. Chadley," he said; "but just as you made it for a reason I have yet to determine and might not find agreeable, I am going to help you for a reason which, if you knew it, you might not find agreeable. I am not motivated to undertake this out of gratitude, as you are, Mr. Chadley. Even if I were in your position, I do not know that I would be. But I shall make the greatest effort to prepare this boy to pass his examinations with high grades. And I shall also give him whatever feeling of confidence I can as we go along. And we shall be together on the project to that extent."

Almost imperceptibly, Fenton nodded agreement. "I did not expect you to feel the same affectionate concern for Ralph that I feel, Mr. Abbott. I would not have required any involvement of your feelings in this matter. I do not believe I would have had to, for I have already detected in you a certain degree of sympathy for Ralph's cause." Fenton smiled a little slyly.

Mr. Abbott did not reply, either to confirm or deny it. He smiled back with as much enjoyment of Fenton's remark on his face as Fenton exhibited himself. Then he said, "I am usually able to put a hundred and fifty dollars in my pocket by the time I return to the campus each fall, Mr. Chadley. That would make my coaching fee three hundred dollars."

"I am agreeable to that, Mr. Abbott," said Fenton immediately, "and I should prefer that you live with our family, although I am agreeable also to paying your room and board elsewhere if you insist."

"I shall be happy to live in Dunmeade, Mr. Chadley," replied Mr. Abbott pleasantly, still smiling. "I shall be interested in observing the family life in a traditional Southern home. When would you wish me to come?"

Fenton blushed. The reference to his home being of interest as a study to Mr. Abbott, embarrassed him. And yet he understood that Mr. Abbott had meant it as the compliment of the Northerner to the Southerner and certainly not as rudeness. Mr. Abbott was given to odd blunt statements, but he was not ill-mannered. In a way, Fenton's intuitive confidence in him was inspired by his frank, unimpulsive personality.

"I should like you to be there ahead of Ralph, if that's convenient," Fenton requested, "and he will be arriving the end of May or the first week of June. I will put it more definitely the first week of June when I write Isaiah again."

Mr. Abbott nodded.

Fenton raised himself to an upright sitting position. "My checkbook is in the desk drawer, as you know, Mr. Abbott. I should like to make a one third payment upon account – to bind our agreement."

"That will not be necessary, Mr. Chadley," Mr. Abbott said. "I don't need any commitment from you. And you have my word that I will arrive on the day you expect me." He thrust his hands in his pockets again and rocked an instant on his heels and then added, in an odd joking way, "I'm going to ask you not to allow me to draw more than five dollars a week against the total amount, if you will, Mr. Chadley. I've never had three hundred dollars at one time in my life. It might go to my head." His face reddened and he gave a faintly snorting laugh of embarrassment and turned to pick up his briefcase to begin leaving.

Fenton was so astonished at this boyish outburst and at the same time so flattered at the confidence and trust placed in him that he could not answer. At last as Mr. Abbott stood awkwardly near the door waiting to be dismissed Fenton managed to say, "Well, under the circumstances, if your money is to remain on deposit, it should be drawing interest for you." He cleared his throat and hoped his effort to match Mr. Abbott's candid joking manner was being successful. "You would be entitled to one fourth of two per cent – that being the current rate." He cleared his throat again awkwardly and smiled. "It might be difficult to compute, however, if you are going to be drawing against the balance every week."

"I'm afraid I can't worry about that, Mr. Chadley," Mr. Abbott declared. "That's the problem of the banker." He raised his brows and laughed and then he looked at his wrist watch. "If you'll excuse me, now . . ." he said.

Fenton nodded and let him go. Then before Mr. Abbott had crossed the small sitting room and started down the corridor, Fenton called out, "Oh, Mr. Abbott!" And when Mr. Abbott stepped inside the room again, he said, "I don't want you to feel that you must abandon the research you meant to do on your thesis this summer. We shall arrange and keep to a rigid schedule concerning Ralph's studies. You will be free many hours of the day, and I shall see you are not disturbed at your books."

A curious sober expression, almost of resentment, came over Mr. Abbott's face. But he answered politely, "Thank you very much, Mr. Chadley."

Fenton hesitated and then he asked, "What is the subject of your study, Mr. Abbott? Our library is rather well selected, I think – due to my father's wide intellectual interests, of course." He was timid suddenly at the very moment he proffered his books for examination and use.

"The title will probably be, 'The Persistence of Institutional Patterns in the Transition from Agrarian to Industrial Society, with Special Consideration of Race Attitudes and Segregation of Women in Educational Institutions, Politics, and Industry.' I haven't presented my subject for approval by the head of the department yet. I'm roughing out a draft first, though that is not the usual procedure," Mr. Abbott said, matter-of-factly.

Fenton did not say anything. He realized the necessity of making some comment. He had inquired, and Mr. Abbott had obliged him with an answer. But he had not entirely understood what Mr. Abbott had said. The length of the title and the seriousness of the sound of it had startled him. He felt unreasonably ignorant and uninformed before Mr. Abbott, who waited in the door, again hoping to be dismissed quickly.

"I'm very impressed, Mr. Abbott," Fenton said simply, when he could think of nothing else. "I shall look forward to reading the published paper and I shall hope that I can understand it sufficiently to realize your scholarship."

When Fenton decided to retire from the bank, he intended the transacting of this business, which was so personal to him, to be kept private until the moment when a proper public announcement of the sale could be made. He felt a keen responsibility toward his customers, particularly those for whom he had personally written loans when their "collateral" was not strictly collateral and their "security" not security but only his faith in them. He had worried about them. He was afraid of a successor who might conduct the bank's business with his eyes only upon the Profit-and-Loss statements and not upon the needs of the individuals who were his customers. But the unexpected visit of three men who gained entry to his hospital room by brandishing an enormous and vulgar floral arrangement before unsuspecting Miss Clancy changed all he had planned.

Mr. Oliver J. Rench, Mr. Jesse Oats, and "young" Mr. Amos drove down to the Doughtry Memorial Hospital to verify certain gossip they had heard and be the early birds with a high shut-out bid for the bank. Fenton recognized their voices in astonishment. He had just had his afternon rest and the blinds were still half-drawn when suddenly Miss Clancy scurried in from the sitting room and began pulling chairs about his bed and fussing over his position. She had been impressed by Mr. Oats's title of mayor of Newtown and the unctuous card on the flowers which dangled on the outside for all to see: "Come home soon; Newtown needs you."

Mr. Amos, who was only a few years Fenton's senior, and whose little girl, Cora Simmons, was one of August's schoolmates, was first to enter. It was obvious that he had been elected spokesman. At least he knew Fenton socially.

"Mr. Chadley," he said, in a tone of deep solicitation, "we have all been mighty distressed to learn of your affliction."

Fenton's ears shrank against the word "affliction." He watched them peering at his eyes, trying to decide whether or not he could see them, whether his dark lenses were to dim the glare or hide his blindness.

"Affliction?" he repeated slowly, "Is that the opinion generally held by my friends in Newtown, Mr. Amos? That I am afflicted?" His voice was quiet and controlled. "I think Dr. Glasson would be rather shocked to hear my little complaint described so. I am very grateful for your concern, however."

Fenton seldom felt real anger. His deep emotions were usually sadness or despair when he was disturbed. But this sudden intrusion upon him by persons with whom he was not friendly shocked him and Mr. Amos's remark implied that his operation had been gossiped about and conclusions drawn which were not the proper concern of strangers. In his indignation he spoke in the manner of his father. Indeed, even his retort might have been the retort of Mr. Chadley; it had so much of his patronizing tone before an insupportable fool. But Mr. Amos was not sensitive. He blustered cheerfully, "Oh, I'm sure everyone knows it's just a temporary setback, Mr. Chadley. I've just always considered anything that laid me up and interfered with the office as being the next thing to death's door. To tell you the truth, Mr. Rench and

Mr. Oats and myself here were expecting you home some time ago. We're all mighty glad to see you're doing so fine." He cocked his eye at the other two as if to say, "He's pretty touchy about it, isn't he?"

"Thank you, Mr. Amos," Fenton said. He waited for the delegation to announce the purpose of the call, for something more than concern for his health had brought them such a distance to see him. There was a restless movement among them.

"Won't you help yourselves to cigars, gentlemen?" he asked politely, "You'll find them on a small table near the door unless Miss Clancy has moved them since this morning."

Lighting cigars succeeded in removing the last restraint which sick-room etiquette had forced upon them and Mr. Rench came to the point with a direct statement.

"We have considerable interest in some confidential information that you are anxious to dispose of your banking interests, Mr. Chadley. I hope you aren't going to hold it against us for trying to get our bids in first this way. Mr. Oats and Mr. Amos and I represent a group of six. We're ready to talk turkey any time you are." He finished with a kind of chuckle down in his throat as if he considered himself quite shrewd and were sure Fenton thought the same.

For a few minutes, Fenton was so taken aback, he was conscious of nothing but the audacity of the men sitting before him. How could such information have got about? He had hinted at his intention to no one but Mr. Starburg, who had refused to accept the idea of such a decision, refused really to discuss it seriously until he was well. Mr. Starburg would not have started a rumor with no more purpose than to provide gossip.

"May I ask the names of the other three gentlemen?" Fenton inquired. He found it difficult to keep his voice steady. It had come into his mind that Mr. Rench, Mr. Oats, and Mr. Amos had coupled some extreme speculations concerning his condition with perhaps a wholly sympathetic, but ill-advised, comment from Mr. Starburg that Fenton was concerned over keeping up his responsibilities at the bank.

Mr. Rench hesitated over the names of the other three men. Fenton waited.

"I am not at liberty at the moment to divulge their identities, Mr. Chadley," Mr. Rench said, apologetically. "They have no intention of entering the managership of the bank, as I have." He paused then, as if this were designed to reassure Fenton and emphasize the seriousness of his own personal interest in contrast to the absentee interest of the others.

Fenton's immediate defensive reaction was to deny intending to sell the bank and so cheat and embarrass them. But in honesty he did intend disposing of the stock, and however he resented the matter having become public, there was nothing to be gained by denying it out of personal disgust for the manners of the persons interested. In the conduct of daily business, his sense of propriety often was affronted. He had realized that there would be some unpleasant moments for him in negotiating the sale of the bank. There were so many memories attached to it. But he was quite unprepared for Mr. Oliver J. Rench, for whom he had neither respect nor tolerance, suggesting himself as his proper successor. His shock and displeasure were evident in his answer.

"It is not my practice to conduct business outside business hours or business premises, Mr. Rench. No doubt you will learn from your confidential informant when I have returned to Newtown. I'm sure you will excuse me from any further discussion now, gentlemen. My regimen here is quite strict." He pulled the black cord attached to his bedpost. "Miss Clancy will show you to the corridor," he said with polite finality.

With firm smiles they repeated the empty expected assurances that he would be recovered and back among his friends in Newtown in no time and that they would be the first to welcome him. And then they moved out behind Miss Clancy, each one in turn surreptitiously glancing at Fenton to see if his eyes followed them.

Fenton stared straight forward.

Then he listened to them tiptoe through the sitting room, as if they were stealing decorously from a room of death. Suddenly, in the corridor, all three spoke at once, and the unintelligible bark of their indignant voices came back to him sharply and then faded out as they hurried off.

Fenton sighed. His anger had subsided, and an overwhelming sense of futility and weakness had come over him. He turned his face into his pillow, half hiding, as if, that way, he were able to escape the world's movement which so tried him. Perhaps I am being too exacting, he thought. And with the hope that, whatever the outcome of this unexpected and shocking call upon him, the customers of the bank would continue to be faithfully served and their best interests minded, he deliberately forced his mind from any further thought on the subject and began to ruminate upon the probable happy effect of Mr. Abbott's presence in Dunmeade upon August.

It will be a stimulating association for her, I'm sure, he decided contentedly; she has never known a scholar.

As for Mr. Abbott, when he had left Fenton and returned to the university, he went to the office of Professor Elwige, up three steep flights of slick worn steps in the old library building in which the Departments of Sociology, Philosophy, and Economics had been crowded together "temporarily" for ten years.

He consulted the schedule of courses typed on a card and tacked on the door molding. Professor Elwige at that moment was holding his last afternoon class, "Problems on the Family." Mr. Abbott wrote the following note and slipped it well under the locked door.

Dear Professor Elwige,

I have very abruptly and perhaps without sufficient consideration changed my plans for the summer. Could I see you immediately after next period? I'll come up from "Statistics" on the second floor.

[He paused, considered, was about to sign his name, and then added] I committed myself, challenged by the job itself; but I'm hoping that you'll decide as I have upon reflection – that a record of the experience might well provide me an important chapter for "the book." Certainly it will be a unique opportunity to observe firsthand an instance of paternalism.

ABBOTT

The days moved swiftly toward the final negotiations in the bank sale. Mr. Rench was not to be put off by Chadley decorum; he had plans which could not wait, plans for the bank. And even old Mr. Starburg, who was disapproving of Fenton's selling at all, was impressed with the offer of Rench, Oats and Amos.

Briefly, in cold figures, their proposition would net Fenton a profit of over four hundred thousand dollars after taxes. The other three gentlemen not named by Mr. Rench during the hospital visit were Gaither Lyndon, Hartley Pickett and a Mr. Otis Duffy, who had recently come to Newtown with Northern capital to open a sock factory.

Gaither Lyndon, once it was disclosed that he was a major participant in the transaction, took a great personal interest in the details. He even paid a call to Dunmeade – one of the few of his life – and proudly reminded Fenton that he had been one of the original stockholders of the Bank of Newtown when it was sold in 1900 to Fenton's father. He had sighed dramatically as if this sidelight on the bank's history held some dear nostalgic meaning for him. Then he had added brightly, "Well sir, Mr. Chadley – like father, like son. You don't shy at driving a hard bargain either, seems to me." His hoarse tonsillar voice was patronizing and reassuring, but the gleam in his small fat-encircled eyes belied his tone. Privately, he thought Fenton could have done a great deal more with the bank in times when even the local shoe clerks were rolling in unclipped coupons. He and Rench intended to clean out the deadwood in the bank's personnel and get in a few live wires. Half the loans should have been called in long ago, or not made at all, along with most of the mortgages on crops and farmhouses. Fenton had been too sentimental.

And then almost as if Fenton had read Gaither's thoughts, he said, "You'll find the trained personnel quite valuable to you, Mr.

Lyndon – particularly Mr. Estes. Banking is not the brickmaking business. There's the element of personal service. . . ." And his voice had risen suggestively at the end. He was sorry Mr. Lyndon had come. He preferred not talking about the bank except when Mr. Starburg came with the lawyers for necessary business. He wanted it soon to be over – all of it. And it would be, soon, after he had attended to the details concerning August's share of the stock which was held in trust.

At last he gave Mr. Lyndon tea and did not urge him to sit longer. And Gaither, clumsily handling the frail handle of a Worcester cup, thought how different things were at Dunmeade with this son its master – how prim and high-toned, as if it were a woman's house instead of a man's. In Mr. Chadley's day, a fine bottle would have been brought out and an occasion made – even if Mr. Chadley had poured with his free hand opening the door latch. Old Marcus had been a cold customer, he thought, remembering the molded arches of Mr. Chadley's eyes from which his glance would come forth as from a dark hole; but his way had been better than this prissy politeness.

At last, Gaither managed his farewell and Fenton stood courteously watching until he was beyond the sycamores, then he eased down to enjoy the last warmth of the spring sun. He did not want to think of Gaither Lyndon. Now, the bank had been sold. And when Fenton thought of the men who were to succeed him, guilt rose slowly and relentlessly in him and he could not dispel it.

Then, quickly, the last details were done and the time came when Mr. Starburg asked him the question he knew Mr. Starburg would ask – "What will you do now, my boy – cut yourself away from the world completely?" The old man had the fear of old men of being left outside the motions of life – even the useless bothersome motions.

But Fenton reassured him kindly, "I could hardly do that even if I wished, sir. There are our interests on Prince River, you know."

Mr. Starburg's face relaxed. "Oh yes, yes," he reflected, "there's the turpentine tract, isn't there?" He was obviously cheered.

"And some real estate of August's," Fenton added, "and of course, the Starburg Mills." He smiled cheerfully at his father's old friend. "And I have an immediate matter to attend here during the summer."

Mr. Starburg's eyes brightened. "Yes?" he encouraged Fenton.

"You remember Isaiah – Isaiah and Maude?" He waited for Mr. Starburg to recall the old household. "They have a son nearly grown now. It was my father's wish that he receive an education in the college here. He entered the boy's name many years ago." Fenton hesitated momentarily. He had never been able to subdue the painful sadness which always came with memory of his father. "I am going to have Ralph come here for a while to prepare for his examinations. He's a country boy. I want to ease the dread I know he feels at entering a strange college so far from his home."

Mr. Starburg was surprised at this disclosure. He said nothing but looked instead at the mounds of veins twisted over the tops of his thin hands. When he replied, it was with a slight quaver in his voice. "Your father had an unusual insight into the cares which concern others not so secure in the world." Then he looked up. "He was always very proud of you. He had every right to be. You do him great credit."

Walter Abbott arrived at Dunmeade in early June, at Fenton's request upon the day before Ralph was due from the East.

He looked up the drive and through the trees to the beautiful missionlike windows on the second floor, and said, bluntly, "It isn't at all what I expected." The windows were purple pink from the shadows thrown by the roof. The whole shape of the big sprawling house on its different levels was lightly haloed by the reddening afternoon sun.

Fenton blushed. "I meant to correct your impression that you were going to visit a traditional Southern home, but we got off on more pertinent topics that day and it slipped my mind." He began to recite Dunmeade's history in a serious, almost tourist-guide's tone.

Walter made no comment. They had walked to the rear garden and were looking through the grove of sycamores stretched in a screen against the street beyond. To the left and just visible by one corner was Gilberta's greenhouse. And near to it was the little summerhouse Mr. Chadley had made into a home for Isaiah and Maude. Then Walter said, looking at Fenton with inquiring interest, "It's rather unusual that Mrs. Chadley should be the mistress of this house, don't you think? I mean after all the changes of ownership? It's rather romantic."

The odd compliment seemed to please Fenton, but he said no more about the house. Instead he commented, "I hope that you will get to know Mrs. Chadley while you're here. She hasn't . . ." He started to say "hasn't many friends" but quickly amended it: ". . . Hasn't a great deal of interest in things outside her home and gardens."

"I don't imagine she welcomes intrusions either," Walter remarked, with a glance at Fenton, "I shall be certain to have a proper invitation before I storm her greenhouse."

Fenton laughed. "I'm sure she'll urge you to come the moment you express interest in her flowers. She's particularly successful with her roses – she has done extraordinary things with a particular rose my father had under cultivation here." He gave Walter the tip to Gilberta's favor with a certain shy pleasure as they walked into the patio. Then he rang for Addie to come for Walter's small traveling bag, which was all he had brought from the station. "I suppose you'll want some arrangements made about bringing your trunk from the station, won't you?" he inquired hospitably.

Walter smiled. "I haven't any trunk," he said. He nodded toward his small bag. "I have everything there." Unconsciously Fenton glanced at the size of the bag and then flushed deeply. He raised his eyes to find Walter watching him. "It will have to be all I need because it is all I have," Walter explained simply. And then as if he were trying to ease Fenton's mind he enumerated the articles in his wardrobe, and concluded reassuringly, "So you see, with my other trousers, I'll have a change when you have guests."

Fenton was almost ill with discomfort. He prayed that Addie would quickly answer his ring. "Mr. Abbott will occupy the guest room in the south wing, Addie," he almost shouted to her when at last she stood in the door.

Addie looked solemnly at the small valise before moving to pick it up. She seemed to want to say something to Fenton but was undecided about speaking before the guest. Then she made up her mind and said, "Mrs. Chadley told me to carry the gentleman's things to the guest room down near the stair that old Mrs. Ventura used to sleep in." She waited passively for Fenton's answer.

"You must have misunderstood Mrs. Chadley, Addie," Fenton said sternly. "Mr. Abbott is to occupy the south guest room. It's young Ralph who is coming tomorrow that we'll put in the room near the back stair."

Addie's eyes did not leave Fenton's. "The little colored boy?" she asked, her lips set forward in a thick pout.

"Isaiah's son," Fenton answered, evading the proper short answer of "Yes." Addie slowly looked Walter up and down from head to toe. Then she reached down and picked up his little bag. As she went into the house, she made an audible sniffing sound.

"I don't think she approves of me," Walter said with amusement. "Her face clearly said '*pas élégant*,' and I'm afraid she is right." He was not in the least disturbed by Addie's discourteous exhibition. But Fenton was quite disturbed. He intended to speak to Gilberta immediately about Addie and the guest arrangements.

"I hope August will be joining us for tea," he murmured. He wanted to change the subject. He took out his watch. It was already late. "I don't know what's keeping Susie with the tray." He was tired and his tone was a little irritable.

"Perhaps I should excuse myself and go to my room, Mr. Chadley," Walter suggested kindly, and then there was a sudden shuffling sound inside and August sailed out on the patio letting the door bang behind her. "Gee," she laughed, kissing Fenton on the head, "Susie's a worse grouch every day. I don't think she'd ever serve us anything if I didn't go out there and find it. She's trying to hide a big caramel cake. What difference does it make whether we eat it for tea or for dinner?" She plopped heavily in a chair with her long legs stretched out in front of her. The pose was unladylike and Fenton tried vainly to catch her eye; but she was in one of her gay coltish moods intent upon exhausting her own exuberance and her eyes darted here and there and stayed upon nothing.

"You haven't spoken to Mr. Abbott," Fenton reminded her firmly.

"I saw him from the kitchen window," she said, still not speaking to Walter. And, as if her mind had willfully bolted off and away from the subject of greeting their guest, she began to babble happily to Fenton about Billy Pickett's visit during the few moments Fenton had been walking Walter about the grounds. "Gee, he was all laced up in his uniform and showing off as usual," she said airily; "he's just gotten home."

"August is referring to a young friend who goes to a military school called 'The Fortress' – which you may or may not know. It seems to be popular with the young men of Newtown just now," Fenton explained to Walter. He was astonished at August's manners. Gossip about Billy Pickett could have waited until another time.

"Where did you go to prep school, Mr. Abbott?" August asked Walter suddenly, looking into his face with innocent interest. Walter observed her expression appreciatively. Each of her random movements and explosive comments is calculated to draw and hold attention, he thought. She's jealous, jealous of a visitor in the house.

"I did not attend a prep school, Miss Chadley," he answered her. "I worked in my father's shoe shop during the day and prepared for my college entrance exams at night, alone." Then he added, still more virtuously, to irritate her after her snobbish question, "I found it profitable. I entered with the highest examination average ever recorded at the time."

"Well, I'm glad it turned out so well since you had to do it that way anyhow," August retorted, sweetly. She was going to be his enemy, a friendly one, of course, but an enemy nevertheless, and she was letting him know it. She was not going to be impressed by anything he said or did. He was only to be put up with temporarily – the way one puts up with a plumber come to repair a stubborn leak. She turned unexpectedly to Fenton and said, "Mr. Abbott is probably expecting a mint julep instead of tea. Everyone in the South is supposed to do nothing but sit around all afternoon drinking mint juleps. He'll be disappointed. I don't think Addie knows how to make one. But I can call O'Smyre out of the greenhouse and see if he knows." She stood up as if she really were going to call her mother's gardener.

Dumfounded, Fenton half arose to restrain her, but Walter Abbott answered instantly, in a warm and patient tone, as if he were speaking to a very small and aggravating child, "I'm really much more curious about the raw corn liquor you are reputed to swill like water in this region, Miss Chadley. You wouldn't have the family fruit jar hidden in a handy place, would you?" He looked about with interest as if he expected August to produce a jug from under one of the chairs.

August turned on him in surprise and for an instant she lost her composure and opened her mouth to speak, and then emitted only a gasp of indignation. "We're all out of corn just now," she said, "but I'll see that we have a fresh supply tomorrow – if you can wait." Her head went up and she stared angrily down at him, still seated comfortably in his chair, observing her with tolerant amusement. Then as Susie struggled onto the patio with the large tea tray, she caught the door before it swung back and escaped into the house.

"There's no apology necessary, Mr. Chadley," Walter said quickly, when Susie had gone and Fenton was trying to speak; "we're going to manage quite all right, August and I." He laughed and took a slice of the caramel cake August had wheedled for their tea. "I'm really not worth her sacrificing this treat, you know."

Fenton stirred his tea. "You're very generous, Mr. Abbott," he said quietly and then he looked away. His eyes had begun to tear. He was not yet strong and his first weeks home from the hospital had not been restful. Scenes, or the anticipation of them, unnerved him. He dreaded now having to speak to Gilberta, as he knew he must, on the matter of Addie's conduct about the rooms for Mr. Abbott and Ralph.

Without meaning to be rude, he hurried tea to manage time to see Gilberta before dinner. Then he escorted Mr. Abbott up the circling black stair to the gallery and the guest chamber to the south.

"I hope you'll be comfortable," he said, "there's a desk, though it isn't a large one. Mrs. Chadley will be happy to make any changes you wish in the arrangements. Please don't hesitate to speak to her."

Walter thanked him and he was about to go, when Walter looked about the spacious, quiet room and said, "I don't seem to see my bag, do you?"

"Perhaps it's in your dressing room," Fenton suggested, and indicated the direction.

But Walter's modest valise was not there, nor in any closet. Fenton's face sobered. "I'm so sorry, Mr. Abbott," he said. "My orders seem to have been disregarded. Please excuse me. Your luggage will be brought immediately."

He left Walter watching him from the doorway and went down the gallery to Gilberta's apartment. For a moment, he hesitated before her door. Then he knocked sharply. "I should like to speak to you," he said, when she answered from inside. He stood waiting for her to admit him.

"Now?" she asked, opening the door. She began to frown. She wanted time for her bath in a leisurely fashion.

"Yes," he said simply. She hesitated a moment and then nodded for him to come in.

Inside, the long silks along her windows billowed lightly with the draft from the open door. The room was fragrant and pale, all its fabrics in tints of greenish blue, an oddly calm and restful room for such a restless nature.

"I've been terribly embarrassed before Mr. Abbott in this matter of his room," Fenton stated directly. "I want to be certain that the fault lies with Addie before I take further steps." As he said it his voice rose and his tone took on a sharp quality not usual with him. "I have seen Mr. Abbott to the guest room in the south wing, where I sent Addie with his bag; but, for some reason I cannot imagine, his bag is not there."

"Mr. Abbott will find his clothes laid out for him in the small room my mother always occupied," Gilberta said. She had placed her gardening gloves in a small hamper in her dressing room and was walking back toward Fenton as she said it. "Is there any reason for Mr. Abbott not being comfortable in that room? It's near the service from the kitchen if he should wish anything." There was a stubborn hostile expression on her face which told Fenton she had countermanded his orders to Addie deliberately.

"I wish Ralph to occupy that room," he said.

Gilberta looked directly into his eyes for a long moment. "Then I hope you are prepared to find me other servants when Addie and Susie leave." She turned then and, with a shrug meant to suggest indifference and resignation, she started toward her hangers to select something cool for dining.

"I am afraid I do not understand you," Fenton said hardly.

"You will when you put a colored boy in the house for Addie and Susie to wait upon," Gilberta answered coldly without turning around. She pulled the mechanical racks out of the closet and ran her hand along the center release to withdraw a peach crepe gown with a single brown flower painted low on the skirt. "Will you excuse me?" she asked, as if there had been no disturbing conversation at all in the room. She moved toward her dressing room.

"May I ask where you intended putting Ralph – if not in the small guest room?" Fenton insisted.

"The storage room next to O'Smyre's toolroom has been

cleaned out and waiting for a week. There's a comfortable bed and August's old chest from her playroom, and the linen is as clean as any we are using." Gilberta shook the dress over her arm impatiently. It was wrinkling. She had a satisfied righteous set about her face and her head was high and challenging.

Fenton walked to the pull on the wall near the door and jerked it three times. It was Addie's signal.

"Would you prefer to tell Addie to remove Mr. Abbott's bag from the small room and take it to him in the south room or shall I?" His face was flaming and he thrust his handkerchief up against his watering left eye and wiped at it savagely. His fingers trembled as he brought them to his side and he stood facing Gilberta in choking indignation. The pulse at his throat beat visibly against his tight collar.

There was a soft tap at the door.

"Come in, Addie," called Fenton. And with her mouth a little ajar with surprise and the instant anticipation of trouble, Addie entered. She had never before seen Mr. Chadley in Mrs. Chadley's rooms. "Yes sir, Mr. Chadley, sir," she mumbled and looked quickly toward Gilberta for reassurance.

"Mr. Chadley wishes Mr. Abbott to be put in the south guest room, Addie. The little colored boy who is coming tomorrow will sleep in the small room," Gilberta said coldly. "Please fetch Mr. Abbott's things to him." Her mouth moved with a sudden twitch over the full lower lip as she finished speaking. She was calm and quite still, her dinner gown limp over her arm; but there was a feeling of violence moving through her as if she were about to pick up a weapon suddenly and strike Fenton without a word. Fenton did not return her glance. His attention was upon Addie.

"If these plans do not meet with your approval, Addie, yours and Susie's, you are perfectly free to leave Dunmeade this evening after dinner and I will give you your wages for the next month. You may discuss the matter with Susie and come to my study with your answer just after coffee."

Addie stared at Fenton a moment and then closed her mouth

and nodded dumbly. She nodded to Gilberta again and backed out the door.

When she was gone, Gilberta said to Fenton, still standing stiffly in the middle of the room: "I hope you have made some arrangements for his meals." She meant Ralph. "I don't think he will be very welcome in the kitchen, assuming that Addie and Susie accept your bullying ultimatum."

"He will be served with me in my study," Fenton replied. He met Gilberta's eyes and for a moment an overwhelming sense of sadness came over him. They had come to an estrangement he would never have imagined possible. He had counted so upon her support in this kindly duty, this willing repayment to Isaiah for all his care and love. He moved to leave, hoping Gilberta would say one understanding word; but she was silent. Then as he turned the knob to the door, she spoke.

"I suppose it was too much to expect that you would consider August; she is not your child. But I am your wife. You might have had some concern for me when you decided to put a Negro across the hall from my bedchamber."

In horror, Fenton stood facing the blank door, squeezing the knob in his fingers for support. He could not turn it or move to leave.

"I shall bolt my door each night," Gilberta finished, "and I shall instruct August to do the same."

The blood drained swiftly down from Fenton's head and he felt himself sicken.

"I forbid you to do such a thing," he whispered, almost inaudibly, "I forbid you." And, ill, he managed to leave the room and go to his own.

Down the gallery, Fenton heard Mr. Abbott whistling as he dressed.

As they dined that evening, there was not a word, not a glance, not even an awkward silence to suggest that there had been discord and distress in the house only an hour before.

Watching Mrs. Chadley as she quietly ordered the service, Walter thought of the serene and graceful ladies of the medieval tapestries with their household pursuits woven into their hands, and their faces smiling, vacant and beautiful.

After coffee, Addie came to tell Fenton that she and Susie wished to remain at Dunmeade. She stood before Fenton with a mournful droop to her features and declared that neither of them had thought of leaving, that only Mr. Chadley's dissatisfaction with their service could send them away.

"Thank you, Addie," Fenton replied, "I'm very glad that you want to help me with young Ralph. You'll be very proud of him one day and I shall not forget any kindness you do him." He said it deliberately, fully aware that she had not mentioned Ralph.

"Yes sir, Mr. Chadley," mumbled Addie, softly, not looking at Walter Abbott, who had discreetly moved to examine the book titles in Fenton's library. When Fenton seemed to have no more to say to her, she backed out of the study and closed the door.

"I think we should be careful, Mr. Chadley," Walter said, when they were alone, "not to isolate this boy. We aren't trying to prove anything, you know. We're only tutoring him to stand his college entrance exams. He must have some companionship and recreation."

"Yes," replied Fenton, "I have been thinking of that. I am going to speak to young Billy Pickett about taking Ralph fishing. Billy goes out to a lake owned by the city. Ralph is accustomed to fishing and hunting and getting out in the woods and I don't want him to feel that he is unnaturally confined here in the house."

Walter nodded. Mr. Chadley had not understood him. He thought of saying it another way, of saying straight off. "Mr. Chadley, I don't think we should separate Ralph from his own people. I don't think you will be helping him that way." But Fenton's almost eager, hopeful expression silenced him.

"I think getting out in the afternoons and going fishing with Billy will solve the problem of recreation, don't you?" Fenton asked.

"Yes," agreed Walter, "that will help a great deal."

"It's been very nice of you to consider this matter with me, Mr. Abbott," Fenton said suddenly, "I'm very grateful to you." He lifted his head a little, as he did when he was self-conscious.

"I don't know that you will understand this, Mr. Abbott," he continued, "but your presence here has something of the feeling of a reunion for me." He blushed and explained, "A Professor Hanley from the university lived with us for many years, and, in fact, wrote his paper for his doctorate in the very room you are occupying. He tutored my brother Lesley and me." Fenton smiled and then added with a certain shyness, "I hope that you will be able to get on with your researches too."

Walter did not answer. If he could have left Dunmeade then, without having spent one night under its roof, without having progressed any further in an association with a family which had begun to involve his emotions in an odd and restricting way, he would have done so and been grateful for his escape. But he could not leave. He could not leave Fenton.

"If you will excuse me," he said, almost rudely, "there are some notes I would like to make before I go to bed." He stood up. He had not made even a perfunctory polite reply to Fenton's innocent and entirely complimentary comment.

"Good night, Mr. Abbott," Fenton said, rising also. In some way he seemed to have offended Mr. Abbott and he did not know how. "I hope you rest well," he said stiffly. "You may breakfast at any hour you wish. The servants are up from seven."

Half an hour before Ralph's train was due from the East, August found Walter Abbott reading in the patio and said, "My uncle would like to know if you would mind going with me to the station. He isn't very well today. He's still resting."

Walter stood up and put his book in the chair seat. It occurred to him that Mrs. Chadley might take her husband's place without sacrificing more than thirty minutes of her time from her flowers;

but he answered August agreeably, "Of course. I'll be glad to go with you."

"Thank you," August said, "I'll tell my uncle and meet you at the car. O'Smyre will be backing it out in just a few minutes." She nodded toward the garage.

Walter went out to the car.

"Do you know the boy we are going to meet?" he asked O'Smyre.

"No sir, I don't; but Miss August will recognize him for you," O'Smyre replied, thinking that Walter was concerned over identifying Ralph. "You just go right on up on the platform with her. Yes, sir." O'Smyre smiled at him in the driver's mirror and nodded his head.

"Thank you," Walter said.

"I used to teach out at the college," O'Smyre confided, after a pause. He was referring to the college where Ralph would go. He watched in the mirror for August's approach. When he saw her, he began to back out the car. "Horticulture was my subject," he finished.

"That's very interesting," Walter said. "Have you given up teaching entirely?"

"Yes, sir. I spent fifteen years out at the college. Then I came here to work for Mrs. Chadley."

"And you like private work better?" Walter asked.

O'Smyre smiled at him in the mirror. "Well, sir, it pays better."

"Yes, I imagine it does," Walter agreed.

O'Smyre got out and held the door for August. Then they drove to the station.

Once on the way, Walter turned from observing the store fronts to find August looking at him intently. She colored, and Walter said in the awkward silence, "I'm rather complimented that you'd let me come with you, Miss Chadley. I was afraid I'd offended you yesterday afternoon."

August ignored his reference to the teatime incident.

"It was Uncle Chad who asked you to come," she reminded him.

Walter smiled. "You might have objected; but you didn't, apparently."

"I couldn't go alone, could I?" she retorted. She glanced at him with an expression of incredulity and scorn. Then she turned conspicuously to gaze out her window at the thickening traffic as they drove through the warehouse district.

At the parking terrace around the station, O'Smyre carefully eased the big car into a space.

"Please hurry – the train is already in!" August commanded Walter. Without waiting for him, she jumped out of the car and ran off through the station.

She was climbing the steps to the platform, when Walter caught up. At the top, she paused and tried to determine the direction of the coaches. Then she walked down the platform toward the end of the train.

"There he is," she said. "He's already out."

Ralph was standing apart from the knot of passengers struggling with boxes and valises at the exit of his coach. Walter hurried behind August and involuntarily raised his hand to wave and beckon, but the boy turned away at that moment to look in another direction and shift his suitcase to his other hand. Then August came up behind him.

"Here we are, Ralph," she said clearly, as if she were speaking up to someone deaf. With a jerk Ralph turned to face the voice and Walter saw the quick passage of a look of terror which crossed his face as he snatched off his stiff new straw hat and bobbed his head up and down in recognition of August. He did not move his eyes to Walter until she said, "We have the car back in the parking section. Mr. Abbott will go with you to get the rest of your things in the baggage room if you want him to." August looked at Walter meaningfully.

"How do you do, Ralph," Walter said nicely, "Mr. Chadley wasn't feeling very well this afternoon. I came in his place. I'm from out of town, too."

"Yes sir." Ralph murmured. He did not look straight at Walter.

"Well," asked August again, "do you have to get any more baggage from the station?"

"No, ma'am," answered Ralph slowly, moving his head back to August obediently, yet not raising his eyes. "Papa said the trunk wouldn't get here for two or three days, thanking you just the same, ma'am." He stood with his straw hat in one hand and his wicker suitcase in the other waiting for August to tell him what she wanted him to do next.

"Then we'll be going," she said, and she walked off rapidly down the platform toward the steps to the street level. Ralph stood waiting for Walter to start too. "Can you manage that?" Walter asked, nodding to the wicker suitcase.

"Yes sir, thanking you all the same, sir," Ralph murmured respectfully. He was ready to go. He kept his eyes just below Walter's face.

Resigned, Walter started forward alone toward the car. After a few steps he heard Ralph following behind him.

In the foyer at Dunmeade, after August had directed Ralph to Fenton's study where Fenton was waiting, she said to Walter Abbott, "I wanted you to go with him to the baggage room for his trunk because it would have saved time. Colored people have to wait." She said it very patiently and observed him with a kindly superior expression.

"It's all just a big nuisance, isn't it?" Walter commented, very sympathetically. "I suppose one of us will have to go back again with O'Smyre when the trunk arrives. It will be the same situation again, won't it?"

August thought a moment. Then she answered, "No, I don't think anyone will have to go back. Uncle Chad will call up and have it delivered."

"That's good," Walter said, as if he were relieved. "Prejudice demands a great deal of extra effort sometimes, doesn't it?"

August did not reply. She started up the stair to her room.

As she neared the gallery, Walter moved into the center of the stair well beneath her.

"Miss Chadley?" he called softly. August paused with her hand on the curve of the black iron banister.

"Miss Chadley," he said, "you really don't mind my talking to you as if you were an adult, do you?"

August hesitated. She looked down at him a moment in silence and then she said primly, "Say anything you like, Mr. Abbott. I make allowances."

Walter smiled. "Thank you, Miss Chadley. It's nice of you to tell me."

August went on to her room.

Inside, she stood with her back stretched against the closed door. Her fingers felt down the frame and fastened on the molding. She pinched it firmly and steadily.

When he had heard the car leave the grounds for the station, Fenton had descended from his darkened bedroom to sit quietly in his father's old wing chair in the study and await Ralph's arrival at Dunmeade.

He waited with his back to the windows and his eyes closed, noting only the soft chimes of the half-hour and thinking of nothing. Then, as the minutes had passed into an hour, impatience and excitement had begun to grow in him. He stirred and listened for car wheels on the drive. Gilberta's hostile and uncharitable attitude had depressed and unnerved him. He felt alone in his undertaking. He roused himself and shuddered slightly, as if he expected the motion to shake off the self-pity which threatened to overcome him. At times, an almost insupportable longing for the spent days of his boyhood filled Fenton, the days when his father had ordered the life of Dunmeade and all of them had been secure in that care – Isaiah and Professor Hanley and even Lesley, who had rebelled against it. Thinking thus, he did not hear the car when at last it made the turn through the gates and passed on to the rear of the house. Voices were already in the foyer when he arose from his chair. He walked to the door and opened it to hear Ralph's strange, timid voice inquire, "Which way is it, Miss August? Begging your pardon, ma'am . . ." And then August's clear reply, "Just ahead down the corridor. Don't you remember? I thought you used to live here."

Fenton stiffened, poising to assume his role of master of the house and welcome his strange young guest.

"Come in, Ralph," he said, cordially, and was about to stand aside at the door so that the Negro boy might enter when suddenly he remembered and, confused, went ahead into the study. "I hope you had a nice journey. How is Isaiah? How is Maude?" He was conscious of his rush of questions and of Ralph's bewildered expression, but his confusion had made him awkward and he had lost the little ease he had summoned for his greeting.

"Everybody is just fine, Mr. Fenton," Ralph answered, "just fine. Papa sends his respects." He looked down at his feet self-consciously. He was still holding his new hat in one hand and his wicker suitcase in the other.

"You must be tired," Fenton said, quickly, at the sight of Ralph's stooped shoulders and touching respectful posture. He was eager to be hospitable and kind. "I'll take you to your room," he said; "you may rest awhile and then we'll have a little supper together right down here. I want to tell you all about our plans. Mr. Abbott, the gentleman who met you with Miss August, is going to help with your studies. He's a teacher. He wants to prepare you for your examination." Fenton smiled and lingered a moment, expecting Ralph to reply, to make some pleased response. But the boy said only, "Yes sir," and continued to stand with his eyes lowered, until, puzzled at his docile, resigned air, Fenton started reluctantly out of the study. Ralph waited a moment, then he followed, discreetly keeping a few steps behind Fenton as he had kept behind Walter Abbott from the station to the car.

At the curving stair, Fenton stopped and looked up to the gallery indicating the direction they would take. "Your father once occupied the room you'll have, Ralph," he said, trying again to draw some response from the boy. "He could keep an ear out for any rumpus Mr. Lesley and I made and it was near his kitchen. There's a back stair just next to it."

Ralph had already murmured "Yes, sir," behind him before Fenton realized the suggestion in what he had said. An almost painful heat began to spread through him. Carefully he climbed the steps, guiding himself by the cold banister. "There's a back stair just next to it," his mind repeated. He could not look back at Ralph. At the top, he paused and tried to speak; but he could think of nothing to say. He moved down the gallery and Ralph followed. At the door to the little room, he said, at last, "I hope you'll feel at home here. . . ."

The last episode of the day took place at twilight in the sycamore grove beyond Mrs. Chadley's garden, where Walter Abbott went to rest against a tree trunk and reiterate his resolution to limit his interests at Dunmeade to the performance of his duties as tutor, and the objective and scientific observation of the family's life.

He was watching the parade of homeward-bound citizens beyond on the sidewalk when a young man walked into the drive and stood looking down at him and said, "I suppose you're the Yankee professor." He was carrying something in a large brown paper sack which he hugged to him in the curve of his arm. He wore duck trousers laced tight to his thin hips and his hair was cut close in a military stubble.

"I am Mr. Abbott," Walter answered, nettled.

"Well, you're the Yankee professor Mr. Chadley hired to teach the colored boy, aren't you?" the young man insisted gazing down at him solemnly.

"I am from New York State," Walter said, with some heat, "but I am not a professor."

"Well, that's your problem," the young man said easily, "all

I'm interested in is making certain you're the party I'm to give this to." He pushed out his parcel in both hands to show Walter and at the movement there was a distinct gurgling sound.

"What is it?" demanded Walter suspiciously, making no move to accept the package.

"White Lightning," was the prompt answer. "August said you asked her to get you a jar." He parted the top of his sack and carefully withdrew a fruit jar of colorless liquid. "You asked her to get it, didn't you?" he asked worriedly. "This is bootleg stuff, you know. My Uncle Hartley would beat my pants off if he ever found out I went after . . ."

Walter waved him to silence and took the jar from him. "Have no fear. Your secret will be safe with me," he promised seriously. "And I am a man of my word, despite my place of birth and calling." He looked up into the young man's face. "And to whom am I indebted for this favor?" he inquired.

"What?" the visitor asked, frowning as he struggled to understand.

"I said I don't think I caught your name," Walter repeated.

"Pickett," the young man supplied – and then he smiled and suddenly put out his hand – "Billy Pickett. You can call me Billy." Then he added, "But you aren't as old as I thought you were."

Puzzled, Walter shook hands and did not struggle to understand how his age conditioned his calling his new friend by his Christian name.

Billy sat down.

"What shall I do with this?" Walter asked.

"Drink it," Billy answered, surprised. Then another thought occurred to him. "Oh," he said, relieved, "you mean what do you do to age it? Use chips. That's what most folks do."

"Thanks," Walter replied. He had been about to confess that he did not drink but now he patted the fruit jar affectionately. "I imagine this will provide me sorely needed consolation at times."

"It sure will," Billy agreed. "It beats gin all hollow. Doc Langley sawed off a man's leg with it once. I mean the doc poured a pint down him and then went to work. There was a little something wrong with the tractor and it backed up and rolled over this man's leg." Billy plucked at a tuft of moss on the ground as he imparted this testimony.

"Well, I am not expecting to need a painkiller," Walter protested mildly, "but I suppose one never knows. It'll be good to have on hand."

"It sure will," Billy agreed again. "Things aren't very lively around here." He jerked his head suggestively toward the house. "You can prime yourself with a little nip in your room and enjoy the conversation a little better. You can sneak down to Beaver Alley once in a while though, if you have to."

"What is Beaver Alley?" Walter inquired and then, at the incredulous look on Billy's face, he knew.

"I wouldn't advise your going down there unless you were obliged to," Billy advised. "Mr. Fenton is a very fine man and certainly has always been my friend, but he is not a man to understand some things and he might fire you."

"I'm sure he would," Walter murmured. "He'd probably consider me unfit to reside under the same roof with his wife and daughter." He kept his face solemn and stared moodily ahead.

"Well I don't know about Mrs. Chadley," Billy said. "She's a married lady. But he thinks August is the innocent little Lord Jesus come again and he might get stewed up for her sake and fire you without notice."

"That would be unfortunate for me," Walter confessed. "I have made my plans for the summer and I would prefer not having to change them suddenly."

"I don't blame you," approved Billy. "Besides, you can probably manage to get along with August until the time is up and then you'll have your dough and can leave."

"Is August difficult to get on with?" Walter asked innocently.

"Oh no," Billy said, "she leaves you strictly alone usually. But she made it perfectly clear to me this morning that she particularly has no use for you. She is in hopes that the corn will make you sick." Then he glanced at Walter with frank admiration and added: "But I can see you know your way around and she is going to be disappointed. It will do her good." His voice had a wistful note in it and Walter quickly gathered that Billy had felt the bruise of August's will upon him.

Suddenly, he popped up and Walter struggled up from the ground beside him.

"I have to get home now. My mother will start calling up people all over Newtown," Billy said and blushed. "She's very nervous. She's always imagining the worst."

"What is the worst?" Walter asked.

"Oh, it varies," Billy said, "but most of the time it's getting hit on the head by a mill hand and being robbed."

"Does that happen often around here?" Walter asked.

"It never has that I know of," Billy replied, "but my mother says that that's no reason it won't." He seemed to be tolerant of his mother's fears and quite undisturbed by the restrictions they placed upon his activities.

"Would your mother be nervous if Ralph went fishing with you this summer? I think Mr. Chadley is going to ask you to take him."

"The colored boy?" Billy asked.

"Yes," Walter answered.

"My mother is nervous even when I take my father out fishing," Billy laughed. "She's sure he's going to rock the boat and drown me. She never worries about him, only me." Then he answered, "Sure, I'll be glad to take the colored boy. I'm going tomorrow morning."

Walter nodded. "Good," he said. "You come by and pick him up. I'll tell Mr. Chadley. Going fishing will do him more good than a Latin lesson. What do you think?"

Billy grinned. "Sure," he said. Then he stuck out his hand. "I'm glad to have met you," he muttered and bolted down the grove to the street.

Walter arranged his parcel under his arm and strode toward the house. As he climbed the stair to his room to leave it, August came out of the drawing room and stood watching him. At the top, he turned around and waved his hand and called, "Thanks." Then he patted the package and nestled it against him suggestively.

"You're welcome," she replied pleasantly and smiled.

Walter went to his room and closed the door.

One morning, toward the end of Ralph's first week at Dunmeade, August went out to the drive where Billy sat parked in his Uncle Hartley's truck waiting for Ralph, and said hospitably, "Don't you want to come in? Addie will give us a cold drink."

"Thanks just the same," he answered, "I guess we ought to get on as soon as possible. I have to get the truck to the warehouse before noon. Is Ralph going to be long?"

"I'm sure I don't know," August said a little sharply.

"Gee," said Billy, eying her, "who ate your cupcake?"

"I don't know what you mean," August said, huffily.

"Nothing. Skip it." Billy jangled the keys on the dashboard. "Want to come along with us?"

"I can't," August answered, putting her foot up on the short running board.

"Why not? We don't mind girls," Billy smiled, "especially one." He looked boldly at August until she turned her eyes away.

"Well, I just can't. You know that," she repeated a little impatiently. She removed her foot from the running board and examined her sandal carefully.

"I don't know why," Billy argued. "You can swim if we turn over."

"Well that would be a fine sight, wouldn't it?" August blurted in exasperation – "Me out fishing by myself with you and a colored boy!"

Billy looked down at the steering wheel. August stared indignantly at his close-cropped head. At last Billy said, "Well, I can tell you one thing I've found out – if you didn't look at

Ralph you wouldn't know he was colored." He raised his head defiantly and stared at August with accusation.

"Well, why are you looking at me!" she blazed. "Everybody around here thinks I've got something against him." She fumbled with her dress buckle in agitation and then finished lamely, "Well, I just think it doesn't look right."

Billy's face drooped and sorrow was written all over it. He had not meant to offend August or blame her for anything. There was nothing to blame her for, of course. She was a girl. He should have used his head and not argued with her when she said at first that she could not go.

"Look, August," he apologized contritely, "I didn't mean to make you mad. I'm just dumb."

August kept her face down and kicked her sandal up and down in the gravel.

"That's all right," she said.

Neither of them spoke for a few minutes. Then Billy, intent on leaving with the air clearer, said cheerfully, "Oh well, it'll all probably turn out all right and then he can go up North and get a job."

"That's right," August agreed quickly. And then she heard Ralph's feet hurrying across the flags of the patio. She backed away from the truck and started walking toward her mother's greenhouse. She was quite a distance away when Ralph got in the cab of the truck beside Billy. August stood watching Billy start the roaring motor. Then as they turned into the street on their way, she waved. "Good luck," she called, trying to make them hear her over the racket of the engine. Billy leaned out and waved back, and then she saw him turn to Ralph and uncertainly Ralph lifted his hand too.

August swallowed. Then, very self-consciously, she waved again.

She walked back to the patio and sat down. It was cool with the early damp still on the flags. The sun was not high enough to strike them yet. She tapped her foot and started herself rocking in the chair. Then she got up abruptly and went into the house. Mr. Abbott came down the hall from Fenton's study.

"Your uncle is just telephoning to see if some friends of yours named Willetts will let me swim in their lake," he said to her. "We've let Ralph off until noon. Mr. Chadley thought you wouldn't mind directing me out there if you were going riding this morning. He says the lake is quite near where you go." He waited for her to reply, to consent. Then, when she seemed to hesitate, he excused her quickly, "But don't trouble unless you were planning to ride anyway. Mr. Chadley was under the impression that you were, and he suggested I drive us out in his car."

"Well, I hadn't really decided," August said, a little surprised and also a little resentful. Unconsciously, she objected to the freedom Fenton was allowing Mr. Abbott with the car. Then she said, "But I suppose it'll be too hot this afternoon so I may as well go this morning."

"Please don't go just to be obliging me," Walter insisted, "I can swim some other time."

August flushed. "I'm not going to oblige you, Mr. Abbott," she said, "I ride two or three times a week."

There was a pause. Then Walter smiled encouragingly and asked, "Well?"

"I'll change now," August said in confusion and went quickly up the stair.

When she came down in her habit Mr. Abbott was waiting for her in the patio. They walked to the garage and Walter backed out Fenton's car and August got in beside him.

As they drove down the block, August said, "It would really be easier if I were to drive. It's a little complicated getting out of town."

"Oh that's all right," he assured her, "I'll follow your directions. I have to learn to get around if I'm going to be chauffeuring us this summer."

Peeved and frustrated, August sat back. "I drive quite well," she said; "you needn't be afraid. And it's not against the law if an older driver is with me."

"I'm sure you do," Walter replied easily, following her hand as she indicated a turn to the highway. "I'm sure you do many things well. I'm very anxious to see some of your drawings."

August did not reply. For the next four miles she mechanically directed him through an underpass and then from the highway onto a country road.

"This is pleasing landscape, isn't it?" Walter commented politely.

"Yes," murmured August, only half hearing him. Her mind was stubbornly engaged in preparing another plan to get her into the driver's seat.

"You'd better let me take the wheel," she suggested helpfully after she had instructed him to make a turn off the country road into a private lane, "it's an awful pig-path from here on. It twists about like a hairpin." She looked at him sideways.

"I'll creep," he said, unperturbed.

Disgruntled, August snatched at a spray of honeysuckle brushing the window. She would direct him to the lake and then she would drive herself to the stables and pick him up again after her ride. She jerked at her leather vest and drew in another half inch on her wide polo belt. She was wearing her best linen breeches and the soft English boots Fenton had had made for her. Her hair was twisted in a short pigtail braid with a narrow velvet ribbon tying the ends in a string bow. She was handsome and she knew it. She leaned back half resting against the door, eying him occasionally with a canny smile. But Walter kept his eyes on the rutted dirt road crooking and turning, as August had said, "like a hairpin." His face was expressionless. He only nodded when at length she said, "It's around this turn. Use your brake. People have run right into the water."

When he had stopped the car, he turned to her and asked, "How are you going to get to the stables from here?" His brows were lifted in a slightly quizzical expression. His tone was one of curiosity, not concern.

"I'll drive myself," she said, "it's only down the road." She reached over to turn on the ignition again; but Walter quickly pulled out the keys and slipped them into a little leather pouch hung about his neck from a cord. "For my valuables," he said pleasantly, patting the little pouch and ignoring the rage and frustration on August's face. He got out of the car and looked about the landscape admiringly. The lake lay in a hollow perhaps a quarter-mile across. Opposite, the hillside rose, green and thick with pines and wild berry bushes. Here and there, as the sun crossed the stragglers by the edge, shadows darkened the surface of the water. Directly below the car was a small bathhouse and before it a little beach of white sand dumped there without plan. Walter opened the car trunk and took out his parcel containing his bathing trunks and towel. Then he poked his head back in the car and smiled at August and said, "Taking a dip with me or walking to the stables?" August stared ahead at the road winding around another tree-shadowed curve and losing itself beyond the thickets. She did not answer. Her chin was high and rigid and her eyes were wide and unblinking. She sat as if she were holding her breath. "Well," said Walter, cheerfully, "if you want me for anything" – and he waved his free hand back to indicate the direction of the bathhouse – "I'll be right below." Then he turned and loped off down the decline to the water.

When she was sure he had reached the bathhouse, she put her head against the cold metal frame of the window and quietly wept out her humiliation and anger. She hated Walter Abbott – his face, his easy-swinging big body, his voice with its hard Yankee twang, everything about him. Into her mind returned a painful memory. She saw again a gang of catcalling neighborhood boys streaming into the Barrons' back yard toward the clubhouse piano crate, with Earl Barron's yellow Yankee head leading, while she watched, deserted, trying to hide herself in the sycamore grove. Her tears stopped and she sat up and shook her head. She looked quickly toward the lake to see if Mr. Abbott had gone into the water yet. He was standing in the sand stretching and slapping his naked chest heartily. She waited until he had waded in, then she opened her door and slipped out of the car and into the thicket and trees by the roadside. When she had rounded the curve and was out of sight, she took off her tight boots and walked back onto the road in her sock feet. "He'll be sorry for this," she promised herself grimly as she made her way around the circle of the lake to the opposite shore.

Half an hour later she had climbed a distance up the wooded hillside and could look below at the little blot of white beach across the water. Mr. Abbott was swimming. She found a spot to spread a nest of leaves and sat down to wait for him to finish his dip and start looking for her. In the end he would try to find the stables, of course. He would pass the Willettses' house if he happened to turn left at the next forks, and ask directions. But if by chance he took the right road at the forks, he would wind back out to the Newtown highway and have to start over again. She watched him surface diving and cavorting in the water and smiled. He would worry when Pop Lindsey told him she had not been at the stables, that he had not seen her at all.

After a splashing race with himself to the middle of the lake and back, Walter slopped out of the water and spread his towel on the sand and stretched out to sun his back. August studied his figure. His legs were long and his neck and shoulders muscular and broad. His arms were stretched so that his hands were down against his knees. He was almost homely, she thought happily. She removed her socks and examined her feet. They were tender and swollen. She would have to soak them in salts when she got home. Feeling a blister, she wondered how long Mr. Abbott would dally before starting to look for her. He probably expected her to ride by on her horse to show off. With chagrin, she realized she had meant to do just that if things had not turned out as they had. She squirmed a little on her pillow of leaves. The damp from the ground was coming through. She stood up and felt under herself. Then she twisted around to examine her breeches. They were damp and stained from the oily green leaves. "Dern," she muttered and wiped at them with her handkerchief, but the stain did not come off. Absorbed with cleaning herself, she forgot Walter down on the warm sand. Suddenly, an automobile horn shattered the woodsy quiet and August straightened up to look out through the trees. A car had eased up behind their car and Walter was wrapping his towel about him and starting toward it. Then a girl in a blue bathing suit jumped out of the front seat and waved him back. Walter stopped and the girl continued toward him. The lady driving leaned out her window and said something to both of them. Then she backed the car away from the Chadleys' car and drove around it down the road. It was Mrs. Willetts. And the cow in the blue bathing suit was Jessie. August would have recognized her long neck and big hips a mile off. She cavorted clumsily across the beach and splashed into the water, squealing for Walter to follow.

August stood in her bare feet staring at them. She should have known that Jessie would bounce down the instant her father told her there was a man swimming around in her lake. She had probably skinned into her bathing suit right in the car to save time. She was jumping all over Mr. Abbott now, pretending she couldn't swim. With all the fat on her, she couldn't have sunk if she had tried! Mr. Abbott was surface-diving and coming up behind Jessie and yelling and splashing in as silly a fashion as she. The whole spectacle revolted August. She wiped at the soles of her feet and put on her soiled socks and squeezed into her boots. Then she started down the hillside and around the end of the lake back to the car. Her feet were blistering and she was about to cry. She wanted to go home.

She was opening the door to the car when Walter and Jessie saw her. "Hey," yelled Jessie, "come on in." August did not answer her. Walter stood up with his knees in the water and waited. August slammed the door and sat there, not looking at either of them. "What's the matter with her?" she heard Jessie ask him. Jessie was wearing a bathing cap over her ears and her voice was loud. Out of the corner of her eye, August saw Walter walk up the beach and pick up his towel and start for the car.

"Do you want to go now, August?" he asked politely, putting his head in the window.

"Mother will be waiting lunch," she said coldly.

"May we drop Miss Willetts? Her mother asked if we'd bring her home . . ." he said. He looked at August's dust-stained legs, Then he looked back at her face. August ignored his question.

"Just hurry, please, if you don't mind," she answered. Jessie was wading out of the water and coming to the car.

"Yes ma'am. Right away, ma'am," he said, smiling. He ran to the bathhouse to change.

"I'll sit on the floor in back, August, so I won't get the seat wet," Jessie murmured, getting in. August did not reply.

"Are you mad at me, August?" Jessie asked timidly from the back. She reached one arm up over the front seat and felt for August's shoulder.

"Don't be silly," August said, shrugging out from under Jessie's fingers.

There was a silence. Then Jessie said hopefully, "I think your visitor is very nice, August."

Walter was coming up the bank, dressed, with his wet suit rolled in his towel. He put it in the luggage trunk and got in the car. "You'll have to tell me which way," he reminded her softly.

"At the forks, turn left," she directed him, matter-of-factly.

Walter slowed down at the Willetts house. "This it?" he asked August. She only nodded.

"Thanks for bringing me home, August," Jessie said politely when she scrambled off the floor of the back seat. "Mother and I would like for you to come and bring Mr. Abbott for a picnic supper . . ." She looked imploringly at August.

"Thank you," murmured August.

"I enjoyed the swim, Jessie," Walter said and held out his hand.

Gratefully, Jessie took it and smiled. "Come out any time you want to," she invited him, warmly. "We'll be glad to have you just any time."

A mile beyond the Willetts house they passed the stables. The white sign shone in the noon sun, NEWTOWN RIDING ACADEMY.

Walter turned to August as he slowed down for directions to the highway. "I'm sorry about the car," he said, "your uncle asked me not to let you drive. I didn't know it was so far to the stables." He waited for her to say something. He glanced at her dusty legs. August kept her eyes ahead and did not answer. She wanted him not to talk, only to get her home quickly.

"I hope you enjoyed your ride," Walter said earnestly, "I would feel less badly if I knew you had." August ignored him.

They drove on in silence until they were in the city limits. Then Walter tried again, for the last time. "I'm really awfully sorry about the car," he repeated, "I thought the stables were quite near the lake. You aren't going to be angry forever, are you?"

"If you're afraid I'm going to tell on you, you needn't be. I don't tattle," August said. Then her voice broke and she jerked her head to look out at the traffic. The velvet ribbon had come untied at the end of her braid and her hair was unwinding slowly. She snatched at it savagely and shook the strands loose with her fingers.

"Look," said Walter, hardly, "let's understand each other." His chin was thrust out stubbornly and his face was flushed. "You don't have to threaten me about anything, Miss Chadley. I'm no happier being in your house than you are in having me there. I'm at Dunmeade only because Mr. Chadley pays me to do what I can for Ralph – which I hope will be adequate for Ralph's needs, of course. But there are a thousand other places I'd rather be this summer. Remember that, when you feel you're doing me a favor by having me around."

August's mouth trembled. "You may go tomorrow for all the good you'll do Ralph," she said softly.

"I hope you're wrong about that," Walter replied, turning in the gates of Dunmeade, "for Mr. Chadley's sake, if for no other reason."

August was silent. She got out of the car in the drive and then waited awkwardly for him to put up the car. Across the back garden in the patio, Fenton was watching Susie lay the cloth for luncheon.

"Billy Pickett telephoned," Fenton greeted them. "He said

they're breaking all the records for bass, so I let Ralph off for the remainder of the day. I didn't think you'd object, Mr. Abbott." And then before Walter could answer, he went on, "Mr. Willetts has rather an attractive place, don't you think?" He seemed a little shamefaced and anxious to change the subject. "Mercy, I've never seen you so disheveled, dear. Are you limping?" he asked August suddenly, looking at her soiled habit and dusty boots.

August smiled and glanced at Walter. "A horse rode me this morning, just for a change," she said, and then at Fenton's astonishment, she kissed him and added, "but I'll survive."

She turned to Walter. "There's a line in the little room next to O'Smyre's tool closet," she said. "You may use it to dry your suit and towel."

Walter nodded. Then he asked, "Could that horse have gone swimming in the Willettses' lake, Miss Chadley?"

For an instant August looked as if she were about to laugh. "I'm sure I don't know," she said stiffly, and she hurried in to change.

So the first month passed and the hot weeks of summer began and Fenton had Ralph breakfast with him in his apartment where Ralph read aloud the financial news before translating his Latin passage, which Mr. Abbott heard later.

In the evening Ralph and Mr. Abbott took a light supper together (in the patio in fair weather) and Ralph identified famous lines from famous English and American poems.

Ralph diligently followed his study schedule, and if he felt his isolation from Addie and Susie, and, at the same time, from the real life of Dunmeade, he gave no indication of it.

One morning, tucking the morning paper into Fenton's magazine rack, he said, "Mr. Chadley used to be very particular about washing down the highdaddy and bedposts in his room, Mr. Fenton. He set great store by a good soaping and waxing and plenty of rubbing. Women haven't got the hand for it." He looked pointedly at Fenton's chests and bed – the pieces which had been Mr. Chadley's and his father's before him, and which Fenton had never changed. Fenton followed Ralph's eyes around the room.

"They look dry, Mr. Fenton," he said.

Fenton cleared his throat. He did not know what to say. Ralph's comment was a reflection upon Gilberta's housekeeping.

"I believe Mrs. Chadley has a man in regularly to rub down the furniture and wax the floors. He is supposed to use some special preparation he has concocted for old furniture."

"Mr. Chadley's things always gleamed like anything even by the lamp on nights when the current wasn't going," Ralph said quietly.

Fenton sighed. "I can speak to Mrs. Chadley about using what you suggest," he offered.

"You don't have to do that, Mr. Fenton. I can do it – one little piece at a time of a morning. Nobody has to know." He looked seriously at Fenton. He understood that Fenton could not interfere with the housework without trouble. He looked longingly at the dull dark surface of wood across the foot of Fenton's bed, and then at his long hands hanging from the sockets of his wrists. He seemed to be pleading for some familiar occupation for them.

Fenton swallowed. "Won't it make rather a mess about?"

Ralph shook his head from side to side slowly. "No sirree, Mr. Fenton. I never spilled suds anywhere in the house in my whole life." Pride lifted his eyes to Fenton's and he nodded.

"Don't you think it would be better if we told Mrs. Chadley what you used on the furniture down at Prince River and let her have the regular man do it?" Fenton argued gently.

"He won't do it, Mr. Fenton. It takes a lot of elbow work and an easy hand – real soft and easy, over and over, 'long with the grain. I know." He moved his own hand back and forth slowly and rhythmically to show Fenton.

Fenton looked away. Then he mustered a kind of sternness to add force to his refusal. "Mr. Abbott says you should make a wonderful showing, if you can go on to the end as you've done so far. It will mean so much to your parents to have you enter with high marks. It will be something for you to be proud of all your life. I don't want you to become tired, Ralph. There's no reason for you to do any of the work around the house." As he finished he allowed the real understanding he felt to alter his tone so that he spoke kindly. He looked back to Ralph. The boy's face wore the sad resigned expression which had baffled Fenton so often in the time since his arrival.

"Yes sir," Ralph said docilely. Then he picked up his Latin primer from the stack of notebooks and texts he had brought in with him. He opened to the paragraph from Cicero which was his translation for the day. "I'll just ask you to help me a little bit with this before I have to read for the professor, Mr. Fenton, if you don't mind."

"Start," said Fenton. He sat back to listen. "First in Latin and then in English, please."

Ralph began reading monotonously and slowly.

For August, the heat of midsummer began an interlude of increasingly disturbing experiences. Mr. Abbott's presence in the house was a particular irritation to her. She longed at times to stand before him and scream and scream in long wailing undiminishing sounds signifying her irritation and impotence to remove him. But of course she could not. Instead she spoke to him in a sharp emotional way which made even her most reasonable retorts to his teasing sound irrational, as if blurted from a hopelessly distracted mind. Most unendurable was the persistence of her mind's concern with him. By day she paid a calculating attention to his every act and word in the hope of discovering some soothing fault in him. By night she dreamed of him in humiliating and degrading fantasies in which he emerged over and over again her conqueror. Enraged and unable with the return of consciousness to obliterate the visions of his intimate dream-acts, she would meet him at breakfast while Fenton took his tray with Ralph, and set out instantly to pick a quarrel.

"Haven't you heard from your family yet?" she would ask, as he put his mail aside, half hid by his plate. She was inordinately curious about his personal life and relationships and he had told her nothing. "Not today, no," he would answer politely.

"Doesn't your family miss you? Mine would write every day if I were far from home. Most other people's would too," she would taunt him, dipping into her melon, not looking at him. She had adopted an air that signified she considered him a peculiarly unadmirable type who knew no refinements and would never know any.

Mr. Abbott accepted her patronizing attitude with pretended indifference. From the time of her quarrel with him following their first trip to the Willettses' lake, he had tried to ignore her; but there was a demanding flirtatiousness beneath her hostility which forced him to listen and to look at her however much he wished to turn away. She had remarkable eyes, he thought, obliged at times to hold his glance against hers. They were not merely the dark purplish eyes of a pretty girl. They were the eyes of a creature within whom a conflict of some kind raged endlessly, for their expression changed with violent rapidity from almost hysterical joy to mournful despair in the space of a few minutes, according to some internal mood independent of their superficial attention. At times, alone with him in the patio, she looked at him as if she were about to attack him physically, not with the idea of injury, but with the strange tender desire of a beast about to suffocate its young by lunging against them. It excited Walter in a way he could not understand, until, embarrassed and impatient with himself, he would make some excuse and go suddenly to his room.

"She is only a child, a little girl," he would repeat over and over, messing through his papers distractedly, trying to take up his work and banish her from his mind, "I shouldn't react to her. She's just an aggravating child trying to get attention."

And then one afternoon Walter discovered that August was not just a child, not innocent, not harmless, but filled with curiosity subtly conditioned by prejudice and therefore ready for either love or hate.

On that afternoon it was quiet and breezes worried the sycamores hiding the grounds from the street. Addie and Susie were taking their afternoon off together to buy some bright pink voile on sale in Newtown. Mrs. Chadley had driven to see a display of rare plants artificially grown by a tubercular South American living east and south of Newtown in the sandy pine section. Fenton had taken Ralph to call on old Mr. Starburg who wanted to see Isaiah's boy and observe the result of Fenton's special care.

"After all," Mr. Starburg had reminded Fenton, "it was I who made the match between his parents – with your father's consent and co-operation, of course."

Even O'Smyre was away, not expected until sunset to water the grass. So except for Walter, who was studying in his room, August was alone in the house.

She went to the kitchen, discovered a strawberry mousse, and after filching a dishful started up the backstairs to her study. Halfway up she stopped to swallow a sampling spoonful, mashing it between her tongue and the roof of her mouth for the taste. Then she dawdled on to the top. A south breeze blew the sheer cascading drapery out into a fan before her as she passed the hall window.

The first room after the stairs was the small room her Grandmother de Ventura had used when she visited Dunmeade. It had never seemed to August a part of the house. No one had ever used it since – until now. She absently took another spoonful of cream and, as she swallowed, she observed the few objects in view through the half-open door. The night lamp had been moved from the candlestand beside the bed and placed on a small desk pulled out from the wall and set with its back to the foot of the bed, so that it was in the center of the room. This was Ralph's room. His things – whatever things a colored boy had – were in it. She stood looking, wondering what Ralph had in his room. Then she glanced up and down the hall, and listened. There was no sound of any other presence. Walter Abbott's door was closed. The soft periodic whir of the drapery blowing in the end window was the only faint disturbance. August put her dish down on the carpet, walked to Ralph's door and went in the room.

For a few moments she only stood in the middle of the floor and looked around at the furniture. It was all familiar to her. And it had only been rearranged slightly to give Ralph better light for his studying. She did not know quite what she had come to see, what she should look for, where she should search in the hope of finding what. She had never had any curiosity about the personal effects of anyone before. She did not know why she wanted to examine Ralph's room. Then she went to the chest of drawers near his bed and looked at the plain black comb-and-brush set on it. Beside them was a round collar box of fine leather, polished and hard. August raised the top. It was lavender watered silk inside. In it lay an assortment of cuff links and collar buttons and shoe laces. She picked up a gold cuff link. The monogram in fine flowing letters was M.C. It had been her grandfather's. Without wanting to be suspicious, August's mind went unconsciously to the question, "Did my grandfather give them to him — or did he take them when my grandfather died?" She picked up another pair. They were garnet and there was a tie pin to match. Fenton had had a tie pin of garnet. As she turned the stone in the light, a funny little physical pain began in her chest, a little squeezing sensation. This was Fenton's garnet pin. Where would Ralph ever go to wear such fine things? Why had they been given to him? It was silly. They would only be stolen from him. The Sunday paper had items every week about the knifings and robberies down in colored town on Saturday nights. Ralph wasn't going to live at Dunmeade forever.

She began to open the drawers to the chest one at a time. Two were empty. Two were slightly filled. The top one held Ralph's shirts. August looked at their clean white muslin. The shirts were handmade. She lifted out one and picked up a separate collar belonging to it. The cuffs of the shirt were double with fine handworked holes for his cuff links. Some of the shirt bosoms were hand-tucked with narrow fine rows of stitching. Astonished at their quality, she opened the pile of one-piece underwear stacked neatly in the next drawer and pulled out a garment from the middle. Perhaps he kept his best things on top and the everyday ones on the bottom, hidden. But the undergarments were made as carefully as the shirts, white and thin with handworked button holes and whipped back seams to keep them from raveling. Shocked and resentful, she replaced the lot and closed the drawers. Ralph's clothing was the clothing of a gentleman, not of a Negro country boy. It was improper for him to dress so. Nothing in her memory helped her to understand what she had found. She did not remember that Maude had made some of her baby dresses of batiste. She did not know that Maude had finished whole sets of table linens for Mr. Chadley. She did not know that her father Lesley had worn fine hand-pleated shirts which Maude had made from the same thin linen she had used to embroider Mr. Chadley's handkerchiefs. It did not occur to her that Maude had made these things for Ralph. It seemed to her only insolence in Ralph to affect such airs and affectations as wearing garnet cuff links and finely made shirts, wherever he had got them.

With resentment increased by her guilt at having wantonly rummaged through Ralph's personal belongings, she made one quick survey of the papers and books on his desk and started to leave. She was not interested really in his progress with his studies. She had no faith in him. It meant nothing to her that he learned quickly and was diligent. Negroes were emotional and untrustworthy. Ralph would get excited at his examinations and forget all he had been taught. He would fail, and all Fenton's time and trouble would have been for nothing. She picked up his Latin primer and looked at his lesson for that day. It was an excerpt from Caesar. She put it down and then she saw his Bible next to it. It was open with a half-written letter by it. August hesitated. Then she picked up his Bible and looked at the passage he had been reading. It was the thirteenth chapter of First Corinthians. Some of the lines were faintly underscored with ink long since faded. It was an old Bible, ragged at the creases of the binding. The lines nearest the end of the passage were most clearly marked. "When I was a child, I spake as a child, I understood as a child, I thought as a child: but when I became a man, I put away childish things." August's eyes ran back up the verses to the beginning. Someone had put a tiny ink star beside the first – "Though I speak with the tongues of men and of angels, and have not charity, I am become as sounding brass, or a tinkling cymbal." She read slowly down through the third verse, underlined faintly too, "And though I bestow all my goods to feed the poor, and though I give my body to be burned, and have not charity, it profiteth me nothing." She looked at the letter. Her fingers were perspiring. She picked it up and held it at one corner only. It was written in ink. Ralph's first letters home to Isaiah and Maude had been written on tablet paper in pencil.

Dear Papa and Mama [she read quickly]:

This day finds me in good health, hoping you are the same. Mr. Fenton is better daily and no one would know of his trouble to hear him talk. Miss Gilberta continues the same but she is nice to me if I come on her in the yard or anywhere.

Mr. O'Smyre took me to his house for Sunday last and I attended church with him and Mrs. O'Smyre. Mrs. O'Smyre cooked and while it was tasty it was not like home to me, Mama. You are the best in the world, Mama.

Miss Susie and Miss Addie treat me tolerably now, Mama, I tell them all about you, Mama. I try to make friends. Today they let me clean the floor spots with soda while Mr. Fenton was out. But he won't let me do nothing to Mr. Chadley's bedstead and things that need it so bad. I asked him like you told me to, Papa. I will ask again to be of some use soon, Papa.

Miss Susie asks to try her hand at shrimp batter like you make down home, Mama. So be so kind and put it down next letter, please Mama.

I have caught twenty-two bass up to now, Papa, but my friend Mr. Pickett has caught thirty, though some I thought undersize for pulling in. Mr. Fenton eats every one I bring home, Papa, with fried corn bread. He is just like you say, a fine man. He is just like Mr. Chadley in many ways. He is a good man. I continue grateful to him and try hard. He is like you say, Papa, my good friend, the best I have in the world.

I have acted the way you said, Mama, and stayed at a distance when in the company of Miss August and not done anything to frighten her. But I do not think it matters what I do, Mama. She has never been my friend. She doesn't change, Mama. She does not want to be a friend of a poor colored boy like me, Mama. But I will give her the handkerchiefs like you want me to on her birthday, Mama, hoping she will take no offense.

The professor continues the same. He asks me lots of questions about you, Papa, and Mr. Chadley. I like to hear him talk. You would not understand a word he says, Papa. He tells me about what the people up North . . .

And that was as far as Ralph had written.

August stared down at the letter and then she looked at the Bible. She turned its cover to the first flyleaf. On it was written, *Francis Prince Wortham*, and beneath, *Elizabeth Wortham Chadley*. At the bottom was inscribed in a fresher hand, *For Ralph Craig on his tenth birthday from his friend Marcus Chadley*. August flipped the leaves back to Ralph's place and replaced the letter as it had been.

She looked down at it, anger rising in her until she felt it knot itself in her throat. Confused, with a guilt she did not understand, she turned in a violent movement to put her back to the room and its contents – and saw, facing her, standing motionless against the doorframe with her dish of mousse in his hand, Mr. Abbott! When he had come, how long he had watched her, she did not know. He did not speak or move to leave, and for an instant she was too startled to do more than stare at him. Then abruptly she started forward to pass him and escape to her room.

"Was it here?" Walter asked softly, moving at the same time to halt her flight.

She stopped again and instinctively lifted her hand to push him aside. Then she dropped her arm and waited for him to move. She did not answer him.

"Did you look in his closet?" Walter questioned.

August did not speak. She swayed a little, almost imperceptibly, doggedly, feeling for escape.

"Perhaps it's in *my* room," Walter suggested. He did not smile, or make any gesture. He did not move. His eyes looked calmly into hers. There was no expression on his face. His tone was neither scornful, nor disapproving, nor amused.

They stood measuring each other, waiting, until suddenly there was a crackle of tire wheels on the drive outside and August glanced over her shoulder toward the open window. Then she said, her voice uneven with a kind of forced control, "Will you please stand aside. I want to go to my room."

Without turning his gaze from her, Walter took a step back into the hall and left the door free.

August walked swiftly past him and down the gallery.

Walter waited until she was inside her room. Then he looked at her dish of uneaten mousse. He went down the servants' stair with it and set it on the kitchen table. Then he went out in the patio and arranged a chair in the shade and sat down. O'Smyre was dragging the hose from the greenhouse to attach the lawn sprinkler. Mrs. Chadley was standing near her car giving some sort of instruction to Addie and Susie, who stood nodding with their arms full of store packages. Sunset was beginning beyond the grove of sycamores. Walter stretched back in his chair and closed his eyes. "I wonder what she expected to find in the boy's room," he thought. "Good Lord, how do they get that way down here? What happens to them? When does it all begin?"

He was shocked. But he was troubled, too. Reluctantly, long before the depressing scene he had just witnessed, he had come to pity August. He had begun to observe the loneliness of her life. It seemed to him that she was drifting alone inside the large sprawling house with no more aim to her voyage than to keep herself moving. She had an unanchored, solitary look about her for all the attention Mr. Chadley lavished upon her. She had no friends. She seemed to desire no social life of her own. What her activities were he did not really know. He had never heard her play the piano, though Mr. Chadley had told him she played as well as painted. He had asked to see her drawings, but when pressed she had declared that they were at her school where she had left them for the summer. As he had watched her more closely he had begun to see what it was that was wrong with her. Too soon she had put away childish things – if she had ever been a child at all. She did not know how to play with anyone, she did not even know how to communicate with another person except in an almost antagonistic, defensive way.

There was a tension about her from impulses held in check which should have been spent in a thousand natural harmless ways – in spontaneous laughter, in flirting with little boys, in primping and fussing with her hair and dressing up in her mother's clothes, in devouring bad novels surreptitiously by the bathroom light, in indulging in any one of a dozen understandable, childish things like any other growing girl. She seemed entirely devoid of spontaneity and the seriousness with which her every interest was watched and diagnosed, and her every word taken up and answered soberly, had turned her into a tyrannical and bitterly lonely girl, susceptible to deep injury from the first unthinking person upon whom her unspent love and affection might fall. She was starving in the isolation of luxury. She had not even a dog or a cat or any helpless thing upon which to lavish the harmless superficial gestures of protection and affection. To the slightest incident, she brought a frightening concentrated attention and beyond that an almost hysterical emotional reaction. He pitied her and in his pity he blamed Fenton for his indulgence and Gilberta for withholding her mother's love from her child.

"If she'll let me," he promised to himself, "I'll help her. I'll be her friend." And then, as he thought it, the preposterous image of August submitting to aid from anyone came into his mind and he laughed. "She'll probably tear me in pieces," he said to himself, "but here goes. It's the least I can do in return for the study she's provided me."

In the morning, Walter lifted a letter from the floor just inside his doorsill. It was from August. It was written on thick velvet-finished notepaper with a small coat of arms embossed in gold at the top.

DEAR PROFESSOR ABBOTT:

I want you to know that I was not looking for anything stolen this afternoon. You were entirely mistaken.

I have a right to go in any room I want to in this house. This house belongs to me. My grandfather Chadley willed it to me when he died. So, that's that.

Sincerely yours,

AUGUST CHADLEY

Walter brought his reply down to breakfast and put it beside August's plate as he passed to the buffet. It was written on scratch paper and unfolded.

August read it as she continued to chew her sausage.

DEAR MISS CHADLEY:

I am afraid I have unwittingly denied you your proprietary right. Hereafter my door shall remain unlocked and ajar. I hope that I shall be in when you choose to call. I enjoy seeing you and I'm sure our conversations will prove to be of distinct value to me.

Most cordially,

WALTER ABBOTT

August crumpled the page in her hand and put the ball in her lap beneath her napkin. She deliberately served herself a second helping of eggs, which she did not want, in order to remain at table while Walter finished his coffee. There was no conversation between them until each arose to leave. Then August said,

"It isn't one of my habits to visit gentlemen in their rooms, Mr. Abbott. I'm sorry."

Walter smiled. Then he said, "I'm not a gentleman, am I, Miss Chadley? By your Southern standards? I'm just a poor Yankee schoolteacher."

August frowned. Then she retorted impatiently. "I don't know what you are . . ." And paused long enough for her meaning to be clearly . . . *and I don't care*. At the foyer, she concluded: "No lady ever goes into a man's bedroom, Mr. Abbott, in case you don't know it." She left him standing there and marched haughtily up the stair.

Walter watched her through the beautiful black iron lace of the curving banister until she disappeared from the gallery.

But she can explore a Negro boy's room, because a Negro is not a man even, not exactly anything – he noted in his mind – and yet I hear both Mrs. Chadley and August bolt their latches noisily every night.

Mr. Abbott's intrusion upon and critical attitude toward her idle examination of Ralph's room not only increased August's antagonism toward him but roused a specific resentment toward Ralph. Ralph had clearly written a criticism of her, the implication of which was that he was the victim of mistreatment and that any efforts he made to ingratiate himself with her would be useless. This accusation, brought into relief by her guilt at having made no conscious gesture to put the boy at ease in his difficult situation, made her fume.

At her first opportunity, she discussed Ralph with Fenton.

"Did you have a nice visit with Mr. Starburg?" she began by asking Fenton, who was just stretching out on his couch near the window, "I forgot to ask you yesterday. I wondered if Ralph managed with him."

"Oh," Fenton leaned back and removed his glasses, "it was all very pleasant all around I think. Ralph is a well-mannered boy, you know. I never expected him to be anything but a success with Mr. Starburg."

"Gee," said August, watching Fenton intently, "it will be just terrible if Ralph flunks."

"Nonsense," murmured Fenton, closing his eyes. "He's going to pass with high marks. I'm sure of it."

"I wish I were," August said wistfully.

Fenton opened his eyes and looked at her sharply. "Mr. Abbott thinks he is doing brilliantly," he said.

August shrugged. "You never can tell about colored people. And he's peculiar anyway. He might blow up the minute he gets in the exam room. Everyone gets stage fright, you know. I always forget everything I know for the first five minutes."

"Fiddlesticks," Fenton said and patted her hand, "you always come out of it in time to get an A, I have noticed, and I'm expecting the same of Ralph." He was relieved that August's fears were based upon something inconsequential.

August colored. It shocked her to hear Fenton voice the same confident expectations for Ralph that he always expressed for her.

"Well," she said peevishly, "I won't be surprised if he flunks. And I think it might be a good thing if he did. Why does he need to have a college education anyway? What good will it do him? He'll just get out of his place and cause trouble."

Fenton sat up and faced her. "I'm astonished at such an attitude in you, August. Indeed, I'm disappointed. I have counted on you from the start to help me. But now that you bring my mind to it, I must say I have noticed how little effort you have made to make things easier for Ralph here." Fenton's face was reddening.

"Well, what did you expect me to do exactly?" she retorted defensively. "*I* can't teach him, can I? That's what you hired Mr. Abbott to do."

"I did not *hire* anyone, August," Fenton said, controlling his voice. "I *engaged* Mr. Abbott and I consider it a great compliment to me that he was willing to come here." For a moment Fenton looked at August with his eyes squinted. Then he put on his glasses. "I think we should have an understanding, my dear," he said more gently. He reached out his hand and drew her to a place on the couch beside him. "You have displayed a singularly unsympathetic attitude toward Ralph from the time you were a little child," he said, sadly, "so perhaps I have only myself to blame for your attitude now. I should have found some way to make you understand our situation. I should have tried to show you . . ." and Fenton fumbled for a definition of tolerance to apply to the case before them. August waited.

Fenton cleared his throat. Then he began with what seemed an irrelevant statement.

"Your father loved Isaiah as much as anyone in the world, dear – after Father and me, of course." He looked for some sign of understanding from August. But her expression was blank and challenging. He tried again.

"It is the duty of a person of means and position to see to the welfare of others less fortunate in the world, dear."

August made no reply. She looked down at her hands. Fenton glanced at her appealingly. Then he began wearily, "These things are always so difficult to put into words. To me, Isaiah and Maude and Ralph have been so much in our family life that it seems strange to have to explain them in the hope of making you see them as I see them. And yet I realize that you have never known any of them and they are really strangers to you, though no one would be more shocked to hear that than Isaiah and Maude themselves. They love you just as they loved your father. When you and your mother came to Dunmeade to live, Maude became your nurse. Ralph, who was a little boy of seven, became your faithful guardian. It was Ralph who taught you to walk. You didn't know that, did you? He was so proud of you." Fenton mused over the scene in his own mind. "Then, after your mother consented to marry me and your grandfather began to be troubled so with his heart condition, he retired to his old home in the East, taking Isaiah and Maude and Ralph with him." He looked at August appealingly as he neared the disclosure he felt obliged now to make. "When you saw them again, you were nearly six years old. Do you remember Father playing the harpsichord for you?"

August nodded. "I remember," she said.

With determination Fenton moved to what he had to say to her. "Because you were only a child, Father and I excused the hostile attitude you showed so unexpectedly toward Ralph. We thought that perhaps you were frightened of him and did not understand his . . ." He stumbled. ". . . His perfectly natural expression of interest in you." Fenton swallowed. "Poor little Ralph was so excited that we had come to visit them that he ran down the walk to carry our luggage and greet us," Fenton hurried now to the regrettable incident, "and he looked down at you so surprised to see how you had grown and asked me, 'Is this little August?' – knowing all the time that it was you; and then – you must have been irritable and tired from the trip, for you said something very unkind and not at all like the sweet little girl you were – you said sharply, 'You call me *Miss* Chadley!' You rebuked Ralph when he had meant no disrespect at all."

As he said it, he dreaded seeing the embarrassment and humiliation he knew must come into her face. But instead, she was expressionless.

"Father and I never found a way to mend things," he went on, suing for a reaction. "You had shamed Ralph and he never dared invite you to play. He had wanted to show you his boat down in the marshes, to take you crabbing on the inlet. He had been told that he could look after you, that you would remember him from Dunmeade. You took to Maude after she had told you a bedtime story, but you remained hostile to Ralph and no one could understand why. You seem to have no sympathy for Ralph in his situation now, dear, and I cannot understand that, either. You never speak to him cordially or ask about his studies. He has every right to expect you to be his friend and protector. If anything should happen to me, I expect you to take my position as guardian to Isaiah and Maude and Ralph as long as you live. It distresses me that you feel no desire or obligation to care for them and to make Ralph feel welcome here."

He waited for August to speak, to declare that she had not understood about Ralph before but that now she did understand and would behave differently.

"I just don't like him," she said simply. "Perhaps if he looked differently and didn't act as if he expected me to kick him any minute, I wouldn't mind him so. But he irritates me, always creeping around so humbly and reading his Bible day in and day out."

"I'm afraid it's your attitude toward him which makes him so self-conscious with you. He senses your dislike. Negroes are very sensitive. They have no one to turn to, if not to us. You frighten him."

"I'm not going to boo at him," August answered, "and I think some of the blame belongs on his head too. He doesn't like me either."

"Now, dear," Fenton said, shaking his head, "your duty does not depend on whether the boy likes you or doesn't like you. That is all beside the point. Even so, you have no right to attempt to attach blame to Ralph to excuse yourself. Ralph would never be so impertinent as to form a critical opinion of you. You know that. Shame on you."

August did not reply.

"You know, dear, it isn't enough for us to see that the less fortunate have shelter and food because it is necessary and we must. We have to *want* to see their condition bettered. We have to have some feeling about them inside ourselves. You have a kind and generous nature. No one knows that any better than I. Would it be asking so much to ask you to try to understand Ralph and help him – more than what you would do for duty's sake?"

Fenton looked at her beseechingly. August stood up suddenly. She nodded her head. Then she turned away from Fenton.

"I'll try," she said with a gruff tremor in her voice. And then she walked quickly to the door and out of the room without another word.

When August had gone Fenton lay down and closed his eyes. He did not know what to conclude about their conversation.

August lived in a private world much as Lesley had done, seeming to need no one yet showing at intervals a frightening need for a confidant and friend. That she came to talk to him occasionally of her own accord relieved him. More and more of late he had felt inadequate to his task of being her sole parent. He was a man and there were times, he was certain, when August needed a dear friend closer than he could be. His mind fought against criticizing Gilberta, but the truth came forward on the surface of his thought to be acknowledged. August needed her mother and her mother had removed herself and he was to blame. And beneath this distressing realization was another which he turned from and tried to suppress in his mind. He had not been honest with August, he had never told her the truth about her father and her grandfather and he never would. Yet he expected her to feel the same close tie he felt to each of the other lives involved unhappily in that old conflict out of which her own life had come. And since he could not ever impart to her any of his special deep affection for Isaiah and Maude and their timid son, Ralph, in a kind of despair his hope fastened upon Walter Abbott to help him in his struggle with August to develop a sense of care for the dependents upon her – Ralph and Isaiah and Maude, and all the other Ralphs and Isaiahs and Maudes that she might not ever know by name. Mr. Abbott could serve where he could not.

After that, when August met Ralph, passing from one place to another in the house, she spoke to him quickly, trying to finish her greeting before he lowered his head and eyes and backed away or stepped aside. But always he defeated her and his murmured respectful response would seem to come from out his shirt bosom as he ducked and moved away from her.

One afternoon, almost defiantly, she managed to say, "Mr. Abbott says you are getting along just fine, Ralph, and I think that's just fine, too," before he escaped completely with his almost inaudible, "Yes ma'am. Thanking you just the same ma'am."

She was still standing in the stair well watching Ralph's retreat to Fenton's study when Walter Abbott came down the circle of the stair behind her. At the sound, she turned and gazed at him inquiringly. Then her eyes measured back the number of steps she had heard, and stopped at a place half up to the gallery. He obviously had been watching her with Ralph.

"Miss Chadley," he said, and he smiled a little ruefully, "your uncle has asked me to help you to develop a charitable attitude toward Ralph. But I don't think I am the proper person for that undertaking, assuming I agreed with Mr. Chadley in what he considers to be a truly charitable attitude."

August regarded him with an expression of mingled annoyance and dismay. She was angry that Fenton had discussed her with Mr. Abbott. On the other hand, she sensed in Mr. Abbott's tone a certain sympathy for her, though she did not know what he meant by his suggestion that he was in disagreement with Fenton. She said nothing.

He stood on the last step, looking slightly down upon her and observed, almost as if he were talking aloud to himself, "Having one's conscience interfering with one's freedom to like or dislike another person is troublesome, isn't it? It isn't very noble to be critical of a helpless dependent, is it? And it's almost indecent for the dependent to feel anything but gratitude toward you for your charity. Inequality complicates things, doesn't it?" He looked at her understandingly and smiled.

August remained silent. She could feel a painful thickness beginning in her chest. She breathed deeply, then opened her mouth to speak, but closed it having said nothing. Abruptly she turned her back on Mr. Abbott and walked away in the direction of the kitchen.

"Oh, Miss Chadley," Mr. Abbott called after her. He came across the foyer until he was before her again as she turned around.

"Mr. Chadley told me that if he and Mrs. Chadley were not

back in time to take you to Quakertown, I might drive you. That is, I might ask you if you'd allow me to drive you."

August looked at him in surprise. She hesitated. Then she said, "I've decided not to go today."

"Have you? Really?" he asked. "Mr. Chadley said you were going to make the sketches for a drawing for your room. I was awfully pleased when he said I might drive you." He looked at her directly and added, "I hoped he wouldn't get back in time."

Back of her ears, the bones of her head seemed to swell, until, unconsciously, she reached to press her fingers against them on one side beneath her hair. Then she put her hand down and forced herself to say calmly, "There's nothing for you to see. I'll just make the sketches and then we'll come back." She shrugged to suggest that he had imagined the sketching to be more interesting to observe than it really was.

Walter smiled. "You're probably trying to tell me you don't want an audience – and particularly me."

Instant embarrassment and a curious confusion spread warmly through August.

"You're mistaken," she objected, "I'm not in the least self-conscious."

"You misunderstood," he apologized quickly. But he did not explain, only turning up his hands slightly in a gesture of defeat.

They stood awkwardly saying nothing.

Then August declared, "Well, we'll have to go right now, because it's already three o'clock."

"I'm ready," Walter said and he held up the car keys to show her.

She hesitated a moment more in one last temptation to decline and disappoint him, and then she ran childishly to the stair and started up. At the gallery, she stopped and leaned over and explained, "I'm going to get my things, you know."

When she returned, she was carrying a portfolio. Walter followed her to the car. She strode ahead and put her portfolio on the back seat. He held the front door for her while she climbed in and settled herself. Then he drove them out of the grounds.

On the highway, August asked suddenly, "Why did you come all the way down here to go to college?" She turned sideways in the seat and sat facing him as he drove.

"Oh, there were several reasons but the deciding one was that I could get a fellowship here. Why?"

"I just wondered. Billy Pickett wants to go up North. All the boys down here want to go up North."

"I suppose everyone likes to get away from home," Walter mused, "or at least thinks he does at one time or another."

"I don't," August said.

"Don't you? I should think you'd like to go to one of the girls' schools in the East."

August shook her head. "I'd like to live in New York, though," she admitted.

"New York is a wonderful city," Walter said. "I can understand your wanting to live there."

"Do you live right in New York?" she asked.

"I wish I did," he answered. He was busy for a while getting from the highway onto a sand clay road, and then he went on, "I live about fifty miles north of the city. It's just a little place." He named it.

She was silent then, but he knew she wanted him to say more, to talk about his home.

"Most of the population is of Dutch descent," he said, "but my immigrant ancestors were English. My great-grandfather used to make shoes for the Dutch gentry all up and down the Hudson. They liked English shoes. English shoes made their feet look smaller." And Walter laughed. Then he complimented her on her riding boots. "They were very well done, I noticed."

"They were made in England by special order," she said proudly. Then she thought a moment. "But my feet are already small."

"I've seen them," Walter said, "I'd like to make a pair of sandals for you when I get time."

Surprised and flattered, August laughed self-consciously and asked, "Can you really make shoes?"

Walter nodded. "And even if I couldn't, my father would make them for you and let me take the credit."

After a silence, August said politely, "I would be very pleased to have them no matter which one of you made them."

Dense foliage filled the woods along either side of the road. They rode up a long gentle hill and looked down before them across two wide plains of cultivated land. The soil under the sun was alternating red and yellow. Below, the valley was crossed by a narrow creek and away to one side of it was a field of corn.

They passed a house. The hounds lolling under the walnut tree in the yard flung themselves out to the road and barked along back of the car for a few yards and then stopped and watched. Walter looked back and saw two women lift their heads from the washtubs in the back yard and stare.

"It's a beautiful day to have to spend over a washtub," Walter murmured sympathetically.

August looked back. "Well, I guess they're glad it isn't raining," she said. "You have to do it in the house when it's raining and hang the clothes all over the kitchen to dry."

It was such an unexpected thing for August to say that Walter was both surprised and impressed. "How did you know that?" he asked.

"My Aunt Grace is always upset when it rains a lot. The clothes get moldy. It puts a lot of extra work on her when they have to be done over and aired again."

"Will we pass your Aunt Grace's house?" Walter asked. "I know your mother's people live out here somewhere."

"That's it, right across there on the lefthand side above the hollow." She directed his gaze with her hand, pointing out the faded house at the end of a long red wagon drive. "And that house beyond it on the little rise is my grandmother's old house. It belongs to my Uncle Rafael too now."

Between the two houses the fields stretched out in yellow and orange ridges. Behind them, below another slope but visible from the road, was a boxlike shack with a crumbling roof, held together it seemed by the strength of a snarled vine.

"That's a sheepherder's cabin," August volunteered, "but the sheepherder is dead now." She stared at it until they had passed. Then she said, "When we get up on the next hill you can stop the car."

When she had climbed up the clay embankment and found a place at the woods' fringe from which she could overlook the shallow valley beginning its drop on the other side of the road, August stood for some time examining the landscape. Walter leaned against a tree behind her, observing her with interest. She was working out the scene she would sketch, he supposed. Then she turned to him and said, "I think it's very funny that there's no smoke coming from the chimney." She looked again across the valley and stretched out her arm toward her Uncle Rafael's house below them. "There aren't any clothes on the line, either, and I don't see William or anyone in the fields."

"Perhaps they've gone in town or to a wedding or something," Walter suggested.

"Perhaps," she said, but her tone indicated that she was not satisfied with any of these explanations.

"They'll probably be back before we're ready to leave," Walter said reassuringly.

"Probably," she repeated. Then she added, "I thought maybe you'd like to stop and meet my aunt and uncle since we're out here."

"I would very much," Walter said, "I'm glad you thought of it."

She opened her portfolio and held it in the crook of her left arm. Then she took a piece of charcoal from her pocket and rubbed down one side of it.

"If you want to sit down, you'll have to get a seat cushion from the car," she said over her shoulder. She began to sketch.

"Thanks," Walter said, "I'm propped here."

"You may talk," she said, after a few minutes scrutiny of the landscape and a few whishing strokes of the charcoal.

"Are you including the two houses in your scene?" Walter asked. "I can't see what you're doing."

"No," she explained, "I'm using the long low hills and those buildings back beyond them. Do you see? There's a silo." She went on working.

"Yes," Walter said, "it appears to be quite a farm. I don't remember passing it."

"It's not on the Quakertown road," August explained, "we are looking at the back of it. It's Mr. Gaither Lyndon's dairy farm. He furnishes milk and stuff for the people that work for him. He has all the latest machinery. My Uncle Chad can tell you about it."

She was busy for a while. Then she scrutinized her sketch, holding it out away from her. Walter could see only the darker strokes in broad outline.

"Mr. Lyndon must have quite a number of people working for him to make a dairy that size worth while," Walter observed.

"He has some grocery stores too," August said, "but they're right in the settlement around his brickyards. They're just for his workers too."

"I suppose he charges them much less than they would have to pay elsewhere, doesn't he?" Walter said, "or there'd be no inducement to buy from him exclusively."

August did not answer at once. She wiped parts of her drawing with a twist of felt. Then she replied, "They don't pay for anything in cash. He gives them credit. Then he deducts what they owe from their wages."

"I see," Walter said.

August made no further comment. Her whole attention was upon her work. Walter shifted his weight against the tree. After a time, he asked, "Does your Uncle Rafael grow any particular crop?"

August wiped again with the felt. "Just a minute," she said and she carefully stroked in a detail. Then she answered, "My Uncle Rafael doesn't grow anything that doesn't grow itself."

Walter laughed. "Who plants the seed? You have to give things a start, you know – except weeds, of course."

"Well, if anything gets done, William does it," August declared. "Pedro is just like Uncle Rafael, only worse. Uncle Rafael is very nice. He just doesn't take any interest in his land."

"And Pedro? What's his trouble?" Walter asked, amused.

August hesitated. Then she said, "I really shouldn't talk about him if I can't say something nice – and I can't. So that should give you an idea."

"It does," Walter replied. "It gives me the idea that you would not miss him if he weren't around." He laughed.

August made a little grunting sound.

"I don't believe any of your relatives have come to Dunmeade since I've been there, have they?"

"No," August said. She let her arm hang a moment to rest and held the drawing in her right hand. She studied it in silence. Then she resumed her work. After a time she said, "We used to come out here to see them quite often when I was a little girl."

Her eyes moved back and forth from the scene in the distance before her to the scene growing on her paper.

"Do you like the country?" Walter asked her. "My guess would be that you do."

"I think so," she answered; "but I've never lived in the country, so I don't know. It's probably different when you live on a farm from when you are just visiting. But I think I would like it. I like the things you eat, I know that."

"So do I," said Walter. "In fact I like to eat some of them right out of the earth, dirt and all – a raw turnip, for instance. Have you ever tried one?"

"Yes," she said. But she did not go on. With his question, an unpleasant memory had come into her mind. She felt herself stumbling through the soft turned soil of the vegetable patch with Pedro reaching for her dress sash, jerking her back and back until she fell between the rows of beanstalks while María ran on to safety and left her to Pedro's tormenting threats to pull up her dress and look at her ruffled bloomers.

"I like to eat tomatoes with the heat still in them, too," Walter said.

"My Aunt Grace's cellar is full of things," August remarked. "She makes wine from their scuppernongs and the demijohns are down there. I like wine. I like it in whipped cream on top of fruit cake for Christmas."

She contemplated her drawing for some time. She touched it lightly here and there after rubbing down her charcoal again.

Then she was ready to go. She put a sheet of waxed paper over her sketch and closed the portfolio and started to the car. When he closed her door, Walter noticed that she was smiling in an odd little inward way which gave her an expression of quiet content he had not seen before. Apparently she was happy with the work she had done. He hoped she would show it to him when they were back at Dunmeade, but he was not going to ask her. He turned the car around in the road at her direction and started back the way they had come.

She watched her Uncle Rafael's house intently as they approached. Walter drove carefully up the rutted wagon drive and around the house to the back porch. "There's no one at home," August said, even before she had got out. "The kitchen door is locked and all the windows are down."

"Couldn't they have gone on a trip somewhere, a vacation?"

"Not without telling us."

"Well, perhaps there's a funeral and they've gone to that."

"My Uncle Rafael wouldn't lock up the house to go to a funeral. He never locks anything."

She stepped up on the back porch and looked in the kitchen windows. She held her hand up to shade the reflection of the afternoon sun on the panes. Without comment, she went to the front of the house and peered into the parlor, Walter following her.

"We'd better go right home," she said. Her pupils had darkened with alarm. "Something must have happened. I have to tell my mother."

She began to run back to the car. Walter ran after her. No real tragedy could be kept secret long from close relatives, he knew, but he felt that that reasonable argument might be more irritating than comforting at the moment, so he helped her into the car and then hurried to start the motor and said only, "We could stop at the house up the road here and ask. They might know something."

August glanced at him in horror. "Oh no," she said, "I wouldn't think of letting people know anything was wrong."

"Yes, I suppose it would be a mistake," Walter agreed quickly. "There's no reason to make one's affairs public." He should have known better than to make such a suggestion. August would never commit the indiscretion of starting gossip among her uncle's country neighbors.

"You didn't notice anyone stirring about down near the barn, did you? I forgot to look," she asked him suddenly.

Walter thought. "I don't remember seeing a barn," he answered.

She sucked her tongue against her teeth. "Isn't that stupid of me," she declared. "There isn't any barn. My Cousin Pedro set fire to it."

"He did?" Walter said, amused and a little astonished too.

"Well," she amended, "the barn burned down and it was my private opinion that Pedro did it — even if he is my first cousin."

"You are quite critical of your Cousin Pedro, aren't you? Hasn't he any good qualities?"

August shook her head.

Walter was about to press her for further information on Pedro's character when he heard her emit a curious faint little cry and, turning his eyes from the road a moment, he observed her face working as if she were about to weep. He said nothing and they drove the rest of the way in silence.

Fenton was having his tea in the patio when they arrived. As they left the garage, August asked suddenly in a whisper, "Do you think I can tell my Uncle Chad? He isn't supposed to be upset. Shouldn't I tell my mother first?"

"I think he'd rather you told him first," Walter answered,

softly. "Why don't you wait until he has finished his tea and then tell him privately after I've gone upstairs."

August looked at him gratefully and nodded. He had suggested what she had really wanted to do but hadn't been certain was best. "Thank you," she said, as they walked through the garden, "I mean for driving me to Quakertown. It was very nice of you."

Walter smiled. "It was a pleasure and I hope you'll let me do it again," he said.

She strode out a little in front of him hugging her portfolio and he saw the stain beginning in her cheeks and down her neck as she blushed.

It was after coffee, when Gilberta had left them sitting together in the drawing room, that August told Fenton of the de Venturas' absence. She had tried at tea to tell him; but before Mr. Abbott had got away upstairs, Mr. Estes, Fenton's old employee from the bank, had been announced and Fenton had gone to meet him in the study.

"Mr. Abbott and I stopped at Uncle Rafael's on our way home this afternoon," she said directly, "but there was no one there. In fact, the doors and windows were locked, so I think they must have gone away. I didn't know they were planning to go off. Did you? I was afraid something had happened at first."

"They've gone to Florida, dear," said Fenton, wearily and resignedly. "Mr. Estes brought me the news this afternoon. That was his business with me." So he had not known as soon as August, really.

"I don't think it was very nice of them to leave without telling us, without saying good-by," August said, angrily. "I don't know why they didn't." She was offended that María had not confided in her, and at least allowed her to share in María's own preparations for the trip.

"I think your Uncle Rafael was afraid some objection would

be raised," said Fenton, "for the purpose of the trip is not one I can endorse. Truthfully I am quite distressed by it all."

"Are you?" August asked. The painful contraction of her heart, which she had experienced in the afternoon before the locked house, returned. "Aren't they coming back?"

"I'm afraid that in time they will be obliged to come back, dear," Fenton said, holding his hands flat and still against his knees.

"I don't know what you mean," August said, shaking her head.

"Your Uncle Rafael mortgaged his property here and took his family to Florida to speculate in real estate. He hopes to realize a fortune." Fenton smiled in a sad way. "I hope with all my heart that he will. But I do not think things will end that way, and I'm afraid that he will lose all his holdings in Quakertown."

"Grandmother's house, too?" August asked.

Fenton nodded. He seemed about to say more, but then, instead, he patted her hand and smiled in a lost and yet curiously hopeful way, as if he were remembering that, despite his own misgivings, some fateful circumstance might yet deliver Rafael de Ventura from the probable consequences of this folly.

"Does Mother know about it? She will be very worried."

"I told her after Mr. Estes had gone. She did not gather the seriousness of the situation and I refrained from impressing it upon her."

"She knows that you won't let anything happen to Uncle Rafael," August said, solemnly.

"Yes, I suppose that's true," Fenton admitted. He did not seem to be complimented.

"I don't think it was a very nice way for Uncle Rafael to treat you. He might have asked your advice."

"He anticipated what my advice would be," Fenton said simply, "and he wished to go."

"Perhaps they'll all come home soon, and nothing will have happened," August said.

"Perhaps they will," Fenton agreed.

"Would you like for me to play something on the piano?" August offered.

"I think it would be very pleasant to hear a little music, dear," Fenton responded.

"I'll play the Mendelssohn," August said. She crossed the floor.

Outside the patio door swung softly shut and, before August began, Mr. Abbott and Ralph passed the drawing room on their way upstairs.

"Come in, come in," Fenton called to them, "we're going to have a concert."

Walter glanced at August for permission. Ralph hung behind him.

"Come in, if you think you can stand it," August said. "I haven't practiced for ages. I'll even let you select a number, Mr. Abbott." She smiled and beckoned him to the piano to look over the music.

Fenton spoke to Ralph and patted a place beside him.

"Now these are the ones I know best, and these are the ones I'll stumble on," August said to Walter, dealing the sheets into two piles. Walter nodded and picked a Schumann song. "Oh, that's for voice," August said and moved it away. "I accompanied one of the boys in his recital."

"I'll sing it," Walter said.

Fenton clapped his hands for the concert to begin and nodded for Ralph to do the same. Embarrassed, Ralph patted his thin fingers together.

"Goodness," murmured August, looking at Mr. Abbott in surprise, "wonders never cease." Then she sat down and with an odd little smile played the first measures. Walter began the words, "*Du bist wie eine Blume.*" His voice was clear and pleasant in tone and he sang with obvious ease. He was properly a baritone, but his range was not hopelessly restricted and he managed the tenor key in which the music had been arranged. He faced Fenton and Ralph and glanced only once at the music for a word cue. He knew the song well.

Fenton leaned back and listened. What a charming scene, he thought. August needed friends in the house. They brought her out. Mr. Abbott seemed to be getting on very well with her. He was a thoroughly fine fellow. Perhaps Gilberta would come down and join them too. Fenton glanced at Ralph. He was sitting straight and tense on his end of the sofa looking self-consciously away from Mr. Abbott and August. Fenton sighed and shook his head. Then he closed his eyes.

"I told him," August informed Mr. Abbott, as they went together up the stairs, "but he knew about it. My Uncle Rafael has taken his whole family and gone to Florida. He's going to go into the real estate business. And if you want to know what I think, Mr. Abbott, I think my Cousin Pedro put Uncle Rafael up to the whole thing."

"You do? Why? I mean why would your Cousin Pedro do it?"

"Because he's never liked being a farmer and having to live in Quakertown. He wants to be a big man and travel about. He has all sorts of ideas about himself. The things he does are enough to worry anyone."

Suddenly, self-conscious at having stressed again her low opinion of her cousin to Mr. Abbott, she changed the subject abruptly by asking, "Would you like to see the sketch I made this afternoon? If it isn't too late?"

"It isn't too late for me," he assured her, pleased. "I've been hoping ever since we left Quakertown that you'd invite me to look at it."

"Well, it's right down here," she said, embarrassed, and flung her hand out in the direction in which he was to follow. "It's in my study."

She went ahead and turned on the lamps.

Walter stood a moment in the door, examining the furnishings of the room and consciously studying her against them. There was an air of virility about her study, though it was obviously the room of a girl. It was neat and plain, with none of the bric-a-brac he had expected to see in it.

August was leaning over what seemed to be an old corncrib, waxed and polished. From it she took an even larger portfolio than the one she had carried to Quakertown.

"That's an unusual piece of furniture," Walter commented. "It's fine for holding your materials, I see."

"It's a dough trough," she said. "You've probably never seen one before. It has a sliding top. It's over there behind the door." Walter looked at the large rectangular table-top leaning against the wall. There were large dark smears in the coarse grain of the wood. "Yeast stains," August said. "They used to knead dough on it."

She waited while he went to examine the top. Then she said, "Perhaps you would like to see some of my earlier things first."

She opened her portfolio on the floor and sat down beside it. "It'll be easier to look this way," she suggested and Walter got down on his knees in front of the first sketch.

"This is of the stables where I ride," she said, picking up a charcoal drawing carefully and holding it out for him. "I'd better hold it for you," she cautioned as he started to touch it, "I haven't fixed it. I don't like to spray anyway. I think I'll get some thin glass to put the pastels and charcoals between."

Walter looked carefully at the drawing.

He made no comment but only nodded. August withdrew another drawing, this time one in brick-colored crayon.

"This is not from life," she said, explaining it. "I remembered the dunes from a trip Uncle Chad and I made East to my Grandfather Chadley's. They are not really as high as I've made them, and they're gray except at sunset. Then they look like red mounds leading in even rows out to sea. Uncle Chad said I thought they looked like the kilns in Mr. Lyndon's brickyard. I don't remember what I said at the time." She looked at the drawing herself. "It was an assignment at school. It's more of a decoration than anything else."

Walter nodded again and made no comment. August withdrew another sketch. It was of a woman's head. She was leaning her cheek against the back of one hand and the opposite side of her forehead and cheek were drawn as if the artist had been looking down at her and the woman had been looking up and listening to something. It was in pencil with the high lights very pronounced in white chalk. The woman was smiling.

"This is my Aunt Grace," August said. "She's very nice. She's listening to my Uncle Rafael play and sing. He sings Spanish songs, you know."

"Has she ever seen this?" Walter asked.

"Oh no," August blushed. She put it away. "She didn't pose for it."

"You should give it to her," Walter said. "I'm sure she'd like it. She'd know you thought a great deal of her. It has real affection for her in it, I think."

"Here's one of my Cousin María hiding from my Cousin Pedro," August went on, holding up the last of the series. Walter moved back from it and August raised it a little so that he was looking up into the scene. It was sharp and bold, all vigorous lines describing a little girl hiding with her back braced in terror against a corner of the house while from the window sill above her a grinning man leaned out with his fingers stretched toward the hair ribbon twisted through the curls on top of her head.

Walter looked at August. She was studying the sketch intently. Then she turned to Walter and before she smiled quickly he saw an expression of deep distrust and fear in her eyes.

"This is Pedro?" he asked.

August nodded.

"He doesn't look any nicer here than you say he is in person," Walter commented. August made no reply. Instead she snapped the portfolio together and put it back in the crib. She did not ask him if he liked her work, and he wondered if perhaps she invited no comment because she was afraid of criticism. But then he knew that if that were true she would not have shown him her work at all. She would have continued to maintain that she had left it all at her school.

"This is what I was working on this afternoon," she began to explain, as she took the sketch from the portfolio he had seen her carry to Quakertown. "I don't know how it will come out yet, but I thought I might size some thin muslin onto large panels of cardboard, and then work a gesso ground over it and do the whole scene in panorama in several panels." She looked at him to see if he understood, and when she saw that he did not, she laughed and began again. "Well, you see," she said, "I am going to make some panels for the wall of my room – like wallpaper. But they won't cross the whole wall, only the part of wall above my bed. Do you see? I don't want to paint directly on the wall and yet I want the whole scene to fit flat against the plaster. If it doesn't I'll bump my head some night jumping up from a bad dream." Then she blushed. "Not that I have nightmares, but I might. I was just teasing." She glanced at him with her head lowered a little. "This is not to scale, of course. I'll have to figure all that out." She spread it down before him. "You see, this part of the scene will be the left corner of the wall space, and then so on." With her finger she divided the sketch with three imaginary vertical lines. She glanced at him to see if she'd made it clear. "It will be a continuous panoramic view. I want to do it in thin oils and just a dull varnish after. I was only interested in getting some details to work with this afternoon. After I've decided about the rest of the room, I'll decide whether I'll keep it realistic or not. I mean the painting." She sat silently looking at the sketch with him and then she added, "It might be nice to have the walls of my room in pale yellow." She said it musingly, really to herself.

Throughout her explanation, Mr. Abbott watched her face with increasing interest. She might have been alone and the words unspoken and only sounded through her mind as she reviewed her plans and her purpose. When she'd finished, he said, "I expected your work to show talent, but I did not know you were a good craftsman too. I'm very glad to have played a little part in the beginning of this project. I hope you'll let me watch it develop."

"It's just messy – the next part," she said, simply. "It isn't interesting. You make glue out of gelatin sheets and dip the muslin in it and fix it to the cardboard panels – after you've treated the cardboard, of course. It isn't very interesting unless you're doing it yourself. I like it." She put the drawing back in the folio and placed it in the criblike dough trough. She was ready for him to say good night and go.

"Thank you for asking me in," he said rising. He wanted to say more; but admitting he was surprised to find her actually accomplished, in an art in which he had been inclined to grant her only superficial talent, would not have been tactful – though in a way it was a compliment to her.

She turned out the farthest lamp and he waited at the door for her. Then they stepped together into the hall. He said good night. "Good night, Mr. Abbott," she replied. Then she smiled at him and said, as he was about to move down the gallery to his room, "Would you be afraid to marry a lady artist, Mr. Abbott?"

The question startled him so that he laughed self-consciously. "Why, I don't think so," he answered. "Is there any reason why I should be?"

"Not to my mind," August said. "But my mother is afraid I'll be an old maid if I grow up to be an artist. So when I'm around her, I just pretend I'm not very interested in drawing anything except for my room."

"You'd rather I'd not say anything about seeing your drawings. Is that it?" he asked.

She nodded. She was still smiling.

"All right," he said, "I'll join your conspiracy to keep your genius secret." And then, on impulse, he reached out and touched her cheek. But she withdrew from the unexpected intimate gesture and turned and went to her room.

Before he had reached his door, Walter saw Fenton starting up the stair from below. He waited for him.

"August showed me some of her drawings just now," he said softly, half turning to see if August's door had closed. "I went with her to the country to sketch this afternoon, you know."

"Yes, she told me," Fenton said. He felt a little for the top step.

"I think you're right to encourage her, Mr. Chadley," Walter said simply.

"I'm glad," Fenton replied. "You can be of great service to her and I shall be grateful to you for any helpful comments you make to her. She has a real gift. You'll see."

"She has something to be thankful for, if I may say so, Mr. Chadley," Walter said. Suddenly he was filled with pity for the man before him.

"Yes," Fenton reflected, "she does have a fortunate background. Both her father and her grandmother were artistically inclined."

"I know," said Walter, "but I am not referring to that."

Fenton did not understand.

"I mean she should be thankful that you are her guardian."

Fenton put his hand to his glasses and lifted them as if, suddenly, they had become an intolerable weight across his nose.

"I think you overestimate my importance to August, Mr. Abbott," he said thoughtfully. "But I am pleased at your compliment. A true artist will persevere, overcome any difficulties, and by the quality of his work demand recogniton of his genius."

"Yes," said Walter, "the artist may never cease struggling to create freely, but unless he can support himself while he develops his art, he has slight chance of seeing a day of honor, Mr. Chadley. Isn't that so? I think it is. And I think that August, if she is going to work seriously to produce something of quality and imagination, is most fortunate in having wealth and the sympathy of her parent to support her."

Fenton was silent. He reached again to adjust his glasses. At last he said, "If you will excuse a personal remark, I should like to pay you a compliment too, Mr. Abbott. It seems to me that for such a young man you have an uncommonly wise and reflective intelligence. My father would have been pleased to have you in Dunmeade."

Mr. Abbott awkwardly inclined his head. "Thank you, Mr. Chadley," he said, and then abruptly, "Good night," and went to his room.

Fenton's immediate reaction to the news that Rafael de Ventura had mortgaged his farms, and gone to speculate in Florida real estate, had been to feel meanly used. But almost in the instant his pride felt the wound, his mind had been caught in a disturbing concern for the final outcome of the whole affair. He did not believe Rafael to be a dishonest man; but he knew that Rafael carried his obligations lightly and would as soon as not allow foreclosure and a forced sale of his properties, not considering that he would be cheating his family of future security. So Fenton considered carefully the various actions he might take to protect Rafael's family from Rafael's irresponsibility. At last he decided to buy up the mortgages, and so exercise some control over the properties for the sake of Lucy and her children. He expected, as a courtesy to him, that the mortgagee would set a low figure as acceptable payment for the interest due to date (the mortgages were only thirty days old), since he would understand that Fenton was not buying up the mortgages as an investment from which he intended to realize a profit.

Having thus decided, Fenton sent a stiffly worded invitation to Mr. Oliver J. Rench to come to Dunmeade to discuss some business of personal interest to him. He received a reply in the return mail.

"I'm having a gentleman in this afternoon," Fenton said to Ralph on the day of the appointment, "I want you in the room, for at a certain point I shall wish you to take some papers I shall pass to you and read them aloud to me. Stand in a good light and read distinctly, taking care to phrase precisely, with the commas and other marks of punctuation. That is very important. Can you do it for me?"

Ralph's eyes grew large. "Yes, Mr. Fenton. Yes sir," he promised.

"Thank you. I'm sure you can. It's at such a time as this that I feel the deprivation of good sight." Then Fenton noticed the anxiety growing into terror on Ralph's face. "They'll be mortgages you'll read to me, Ralph," he reassured him. "I want to be certain I understand all the clauses. That's all."

So, after a decent interval of conversation during which Mr. Rench drank two whiskies and acquainted Fenton with some trifling and coarsely related items of gossip from the business section, Fenton said directly, "Mr. Rench, certain information concerning Mrs. Chadley's brother, Mr. de Ventura, is responsible for my presumption upon your time today."

Mr. Rench grinned. Then he reached unceremoniously into his pocket, withdrew the two mortgages, patted them affectionately and laid them across his knees in full view. Then, suddenly catching sight of Ralph in the corner, he instinctively put his hand over the papers. He looked at Fenton questioningly.

"Ralph is acting as my confidential secretary this afternoon, Mr. Rench. Proceed," Fenton said, matter-of-factly.

Mr. Rench turned around in his chair and stared at Ralph. He had heard a tale about the Chadleys when he had first come to Newtown. He had heard that old Marcus had tried to register a darky at the Briggs Arcade. Then he'd heard a cock-and-bull story to the effect that the Chadley boy who had died in the army camp had had his funeral preached by that same darky. This he had discounted as pure bosh. Old Chadley hadn't sounded the sort who'd allow that, not from descriptions of his highhanded ways in everything else. Nothing less than a bishop would have been good enough to conduct services for a dead Chadley. And yet, sitting here in his right mind, he had just heard the stuffiest, I-am-thy-better character the Lord had ever given breath say, without a blink of his eye, his black boy was his confidential secretary! If Mr. Chadley had said, "Pay no attention to Ralph over there. He's half-witted and not interested in anything but scratching and figuring out a way to steal a swig," he could have talked all day. But this! It was indecent of Mr. Chadley to have his Negro witness their private business transaction and claim that he could understand it.

"I'm sure you have some figure in mind for me to consider," Fenton said crisply, his gaze deliberately high above the mortgage papers. He was impatient at Mr. Rench's long attention to Ralph.

"I am not certain I have anything to sell, Mr. Chadley," Mr. Rench said, swallowing the last whisky in his glass. "There was no agreement allowing for prepayment." He observed Fenton with a gloating smile which said clearly, "Now that I've got a Chadley in a hole, I shall not miss the opportunity to spit in his face."

"Then I have misunderstood your putting the de Ventura mortgages out before me," Fenton said shortly. If Mr. Rench were expecting him to plead for the privilege of purchasing the mortgages and haggle like a common tradesman, he was to be disappointed, quickly. "I am sorry to have brought you out," Fenton said coldly and prepared to rise and end Mr. Rench's visit.

"You have misunderstood me, Mr. Chadley – indeed you have," Mr. Rench protested placatingly, spreading his hands and patting the papers on his knee. "I meant that perhaps you would not be in the market for what I have here when I have told you the terms." His smile coated the stirring of his hatred of all fine-gentlemen-in-business. Particularly he hated this stuck-up prig of a Chadley sitting before him, this polite bully in his proper clothes.

"The price is substantially less than it would be if the mortgages had been running twelve months, is it not?" Fenton challenged him. Certainly it should be. He did not understand the threat beneath Mr. Rench's comment.

"No, Mr. Chadley, it is not," Mr. Rench leaned over and said softly.

"Then you were correct in your assumption that you had nothing to offer me," Fenton snapped. "I beg your pardon." His face had whitened. He placed his hands on the arms of his chair to push himself up from it.

"But the terms are quite understandable, Mr. Chadley," Mr. Rench objected quickly. "There is a good possibility that the property will turn out a valuable asset to the buyer in the event of a foreclosure sale. The neighborhood of Quakertown is straining for wider development now that Mr. Lyndon has put up his dairy. In a few years it could meet the boundaries of Newtown.

I am interested in acquiring good property at a low price too, Mr. Chadley. I am a prospective bidder." He raised his stubby brows melodramatically and fixed his mouth in a thin grin as he watched Fenton.

"The neighborhood of Quakertown has not had a house built in it for fifty years, Mr. Rench," Fenton retorted indignantly, "and the city of Newtown is growing in the opposite direction. I am interested in keeping these properties in the family to protect my wife's sentimental interest in her birthplace. That is all." He gazed coldly at Mr. Rench and hoped that his tone had been particularly firm.

"I assume from that remark that you expect Mr. de Ventura to default on the mortgage payments," Mr. Rench observed in a tone nearly gleeful.

"Mr. de Ventura is not a dishonest man, Mr. Rench," Fenton said shortly and hardly, "but he is completely innocent of any business experience, and is likely to underestimate the seriousness of the transaction he has completed with you. I strongly suspect that he was persuaded to mortgage his farms by someone who surmised his innocence and exploited it."

Mr. Rench laughed. It was clear that Fenton's accusation was directed at him. There was a sudden silence. And then, coldly, Mr. Rench said, "In addition to payment of the principals, full interest on each mortgage for the entire terms will be required to satisfy the mortgagee, Mr. Chadley." He observed Fenton without a flicker of his lids.

Fenton leaned back in his chair and stared in dismay. This was the man into whose hands he had sold his defenseless debtors when he sold the Chadley Bank! His horror sickened him. All his anxiety for the welfare of his poorer customers was confirmed now in this one revealing demand.

"Well?" asked Mr. Rench.

"I decline to buy the mortgages, Mr. Rench," Fenton said. "And before I ask you to leave my house, I am going to tell you that I have received an inquiry about you from the membership chairman of the National Association of Bankers and Manufacturers." He waited while the significance of this caused a growing red to illumine Mr. Rench's face. The muscles in his jaws constricted. "I shall report this afternoon's interview and I shall demand that your name be withdrawn from the list of new candidates being considered."

Fenton stood up and walked abruptly to the door. "When I have done that, Mr. Rench, I shall call a meeting of the executive council of the Bankers' and Manufacturers' Club here. I shall request that your membership be suspended immediately pending an investigation into your business practices. . . .

"Ralph will show you out," he concluded. "Please excuse me."

He left Mr. Rench standing and went down the hall to the stair. He hesitated a moment at the first step. Then he felt with his hand along the cold black banister, raised his chin and started up to the gallery and his rooms. At the top of the stair, he heard Mr. Rench crossing the foyer to the front door. He looked back a brief instant, drawn by some irresistible impulse to observe the man's ignominious departure from Dunmeade. Mr. Rench had paused also – on the threshold. He twisted his head up to locate Fenton looking down upon him from the stair.

"Times have changed since you were a banker, Mr. Chadley," Rench said. "They had changed long before you had the sense to realize it and get out. I hope you won't be disappointed in the results of your letter to the National Association of Bankers and Manufacturers, Mr. Chadley."

Fenton did not reply.

"Good afternoon," Mr. Rench said and nodded and then went out the door.

Upstairs, Fenton removed his clothing and drew the blinds and lay down across his bed. He wanted at that moment to lie suspended in some peaceful state of the spirit where he would neither feel nor hear nor be conscious of anything in the assaulting world about him.

But before an hour had passed, he was called to the telephone. It was Gaither Lyndon.

"Rench has told me about the little business misunderstanding you two had this afternoon, Mr. Chadley," Gaither began in his wheezy voice. He sounded as if he were about to laugh ha-ha-ha and slap Fenton across the back at the silly joke of two businessmen having a serious argument. "I told him I knew you better than to believe you'd hold a grudge overnight even." He waited for Fenton to confirm his confidence. Fenton did not answer. Then sobered somewhat by the lack of response, Gaither finished, "I'm having the de Ventura papers sent over to your house immediately, Mr. Chadley – if that's convenient. You can send your check for the principals involved and interest earned to date any time you're ready."

Fenton did not make any comment. Nor did he thank Mr. Lyndon for his intercession.

Gaither cleared his throat and waited for Fenton to say that he would not make his condemning report on Mr. Rench to the National Association of Bankers and Manufacturers. But Fenton volunteered no promise.

As a last attempt to patch up the situation, Gaither said whimsically, "Rench is a little high-pressure, you know Mr. Chadley – he's not used to us country folks here in Newtown. He'll find out we can get as much done as he can without half the noise. Isn't that right, Mr. Chadley?" And again, his voice had the ha-ha-ha jolly quality in it.

"I shall expect the papers this afternoon," Fenton replied, "Good day, Mr. Lyndon."

When he had hung up, Fenton went to his desk to compose the letter he had threatened to send. He selected his paper and wiped the tip of his pen.

"In regard to the candidate proposed from Newtown," he began to word the letter in his mind, "I should like to enter a strong objection – " Then he reconsidered. "I formally protest any consideration of Mr. Oliver J. Rench, the proposed candidate from Newtown," he wrote decisively. Then he stopped. A thin, cool sweat oozed out across his forehead and he reached up to feel it. He looked down at the line he had written. There was no reason to write the letter now, he recalled with relief. There was no reason to be arbitrary, to continue a dispute which no longer existed. He crossed through the line, then tore up the letter paper and dropped the pieces into the wastebasket.

Walter Abbott began his preparations to be gone from Dunmeade by early September. When he had seen Ralph through his examinations, he would be free to go North. He had obtained an appointment to teach in a small college and though this first position was not challenging, it was a triumph in that he had managed to get it his first year out, with the disadvantages of youth and no record of previous teaching experience, except for laboratory assistantships in his own field. He came to Fenton's study with the letter of appointment in his hand and blushingly held it out. Then, instantly embarrassed at having given Fenton something difficult to read, he recited the brief contents word for word without ever looking down at the letter in his hand.

Fenton smiled. "It's splendid news, Mr. Abbott," he said generously, "I'm very happy for you. I hope it is to be the first step in a career distinguished by service to others, and intellectual reward to you. I shall hope to hear from you often and each time a report of success. I'm going to let Mrs. Chadley know, now, if you'll excuse me." He moved toward the door. "We shall certainly have a celebration this evening."

So, at eight o'clock, Fenton and Gilberta and Walter and August drove in to Newtown to dine at a table reserved near the string orchestra in the Neapolitan Room of the new Hotel Dixie Belle. Even Gilberta responded to the news of Mr. Abbott's appointment to a college faculty. She was quite gracious and without her usual preoccupied air. She accepted Fenton's invitation to dance so that Walter would be free to ask August. And then, when she had sat down again after her two-step with Fenton, she said to Walter, "I'm glad that you will be leaving Dunmeade with such a pleasant winter to look to, Mr. Abbott."

She said it gracefully and sincerely but it seemed to Walter that she was really saying only, "I am glad that you will be leaving Dunmeade." And then before he could reply with more than a thank you, the broiled shrimp was brought on and Fenton had to explain again about the wine to be served with the roast. The waiter was new to his trade and a local man and he could not understand how he was to serve spirits when it was against the law. "I have sent down the wine from my own cellar," Fenton murmured as discreetly as possible. "Please consult your captain or send him to me. . . ."

Seeing the humor of their situation, they all laughed and began to watch to see what the waiter would do to ease his conscience when he was forced to serve the Bordeaux. And then, before the disapproving trapped look of the man, Fenton felt obliged to say, "We are celebrating a special occasion this evening" – an explanation which only served to muddle their relations with the waiter still further. He looked with disapproval at August's young face and tightened his lips as he examined Walter's mature stature. August and Walter looked at each other in surprise and Fenton blushed and pushed at his glasses helplessly. Only Gilberta enjoyed the misunderstanding without discomfort. Quite unexpectedly she smiled and nodded toward her daughter as if to corroborate the waiter's misunderstanding of the whole situation.

"Would you care to dance?" Walter asked August in confusion. And equally anxious to do something to change the foolish appearance she was certain they presented, August stood up and rather bolted toward a spot on the floor away from the musicians and far from her mother and Fenton.

"Have you ever!" she exclaimed into Walter's ear.

"No," he responded emphatically, "I can't say that I have. But now that I am getting accustomed to the idea, I can't say that I object to it either. It's a much more entertaining position to be in than just a departing friend. Don't you think so?"

August stiffened and moved her head back so that her forehead no longer touched his chin. Her hand, which had lain relaxed in his left arm, began to close into a fist and she noticeably separated herself from him so that in a few moments they were waltzing about the floor maintaining twelve inches of space between them.

"I think it's perfectly silly. Perhaps you are enjoying it, but I most certainly am not," she sniffed haughtily and Walter knew that she was lying. She had the rattled and rosy look of a young woman who has just been pleasingly kissed without a struggle and is about to slap her admirer in a purely reflex action.

"Well I hope you are enjoying this dance," Walter said, "because I am. You dance beautifully."

August did not know quite what to say. She cleared her throat softly and uneasily and then managed formally, "Thank you. I think you dance very well too." Unconsciously she eased back into their first natural dancing embrace.

When she returned to the table, she said, "Mr. Abbott dances very well for a professor – so you needn't be afraid, Mother."

Walter squeezed his lids together in a grimace. When he opened his eyes, he said, "Thank you, Miss Chadley. We are properly grateful."

By dessert, Walter had danced dutifully with Gilberta and brought her back to Fenton with a puzzled expression on his face as he regarded her walking before him to the table. All the time he had held her lightly and guided her about the edge of the dance circle, he had had a curious feeling. It was the first time he had ever been near her, physically near her, and he had immediately sensed a peculiar and persistent thing about her. Quite unreasonably, it seemed to him that he was holding a soft and yielding animal in his arms which might in an instant and without warning change and jump at his throat. She danced with such slumbrous indolent movements she seemed almost to be swaying rhythmically in her sleep, and he was afraid of rousing her for fear that sudden sharp consciousness would bring some shocking gesture from her. And then when the music had ended, she had smiled politely and distantly and clapped her hands discreetly with the other dancers and moved away from him toward the table. She became Mrs. Chadley again as he had observed her every day for the weeks he had lived in Dunmeade – removed from all other lives around her, wholly attentive to her own interests and duties. But the impression of the fierce but slumbering animal nature in her that he had sensed remained with him, and he caught himself glancing at her sharply at odd intervals to try to surprise some look on her face which might further confirm his feeling.

Back at Dunmeade, when they were saying good night and Walter had thanked Fenton and Gilberta, Fenton said, wistfully, "I'm sorry we waited until you were leaving us to discover what a delightful time we could have supper-dancing. But of course, I was not really well earlier in the season." Then he brightened, "We'll have to make Mr. Abbott come back to Newtown soon again, won't we, August?"

And August unexpectedly answered, "Perhaps he'll come back for Christmas, if he wants to." Then she laughed shyly.

"I'm glad you'd like to have me for Christmas," Walter replied seriously. "I'd like to come – if I have enough holiday time to allow for the trip." And then, on an impulse, he turned to Fenton and Gilberta and said, "Couldn't all of you come North for Christmas with me? You've never been North. You'll be crazy about it." He looked at August leaning against the black iron banister. "They'll be crazy about you."

He stood waiting for an answer, his expression eager and hospitable.

Fenton blushed and looked to Gilberta to accept. But Gilberta only gazed at Walter with her mild indifferent smile, which clearly said she had only half heard him and was waiting to climb the delicate stair to the gallery and her bed.

"That would be a lovely trip I'm sure. Wouldn't it, August?" Fenton said, trying not to sound too anxious to go. "Perhaps we can manage it, if it doesn't cut into your school too much." And then, suddenly, the idea seemed to die just as it had risen, and each of them smiled awkwardly and encouragingly at the other, denying the truth evident to him – that the Chadleys would not go North for Christmas nor Mr. Abbott return to them. And then they began to move together up the stair.

On the morning following the farewell dinner to Mr. Abbott, Ralph came to go over his lesson with his face blank and his mind so adrift that Walter had to speak sharply to him to recall his attention. Then he read his Latin listlessly and without interest and when the hour was done sat silent and waited for his next assignment.

"We aren't going to have school tomorrow, Ralph," Walter said suddenly, "I'm going hunting with you and Billy Pickett. I've been promised a hunting trip before I leave here and tomorrow is as good a day as any. Does that suit you? I've never shot anything but clay pigeons at the County Fair but Mr. Chadley says that you're a crack shot. Will you take me on for an afternoon?"

Ralph looked away toward the street beyond the sycamore grove. The Rolling Grocery was just turning into the drive of the Barrons' house.

"It's not the season yet, Professor," he murmured wistfully in a voice so low that Walter could scarcely catch what he said. "I don't think you can get enough birds here anyway to make a meal. Birds come from down home, down East."

Walter did not know what to say. He was anxious to find something to do with Ralph to fill the few days waiting until the examinations were taken. He wanted also to reassure Ralph, to remind him that his interest in him had not lessened, that he was not involving himself in his own plans for departure. He wanted Ralph to understand that he was not deserted.

"Mr. Chadley said there was some kind of hunting going on almost all year. I heard shots in the woods at the Willettses' lake the last time I was there. They must have been hunting something," he argued hopefully.

"Yes, sir," Ralph murmured.

"If Billy Pickett is agreeable, would you mind going? So that I may have the experience?" Walter persisted.

"No, sir," Ralph said and looked up at Walter just for an instant to let him see that he was willing. His eyes were large and vacant.

"That will be fine," Walter said, "I'll call Billy."

But Billy Pickett was not at home when Walter called. He had driven down to The Fortress to a pre-school conference of cadet leaders.

Walter was disappointed. Ralph's apathetic attitude had begun to disturb him. The Negro boy had about him an air of resignation, as if he were expecting some deep disappointment and had already prepared his mind to accept its inevitability. Walter was unable to reach him, to arouse in him any of the exhilarating excitement he himself had always felt upon entering a new phase of his schooling. Walter enjoyed learning. He enjoyed mastering a new subject. He had what Professor Hanley had had in his way of teaching Fenton and Lesley, an enthusiasm for his own interests coupled with a generous insistence upon sharing his knowledge with others. It came from an unconscious conviction that what he imparted to others, of what he considered valuable and good, would unquestionably enrich their lives. Learning was an ennobling process to Walter, and its own end. He wanted to encourage Ralph to go on reading and studying and thinking all his life, even if he ended earning his living at some physical labor in which there could be no reward beyond the dollars of payment. He tried to impart this hope to Ralph but Ralph only listened to him considerately and made no comment. Walter had not been able to determine whether or not Ralph had any desire to keep fresh the interests which had occupied them all summer. Certainly he showed no enthusiasm for entering the college, which could not have been derived from a fear of not passing his examinations, for he had proved a good and thoroughly diligent student, and not without pride in his ability.

When the day came, Walter drove to the college with him; but only O'Smyre, who had once taught there, took Ralph in.

Then O'Smyre returned and sat with Walter in the car with the doors open to catch the breeze. It was a blue, hot September day. The buildings still had the bare look of summer with only a handful of instructors back on the campus before Registration. Some workmen were busy cleaning windows and mending spots on the roofs of the buildings.

"Would you like to step inside, Professor Abbott?" O'Smyre finally asked when the first hour was over and some of their own excitement had subsided. "There's not much to see. It's about like any other school — but it might pass the time a little to look around."

"I'd like to see your greenhouse, O'Smyre," Walter admitted, stirring himself a little from the slouched position he had taken diagonally across the back seat.

"Oh, the horticulture department is out at the farm — we have a fine practice farm for the students about five miles out the highway, you know. My work was out there." He looked toward the windows where Ralph would be and added, "I wouldn't want to drive away from here just now. . . . Not while the boy can see us. He takes this mighty seriously. He looked to me like he was about to jump the track in there at first until he got used to Professor Duggin."

Walter nodded.

"Would you like me to get us a Coca-Cola, Professor Abbott?" O'Smyre asked as noon approached and the sun came down on the top of the car. O'Smyre let off the brake and they rolled back into the receding shade. "I just have to go down in the basement of the building to get it. There's a sort of commissary down there — mostly an icebox." He smiled. But Walter thanked him and refused.

Another half hour passed. Then suddenly a bell rang through the building and with no more warning than that the time was up, they looked toward the entrance to see Ralph already coming down the steps toward them. He walked sedately and appeared not to be looking at them as he approached. He had a curious little air of self-conscious indifference about him. He walked a little faster as he came closer as if he thought Walter or O'Smyre were intending to come to meet him and he wanted to forestall them. But Walter and O'Smyre did not move. O'Smyre pushed open the door opposite him and, without saying a word, Ralph got in and O'Smyre started the motor.

"All through?" Walter asked. "Nothing this afternoon?"

"No sir," Ralph replied, and volunteered nothing more.

Once Walter looked up to catch O'Smyre looking at him in the mirror when they came to a stop in traffic. O'Smyre's expression framed the question, "May I ask him about the examination or not?" Walter shook his head. And they arrived at Dunmeade not knowing even how Ralph thought he had got along.

And then a curious thing happened. Ralph left them at the garage and ran ahead into the house. And as Walter crossed the garden to the patio he looked up to Ralph's windows above the kitchen wing and for a moment saw Ralph standing there watching him before he moved back into his room. He had not stopped to report his arrival to Fenton, who was waiting.

Walter went into the house and down to Fenton's study.

"I wanted to let you know we're back," he said, putting his head in when Fenton answered the knock.

"Yes?" said Fenton eagerly, "I've been anxious. How did things seem to go?"

"I don't know really, Mr. Chadley. O'Smyre and I waited outside in the car and when it was over Ralph came out and said he did not have to return in the afternoon. Beyond that he has said nothing."

Fenton frowned. "I hope nothing went wrong. Does he seem upset?"

"I don't think so," Walter said, considering, "but I don't know. Perhaps he's just tired. It's a strain. He probably needs to collect himself a little."

Fenton nodded. "I'll take a light lunch with him in here" — and he rang for Susie.

But Ralph disappointed Fenton. He did not come down to the study for his lunch. He asked to be excused. Then, late in the afternoon, he came to speak to Fenton. He had freshened himself and changed his clothes.

"Well, Ralph," Fenton asked cheerfully, "I'm anxious to hear how many we guessed." He meant how many of the questions they had guessed would be in the tests.

Ralph worked his hands. He was always uncomfortable when he sat in Fenton's presence without a study book.

"Well, sir," Ralph began methodically, "first they gave me the Caesar."

He went on to recite the questions for each subject. His tone was curiously impersonal and he made no comment upon his reaction to the examinations. Fenton wanted to ask him if he thought he had made a good showing; but instead he declared, as he often had: "Well, I know that when we get the grades they'll be splendid, Ralph. I'm anxious to send the good news on to Isaiah and Maude." He reached over and put his hand across Ralph's locked fingers and patted them reassuringly. Ralph bowed his head slightly and did not answer. When he looked up he turned his head to the side and tried to hide his face as he got up to leave; but Fenton saw the tears hanging in his lids. He thought that Ralph was moved by a feeling of gratitude toward him. But when Ralph had got to the door and was waiting for Fenton to dismiss him, Fenton saw something else in his face. It was a look so mournful, so suggestive of an awareness that he was condemned and lost, that Fenton was shocked. He tried to smile at Ralph as he let him go, but in his dismay he could not, and Ralph left at his nod.

Except for the minutes when she quickly ate her breakfast at table with him, Walter did not see August alone from the evening of the farewell dinner until the afternoon of his departure. By the time of Ralph's examination her school had been open two weeks and she had spent her evenings in her study at her homework. But it seemed to Walter, as the morning approached when he could telephone for the result of Ralph's tests, that August tried to avoid meeting him at all. She was always done with her eggs and muffins when he got to table and within a few minutes she had left to meet O'Smyre at the garage.

"You're afraid I'm going to talk to you about Ralph and you don't want that, do you?" he asked her instantly the moment he'd sat down to his last breakfast in Dunmeade. "I'm leaving at six this evening. I'm going to report the grades before I go. I've been wanting to say some things to you, only a few things – but you've avoided me."

August stood up and took her new notebooks and textbooks from the chair seat next to her.

"I haven't avoided you," she said. "I never avoid anyone. You may say whatever you like. I'll simply be glad when it's all over and we can settle down to normal around here again."

"I think you mean by that that Ralph is going to fail and return to his home and leave you to go on with your life without the problem of his presence. Don't you?"

"I don't mean anything exactly," she said, "I'm not a prophet."

"You were trying to be, earlier in the summer when you predicted that he would blow up at the last minute. Don't you remember that?"

"Mr. Abbott, I don't want to argue with you about anything. I have to go now. I have to go to school." She said it as if she were straining to maintain a quiet tone against the impulse to scream and burst into tears.

"I know," he conceded, apologetically. "I know you have to go. I'm sorry." He sighed. "I'm anxious for the boy. It seems important to me to try to make you . . ." He did not finish. He got up and went to the buffet and served himself some bacon and took a slice of toast. With his back to her, he said, "I think you are a person of uncommon sensitivity and understanding. I've gathered that only lately. Since looking at your drawings, really. I think that's why I've been disappointed that I'm going to leave Dunmeade before I've been able to say the things I've wanted about Ralph." He paused and waited, hoping she would speak before he turned around. But she was silent. And then when he took up his plate and went back to the table, he saw that she had gone.

He finished his breakfast and then, when Fenton went into the garden with Ralph, he walked down to the study telephone and made his call to the college.

"Yes, Mr. Abbott," the Dean's secretary answered to his inquiry, "Ralph Craig averaged well above 90."

"Do you have his separate grades?" Walter asked.

"Not in this office, no. I'm sorry. We can only give the information that he has met all the requirements for entrance and is to be admitted."

"Thank you," replied Walter and hung up.

He walked out to the patio and stood there looking across the flags. So, now Ralph was entered in the newly-named Henshaw University and August's doubts had been proved vain and Mr. Chadley's hopes had been realized and his, Walter's, task was done.

At that moment, he felt a deep relief. So close upon that feeling as to be confused with it, he felt a kind of regret that the effort was done, and, surprised, he realized that he dreaded the hour when he would leave Dunmeade. He straightened and matter-of-factly looked about the lawn to locate Mr. Chadley and Ralph. Then he made off briskly to where Mr. Chadley rested in a slat-back chair beneath the heavy, already darkening foliage of the trees while Ralph read beside him from the *Wall Street Journal.* As he approached, Ralph moved uneasily on his little stool and tried to rise, but Walter smiled and waved him down and then easily slipped cross-legged onto the cushion Fenton had discarded.

Ralph finished reading the analysis of the week's stock quotations and Fenton opened his eyes and replaced his glasses and spoke to Walter.

"It's going to be a nice fall, Mr. Abbott," he said. "I'm sorry you must leave us. We're going to have our beautiful Indian Summer now."

"I know," Walter said, "I've always arrived here in the autumn until this year."

"That's right," Fenton nodded, "I'd forgotten that. I don't know why I continue to think of you as a stranger to the South. You aren't at all."

"No, I'm not," Walter said. "I suppose I'll have attacks of homesickness after I've left it." He laughed and added teasingly, "You've heard the story of the prisoner who wouldn't leave his cell when he was finally released because he missed digging in his secret tunnel every night to escape."

Fenton looked at him inquiringly for a moment and then his face cleared as he understood the joke and he laughed.

"I hope all of you are going to be good correspondents this winter. I'll be at the school post office bright and early every morning looking for letters from Newtown. How about it, Ralph?" Walter poked Ralph gently against the knees. "If you send me your homework once in a while when you want to go out with the girls, I might do it for you by special delivery. How is that for an offer?"

Ralph looked down and grinned self-consciously and worked his hands.

"Henshaw University is going to have lady students this year, you know," Walter went on, "and you're slated for trouble right from the start. Honor students are as much in style with the ladies as athletes these days, Ralph. With your entrance grades, you'll have to fight your way in and out of the buildings to get to class on time." Walter winked at Fenton. Ralph slowly raised his head and stared at Walter. Fenton tilted his head a little as if he were waiting for Walter to repeat what he had said to be certain he had understood.

"You will be entering Henshaw University with an average of 'well above 90,' to quote the Dean's secretary," Walter said. "And now, I should like to be the first to congratulate you. Your old teacher is proud and honored, Ralph." He scrambled up and took Ralph's hand as the boy awkwardly rose from his stool stuffing the *Wall Street Journal* under his arm to free his fingers.

Fenton stood too and came toward Ralph, after putting his

handkerchief to his eyes a moment conspicuously cleaning his lenses. Then he caught Ralph at each shoulder and held him off from him a moment and then shook him a little roughly and at last said, "That's just splendid, isn't it?"

Ralph looked over Fenton's head into the trees and said nothing. He swallowed twice and strained down in his throat as if he were clearing it to speak. But not a word came.

"We must call O'Smyre right now and send the telegram to Isaiah and Maude," Fenton said, remembering and reaching into the inner pocket of his house jacket to bring out a white envelope. "I have already written it all out. It's right here," he said eagerly. "But perhaps you would like to say a few words of your own, Ralph?"

"No, sir, Mr. Fenton, thanking you just the same," Ralph murmured, "you know best."

"You had no doubt at all as to what the telegram would say, I notice, Mr. Chadley!" Walter commented, smiling.

"None, Mr. Abbott," Fenton answered, "I've been wording and re-wording it all week. How does this sound?" He held the white envelope close to his eyes and read aloud:

"All required examinations passed with best grades. Entering college on Monday next. Know you will enjoy happy thanksgiving this day. Letters will follow giving details."

The message was signed with the names Ralph Craig and Fenton Chadley.

No one spoke. Fenton looked first to Walter and then to Ralph for approval. Walter said, "It sounds very well, Mr. Chadley." Then he looked at Ralph. "That's the story, isn't it, Ralph?" he said. He wanted to help the boy to speak, to say something to please Fenton.

Ralph opened his mouth to answer, turning his head quickly from Fenton to Mr. Abbott and back again to Fenton. With his features working with emotion, he stammered chokingly, "Begging your pardon, Mr. Fenton," and ran from them to the house.

"Goodness me," murmured Fenton, "I suppose the boy is overcome." He seemed to be apologizing to Walter for Ralph's behavior. "I know he feels deeply his gratitude to you, Mr. Abbott."

Walter looked away from Fenton. Slowly and persistently the gnawing of a deep indignation began in him for Fenton's obtuseness. He stopped to pick up the *Wall Street Journal* which Ralph had dropped. He did not want to answer Fenton.

"I'm going to take the six o'clock train, Mr. Chadley," he said, when they continued to stand there awkwardly. "I haven't any money for my ticket and my meals en route, so I'll have to trouble you to pay me some of my salary in cash."

Startled, Fenton flushed and replied quickly, "I had expected to make payment in cash, Mr. Abbott."

"I'd prefer not having the entire amount in cash, if you don't mind," Walter objected, "I only need enough for my traveling expenses."

"What do you estimate your expenses will be, then?" Fenton asked.

"About thirty-five dollars, allowing a little for an emergency," Walter said.

Fenton nodded. Then after a moment of hesitation, he said, "I think if you'll excuse me, I'll attend to it now," and he pushed at his glasses and then started across the lawn to the patio. Half there, he turned around and came back.

"If I'm not mistaken, Mr. Abbott," he said with obvious difficulty and embarrassment, "thirty-five dollars is about the amount you'll need for your ticket, with sleeping accommodation tonight. Shouldn't I make it at least fifty dollars?"

Walter shook his head. "I shan't be traveling in the Pullman car, Mr. Chadley," he said, "but thank you."

"Not at all," murmured Fenton. He walked away straighter and more rapidly than when he had first moved toward the house.

"Heaven help you," Walter thought, following his back, "heaven help you if you ever leave this shelter." He looked at the perfect garden and the arranged paths and the sun on the greenhouse windows. Then he looked from the sycamore grove to the street beyond it and the world. He drew a long breath and with it violently threw off his pity as if Fenton had unfairly put it upon him like a blinding veil.

"Your hope lies in August, Ralph," he said, almost aloud, "and not in this gentle protector who keeps you weak and grateful and isolated in his care."

When he was ready to leave, Walter set his small valise against the banister at the top of the stair and walked down the gallery to Ralph's room. He knocked and said as he did so, "It's Mr. Abbott, Ralph." Inside, he heard Ralph push a chair and crumple a paper. "Yes, sir," the boy answered. Then he came to the door and opened it and stood self-consciously awaiting Mr. Abbott's indication that he wished to come in.

"Would you like to see me off, Ralph?" Walted asked, "O'Smyre is ready to take me to the station."

Ralph looked down at his feet. "I'm not dressed up, Professor Abbott. Thanking you all the same," he said, apologetically, pointing to his everyday pants and bedroom slippers.

"You don't have to be," Walter said. "Just put your shoes on. Hurry. I'll meet you at the garage in ten minutes." He started back to the stair and his valise.

"Is it all right, Professor Abbott?" Ralph called after him, softly. And when Walter had turned his head around and paused, he said, "Did Mr. Fenton say I could go?"

"Yes," said Walter, so firmly as to be almost harsh, "Mr. Fenton wants you to go."

"Yes sir," said Ralph, and he stepped back into his room as Walter repeated, "Hurry now. Just put your shoes on."

Before he had reached Fenton's study, Fenton came out and stood waiting for him with his hand holding back the door to invite him in.

"I've been expecting you, Mr. Abbott. I listened for you," Fenton said. "You have only twenty minutes, you know." He glanced at the clock and went to his desk.

"I stopped and asked Ralph to accompany me to the station," Walter replied, watching Fenton. "Ralph and I met at Newtown Station. My departure concludes our relationship – or rather, one phase of it."

Fenton cleared his throat. With his back to Walter he said, "I think it was very kind of you to invite Ralph to see you off, Mr. Abbott. In fact, I intended mentioning to you that I have observed your tact and consideration all along and that I have been particularly appreciative of your spirit." He took up the envelope waiting on his desk and the clip of bills beside it and turned around and walked to Walter with them offered out to him.

"Here is the cash you requested, Mr. Abbott. And here is my check for the balance due you."

Walter put the bills in his trousers pocket and the envelope in his inside jacket pocket. Then he held out his hand.

"Good-by, Mr. Chadley," he said.

"Good-by, Mr. Abbott," said Fenton. "I hope you will come back to Dunmeade soon. We shall miss you, sir."

Stiffly, and without saying anything more, Fenton walked with Walter to the patio and stood on the flags watching until the car had turned into the street. Then Walter waved to him from the back window and Fenton raised his hand and Walter was gone from the beautiful and secluded house.

"Is Newtown much changed from the time when you lived here as a child, Ralph?" Walter asked as they passed from the narrow streets of the warehouse district to a recently broadened avenue leading to the station.

Ralph thought with his usual solemn look, glancing at the buildings through his window. He shook his head.

"No sir," he said. "It looks just about the same except for having more people."

"Mr. Chadley's father had a lot to do with the development of the city, I'm told."

"Yes, sir," said Ralph.

They drove into the station parking section. Then Ralph said suddenly, "He was a big man," and a curious pride was in his voice. He hesitated and then he added, "Mr. Fenton is a big man, too."

"Yes, that's right," Walter agreed, looking at him with pity.

"You have five minutes, Professor," said O'Smyre; "I don't mean to rush you." He opened Walter's door and took the little suitcase and started on to the train. He was carrying a long rectangular shallow box under his other arm.

"Aren't you coming to the platform?" Walter asked Ralph.

The boy shook his head and drew back into the depths of the limousine. "No sir, Professor," he said, "thanking you all the same. I guess I'll stay here."

Walter reached in and took his hand.

"Well, here's good luck to each of us, Ralph. I'm going to a strange place, too, you know."

"Yes, sir," Ralph murmured. "Good luck, Professor Abbott."

Walter drew a scrap of paper from his pocket and put it on the seat beside Ralph. "That's where you're to write me and send me the copies of your grades." He turned and ran to the steps leading to the platform.

At the door to the first coach he saw O'Smyre.

"I put your things inside, Professor." O'Smyre urged him in as the conductor called out, "All aboard!" The shrieking and whistling began and a shot of steam from under the car rose between them.

"Look after the boy, O'Smyre," Walter called as he moved off. O'Smyre raised his hand.

Walter looked down the aisle of the half-empty coach. He located his valise and sat down on the cinder-filled green mohair seat and watched Newtown slide out of his sight. The twilight of Indian Summer had begun and the first red-and-orange fields of the outskirts glowed beside the train. The conductor came into the coach and Walter reached for his money in the clip. When he had paid for his ticket, he opened the envelope Mr. Chadley had given him and put his ticket in it. Then he saw the check, the amount for which it was drawn, and the note fastened to it.

DEAR MR. ABBOTT:
I have taken the liberty of increasing by a hundred dollars the money which is due you. It is small payment indeed for the privilege of being your most grateful employer and I hope you won't refuse it.
With all best wishes,
Sincerely yours,
FENTON CHADLEY

Walter slapped the envelope and the check and the note and his ticket against the seat edge and pressed his other hand against his eyes, holding his lids closed until his feeling of helplessness had subsided. Methodically, he put the ticket, check, and note into the envelope and into his jacket pocket. Then he reached to the rack above for his suitcase. Before he found his stationery, he had composed his answer.

DEAR MR. CHADLEY [it would read]:
I am two miles out of Newtown and have just discovered the evidence of your generosity. I cannot accept the additional money. I count my stay at Dunmeade and my experience in tutoring Ralph as being of particular value to me in my present sociological studies. I consider myself in your debt rather than you in mine. Without any intention of offending you, I shall return the excess amount when I have reached my destination and opened my first checking account.
Very truly yours,
WALTER ABBOTT

It was when he had difficulty tossing his valise back onto the rack that he noticed for the first time the long shallow rectangular box. He looked to see to whom it belonged so that he might shift it to better accommodate his bag. But there was no one sitting near him. Then he lifted down the box and saw his name written in crayon across the cardboard. He turned it over and saw his name in crayon again on the other side. At each of the four corners on each side was printed the word *fragile*. Cautiously, he shook the box. The contents made a slight, even, shifting sound. He sat down and held the box on his knees. Then he tore the carefully applied tape from the edges and opened it and removed the packing tissue which wedged the contents firmly in the box. Before he looked down at the letter, he knew from whom the present had come and he knew what it was. Excitement at the idea of it and the compliment to him whirred inside him and his heart struggled oddly. Conscious of his agitation and aggravated by it, with forced calm he held out the letter before him and, refraining from examining what was beneath it, he read:

DEAR MR. ABBOTT:

I will be at my music lesson when you leave so I have given this to O'Smyre to deliver when you get on the train. I hope you will like it because I think it is the best one I have done so far. I only finished it night before last. You have been thinking all along that I did not like you and did not want to be friends. Well, maybe that was so when you first came but I think we got along perfectly all right by the end of the summer. You were not very polite to me either at first. I want you to have this picture if you want it and I want to thank you for helping Ralph. You did a lot more than Uncle Chad paid you to do and if he never makes anything of himself it certainly will not be your fault. So remember. And if you ever come to Newtown, I hope you will come to see us.

Sincerely yours,

AUGUST CHADLEY

The lights came on in the coach. Walter held the letter out under the glare of the specked globe above the aisle and read it again. Then he put it on the seat and withdrew the framed drawing from the box.

When he had tilted it back and forth and found a position in which it was free from reflections upon its glass, he held it steady and looked into the pastoral scene which he had viewed with August from the hill in Quakertown. Wide and undulating, the rolling fields moved down into a valley and then rose again behind the deserted de Ventura farms. And on the last height, like a broad spreading crest of white foam upon a wave, was Mr. Lyndon's fine immaculate dairy, its cylindrical silo, its low rectangular sheds, its dome-roofed barns blazing in the spread of sun over its hill.

Walter examined the drawing more closely, an unfamiliar tension beginning its faint pain about his ribs. The faded browns and grays of the two de Ventura farms melted them into the shadows of their hollow, like shabby women slipping into dim alcoves. The ring of bright fields about them, and the rolling colored swells of earth leading to the crown of Mr. Lyndon's dairy upon the hill, exposed their desertion. Sure and unfaltering had been the hand which had drawn their disgrace and set the white dairy like a quicksilver creeping down upon their backs!

A kind of joy came over Walter. Suddenly, in a quick movement, he turned the drawing face down and would not look at it again. He thought foolishly, "He builded better than he knew; the conscious stone to beauty grew." And then he laughed, for at that moment, he became aware of the ridiculousness of his conceit!

⁂

Walter Abbott was only a day away when the catastrophe, toward which they had been moving with such blindness all summer, befell Dunmeade.

In the shock of the first hours after, neither Fenton, nor August, nor Gilberta (each for his own reasons) could mark it anything but a calamity Dunmeade ill-deserved. But guilt first pricked at August, who reached out to Mr. Abbott as he moved farther and farther away from her, unconsciously seeking his explanation as she described the tragedy to him.

DEAR MR. ABBOTT:

I am writing to tell you the terrible thing which happened here today. I will start at the beginning.

Billy Pickett got back to Newtown soon after you had gone to the station. (He was sorry he did not get to tell you good-by and wants to be remembered to you.) He called up to ask if Ralph wanted to go hunting this afternoon in those woods beyond the Newtown Lake. He said it would be the last time he would be able to take Ralph anywhere because he has to register at The Fortress on Monday.

Ralph did not think he could go because he had to report at the colored college this morning and did not know how long he would be there. But he got back by noon and called up Billy Pickett and said he had changed his mind. Uncle Chad was glad he had decided to go because Ralph was looking mopey and going hunting is something he is used to doing down on Prince River, where he is a very good shot.

Well, the next thing, about two hours later, Billy phoned from a gas station out there and said Ralph had been hurt very badly in an accident and he was driving him in town to the Doctor's Clinic. Uncle Chad went straight to the hospital to meet them and saw Ralph taken inside just covered in blood and unconscious. Billy said that one time, on the way in, he thought that Ralph had died.

While Ralph was in the operating room, Billy told Uncle Chad how it had happened. He said that they hadn't had any luck and had turned back and were going through a barbed wire fence. He was ahead and to the left hand side of Ralph. Suddenly he heard Ralph's gun go off. He said he looked back and saw Ralph stumble against the barbed wire and then the gun went off again although Ralph was almost clear of the wire with only one of his feet tangled in it. He was holding his gun close to his side, muzzle down, and did not drop it when it went off. Billy ran to help him and he said Ralph just sank on the ground and lay there with both his legs shot and didn't even moan or groan. Billy tore up his shirt and wound the rags around Ralph's legs. Ralph bled so that Billy didn't think he'd be able to drag him all the way to the road; but he did.

Ralph came to before Uncle Chad left the hospital and told him it wasn't Billy Pickett's fault. (He was afraid he had got Billy into trouble.) He said he just wanted to go back home now to Prince River. But he thanked Uncle Chad for giving him advantages. Uncle Chad is very upset, as you can imagine. He was very ambitious for Ralph and everything looked as if it were going to come out all right until this.

I hope you are not thinking that this is what I meant when we talked about Ralph once and I said I bet something happened at the last minute to spoil everything. I certainly didn't mean anything terrible like this. I am very sorry about it.

I hope you like your school.

Very sincerely yours,

August Chadley

August did not record her mother's reaction, because she had not examined into it.

Gilberta, since the dispute over Ralph's tenancy of the small room, had never reminded Fenton of her prediction that he would regret treating Ralph in a way improper toward one of low station. In her first indignation that Ralph had brought them scandal, there was a temptation to attack Fenton. But when, in an unexpected gesture of charity, she went with Fenton to the hospital and looked down at Ralph, observing with horror and yet admiration the result of his foolish and improper display of courage, she kept silent, satisfied that he had triumphed over Fenton, that he had, in his strange and ugly way, punished Fenton for unseemly ambitions.

Fenton's reaction was not a single one. He pitied Isaiah and Maude, to whom, it seemed to him, the cruelest and most unjust blow had been delivered. But because he had so generously and so earnestly tried to better Ralph's condition, encouraging in himself a true guardian's affection for Isaiah's son, he pitied himself also. Ralph could not have invited such injury with such consequences without first having removed from his heart all sense of gratitude and obligation toward him, his benefactor.

Only in the kitchen at Dunmeade was the grief instant and unquestioning. Susie and Addie each became in her sorrow his grieving mother, as much his mother as Maude. And O'Smyre, silent, his friend from that frightening first day of his residence at Dunmeade, went to the hospital night after night, to sit the darkness through, outside his room, waiting.

In a week, August received a reply from Walter Abbott, but not before he had written first to Ralph in care of Fenton.

"I wrote to Mr. Abbott," August confessed self-consciously to Fenton, "I thought he ought to be told how things turned out. He tried to help Ralph." She had felt her skin gather and moisten around her hair's edge.

But Fenton had only said, soberly, "I think that was a very thoughtful thing to do, dear." Fenton's despair had been underscored by his having received Mr. Abbott's letter refusing the little bonus he had wanted to declare for the summer's work.

August went to her studio and sat by a window to read:

DEAR AUGUST:

I have been pressed for time and so have written first to Ralph, with the hope that it would cheer him to know that though I am a long way from him, I am still his friend and "old teacher." You were good to inform me immediately of the accident. I do not know quite what to say to you about it or whether I should say anything at all. Although you did not say so, I have come to the conclusion that Ralph's injuries were not accidentally sustained. Unfortunately, knowing Ralph as well as I came to know him, it is not difficult for me to think that Ralph looked with despair upon his world, a world in which he found his security dependent upon the good will of one white family. Negroes are, in a tragic sense, still strangers in our white world. It must be a hospitable world for all Negroes before Ralph can feel secure in it, and he knows that. I think his accident settled his problem for him forever. He won't be forced to live up to

Mr. Chadley's high hopes and faith any longer. He can return to Prince River and hide in the marshes for the remainder of his life, for whatever peace there is in that escape from choices and decisions.

I know that each one of you has asked the question I have asked myself. "I wonder if I could have done anything to prevent it?" It is a hard answer to find, isn't it, August?

You do not need to reply to this letter. In a few days, I shall write again – about the "early Chadley" which is my most valuable possession! It deserves more remarking upon than I have time for at this moment, for I hear the last bell for supper ringing.

I hope after that to hear from you that Ralph is recovering and will be able to go home soon. My respects to Mr. Chadley.

Devotedly, your friend,

WALTER ABBOTT

Suddenly August began to weep. What right had Mr. Abbott to insinuate that she and Uncle Chad had driven Ralph to do what he had done? How had such a suggestion got into her letter? Of course, when it happened, everyone had thought Ralph might have avoided shooting himself the second time, but no one had come out and said he had done it on purpose, that he had meant to have the accident. They only thought he could have been more careful. They only blamed him for getting in such a mess after all that had been done for him.

Why is it my fault? she demanded, the question its own answer. She became aware of a sharp, strange, and suggestive agitation in her. It accumulated, stormlike, into a climax of painful emotion and then was gone, leaving her with a deep and shameful embarrassment, as her shocked senses identified it.

For a moment and only a moment, she had confronted life as Ralph!

With horror she stared out into the room and her lips formed the silent words, *What in the world would I do?*

During the year which followed the market collapse, Newtown kept a public countenance of cheerful faith in Business to right itself and to proceed with its hike over the rainbow to the pot of gold. Smoke ballooned reassuringly from the mill chimneys and any downtown stores which had gone into bankruptcy were ignored, except in one instance where the glare of the sun's reflection in the vacant show windows created a traffic hazard at an intersection.

Scandals exposed during the crisis were rationalized, so that, gradually, deliberate and indefensible dishonesty came to be thought of as innocent intention betrayed by freakish circumstances. Two attorneys who were discovered to have "borrowed" from estates in their trust to speculate for themselves in stocks were finally sympathized with as victims rather than offenders. They had been trapped and made to look common thieves. Such was not the case, of course, for they were good citizens, good husbands, good fathers, and regular churchgoers – as devoted to upholding decent practices as the beneficiaries they had robbed.

But with another autumn, a sobriety could be noticed upon the face of the city. Business had not righted itself and proceeded with its hike toward the pot of gold. Hundreds of farm mortgages had been foreclosed and the old Chadley Bank, in the grasp of Mr. Rench, had become a landowner and a landlord. The farmers had become tenants in their own houses upon their own lands, even more disgraced in their failures by there having been no buyers for their properties at the public foreclosure sales.

Near Newtown, small mills which were the whole of a town sometimes, first cut hours, then payrolls, and finally, production entirely, if reorganization failed. That particular autumn – the leaves gone earlier than usual and the damp wind of winter already rising suddenly here and there for a day along the plateau – the workmen going to Boxie's River Webbing Mill stopped in the dawn to stare at masses of dead fish pitching over the dam to catch below in the rocks, or float in the shallows along the banks. Within an hour, staring crowds lined the water's edge for half a mile on either side of the mill. Work was halted. At noon the owner made a statement which the Newtown newspaper carried beneath the headline *Mill Wastes Pollute Boxie's River*. He declared simply that with the falling-off of business in the general hard times, he had kept up his payroll in lieu of buying improved machinery. That was the true, depressing story. Later on in the winter, he obtained relief from his problems; his mill was bought by its great competitor, the Starburg Mills of Newtown, and he became its manager, salaried, and relieved both of burden and possession.

By autumn before the national moratorium on banks, the de Venturas (with the exception of Pedro, who had abandoned them) had slipped home to Quakertown, neither embarrassed at their condition nor grateful to Fenton that their farms were still theirs to claim. Their escapade was never referred to, either by them or by their caretakers, the Chadleys.

In the light of subsequent events it began to appear that Fenton, in 1929, had been very shrewd; and as the days darkened with worries for certain other men with whom he had once dealt, there came to be a disagreeable feeling among them that he had outsmarted them. However, instead of applauding the business astuteness with which they were now crediting him, and respecting him for what they considered to have been a slick operation, they were aggrieved and resentful, as if he had profited unfairly from some unnatural prophetic ability they had not attributed to him before. It was hard to believe that their former low opinion of his abilities was unfounded and that, better than they, he took his advantages during the rising market. Gaither Lyndon even said to him once during the sour days of the bank's dissolution, following the holiday, "I certainly had you cut out wrong in my mind, Mr. Chadley." He always breathed wheezily over the "Mr." He had never been comfortable calling Fenton Mr. Chadley when he remembered him as a boy in his father's bank. But there always had been something about Fenton which compelled all men to call him Mr. Chadley, and it had nothing to do with his having come into his father's high place. "It's right funny, isn't it?" Gaither went on, "I've known you almost all your life and you've always worn those special glasses but it never came to my mind that they made you see farther than other folks!" A great asthmatic laughter pushed out into Fenton's face from Gaither's irritated throat. He enjoyed his own wit like a pig nosing for a corn grain it has coughed from its own windpipe. The muscles of Fenton's eyes contracted painfully and he closed them. He had not been able to smile even.

Dunmeade's time spans were always marked with climaxes peculiar to it, the events within its walls fitting in small sharp pieces inside the large frame of events around it.

When he gave up the bank, Fenton was faced with a task he had only half anticipated – the filling of his hours of the day. There was nowhere he must be at a certain time. He had no contact with the daily business struggle going on in the city. His fortunes were not affected by the decline of business in general even though his earned income from various holdings was less during the crisis years. His resources were so great that he could have weathered many more years of diminishing receipts and not known real alarm. In desperation and boredom he began to make frequent trips to the East to watch over the affairs of the Wortham Turpentine and Lumber Company. And these trips, even when they did not materially result in a conspicuous increase in the profits of that firm, brought him some relief from idleness. And he saw Isaiah and Maude and Ralph. His concern for them was great. The club which had leased Mr. Chadley's old house (willed upon his death to Isaiah) had disbanded, its members no longer able to afford such luxuries as a private hunting and fishing club. Fenton made up the loss in income to Isaiah out of his pocket. He had suggested that Isaiah sell him the old homestead but Isaiah had declined, hoping that times would improve soon and that he would no longer be dependent upon Fenton for help. He was sure that soon Fenton and all the other Fentons in the country would straighten out the difficulties and put an end to hard times, and that the property Mr. Chadley had left him would be rented again. He was old and with age and service to the Chadleys he had changed from the courageous man who had stood once in the swampy clearing and demanded consideration for the squatters. He was brought to final defeat by Ralph's cruel triumph over them all and though he had not examined his attitude and therefore had not noticed the parallel, he was reacting to his relationship to Fenton just as Ralph had done. He was accepting, even desiring paternal care, slipping deeper and deeper into dependence and shying from having to take the responsibility of making even a decision regarding his property. With the property in his possession, he could always in the end turn it over to Fenton in payment for all the years of support he might have required.

In a strange way he was not afraid for Ralph, for what he might face in a future without him or Maude. Ralph's self-inflicted injury was like some sort of badge declaring freedom and independence of his person. He would never be corrupted in his peculiar privacy by the needs and fears which swayed the decisions of others. He was apart and whole with his maimed legs in a way that the upright would never be. He had got free of the mania for independence because he had understood that it had nothing to do with physical demonstration. He was in another world and lived in it in the image of himself which he loved best — a free and roving human apart from other humans, black and white. Fenton, or someone, would always care for Ralph the cripple, Isaiah knew.

In the summer of 1932, returning home from a trip to the East, Fenton experienced a shocking sensation as he drove into Newtown. Though he approached it from the same highway he had always used, it seemed to him that the whole aspect of the city had changed since his departure a few weeks before. The buildings seemed suddenly telescoped together in an ugly huddle of unlike and incompatible architectural forms, and the brick factory of Mr. Lyndon (for he drove along it) seemed suddenly to have pressed down so closely as to be almost in the business section. He had always thought of it as being on the outskirts. There was an ugly barrenness to the streets, since there were no longer any trees to shade the sidewalks. Fenton himself had voted for the widening of the streets but he had never thought that the great quiet elms and light-leafed maples would be missed and take with their uprooting something fine and firm from the visual structure of the place he called home.

It brought an uneasiness into his mind to have noticed the ugliness of Newtown for the first time. He had never thought of it as being either ugly or pleasing before. But it seemed to him suddenly that there must have been a time when it had had some beauty, urban and crisp and unlike a village, of course, but not as it was now. He remembered something that August had said once about a party she had come from. "It was supposed to be fancy dress," she said, "and everyone tried to outdo everyone else on originality. But I kept thinking we all looked as if we were at a 'tacky party.' There really wasn't any difference, the taste was so terrible." He entered the gates of Dunmeade a few minutes later with a nervous relief to find that his own grounds still spread smooth and well-tended and full of growing flowers happily arranged together to play up the beauty of each separate variety. There was order without any sacrifice of individuality.

August was playing on the piano when he entered the house. It cheered him to hear her. She did not frequently sit down to the instrument since she had ceased to study music. He felt a certain sadness about it, for it told him, more plainly than any protest from her could ever have done, that the practice hours she had once spent had been for his sake only and were to her a sacrifice of her time to no purpose. And so when she went to the piano of her own accord and played for even a few minutes, it pleased him.

"There's been someone to see you," August called out to him. She came into the hall out of the drawing room and kissed him and felt along his arms and cheeks in an appraising way to see if he had lost weight. It was a routine she went through after each of his trips and though she laughed as she slapped and pinched and considered, he knew she was really seriously inquiring when she asked, "Did you wear yourself out? Are you the same man who left?" His health was a matter of concern to her.

"I had a very good trip, thank you," he said self-consciously, "I feel very fit, really. Nothing has happened in my absence, has it?" He was asking if everyone in his household had kept well, but he had grown sensitive over his own weakness in contrast to the seemingly unchanging robust conditions of the others and he never used such words as illness or health.

"Addie had the last of her teeth extracted – you know, the one that hung down in the middle like a rabbit? And now she has plates," August said. "She grinds on them furiously sometimes." August began to laugh. "She went around in the kitchen with nothing at all in her mouth until Mother caught her and made her start wearing the false ones. They're beauties. Wait until she whistles through them trying to say soufflé!"

"I shall take particular care not to notice," Fenton replied.

"That's because you're very different from me. I think it's funny. It can happen to anyone. And it does usually, sooner or later." She reached for a card on the tray on the small Queen Anne table by the stair. It was the only card.

"Here's the name of the man who came to see you. You just missed him."

Fenton brought the card up near his face. Printed on it was a name with which he was familiar only from having read it at times in the newspaper when there had been a college graduation exercise. It was an inexpensive card and the lettering was not embossed.

"Dr. Claude White?" he read out questioningly and looked at August. "Isn't he the president of Marion College?"

"I think so," said August. "He looked like the president of something." She put her fingers up to her cheeks and indicated deep folds beginning at each side of the nostrils and running down to the chin.

"Thank you, dear," Fenton said abruptly. "I'll see to it later." He hurried up the stair away from August. She had a chilling way of picturing faces. He did not know what it was that made her see them so unflatteringly. And then, fearing he might have offended her, he looked back from the gallery and started to say something. But August was standing before the gilt-scrolled looking glass by the door examining her own image as she pulled up her eyelids at the outer corners in imitation of an oriental.

"I don't like my own sometimes either," she said, clearly for Fenton's benefit, knowing he had stopped on the upstairs hall. "I have a date tonight and I'm going to have to go out looking the way I've looked all my life. And he's known me all that time too. A pity, isn't it? But he'll be looking the same old way too, so I guess it'll be even Stephen."

"I really don't understand you sometimes, dear," Fenton said, his hand on the black iron rail of the gallery.

"That's good," August replied and laughed and then she darted back into the drawing room and took up playing her piano composition where she had left off, delivering the runs in a loud and abandoned fashion.

Fenton went to his apartment. He wanted to lie down awhile before tea. He was really quite tired and he sometimes had a strange feeling of dizziness come over him, as if nothing about him were quite real and he were not in command of himself. August had upset him. And yet he told himself sternly that he should not be surprised at anything she said or did. She was almost seventeen, at that treacherous period in her life when everything was a little out of focus to her and she behaved accordingly. He must bear with her and show no impatience with her struggle to maturity. What most annoyed him was her prepossession with her appearance and her habit of making almost disgusting remarks about her features at times. The truth was that she was nearly beautiful with a rare, odd strength about the modeling of her face which, when it was in repose, had an almost breathtaking quality to it — as if one had suddenly confronted in a shop of trifles one purely executed marble head. Gilberta, too, was aware of it for he had seen her once observing August in the same way she quietly examined a perfect blossom, seeking the secret of its symmetry in the surprising contradiction of its tints and shades of color. Fenton sighed and drew his curtains apart to let in the breeze and then deliberately turning his mind from the contemplation of anything which would keep him awake, he stretched himself slowly across the summer cover of his day bed, found the best position, and went to sleep.

Dr. Claude White came back to Dunmeade at Fenton's invitation on the following afternoon. Fenton escorted him to the study and there heard the business which had brought him.

While their conference lasted, O'Smyre, close enough at times to the windows to hear their voices, mowed the grass at that side of the house and pulled the weeds from the border. Dr. White's business kept him with Fenton nearly two hours. When the educator left, Fenton went back to the study and, closing the door, though it was warm with no draft to relieve the stillness of four o'clock, took out some papers from his safe and carefully went over them, making notations of figures on a clean sheet of paper which he left in his desk drawer when he had replaced the documents in the safe. The next morning, he drove to Marion College, which was nine miles southwest of the city and had once been in the country. It was now the center of a village inhabited by its teachers and other employees who, as the school had grown, had moved from the original dormitories for them on the campus and built small stone or clapboard houses.

It might have been hundreds of miles from Newtown. The rising hills which began the range of mountains to the distant west were visible from the steps of the central building.

Fenton entered the old unpainted plastered hall, stood for a moment debating the door at which to knock, and then heard his name called. He turned to see Dr. White coming up the steps to the stoop behind him.

"My office is down below, Mr. Chadley," he said, "the English faculty uses the small rooms here for student conferences."

"I see. Thank you," said Fenton, and he went back down to the sand walk and accompanied Dr. White to a room at the end of the building on the ground floor to which there was an outside door reached by a narrow private path.

Inside, it was cool, one window shadowed by morning glory vines which had worked their way over the old ivy climbing the brick corner of the building.

At that moment, a strange and happy excitement began to grow in Fenton. He sat down beside Dr. White and opened his small briefcase.

"I hope that we have before us a long and successful association, Dr. White," he said.

The two bent over the papers.

The end of summer had come and August had returned to school for her last term before Fenton asked her in to the study to tell her of the decision he had come to and the arrangements he had made as a result of Dr. White's visit to Dunmeade. While he did not expect August to react in any way except favorably to what he had done on her behalf as her legal guardian (for the reasons he would give her), yet he had postponed asking her to come in for a talk at least three times. For buried beneath all the logical and finely inspired reasons for taking up what he knew was a good work and a reward in itself, there was the consciousness that he was going to use the project to hold August to him.

He had dutifully and carefully built an independent mind within her; and then as the time neared when she would come into her inheritance, he had begun to understand that it might become the structure upon which his own tie to her would be broken. And his tie to her was necessary to his life. He had become frightened of the thought that she would go away. He did not know where she would go or even whether she might consider it necessary simply to demonstrate her physical independence when she came into control of her inheritance. He tried on one or two occasions to draw her out, to lead her to confessing what private hopes or aims she had. But August did not take up his leads and if she had any intentions she did not disclose them. She appeared to be unaware of the significance of the day which they were approaching. And this alarmed him more than if he had met with opposition when he began to persuade her to cut the cloth of her ambitions to fit the old and comfortable shape of residence at Dunmeade. He began to prepare himself with arguments to keep her. He would build a studio for her, even add a wing where she might live more privately and undisturbed with her painting. And then he remembered that the house itself would belong to August, did already, and he was not in the position to proffer this inducement. And he recalled with a shock that he had once suggested to her that she deed the house to Gilberta. He had been so short-sighted as to inspire her to give up her home—which would in a single act have cut her free from the obligation to tend the one common physical root between them all. He did not know whether she remembered or not, and he was afraid to recall it to her mind even for the purpose of telling her that he had reconsidered the wisdom of making her mother such a gift.

She sat down opposite him and assumed a serious attitude when he told her there was a business matter he wished to discuss. He smiled a little at the sobriety of her expression and was about to reassure her that it was not a disaster he had to report when suddenly she said, "What's the matter? Aren't we rich anymore?" She was not being flip and she had not said it lightly. "I don't care, you know," she said before he could answer. "I've thought about it. It's really a terrible burden to be as rich as we are. I think it has been a terrible burden to you." She looked at him directly and repeated again, "I've thought about it." She drew her breath quickly and then as if letting the words spill out as she exhaled, she said the rest of it, something she apparently had been preparing herself to say for some time. "It's going to ruin Billy Pickett's life. He isn't going to be a doctor. He says he isn't going to study medicine and then dishonor his profession by just becoming an authority on patent medicines so he can endorse the

Pickett advertising." She caught her breath again and held it as if this confession had exhausted her and she were pausing for strength to go on. Then she finished, "He doesn't have to know anything to be a quack like his grandfather, so he's not going back to school this term. If he has to end up learning to take care of his family's money and how to run the factory, then he will. But he isn't going to be a doctor just to see they're not sued for false claims and watch over the chemical department. He isn't going to be a doctor if he can't practice. He would have no self-respect. And no one else would have any respect for him." She sank back into the chair then and seemed to pull herself inward as she concluded softly, "So some people's lives can be ruined."

Fenton was so astonished and so unprepared to hear what she had told him that he was speechless. He had seen Billy Pickett throughout the summer when he had come to take August swimming or dancing. He had talked with him often about his preparation at the university to go North to one of the great medical schools. He had been fired with the excitement that moved Billy when he described his work. He knew that Billy believed already that he was a doctor, that within he was and could never be anything else. He could not imagine what had happened at the Pickett's to bring Billy to the decision August had so hardly quoted. With the shock of being turned aside from his own purpose, and in such a way, it gradually came over him that he was being accused. The tone of August's voice and her own anger – for this was anger with August, told him that he was one with the Picketts in her view, though she did not say so. Indeed she had implied sympathy for him at the opening of her tirade but by the time she had finished, it was clear that she admired Billy for not compromising his principles and she suspected that such a time of decision had probably come for him and he had not been Billy Pickett. And because his guilt about the bank was so deep and so close with him always, he imagined that she had decided that if he had ever wanted to continue to be a banker, he would have found help in his crisis and gone on with the only profession he had ever had.

"I am so sorry," he finally murmured, not knowing really to which he referred—her disappointment at Billy's defeat or his own, or his sorrow over both.

When he turned back to her she was standing at the mantel and had picked up one of the *bocage* figures. She was tracing the glazed leaves and flowers behind the shepherdess with her fingers. Without looking at him she said reflectively, "I suppose that if I had been a boy I would have been going into the bank with you by now and you wouldn't have decided to sell it when you had to have your operation."

It was too much for Fenton to protest with calm. "Oh, *no*," he shouted in pain. And then, ashamed of a violence so unnatural to him, he went to her and took away her free hand from the figurine and clasped it in his. "Oh, no," he repeated, "you are mistaken." And to relieve himself at last of the pattern of scheming to hold her, he faced himself and denied forever his right to indulge his own yearning. "Oh, no," he said still again. "You have always been free to do with your life whatever you felt called to do. I have thought only to care for you in your dependence upon me. When I am no longer here, you and your mother will be as safe from unscrupulous exploitation as I could make you. Soon, you will come into your property from your father and grandfather and while I am living I will continue the management of your affairs. There will be no responsibility upon you. You will be free, as you always have been, to use any amount you can afford, to do anything you like."

She looked steadily at him, letting her hand rest in his without responding to the pressure of his tense fingers. She said, "It's the way you have always looked after Isaiah's property and money from Grandfather too, isn't it?"

And innocently Fenton nodded. Then he added, "I have tried to improve his circumstances too, just as your grandfather did."

They were silent. And then, another thought occurring to Fenton, he reassured her, "There will be no cause for you to be burdened with the physical welfare of Isaiah or Maude or Ralph, if I am not here. I have prepared against that eventuality too.

They will be watched over by the same trustees as you and your mother. You may rest your mind there."

"And if I had been a man?" she asked quietly, still pursuing the answer he had not given.

"But you weren't a man, dear," he said, "and there is really no argument."

"Why isn't Billy Pickett free to be a doctor and practice?" she asked.

"Because the circumstances are not the same at all, dear," he answered; and then he amended: "But of course I shouldn't venture any opinion really. I don't know the exact situation."

"The circumstances are different because he is a boy, aren't they?" she persisted.

Fenton sighed. And then he replied, cautiously, "Of course, dear, every father hopes that his son will grow up to want to continue the family interests and take his place."

"But girls are not expected to do that," she said as if concluding Fenton's explanation and no longer questioning him.

"It is not possible to expect it of them," he said; "they are not the same." And then lamely, aware that his reasons were not quite satisfactory yet to her, he added, "It isn't right. They are women."

"Then it would have made a difference if I had been a boy," she went back. "It might have," he conceded. And then quickly, "But I would not have tried to persuade you to come into the bank with me. You would have been free to select your own profession. At least I would have tried to make you feel free."

August suddenly put the *bocage* figure back on the corner of the mantel and pulled her other hand from Fenton's.

"What was it you wanted to speak to me about?" she asked. She waited with a strange, inquiring, almost suspicious stare, while the undissipated surcharge of hostility which had risen in the air seemed to solidify into a felt but unseen wall between them.

Fenton knew that he could not tell her now. The things which had been said had loosed barbs of distrust, the import of them yet only half determined, but lodged surely like clots against the septa of their hearts, the impulses of love and trust weakened.

With such damage, the course of each one's relationship to the other must be rerouted around the lesion, and time and no further irritation would be required for that.

He lied with half the truth.

"I wanted to tell you that in the past month I have undertaken to assist Marion College to continue its existence," he said. "In the present financial condition of the country, several small colleges have found themselves in desperate straits. Dr. White approached me in their eleventh hour, so to speak, and after thoroughly examining their books and familiarizing myself with their curriculum, I came to the decision to aid the college substantially."

August nodded with a mixture of relief and puzzlement in her expression. Fenton had never discussed his business transactions with her except in a general way. It was not evident why he had made such a point of telling her this. But what was needed to explain to August why it was important for her to know all this was the one fact which it was now impossible for Fenton to disclose. The large loan he had made to Marion College had been August's money as well as his own – for reasons very private and critical to Fenton. He had hoped to involve her interest in saving the institution, and through it to excite her into studying there herself – and so remaining at Dunmeade. And he rushed on now to explain his making the loan at all, as he had prepared to explain it had he told her all the truth.

"I went very thoroughly into the causes for the drop in student enrollment, and it seemed to me that if there were fewer students going to college now, then those who were able must be induced to come here by special attractions. I made it a provision, in granting the financial aid, that a department of music would be established and also a department of art and one teaching secretarial courses. Students enrolling in these departments would be special students who would be able to complete enough study to be awarded a certificate at the end of two years if they were not able to remain four years to earn a degree." He looked at August hopefully. In spite of his depressed spirits, a note had come into his voice which gave away the happiness which was growing in him as he developed his plans. The college was becoming his own, and he spoke of it as a parent of his first infant, beginning to imagine its future in terms of what he should do for it and the inevitable use it should make of its advantages.

"Of course, it is a large undertaking. Space must be arranged, perhaps a new building erected. And there will be new teachers. But I am very hopeful of success." He blushed and concluded, "If we build a better mousetrap, you know?"

"I think you're going to be quite busy," August said.

"Yes," said Fenton.

He waited for her to say that she approved, or that she would be glad to help.

But she made no other comment. She was looking past him to the window. She seemed to be waiting for him to elaborate further or else allow her to go. Finally, in a desperate impulse to catch her interest, he said, "I've been wondering if I ought not to take this up with Mr. Abbott." He had not thought of it until that moment.

August did not break her stare toward the window. She seemed to be reflecting. Then she said, "I suppose he'd be very glad to get a better job."

The tension in Fenton broke and subsided at last. She had suggested what had not yet come into his own mind. He had meant only that it might be advantageous to discuss the plans with Mr. Abbott for the sake of his advice.

"Yes, I suppose he would," Fenton agreed quickly. "I have not written him because I felt we should be further along before I suggest he give up his present position. I'm afraid it will take until the spring term to organize and set up the secretarial department, and probably until next fall before we can offer the courses in the other new departments. And there's a new catalogue to be issued by summer, and we shall need to get the names of spring graduates from the high schools."

"You seem to know a great deal about it," said August.

"Dr. White has very generously allowed me to participate in

planning these small details of promotion," replied Fenton, embarrassed at exposing to her the involvement of his interest. A strange serenity for the final outcome of it all had begun to settle in him. He wanted to talk on and on, now.

"Did you want me to study art there?" August asked abruptly. She observed him again with that odd, suspicious inquiry in her eyes.

"I think that would depend upon whether or not you want to study art at all, wouldn't it?" Fenton replied easily. He was in command of himself at last and he was capable of employing some of the shrewdness he had once used in the conduct of the bank's affairs. "The department of art will be organized mainly to prepare students planning to teach in the grade schools. Your old teacher, Miss Applewhite, no doubt took some such courses along with her required work for a teacher's certificate."

August was silent. She seemed to be thinking over what Fenton had said, with a certain puzzlement and rejection of it, for she frowned suddenly.

But at that moment, a wonderful idea came to Fenton. "I wonder if Mr. Abbott might not be interested in working on the catalogue," he said, and as he said it, was aware of an excitement filling him which he struggled to restrain. A curious and not altogether wholesome suggestion was in his mind. He was offering August Mr. Abbott, loosing him like a tempting bait from a treacherously slackened line.

"I have no idea," said August. She was not going to encourage Fenton.

"I think Dr. White might welcome a special assistant for this task. It involves helping him to work out the new curriculum also, you know. One of the teachers presently on the faculty will have to take it on as extra work unless someone is engaged."

He pretended to mull the idea in his mind and looked away from August and removed his glasses and began to wipe them with the tissues he kept in his pocket. Then he said crisply, his decision clearly expressed in what he asked her. "I suppose I should address a letter to Mr. Abbott at his school. He has no doubt returned by now from his vacation."

A rapidly deepening color had begun to spread up into August's face from her throat until by the time she spoke, her cheek bones seemed to press out in two brightly pink spots. "I think he's in New York doing some work on his thesis," she said, "I don't think he plans to go back to the school."

"Is that so?" said Fenton, surprised. "I'm afraid I must have misunderstood you earlier when you said something about the possibility of his being interested in a better job. I took it to mean that you thought he might prefer coming here to remaining at his school. I didn't know he had resigned his position.'

"He didn't resign. He knew they couldn't afford to keep him and he just made other arrangements before he was let off." She was breathing rapidly with slightly noisy intakes of air through her nostrils.

"I scc," murmured Fenton, "I didn't know you had heard from him recently."

Without warning, August walked to the door. "I'll get his address," she said, and without another word, escaped.

Fenton stood still beside the fireplace. He heard her sharp running steps up to the gallery and felt the faint vibration of the door slam after. Then he sat down, not quite certain if he was really to wait. He was confused. Thc slightly unpleasant thought of the bait came into his mind again. He was still holding his glasses in one hand. He put them on. Then, as if with placing his thick lenses back before his eyes he were able to clear his internal vision, he saw the net with which they had drawn each other in. "Oh dear," he whispered to himself, and relaxed upon a buoying elation.

~

So Walter Abbott returned to Dunmeade.

He came in the wet of November when the trees had dropped the last of their shriveling leaves which lay soaked and pressing solid into a cover over the grounds of Dunmeade. And Fenton, in the patio waiting for him, with a raincoat held above his head as protection against the fine swirls of misty rain, thought, as Walter stepped from the car with O'Smyre, "He must have been somewhat older than I thought. Or he has changed considerably in three years." He stepped out to meet Mr. Abbott.

"Welcome home," he said, blushing. "We are happy to have you here again."

"Thank you, Mr. Chadley," Walter replied and took Fenton's hand. "You are looking very much better than when I left." He laughed and added, "That's what every man should do if he can – retire while he's still young."

"Yes, I suppose so," Fenton said quickly. The remark had upset him. He let them stand a moment in the mist, holding their smiles upon their faces. And then he got himself together and put his hand out toward the door to invite Mr. Abbott in before him.

"August wishes me to tell you that she is unavoidably detained in a history class this hour at her school, which will account for her not being here to greet you," he said stiffly as they walked in. He had meant to repeat August's message and enjoy laughing at it again with Mr. Abbott, for he was certain the wit of it would be as apparent upon repetition as it had been to him when August instructed him. But somewhow the humor had died from it and Mr. Abbott accepted August's regrets literally and then inquired after Gilberta's health.

"Mrs. Chadley is not as well as she might be," Fenton answered, and then, at the expression he took to be concern in Walter's face, he quickly explained, "Oh, it isn't anything serious, really. It's her back. August and I have decided it's an occupational malady of a sort. We cannot get her to desist from hoeing and digging and pushing a wheelbarrow full of transplantings and one thing and another, all of which results sooner or later in a very painful lameness in her back. And in weather such as this, she is scarcely able to get up and down the stair." Fenton was really quite out of sympathy with Gilberta on this matter and his voice had a kind of indignant snorting sound as he finished, "It's quite ridiculous. O'Smyre is there to do all that sort of thing and now there's an extra colored boy besides. He comes over from the Agricultural College three times a week to get practical experience."

Walter could not restrain a smile. "Mrs. Chadley goes about her separate occupation, doesn't she. I remembered her whenever I came to the lines, '*She dwelt among the untrodden ways . . .*' in English Lit." Then, to Fenton's questioning look, he said, "Oh, I taught various courses before it was all over, Mr. Chadley. As the budget shrank and teachers were dismissed, those of us remaining took up the slack, so to speak. I taught Hygiene one quarter." He laughed and then finished, "But I don't think I was a satisfactory instructor. I wasn't asked to repeat the course. What was wanted was inspiration rather than facts, I suppose."

They were still standing in the foyer and, in the silence following this discomforting speech of Mr. Abbott's, Fenton remembered his duties and said, "You're to have your same room, I believe. Shall we go up?"

For a moment Walter hesitated, as if he wanted to say something. But Fenton had started and so he turned to the stair. O'Smyre came in from the kitchen with Walter's two bags and started up behind them.

When he had left Walter to go to his own apartment to freshen himself before luncheon, Fenton paused at his door and looked back. He had meant to tell Mr. Abbott that Addie or Susie would unpack and press out his things later and he needn't trouble with them now. But he saw that Mr. Abbott had come out to the gallery and was leaning over the black iron banister, apparently looking at the front door. Walter raised his head quickly when he became conscious of Fenton standing in the hall, and in an easy voice called down to him, "I thought I heard someone come in. I thought it might be August." Then he went back into his room before Fenton could reply, "We don't expect her usually until after three o'clock."

Fenton was still ruminating upon the incident as he brushed his hair. It had seemed odd when he had stated that August unfortunately could not be at home to welcome Mr. Abbott. And yet, of course, it was possible that Mr. Abbott had thought August in the habit of returning for luncheon. In a way, he was pleased that Mr. Abbott was so anxious to see her again. And yet, since that unhappy discussion he and August had had in the study, Fenton had been conscious of a slight uneasiness within his mind when he thought of August and Mr. Abbott. She had kept to herself the knowledge of the young teacher's changed circumstances and he wondered if she would have told him at all if things had not gone as they had that afternoon. But of course, she might only have been exercising polite discretion, allowing Mr. Abbott the privilege of apprising Fenton of his goings and comings when he saw fit. Still he wondered sometimes about their correspondence. Insofar as he knew, their exchange of letters had been infrequent, and certainly the letters themselves must have been simple friendly recountings of events in their lives. No doubt, however, August had written of Billy Pickett's change of plans and perhaps even described Billy's temporary sense of frustration. But that was understandable and he was sure Mr. Abbott had overlooked whatever prejudice was evident in August's account of how Billy had come to dramatically renounce his medical studies.

Fenton completed his toilet and then went downstairs to arrange some notes he had made to give Mr. Abbott before he drove him out to Marion College to meet Dr. White.

Dr. Claude White was a man nearing sixty. He had spent nearly forty years of his life as a teacher and administrator. He had become the president of Marion College when he was thirty-five, by the unanimous decision of his board of governors and trustees, half of whom were nonresidents of the state. He had served the college diligently and well through a shrewd knowledge of the limitations of the nonprofessional educator's mind and his natural suspicion of the advanced scholar. He had had a happy career and he presented to the observer a perfect image of the modest teacher always conscious of his trust and always respectful of it. But along with his gentle manner of speech, he could suggest with unmistakable firmness that he believed there were fields of study which it was not prudent to lead the very young to explore. And when he was pushed to add certain new courses to the curriculum for the sake of advancing the scholastic and financial position of the college, he could be very regretful and stubborn. Had he not been desperate for the substantial financial help which Fenton was willing to give the college, he would never have sanctioned the inclusion of an art course in the requirements for a degree in education – more specifically, a certificate to teach in the grade schools.

The students who attended Marion College were women, and most of them were enrolled with the intention on the part of their parents of inspiring them to become primary grade teachers. Not infrequently, as many as three young ladies from the same family would be attending at the same time. School teaching was a refined and acceptable profession for women, but why it was necessary for them to be taught to paint and draw, in order to teach their future charges the history of the world's great paintings or how to cut out paper flowers to keep idle hands busy between arithmetic and grammar classes, was something Dr. White could not see. It seemed to him to be bringing into the classification of a worthy pursuit an activity unsuited to the natural inclinations of women and, not only that, an activity about which there had been from time immemorial a discrediting atmosphere of unwholesomeness and frivolity.

However, when he became aware of the decision in Fenton Chadley's mind to measure the sum of his support against the admittance of the courses he had specifically suggested, Dr. White bent before expediency and persuaded his equally alarmed trustees to do the same. And a few days after, he was mollified and helped to accept the forfeiture of his sovereignty by observing what he had not suspected in Fenton's life – a hidden cross to bear. He took Sunday-night supper at Dunmeade and was shown August's drawings and paintings in the room upstairs which had been given her to use as a private studio. He understood much after that. He was conscious of the absence of any of her work on the walls of any other room in the house. He began to develop a deep forgiveness and sympathy for Fenton. He wondered, as he looked at the breathtakingly ugly forms of August's figures and the overly bright demanding landscapes, what end it would all come to for so kindly and respected a man as Mr. Chadley. And he resolved then to help him to channel this wayward talent of August's into a safe harbor. Together, they would provide the girl with purpose – teaching.

It was while in this mood that he agreed to allow Fenton to bring Mr. Abbott from the North to assist him. And on the afternoon that he waited for Fenton to drive Mr. Abbott out to Marion College, he was conscientiously engaged in reviewing the applications of instructors for positions in the department of secretarial training.

He had had some reservations about teaching young women stenography and typewriting and encouraging them to take positions in business offices too. But Mr. Chadley had pointed out that it would be charity to provide women with some respectable means of supporting themselves and perhaps children who might be dependent upon them if they were widowed suddenly. The field of teaching was becoming more crowded, and he had suggested tactfully that certain young women, through no fault of their own, were intellectually unsuited to that calling. Dr. White had had to agree on this point, as every year a few students, despite outside coaching, had fallen by the wayside. This had always occasioned great distress in the parents and shame in the girls. Having earned a secretarial certificate at some respected institution such as Marion College, they would certainly be put in the way of obtaining employment in the better type of business offices. He was certain that he could rely on Mr. Chadley's wisdom in recommending that they offer secretarial courses. Mr. Chadley had been a businessman himself, and had described the type of employment he had offered young women in the clerical department of his bank. Mr. Chadley had directly stated that no irregularity in the relations of the young women to the young men in his bank had ever been reported to him. Dr. White wished to protect himself in every way against any accusation in the future that he had provided some honest and innocent girl with the opportunity to succumb to human temptation.

He went to the window of his basement office when he heard steps on the sand walk. Looking out, he saw Mr. Chadley and a tall, athletically proportioned younger man who wore no hat and whose hair had been cropped close to his head in the fashion of prison inmates. He wore what appeared to be a suit of unpressed sacking and his socks, which could be clearly seen as his trousers flapped against his ankles with each step, were plaid, with green and yellow predominating in the color scheme. But he wore glasses. *That* was reassuring. Dr. White left the window and went to the private entrance door to welcome his new assistant. It was two o'clock.

August first saw Walter Abbott again as he walked around the circular sand drive from the garage to the patio. She heard the car drive in and went running from her room to a window in the little bedchamber Ralph Craig had once occupied. Like Dr. White, she observed the close cut of his hair, the seemingly deliberate lack of fit of his suit, his Argyle socks, and at last his heavy rimmed glasses. He might at that moment have been a stranger whom she had never seen before, so surely did his appearance suggest a foreignness to Newtown. And then he raised his head as if he had known she would be standing there, and sure that he had seen her, she threw up one hand awkwardly and waved. He smiled and called out, "Hello," and pointed before him toward the door. He wanted her to come down. She had changed from the velveteen dress with the linen collar which she had worn to school, but she had not yet arranged her hair. She nodded to him and ran back to her room. She had meant to part her hair in the middle and draw it tight over her ears and into a gold barrette on her neck. But there was not time, not now. He would know that she was making a special effort, that she had planned to look a certain way. With an almost arrogant lack of care to the details of setting the one pin in place which held her hair smoothly from a wide side part, she brushed the loose ends into a smooth roll touching her shoulders and went down the gallery and down the stair to meet him.

He was standing in the foyer just in front of Fenton, waiting. He had not gone into the drawing room. "I'm very glad to see you again," he said. He might have been host and she the newly arrived guest. "It's been a long time, hasn't it?" And she did not need to agree or make any other reply for very naturally, as if it were expected, he kissed her.

August was so astonished and so embarrassed that she began to laugh out of self-consciousness. "Goodness," she said, and then she said again, "Goodness."

Fenton cleared his throat with a little cough. And August, because she had been prepared to do it and Mr. Abbott's unexpected greeting had confused her, held out her hand formally to him and said, "I'm very glad to see you too." Then still agitated, she explained without there being any need to, "Mother will be down in a moment," and started to lead the three of them into the drawing room.

But Mr. Abbott did not follow. "I think I should clean up a bit, now," he said, "if you'll excuse me." He went up the stair, almost running.

Behind him, August and Fenton deliberately avoided each other's eyes. They sat down in the drawing room without any intentions and in a few minutes were joined by Gilberta.

"Mr. Abbott has arrived," said August.

And Gilberta replied, "Yes, he was in time for luncheon."

"He's just excused himself to change his clothes," explained Fenton. Then, after removing his glasses and rubbing one eye carefully, he replaced them and said, "Perhaps I should take this opportunity to change mine." He bowed slightly to the ladies and walked sedately out of the room.

"Have you made the table arrangement, yet?" August asked her mother mildly.

"No, I was just going to do it. Do you want to help me?" She looked at August with a calm appraising eye. August was picking at the narrow fringe binding the upholstered arm of the chair. "You usually do your hair a little more becomingly for that dress, don't you, dear?" she asked matter-of-factly. She stood up with a stiff elevating movement as if she found it difficult to rise.

"I wish you would go to someone who can do something about your back, Mother," August said irritably.

"Yes, I know," said Gilberta, unruffled. "Do you want to help me with the flowers or have you decided to recomb your hair?"

"I think I'll go upstairs," said August, "but I'll be down to help you before you've finished." Then she fled.

As she passed Mr. Abbott's door, August was consciously alert to detect sounds from within — the shower running, or Mr. Abbott moving about. But there was no indication of any movement within. All was quiet behind Fenton's door, too. She went into her studio and sat down on the stool before her easel. There was a still-life charcoal drawing pinned to a board resting on it. She looked idly at it. Her breathing was short and shallow and she suddenly shuddered and drew a long sigh. "This is silly," she said to herself. She picked up a stick of charcoal and began to shade one side of a plate in the drawing. Then she put down the charcoal and wiped her fingers. "This is really too silly," she said again, beginning to grow angry. Then she got up abruptly and went back downstairs to the pantry to help her mother arrange a low flat dish of flowers for the table. "I decided to leave my hair the way it is," she murmured before she was questioned. But Gilberta only looked down at her charcoal-smudged fingers as she picked up a fern frond to cut.

Upstairs, almost above them, Walter Abbott slowly and carefully shaved his face. When he had stung some color into the newly shaved areas with particularly vigorous slappings of lotion, he sat down in a dainty velvet-covered boudoir chair by the window and stared out at the rigid tree branches.

"What in thunder ever made me do that?" he growled, for the first time allowing himself to think of the greeting he had given August. "I don't even kiss my own sister at the station!" He was upset, but his anger was not really directed against himself. It was directed against the Chadleys, this family which had always angered him with its pitiable restraints and formalities. They were dishonest. His mind repeated the accusation. They were dishonest. Inside each one of them were drives and impulses for self-expression which were so passionate and undeniable that they were capable of destroying each other in the conflicting currents of their needs. But not one of them could kiss an old friend, or even each other, without giving that simple demonstration of regard the air of impropriety. He remembered the first night he had ever spent in Dunmeade and his dreadful urge to escape. The same sense of dangerous involvement was coming over him again. He had his final work to do, his thesis to complete. The back of his neck began to ache with straining forward to see the tree branches through the sudden gray dark of early evening. He should not have come back here ever again, however much he needed work. He had had no right to come. He had tricked himself with reasoning that Truth had the right to employ any means to show itself. He had come to finish his spying and reporting. He jerked himself up and rammed his arms into his shirt. He wanted to get downstairs to speak to Fenton. There was at least one thing he could do. He could move out of Dunmeade. He would do that. If he had come back for the last material for his paper, he could make his observations from at least the distance of the college to this house. He twisted his tie and knotted it. Then suddenly he went to the mirror in the bathroom again. He stood looking at his face reflected there. Then impatiently he snapped off the light. He looked his age all right, even older.

Mr. Abbott had no opportunity to speak privately to Fenton before dinner. The Chadleys were in the drawing room and Fenton was standing beside a large silver tray which held an assortment of filled crystal decanters and one unusually beautiful enameled glass carafe of water.

"I'm afraid I don't know the recipes for making those elaborate cocktails that are so fashionable in the North," he confessed smilingly when Walter had seated himself. "But I have a ripe Bourbon whisky to offer you and the ladies will have a glass of sherry with us."

"Whisky and water will be quite welcome," said Walter. He looked at August and Mrs. Chadley sitting together on the sofa. Suddenly August began to laugh and then, remembering, Walter laughed too. Fenton looker around quizzically and Gilberta frowned slightly.

"Don't you remember my efforts to teach Mr. Abbott to drink corn liquor?" August asked Fenton. And Fenton's face began to color. "You were something of a trial to Mr. Abbott at that time, I'm afraid, dear," he murmured and unstoppered the sherry.

"I was probably more of a trial to her," suggested Walter. And August, still laughing, agreed. "I'm not very quick to take in strangers," she said.

"But once in?" Walter asked.

"They have plenty of room," August dodged with unexpected artfulness. And then she walked over to Fenton. "Never mind ringing for Addie," she said to him, "I'll serve us." She took up her mother's sherry and a little silver basket filled with beaten biscuits.

At the table, Fenton could no longer resist discussing the project of the college. It was never out of his mind. And indeed, watching the almost childlike excitement which brightened his face when he mentioned the plans, it was not hard to go along with him.

"I have particularly wanted to ask if you have any one to suggest as the art instructor – a person who has some ability at organization, you know," he asked Walter.

For a few moments Walter thought. And then he said, "I know of an artist who has done some teaching at odd times when he needed money, but whether or not he can organize a department or even a course is something else again." He buttered a light roll and ate it in two bites. Then, without looking up from his plate as he filled his fork with escalloped potato, he said, "He'd be perfect for August, but I doubt if the other students would be advanced sufficiently to benefit from his instruction. I may be wrong, however." Then he said directly to August with a smile, "You'd have a merry time with him but you'd learn something about painting. *His* heart has never taken in friends or relations, much less strangers. The only thing it loves is a tube of paint and a roll of linen."

An odd expression had come over August's face and she looked as if she were about to push herself away from the table and flee. There was a silence.

"Is he a well-known artist?" asked Fenton.

"In some quarters," replied Walter. He did not understand why something he had said had so disturbed August.

"Are we familiar with his name?" persisted Fenton.

"I don't know," said Walter. "It's Aaron Aitken."

"I don't believe we know of him or his work," said Fenton.

The conversation seemed to be ended, when suddenly Mrs. Chadley said to Walter, "His drawings have a somewhat botanical aspect, although I don't believe he means them to be representational."

Walter stared at her in astonishment. August stopped picking methodically at a chicken breast and turned to look at her mother. Fenton coughed.

"He always exposes the inner structure of a flower, you know," Gilberta continued, still addressing Walter. "I wonder if he grows the models he uses."

"I don't imagine so," said Walter, trying to answer her, "I don't think he lives in one place long enough to grow anything."

"Colchicums root very quickly and can be grown in a container on a window sill," said Gilberta.

"Even so," argued Walter simply for the sake of making some reply, "I think he probably goes to the botanical gardens to do his sketching and then relies on some text for his impression of the internal structures."

"Probably so," conceded Gilberta and said no more.

Rallying at last, Fenton said to Gilberta, "Perhaps we should look into purchasing some of Mr. Aitken's work." He wanted to ask Gilberta where she had seen the drawings but knew he could not. "Is it your opinion that he is a very good artist, dear?" he asked Gilberta.

Gilberta rang for Addie, and when she had ordered the platter to be passed again, she answered Fenton. "Yes."

During this surprising conversation August had ceased eating and now laid her fork and knife across her plate. She had turned a little pale and her lips were set stiffly in a defensive pout. Drawn to look at her, Walter thought, "The animal at bay." He had begun to surmise what he had done to her.

"Then I think we should discuss the possibility of bringing Mr. Aitken to Marion College, Mr. Abbott," concluded Fenton. He hesitated and then he said with that simplicity with which the artless have always tyrannized over the sophisticated, "I am just realizing my inadequacy to advise Dr. White on many of the appointments we shall have to make. But I am not fearful of making a mistake, not with you beside me, Mr. Abbott."

"I am as much air as matter, Mr. Chadley," Walter said when he could open his mouth. "Don't lean too heavily upon me." At that moment he wished with all his heart that he had not come back to Dunmeade. He had begun to sense a tide rising about them all. He looked at August sitting silently before him, and suddenly he thought of Ralph Craig.

Much later he asked August if he might see the work she had been doing. He wanted to be alone with her. He feared at first that she would refuse; instead she seemed glad of an opportunity to make a polite escape from further family conversation and obligingly led him up the stair. She walked ahead of him to her studio.

When she had turned on the lights, she stood in the middle of the room and nodded toward a group of drawings together on a wall. She said nothing and let him go alone to examine them. He stood for a long time before them studying each one. Then, with his back to her still, he said, "You are dealing in each one with the problem of space between near and far objects in interior scenes. And you are trying to get the same feeling of great distance that there is between the horizon and foreground of a landscape, suggesting to the observer the same consciousness of things out of reach. And you have tried to do it with almost too carefully simple lines." He turned around then and looked at her to see how she had received his comment.

"I don't think they're very good," she said.

He waited for her to say something more, but she let them both stand there looking at each other in silence. She did not want to discuss the drawings. She seemed to be waiting for him to thank her and go.

"Do you know how your mother happened to be familiar with Aaron Aitken's work?" he asked her.

"She has a number of books on flowers," said August. "Perhaps he did the illustrations for one of them."

"He isn't a botanical artist," Walter objected. "He's almost surrealistic."

She accepted what he said and offered no further explanation. He felt himself beginning to struggle to hold her in the room a little longer. He had not yet come to what he wanted to say. But she was not going to help him.

"I hope that my suggestion that Aitken would be a good teacher for you did not — " and he faltered. "I suppose I assumed that you were planning to study. I've always thought that you wanted to be a painter. And I know Mr. Chadley has always — " and again he left off completing the sentence, failing in his apology. "I haven't talked with you about what you plan to do after graduation in January."

"I don't need to make any plans," she said. "All the plans will be made for me." She went to the light switch and stood there with her finger on it waiting for him to leave the room.

When he was beside her at the door he said, "I'm very sorry if I've made difficulties for you. I don't know what I've done, but I've done something, I know."

"Good night, Mr. Abbott," August said, and abruptly she left him to go to her room.

Walter went back to the drawing room. Fenton was alone, sitting in a wing chair with one of the lamps pulled close beside him to illuminate the fine print of the newspaper he was reading.

"I always have to wait until Mrs. Chadley has retired before I do this," he said smiling. "She gives me frequent lectures on the impropriety of this light for reading. But I suspect that she simply objects to my disarranging the furniture." He almost laughed, as a child who was taking delight in being naughty.

"I have been thinking since this afternoon, Mr. Chadley, that it would be better if I engaged a room in the neighborhood of the college," said Walter directly. "I think I'm going to have to be quite close to my work and it would be more convenient for me. I think Dr. White would prefer having me out there too."

As he said it, Fenton looked at him with surprise and a faint annoyance on his face. He had put his newspaper on his knees and was working one of the corners back and forth with his fingers. He considered the suggestion. Then he said, "I had planned to put one of our cars at your disposal, Mr. Abbott. You would be quite free to keep whatever hours were necessary to further your work. And I think Mrs. Chadley has already spoken to Susie about leaving a little supper out for you on evenings when you might be detained. You would not in any way be discommoding us."

"I'm sure I would be made to feel quite at home, Mr. Chadley," Walter said easily, keeping any argumentative tone out of his voice, "but I think it would really be better if I lived within a few minutes' walk of the campus. One of the faculty members probably has a small spare room I could rent and no doubt would help me arrange to take my meals somewhere."

"Yes," agreed Fenton, "I'm sure everyone will try to make you comfortable." An expression of deep disappointment and helplessness had replaced the surprise and annoyance on his face.

"I'll speak to Dr. White about it first," said Walter.

"Very well," agreed Fenton quietly. "O'Smyre will drive you out after he has taken August to her school tomorrow morning. I believe you have an appointment with Dr. White at 9:30?"

"Yes, that's right," confirmed Walter. He stood then and was about to say good night when Fenton asked him, "I was wondering if you would undertake to locate your friend, Mr. Aitken, the artist, for me. I should like to write to him immediately."

"He can always be reached through Thomason Gallery, which shows his work in New York, Mr. Chadley. But shouldn't you first discuss having such an artist with Dr. White? Dr. White may prefer having an instructor who is more academic, both in his own work and in his teaching methods. I'm not sure Aaron Aitken is your man." He saw the blood suffuse Fenton's skin to a dull pink and he knew he was making him angry, but he went on, "Aaron Aitken is quite advanced in his views on art and he might be useless to your purpose, even if he consented to come here."

"I should still like the privilege of corresponding with him, Mr. Abbott," Fenton said softly as if he were maintaining his poise at great effort. He took out a small notebook from his pocket and wrote down the name of the gallery. Then he got up and brought a magazine from one of the tables to Walter. Very carefully he turned the pages until he came to a section of reproductions of flower paintings and watercolors from the seventeenth century to the present time. Shown in the latter classification were three of the strange, smooth, pastel-colored studies of single blossoms by Aaron Aitken. The interior life structures of stem and flower were laid bare and delicately drawn as if the artist were letting the beholder inquire for himself into the secret of the flower's life. They had an unreal and mystic quality, though, to draw them, the artist had split them in longitudinal sections in the way of the scientist. Walter looked down at them in silence. Then Fenton flicked backward through the pages to the cover. Walter read the title of the magazine: *Town and Country Gardens.*

"Mrs. Chadley tells me that there is some piece or other of this sort in each issue. Frequently she consults the illustrations to suggest new flower arrangements for the house here. And she says the recommendations on certain greenhouse procedures are quite invaluable to her." Fenton handed the magazine to Walter. "Mrs. Chadley thought you might like to look at this copy."

"Thank you," said Walter.

"If Mr. Aitken can teach our young ladies to inspire their future grade school pupils to draw like this, we shall be forever grateful to him. I remember some of August's cut-outs as being quite dreadful. And I have come to think that they were the result of uninspired teaching. How can one lead a child to consider the beauty of his world if one is blind to it oneself?" He smiled reassuringly at Walter then and said, "I don't think you need to have any reservations about our bringing Mr. Aitken here."

"Perhaps not," murmured Walter. He was tired. He wanted to hear no more and say no more. He told Fenton good night.

When he reached the gallery and was entering his room, he heard August's voice again as if it were trailing down to him from the door of her studio: *All the plans will be made for me.*

❧

In the morning he met August at breakfast, just as in the days when he had been in Dunmeade to tutor Ralph. She had served herself and not waited for him, just as had been her habit then. After exchanging greetings with her, he went to help himself to sausage patties and eggs and coffee.

"We have hothouse strawberries all winter—courtesy of Mother," she said with an odd kind of brightness while he was serving himself. "Don't you want some first?"

"I don't think so, thank you," declined Walter.

"She grows vegetables too, including asparagus," said August.

Walter sat down across from her and began his breakfast.

"How are your cousins in Quakertown?" Walter asked.

August laughed. "Did my telling you about mother's vegetable growing remind you of them?"

"Yes," Walter admitted.

"We don't see them very often," August answered his question. "I suppose they're all right."

"I thought there was a girl you were very fond of?"

"María? Oh yes, I like María. I like my Aunt Grace, too. And William is a very sweet boy."

"Who's left?"

"Pedro and my Uncle Rafael."

"I see. I remember you have never cared particularly for Pedro, but what sin, in your estimation, has brought your disrespect for your Uncle Rafael? You described him once to me and I thought he sounded very attractive. You were afraid then that Pedro was playing his father for a sucker, to put it in plain language."

"It was the two of them together who played us for suckers," said August.

"Oh dear," laughed Walter. Then he saw that August was not laughing with him, nor even smiling. "I'm sorry," he said.

"That's all right. I suppose we shouldn't have expected gratitude from someone who has no sense of responsibility toward his own dependents. Uncle Rafael thinks the world owes him a living just for the privilege of having him live and breathe in it. He never thanked Uncle Chad for paying up his mortgages."

"Perhaps he's ashamed and doesn't know how to thank Mr. Chadley," Walter suggested.

"Oh no," objected August sharply, "he just thinks Uncle Chad would have been in the wrong if he *hadn't* paid up the mortgages. He doesn't see any reason for thanking him because he did."

"I'm afraid your Uncle Rafael is one of many who go through life surviving through the practice of that theory. Money doesn't mean anything to them, they tell you with a touch of self-righteousness. But what they really mean is that *your* money, which they cause you to spend on them with each new crisis in their lives, doesn't mean anything to them."

August took a last swallow of her chocolate. She stirred up the puddled sweet residue in the bottom of the cup and spooned it into her mouth. "Yes, I guess that's the way Uncle Rafael is," she said. Her face was impassive.

At that moment, O'Smyre put his head into the room from the serving pantry. "Miss August, if you don't come on we're going to be late again," he said and did not wait for a reply.

August ran to the foyer to get her coat and books. Then she ran back to the dining room, nearly colliding with Walter who had gotten up to go with her. "Finish your breakfast," she said and pushed him aside. "O'Smyre will come back for you. I can't wait." She went through the pantry door into the kitchen and out to where O'Smyre was warming the car engine in the drive. Walter heard the door slam and then the wheels on the crisp cold sand. He rang and asked Addie for some hot coffee. When Addie brought back the silver pot, she stayed to talk.

"Miss August has grown up since you were here, hasn't she, Professor?" she asked smiling. She wanted him to say something complimentary to August.

"Yes, she certainly has," agreed Walter, "and I think she's even prettier now." He poured too much cream into his cup.

"Yes, sir," said Addie, satisfied. Then she offered, "Don't you want me to get you a hot biscuit for one more sausage cake, Professor? Susie always makes a few biscuits along with the toast."

"That would be very nice, thank you," Walter accepted, "if I won't be depriving you of your breakfast."

"Yes, sir," Addie said and brought the biscuits and sausage from the pantry immediately. She had had a plate waiting. "A large man like you needs a hearty meal to start the day, Professor." Happy, she watched him eat the sausage between the biscuit in the style best suited to enjoying that combination. "The vittles out at that college aren't fit to eat, Susie was telling me," she said mildly. "You would do better to stay right here and let Mrs. Chadley see to you."

Startled by this unsolicited offer of her advice, and then amused, Walter replied good-naturedly, "I'll be here every Sunday that Mrs. Chadley invites me and perhaps I can eat enough to carry me through the lean week ahead."

"You won't be putting any extra work on Susie and me to stay here. There's always plenty cooked if you come home too late to sit down with the family," she argued. Her face drooped in disappointment.

"Let's see how things turn out, shall we?" Walter asked and got up to get his coat and briefcase. O'Smyre had returned and the car was standing in the drive outside the windows.

"Yes sir," said Addie, resigned now to defeat. She went back to the kitchen.

On the way out to Marion College, Walter asked O'Smyre, "Is Addie in the habit of eavesdropping on private conversations in the house?"

O'Smyre burst into laughing. "Professor, I'm telling you – if there's any little thing you want to find out about anybody else in the family, just go to that Addie! Those big flip-flop ears of hers are in the wind day and night. She's got it into her mind to make a match between you and Miss August and she's going to be watching you like your own mother never watched you when you were a helpless baby!"

"Oh, good heavens!" Walter almost shouted. The top of his head suddenly felt as if it were drawing away and leaving his brain exposed.

"Yes sir, that's what I'm telling you, Professor," O'Smyre repeated, still laughing.

They drove into Marion College and O'Smyre drew up into a prepared gravel parking space where two other cars were standing. He carefully maneuvered Fenton's big sedan close to the side of the main building. "This won't be much protection, Professor. But it will help some in case of rain," he said.

Walter did not understand. "You're not leaving the car, are you?" he asked.

"Yes sir," said O'Smyre. He opened the back door for Walter and then handed him the keys. "Mr. Chadley said I was to leave the car with you. He said you knew how to drive back to town but if you didn't I was to tell you before I left you."

"Oh no," protested Walter, "I can get a ride in with someone from out here. There's no need for me to have the car. How are you going to get back to the house?"

O'Smyre pointed out to the road. There was a small country grocery just past the entrance to the college, and beside that, a post office. "I'll pick up a ride on one of the grocery trucks or with the postman if nobody's looking," he said smiling. "Anyway, Mr. Chadley gave me some money. I can pay for a ride on the bus if I have to wait that long."

"I don't like this, O'Smyre," said Walter.

"Yes sir," O'Smyre said noncommittally. He was going to follow Fenton's orders. But he stood respectfully waiting for Walter to finish his protests.

Walter looked at his suddenly expressionless face. He was completely Fenton's obedient servant. "I suppose Mr. Chadley is the boss," said Walter, unable to keep an edge of sarcasm from his tone.

"Yes sir," O'Smyre agreed, "that's right, Professor."

"Very well," said Walter. "Thank Mr. Chadley when you get back and tell him I'll be careful." He was ready to go into the building. He put the keys in his pocket.

O'Smyre smiled then, relief sliding over his features like a kind of illumination. He tipped his cap. "Yes sir," he said, "I'll tell Mr. Chadley."

Walter walked away from him to Dr. White's private entrance. He heard O'Smyre start down the drive to the road.

~

When he returned in the afternoon, Walter informed Fenton that he had engaged a room in a farmer's house near the college and also had arranged to take two of his meals with the family.

"There's a telephone," he said. "It's a party line with five other families on it, but I don't think you'll have great difficulty putting in a call to me. Farmers aren't given to holding long conversations." He gave Fenton the number along with his new address.

"I'm sorry you felt you had to make this move, Mr. Abbott," said Fenton, writing down the information in the address book on his desk. "However, I expect that your judgment was carefully considered."

"Thank you," said Walter. He laughed then. "I think Dr. White suspects me of moving in on him to do some sort of spying for you."

The casual humor of this comment did not infect Fenton. He was shocked. "I don't think I understand you, Mr. Abbott," he said slowly. "You gave me Dr. White's need of your constant presence as the reason for your taking a room near the college."

"That is the reason I gave Dr. White also," said Walter easily, "but Dr. White considers me your special representative. And since the expansion of the college teaching curriculum is sponsored by you and you brought me here, Dr. White suspects, I think, that you wish a closer supervision than you have indicated to him."

Fenton's face had become stern, but he kept his hands loosely resting on the arm of his chair. And when he spoke, it was in a carefully soft tone.

"Quite an investment is involved in the building up of Marion College, Mr. Abbott. I am sure you are not unaware of that. And I don't think I am presuming beyond my rights when I take the precaution of engaging the best person I know to help organize the new courses."

Walter sighed slightly and smiled. "I take that to mean that Dr. White is not entirely incorrect in supposing that I am here to underwrite your investment, Mr. Chadley."

"In view of the recent history of the college and its financial plight which brought Dr. White to see me, I think I may be considered justified in securing my investment. And by improving the curriculum, I mean broadening it to include courses which will draw students who otherwise would not enroll there. We are in desperate times, Mr. Abbott. And in such times, concessions must be made. I thought Dr. White was as convinced as I of that."

"I think Dr. White is convinced of the necessity of making concessions, but he is a man who has lived a long teaching career in the atmosphere of inspirational classical study. I think he is dreading the day when a truck drives up to the supplies building and unloads fifty typewriters and ten adding machines."

"It will be as strange a sight to me, Mr. Abbott, if I am there to witness it. I have never attended a public school or even a college. August's father and I were educated by private tutoring. And we were well instructed in what you have termed the inspirational classics. I daresay that I am as fit to teach Greek and Latin as Dr. White. So it is not without consciousness of the changes that our times are forcing upon us that I am insisting upon this modernizing of the college's curriculum."

Fenton had risen as he spoke. He removed his glasses suddenly and wiped the moisture which had oozed along his eyelids and beaded his lashes.

"I hope that my insistence upon additional courses will prove to be the saving of this institution, Mr. Abbott. There were other investments I might have made which would have brought me a greater return in dollars, and with less risk, even in these times. This crisis will pass. But I had some altruism in my motive in investing in an institution of learning. I will be grateful if you will accord me your recognition of that."

As he said it, there was a quick sharp knock at the door. Both Walter and Fenton turned and stared. Coming at that moment, the threat of intrusion was startling and unwelcomed. All that needed to be said had not been said. The knock was repeated. Fenton put on his glasses and called out, "Come in, please."

August and Billy Pickett came into the room.

"We heard your voices," August explained. There was a curious look of distaste on her face as she spoke and she addressed herself to Fenton.

Walter stood up. "How do you do, Billy," he said, and offered his hand.

"Fine, Professor," Billy replied. "How are you?"

"Glad to be back in Newtown," Walter said and forced himself to smile.

There was a silence. Then August asked if Mr. Abbott would

care to go to the basketball game at the Newtown High School. "I interrupted you because we thought that you might like to go with us to the dinner before the game," she said, "and if you would, we must start now. It's at six o'clock downtown in the hotel dining room. This game opens the season."

"By all means, go if you like, Mr. Abbott," Fenton urged, for Walter had looked to him for permission.

"Thank you," Walter said. And then to August and Billy, "I'll just keep you waiting a minute." He left them and went to his room.

It was not until he went to the bachelor's chest between the windows to select a change of cuff links from his case on top that he saw the note slipped half under a silver ash tray. He looked at it a moment without picking it up. The paper was familiar to him. Then he opened it slowly and read the short paragraph.

> Dear Mr. Abbott:
> Let's not get off on the wrong foot again. I tried to talk honestly to you about the de Venturas this morning at breakfast because last night in my studio I was in one of my shut-up moods. I have no doubt that you are my friend. I want you to know that. And I hope you are not moving out to the college to get away from me. I am much more grown-up than you probably realize and I don't play games any more. I am just upset about something. It isn't anything I can explain. I hope you will reconsider moving out of Dunmeade. You are really very welcome here.
>
> August

Walter turned the note over and wrote quickly on the back: *I was only trying to tell you last night that I was aware of having added to some trouble you were already in. I am upset about something too. And that is the real reason I am going to stay out at the college. Someday I will tell you about it. I will have to.* Walter.

He put the note in his pocket and went downstairs to where Billy and August were waiting for him in the foyer.

When they had fitted themselves in closely in the front seat of Billy's car and Billy was busy with the gears as they started out of the drive into the street, Walter pressed the note into August's hand. Without looking at him she slipped it into the big pocket of her coat. They proceeded in silence to the center of town.

And then, as they were parking the car a block from the hotel, Billy said, "I don't know why I'm going to this game, Professor. Newtown High is not my alma mater." He laughed in an odd nervous way and shot a glance at August.

"Billy doesn't know how to make a sacrifice with good grace, Mr. Abbott, but he's learning," August said, and her expression suggested that there was more in her retort than just a sharp reply to Billy's complaint.

"There's no point to some sacrifices," said Billy. He locked the ignition and started to get out. Then he kept his hand on the door handle and said, as if it had been squeezed from him, "In this case, I'm just here to lend respectability to the outing. August was afraid people would talk if she brought you alone." He got out quickly then and stood on the sidewalk and waited until Walter and August joined him. August's face was set in the cold form of anger. The three of them walked in silence up the street. Inside Walter, an old familiar and disturbing sensation had begun. "Oh my sainted aunt . . . !" he breathed into his scarf. "Don't let me add *this* to it! She's only a young girl!" He began to walk faster and the others went along with him.

"This is it, Professor. Hold it," Billy said. "You're about to go past the door through which the biggest drunks and you-know-whats in Newtown enter. Step right in." He waved Walter in ahead of him with August. The lobby lights were faint hazy circles of yellow pinned regularly to the gilded columns. They were strangely impotent to illumine the half-dark of six o'clock. August went to leave her coat and Billy and Walter handed theirs to a Negro porter standing beside an improvised rack by the dining room door.

When Billy lit a cigarette and offered one to him, Walter shook his head.

"I wish you would go back and take your medical degree," said Walter directly. "Things might be worked out for you with a diploma and a title already on your side."

"August tells the tale very dramatically, Professor, just the way I told it to her," said Billy, with a slight bitter shortness to the words. "She doesn't tell you that I have no guts."

"Making a stand at all took guts," Walter objected quietly. "Then you laid down the gun. You should go back to medical school. When you're out you can crusade for the manufacturing of legitimate drugs. The plant will be yours one day. You can use it to serve mankind properly. There's honor and reward for you there, Billy. Think it over."

August was coming toward them. There was a thin fair-haired girl with her. The girl was giggling and gesturing dramatically with her thin hands and glancing animal-like about her for an audience.

"You know all the answers, don't you, Professor?" Billy said, pressing out his cigarette in a great pottery jar filled with sand. "I should take you down to give that one to my mother and Uncle Hartley. They'd love to hear you tell them how easy it would be to convert a million-dollar patent medicine factory into a laboratory for making quinine. I'd like to see your estimated profit and loss statement on the first year's operation. It would be worth framing!"

"Consolidated Drugs isn't doing too badly," said Walter. "They manage to eke out a small financial gain over the expenses of manufacturing anti-malarials."

"You've forgotten the most important thing, Professor. *The public* BELIEVES *in Pickett's Products. In thirty years, faithful users have never reported a case of pneumonia developing after the first dose at the sign of a cold. . . .* Don't you ever read our ads?. . . *Pickett's Products are not dangerous drugs, they're old family remedies – tried and true!* The next part is left out. They may not cure you but they won't kill you either. *The public* BELIEVES *in Pickett's Products!* That's the slogan that gets 'em. And it's got me too, Professor. But thanks for your time." Billy blew a tobacco shred out of his teeth.

"Miss Amos, this is Mr. Abbott," August introduced Walter to the thin blonde girl.

"Hello, Cora Simmons," said Billy.

"Hello, Billy," the girl drawled softly and breathlessly and took his hand in hers. Then, looking back over her shoulder, she smiled nicely at Walter like a child courting the indulgence of its grandparent. "It's mighty nice of an older man like you to come out to our little High School affair, Professor." Again she glanced in her animal-like way to see what audience had appreciated her scoring. Her eyes stayed for a brief second on August.

Walter felt his scalp tightening over his head. He smiled at her boldly and looked slowly up and down her immature and bony frame. "I don't think it's going to be any effort for me to enjoy your company, Miss Amos. No one would ever suspect you of being only a High School girl."

Cora Simmons flushed and switched her colorless hair in an abrupt removal of her attention to Billy Pickett beside her. Then she giggled and said something under her breath to him and Billy laughed.

"She's a skunk," said August, suddenly slipping her hand into Walter's, "complete with white stripe beginning at her head."

"She loves you, doesn't she?" Walter commented.

"Very much," August replied. "She always has. Almost as much as I love her!"

They went into the dining room and found their places. The tables had been arranged to form a large letter N spread along the row of silk-hung windows which looked out upon the street. The regular hotel guests on the opposite side stared with annoyed interest at the gathering throng of jabbering, self-conscious students picking up and putting down the monogrammed home-made cards standing at the plates. Finally all were seated and the High School Principal stood up from his chair at the top point of the letter N and addressed them. He was a freckled man with close-cut fuzzy red hair. When he had said his few conventional words for the occasion, he hesitated a moment and then decided against what had been in his mind to say in conclusion and suddenly sat down. The students applauded and then nervously looked at their plates to see what first course had been served them. It was grapefruit.

Walter whispered to August, "I think he was about to pray that you would win the game tonight."

"He's all right," said August. She was embarrassed and ill at ease, as if she were seeing herself and her contemporaries in all their childish awkwardness for the first time. She began to eat her grapefruit.

"I hope you're not sorry you brought me," said Walter softly. He did not look at her but his tone was tenderly understanding of her feelings at the moment.

"I read your note in the powder room," she said. "Thanks."

"I want to talk to you," Walter said. And then the girl to his right passed him a basket of soft hot rolls. August leaned around him and introduced him to the girl. "This is Mr. Abbott, Catherine," she said. "He's a visitor."

The girl nodded shyly and buttered her bread. Her hair was tied on her neck with bright red and blue satin ribbons.

"Catherine goes with the captain of the basketball team," August explained nicely when she saw Walter notice the ribbons. "She's wearing our colors."

"I suppose you're pretty excited tonight, aren't you?" Walter asked her.

Catherine ducked her head and laughed, "Yes sir, I guess I am," she murmured.

Then August introduced the boy who was sitting on her left and with great ease the boy, whose name was Arthur Busby, gave Walter an account of the team's previous record and named the players on the present team and recited their good and weak points. In his opinion, the game they were about to witness would be a walkaway for Newtown High. "As long as we've got old Beany Hammond with us, we'll sail right through to the championship," he said confidently between mouthfuls of creamed chicken and peas.

"Beany Hammond is the captain," August explained and nodded toward Catherine wearing the bright satin colors.

When the dinner was over there was a sudden hurried scurrying to collect coats and caps and get to the High School. August and Walter waited at the lobby door for Billy Pickett and Cora Simmons Amos. When he saw Billy's head in a knot of boys and girls clustered just outside the entrance, Walter took August's arm and guided her out to him.

"Oh hello," said Billy, "we were waiting out here for you. I'm going to ride out with Cora Simmons and some of the others. Here are the car keys, Professor. August will direct you to the field of battle." He put the keys into Walter's hand and turned away without waiting for an answer.

"Do you think Billy doesn't like me?" Walter asked, trying to tease them past the moment's embarrassment. August's lids were half closed in a stare at Billy's head moving off away from them to the street.

"Mr. Pickett is going to pay dearly for all this," she promised Walter grimly.

"Don't be too rough with him. He's having a bad time of it these days," Walter said easily, his hand at her elbow moving her forward to the street. "Let's find the car." August stepped aside from him and walked in silence down the block.

When he had helped her in and started the motor, Walter asked, "Do you still want me to go to the game, August? If you'd rather be with your friends you can drop me off and drive the car on to meet Billy. I have the feeling I'm spoiling the evening for you. I don't want to do that."

"If there's something else you'd rather do than go with me I'll be glad to let you out at the house," she answered. Cars began to pull from the curb and move past them from behind into the street traffic. They were filled with students talking loudly and calling out to others still standing on the sidewalk.

"There is nothing I would like to do more than what I am doing now," he said.

"When you get to the stop light ahead, make a left turn," August directed. Walter nodded. He carefully brought the car into the lane of automobiles, all going toward the stop light ahead and all making turns to the left.

"Shall I just follow along?" he asked. She had moved away from him to lean slightly against her door. She was looking out the window.

"Yes," she said, without turning her head.

They drove nine blocks in silence. Walter held the wheel loosely in his fingers. The line ahead inched slowly on catching every stop signal. A strange tension was beginning to tighten all his muscles. Back in his throat a near pain had begun and he swallowed noisily with not enough saliva in his mouth. A feeling between them and around them was beginning to press upon him and he felt once in the silence as if he were going to yell "Hey!" or something equally meaningless to interrupt its progress. He wanted to look at her, to examine her expression. But he kept his eyes on the tail light of the car ahead.

"We're only a block from the school now," she said. "Instead of stopping with the others, go past the buildings. There's a dirt drive just beyond which will take us back of the gymnasium. There's a parking space the coach uses. It's really for the use of the workmen on the grounds. They bring their trucks in that way."

Walter followed her instructions and drove up a slight long incline from the street which curved around the three main buildings to terminate in a gravel rectangle behind the gymnasium and cafeteria. Three other cars were parked there. The ceiling arc lights inside the gymnasium shot paths of white down through the windows which lay across the dark like streamers. Walter slid the car up to the peeled log guard.

"Now we only have to step inside and afterward there won't be all the waiting for others to move out ahead," said August. She opened her door and stepped out and Walter met her by the rear fender. They were in one of the alternating stripes of shadow between the ribbons of light on the gravel. Walter stood there waiting for her to indicate the path. A thin clacking sound of laughter suddenly came from inside and there were sounds of the ball smacking flatly on the floor as the teams warmed up. August drew her breath and stretched in an abrupt fixing of herself for entrance into the crowd.

"It isn't such an ordeal, is it?" asked Walter softly, and he came closer to her. She did not move. He could not see her face. Very easily, as if it had been decided between them long before and they had come steadily to it, he put his arms around her and held her against him. Another whoop of voices came from the gymnasium. She stiffened against his arms and he drew them tighter to oppose her escaping. Then he kissed her.

⁂

On the following morning, which was Saturday, August did not come down to breakfast early; she wanted to avoid meeting Mr. Abbott before he left with his suitcases for Marion College. Half formed in her heart was the hope that neither her mother nor Fenton had invited him to spend Sunday with them. She had slept in a strange and fitful way, slumbering deeply and then waking suddenly, off and on throughout the night. She only half-remembered the basketball game. It had been a kind of distracting and irritating demonstration she had been forced to watch, while all the time a tension and desperation was mounting in her until she had located Billy Pickett sitting in another section from them and sent Mr. Abbott to give him the car keys. Her whole thought had been taken with insuring her not having to drive home with Mr. Abbott alone. She was aware that they could have met Billy after the game, but she wanted to stop any intention Billy might have of going off with Cora Simmons Amos again and leaving his car at their disposal. The ride home, however, with Billy analyzing the plays and accounting for Newtown's loss of the game (all the while a smile of obvious detachment and superiority on his face) had been nearly impossible for her to bear. She had wanted to slap him. Always her anger at other men took the form of a deep desire to punish Billy. Billy told her good night as if he *knew* and were tenderly promising with the amusement in his eyes to keep her secret. "Thank you, Billy," Mr. Abbott had said, in his unruffled tone. "It's been a grand evening. I wouldn't have missed it for the world." August had leaped from the car and gone quickly through the patio and into the house. She had left the gallery light for Mr. Abbott to turn out. Then she had stood in her room in the dark and waited to hear his step, and his door closing. But he had not come directly. After a time, she decided that she had missed the sound of his feet on the stair, and with a kind of shaking sigh, she went about removing her clothes for bed. Much later, when she could not sleep and a sickening hollowness seemed to be expanding from her stomach up through her chest so that she was urged to vomit, she got up quickly, put on a quilted robe and went downstairs to the kitchen.

And there he was.

The kitchen was dark and he sat at the servants' table with only the light from the pantry beyond to help him see the sandwich he was eating and the glass of milk which stood sweating moisture into a coaster.

"This is the one I made for you," he said, getting up, "but I've eaten most of it too now." He was in a dressing gown and the round neck of his blue cotton pajama jacket exposed a fringe of hair high on his chest. He had taken off his glasses and he looked more as he had looked during that first summer at Dunmeade.

August went straight to the refrigerator. She took out a bottle of chocolate milk which Susie kept in the back for her. "I only want a glass of milk, thank you," she said, going methodically to the pantry for a glass. And then when she had replaced the bottle, she went around the opposite side of the table from him to get to the door. He still stood, as if expecting her to take a chair and join him. "Good night," she said.

"Good night, August," he replied to her back as she left him.

When she was in her room, she set her drink on the candlestand by her bed and sat down to drink it. The heat had gone down and she shivered. The milk was too cold. With a desperate gesture, as if with throwing off her robe and kicking her slippers onto the floor she were ridding herself also of his disturbing presence there in her mind, she threw herself into bed and grabbed the covers about her and left her glass untouched. "Oh, my goodness," she cried and rocked herself in a knot of her arms and legs beneath the slowly warming comforter.

Now in the morning, she lay still listening for the sounds of the others up and moving about the house. She had not yet heard the car leaving. But that would be hard to hear, for her room was not in the back above the drive, and her door was closed. At last she heard her mother talking in the hall with Addie. She was on her way down to start work with O'Smyre. It was ten o'clock by her small clock in the porcelain case with the blue porcelain flowers baked around the face. It was safe now to get up and go down for her breakfast. She was painfully hungry. She did not dress, but only brushed her teeth and wiped over her eyes and nose quickly with a wet cloth and combed her hair. She went down the gallery tying the cord of her quilted robe and scuffing her feet against the carpeting to get her slippers on securely. Then, as she reached the bottom of the stair, she heard Fenton say from the dining room, "Such a sacrifice was not really called for, but I'm afraid he had dramatized his position to the extent that argument was useless with him. He must not really have wanted to study medicine." He was talking about Billy Pickett. Instantly, a choking sensation began in August's throat. Fenton had no right to speak of Billy at all. He had not talked to him. He had not tried to understand. He had turned away from Billy's problem as if even hearing that Billy had left school only stamped Billy as unreasonable, his feelings not to be considered. He had not, from the afternoon when August had told him, inquired after Billy's state of mind or expressed a hope that all the difficulties in the Pickett family had been worked out without pain and frustration to anyone. Filled with anger and a sharp urge to protest the unfair judgment Fenton had just voiced, August went boldly into the dining room and then stopped abruptly beside the serving table. The person to whom Fenton had addressed his remark was Mr. Abbott. He had not left the house. He was sitting across the table from Fenton, enjoying a generous serving of Susie's pancakes.

"Good morning," they said in unison.

"Good morning," August responded sullenly. She stood where she was, looked hardly at the cheerful smile each had on his face for her, and then turned and left. But she had only reached the stair again when Fenton caught her.

"Please come back and eat your breakfast, dear," he pleaded understandingly. "Mr. Abbott will take no notice of your dishabille."

"I'm not interested in what Mr. Abbott does or does not notice," she said, beginning to take two steps at a time. Then from the gallery she leaned over and, looking down at him standing helplessly watching her from the circle of the well, she said, "I don't think you had any right to say what you did about Billy Pickett. You haven't even spoken to Billy about it. You haven't tried to see his side. You pretend to like Billy. But I know you don't. You don't like anyone who disagrees with what you think he ought to do." She drew her breath back through her teeth in an odd liquid sound as if it had passed through tears of words unsaid. Then she pushed herself back from the black iron banister in a crude movement of shrinking away from Fenton below her and ran down the gallery to her room. Without stopping, she went into her bathroom and began the water in her tub. With a savage jerking of her robe and pajamas from her body, she seemed to free herself from all restraint, and, with a curious moan, stepped into the water and stood fixed, watching it rise to her ankles before she turned the shower above her too and then screamed with relief into the roaring sound and bent her back under the rushing stinging spray.

August left the house with exaggerated urgency. She had no destination. She had not planned her day; for, until the confusing events which had seemed to begin with Mr. Abbott's very arrival, she had dimly anticipated that on his first Saturday in Newtown she might take him riding with her. There was a place she wanted him to see, an abandoned gold mine four miles from the stables. She had been there twice since she had found it in the summer. But she had been afraid to go at sunset alone, and it was in the twilight that she wished to examine its exciting form with the shadows from its mutilating structure further depressing the spoiled terrain. They could have carried a "Thermos" and some sandwiches and watched the dark start in its silent scar and then spread out to them. She could have made a quick broad sketch in chalk. Sundown came at five and they would have been home at eight.

But now, she would never risk going to an abandoned gold mine with Mr. Abbott. She would not lead him there even in the brightness of twelve o'clock noon. She dug her hands fiercely into her pockets as she strode toward Newtown, and her breath came dryly and painfully into her nostrils from the cold November air. It was the first time in her life that she had walked into the city. She had not really determined her direction for an exact purpose. She had been intent only upon leaving the house without encountering anyone in the family. She had cautiously proceeded in her removal from Dunmeade as if she had been trying, without detection, to rob it of one of its treasures. And she was nearly faint with hunger. The route to the city was in the opposite direction from the one Mr. Abbott would travel to get to Marion College. She could buy her breakfast in a café and be safe from the threat of meeting him unexpectedly on her way there or back.

Seven blocks from home she realized that there would be no cafés on the side of Newtown she was approaching. She would have to turn south and east and direct herself below the department stores and office buildings unless she wished to go to the hotel. Quite abruptly and with irritation, she changed her direction and turned a corner and crossed the street – so close behind a gravel truck, that, had it slid backward even a foot as it stopped at the traffic light, she would have been struck. Propelled by both her emptiness and her imagined necessity to escape the confusion of relationships at Dunmeade, she walked too rapidly and a sharp pain began in her side and spread upward through her ribs, drawing her over into a sudden stoop to ease it. She stopped and began to breathe slowly and easily, waiting for the tension in the muscles of her side to relax. She looked about her deliberately, self-conscious at standing there in pain. It was a neighborhood she did not know. Or if she had ever known it, she did not recognize it. It was entirely strange to her. The yards before the houses had been foreshortened, chopped off to allow for widening the street. And the houses teetered forward bonily over raw steep banks as if they were about to fall upon the new narrow sidewalk. Suddenly a little boy raced shrieking around a porch, stumbled down the steps, then stopped short on the edge of the bank and gazed at August. His pursuer, a girl only a few years older, caught up with him and with violent jerks of his coat belt in her hands, succeeded in dragging him backward to the steps. Throughout his capture and return to the prison of his porch, the little boy gazed steadily at August, as if by the intensity of his stare he hoped to make known to her the serious consequence to him of finding her unexpectedly obstructing his flight. She walked on slowly and at the corner looked back. The little girl was methodically fastening a wooden extension fence across the porch opening to the steps. The boy was still staring after August.

Before she reached a café in the business district, August passed the new drugstore of the Wallow chain which occupied the space once leased by a local merchant of men's clothing and furnishings. Still visible on the glass door was the stain of the block lettering which had read *Parker Houston,* and beneath, in flowing script, *The store for men of taste.* She went into the hot damp of the drugstore, with its combined odor of steaming coffee, grilling cheese sandwiches, drugs and cosmetics, and sat down in a booth separated from the fountain customers by a temporary partition of boxes of stationery pyramided two feet high on a center aisle counter. In red and blue show-card colors on a sign against the top box was printed: IF YOU CAN'T CALL — WRITE! (The Wallow chain drugstores were known for their snappy advertising and the running of regular *specials* on regular stock, a selling technique devised to protect them against charges of price-cutting.)

It was ten minutes before one of the boys at the soda fountain saw August and came to wait on her. There were no waitresses. In that ten minutes the mood which had motivated her flight from the house changed. She sat stiffly staring at the mound of stationery, crowned by its vulgar sales come-on, seeing nothing before her and losing even the hunger which had hurried her in to that place. It seemed to her at that moment, when her mind slipped from its momentary numbness and began to roll cloudy and just-forming thoughts into her consciousness, that no instruction and no experience in her life had ever prepared her to defeat the emotion which was solidifying into a threat to her very mastery of herself. She had fallen in love with Mr. Abbott and she knew it. She knew without looking in upon herself, without making any examination, that it had happened long ago. Much worse than that, she knew that her fear (and it was fear which made her run from him as she desired to be close to him, antagonize him when she wished only to please him, reject him when she suffered to invite him) was the old and female fear that he did not feel as she did, and never would, despite his recent overt demonstration. He was a man. Impropriety was allowed him without the threat of punishing consequences. She was alone in a trap — or so she believed — the shape of which she perceived, but as yet could devise no means of escape from.

"I've got to get rid of him," she cried silently into the terrifying conclusion her mind had at last confronted her with; "I've got to. I've simply got to!" Then she looked up into the face of the boy from the soda fountain, saw him waiting there for her order, wiping his fingers on his spotted apron, and she said, "I'm expecting someone. I'll order later."

"Sure," he replied and left.

Then, when she was certain he was back behind his fountain, she got up and quickly walked out of the drugstore.

Then she went home.

August had the afternoon to sink and float and sink again in the filling lake of emotion which characterized her awakening to love. No one was in Dunmeade. Her mother was in her greenhouse and Fenton had gone to a kind of business meeting at the Starburgs'. As the lists of unemployed in Newtown had lengthened, those who could promoted projects to give work. On this day, Fenton, Gaither Lyndon, "young" Mr. Amos, Vincent Starburg, and Charles Willetts, his cousin, with Hartley Pickett and Mr. Jesse Oats (who had, after his term as mayor of Newtown, become the most committee-minded citizen in town) were meeting with old Mr. Starburg to discuss the raising of a memorial to honor the Newtown dead of the late war.

Old Mr. Starburg, whose idea it was, favored erecting a building which would be primarily an auditorium but would have also a banquet hall and kitchen. He wished to entice first-rate musicians, lecturers and traveling theatrical troupes to Newtown. Except when induced by special terms for special occasions, none had ever come, because they objected to the lack of conveniences and of an acoustically suitable hall. Mr. Starburg remembered the early days of Newtown when there had been an opera house and they had put on an amateur performance of *The Fireman's Heart*. People should get together more often and do things together, he felt, and that was why he wanted the building to have a banquet hall and kitchen in which to hold rallies and bazaars and local anniversary celebrations. He thought it was time to end having to borrow the basements of the various churches or throw up the undertaker's folding chairs in the hotel ballroom.

Along with these good reasons for making the memorial a building, there was the inciting jealousy of Newtown for the success of the handsome new music hall in nearby Huntsville.

It had been a gift to the town from the Continental Tobacco Company when that firm had needed to reduce its taxable income. The Newtown crowd had first derisively referred to it as "the tobacco barn," and avowed that any long-haired musician wanting "curing" of the urge to make a public spectacle of himself and disturb the peace with his noises had only to perform once in the Huntsville "barn." However, Newtown's coarse witticisms soon ceased to amuse when the great Huldah Jurgensen sang twelve encores to a foot-stamping Saturday-afternoon audience and even the barefooted farm boys, standing half in the entrance doors and half out, were stirred suddenly into beating the crowns out of their hard-shell straw hats!

That afternoon, when August had Dunmeade to herself and spent from noon until teatime examining into the condition of her startled and defeated heart, Fenton and the others at the Starburgs advanced their plans to deciding that an appropriation amounting to one third the total cost of the project should be made up between themselves. The balance, they decided, should be obtained from state and federal funds available to create work for the unemployed of Newtown and its environs. Mr. Lyndon volunteered the brick, Mr. Oats the ventilating, heating and plumbing equipment, "young" Mr. Amos (and his partner Mr. York, of course) the electrical wiring and acoustical equipment – and each of the others, cash, to buy the ground and clear it. And they had a site in mind.

These plans concerned August, though she did not know it that November afternoon when she grasped at her drawing so desperately to help her past the pondering, the reproaching, and the measuring of her heart in its sick first swelling. She looked often out of the window of her studio at the mist which had risen fresh and even in the early afternoon but now was splitting in altering thick ribbon shapes as it died before a twilight colder wind. She had tried to go on with her charcoal studies of interior scenes. But she could not direct her thoughts away from Walter Abbott. She listened at intervals to hear if someone were coming up the stair – not her mother or Fenton, but him. He might have forgotten something and come back for it. But she knew this was not really likely, for she had already gone into his room, seen the cleared and freshly dusted surfaces of the chests, resisted the temptation to open the closet door and then, confused with the crossing and opposing reactions of relief and frustration, run down the gallery and closed herself in her studio.

I really don't want him to be here, she explained to herself, I just want to know what he's doing. And then she remembered her stairway scene of the morning with Fenton, and the guilt at having struck at him so arbitrarily, allowing him no defense, bit into her massing distressful feelings and refreshed the irrational edge of anger which had outlined all her reactions that day.

I know why he didn't care if Billy never became a doctor! she said to herself – as if, with her senses quickened in the fire of love for one man, she had illumined the perfidy of another – Uncle Chad is a big stockholder in the Pickett business. *That's* why! He *wanted* Billy to come home and learn to run the company!

She perceived in that instant of strangely inspired revelation, the real, the bright, the unextinguishable flame of truth. Her internal eyes, which had come so unexpectedly upon this ugliness, fixed and would not be moved.

I shall tell Mr. Abbott! she promised herself, joyful at discovering an excuse to seek him. I shall tell Mr. Abbott something he doesn't know.

But August was unexpectedly enjoined from carrying out that threat to reduce, in Mr. Abbott's mind, the importance of Fenton's opinion on the change in Billy Pickett's plans. The rare and paining rage which had prompted it withered in the shock of news which Fenton brought to Dunmeade at the end of that day: Old Mr. Starburg, just as the committee meeting was concluding, fell forward in his chair, and, with no other warning than the uttering of a soft sigh, almost as if in relief at having gained that strange last threshold, died.

His death occasioned in Fenton a desolation of spirit, for Mr. Starburg had been to him his only other parent. The abrupt discontinuance of that affection he had known from Mr. Starburg since the days when he had been a small boy, shocked him deeply.

The great mills closed, and Newtown honored the memory of Lucius Starburg with a minute of silence; and his life was remarked upon with praise and regret at its ending. And his death seemed to invest with poignancy the plans they had been about in the hour of his passing. Fenton and Vincent Starburg and Gaither Lyndon and the other three pressed forward the realization of a war memorial auditorium.

It had not been a gay holiday season at Dunmeade. Susie had come down with an attack of rheumatism and was confined to the servants' house. Addie, uncharitable with extra service upon her, had rationed Susie's holiday sweets and eggnog on the excuse that rich foods would increase the painful symptoms. This had caused a falling out, Addie complaining to Gilberta that Susie had threatened her with the walking stick which Fenton had provided her to limp about on.

In addition to the gloom which Susie's indisposition caused in the kitchen, Mr. Abbott left unexpectedly to spend the holidays with his supervisor at the university. He had not anticipated that the Chadleys would expect him to share the family celebrations at Dunmeade and he was visibly embarrassed at the disappointment which Fenton could not conceal at his announcement of his departure.

"I have ordered a blue spruce from New England for our tree," Fenton tempted him childishly. "We had one years ago when August was a little girl. There had never been such a tree in Newtown. It excited considerable admiration."

"I'm sure that it did, Mr. Chadley," Walter said, "I've seen some magnificent trees in Vermont and Maine."

"Perhaps you will return to Newtown before our spruce has had to be taken down," Fenton said, and it was an acknowledgment of defeat.

"I hope I will," said Walter.

And that had been all, except a good-by which August came downstairs to say to him.

"You're getting away just in time, Mr. Abbott," she informed him in a curiously sharp teasing tone. "Billy Pickett has his winter cold and you were in danger of having to receive with me at a little open house I'm going to have for some of the young crowd."

She was dressed in a claret-colored wool jumper with her small waist strapped in a wide matching belt. She was conscious of the beauty of her figure and leaned against the black iron banister of the stair with a kind of indolent invitation to admire her.

Fenton looked at her in surprise. She had said nothing to him or to Gilberta about wishing to give a small party. She seldom entertained.

But Walter replied defensively, "Had I known I was to be pressed into such pleasant service, I would have made arrangements to oblige you."

"Do you know how we can avoid misunderstandings in the future" she asked him, with flirtatious suggestiveness.

"Yes," he said, directly, gazing at her with amusement and approval of her tempting female arrogance, "I can consult you first for my orders, before I dare to make any other plans."

"That's correct," she confirmed and laughed. Then she came down the last step and offered him her hand. "You will have to wait until you return for your Christmas present. I haven't got it wrapped yet. And besides you don't deserve my conveniencing you."

"Merry Christmas, ma'am," he said, in mock contrition.

And then he left and Fenton and August stood looking at the door close behind him.

"I'm very glad that you are going to entertain a few friends during the holiday season, dear," said Fenton.

"I'm not going to," August stated bluntly, "I was just saying all that." She started back up to the gallery and to her studio. "I'm glad Mr. Abbott isn't going to be here. He gets in my way. I never know what I'm supposed to do about him. He's too young for your company and too old for mine."

"Yes, that is somewhat the situation, isn't it?" Fenton agreed, reflectively. But August had already got beyond hearing the soft murmur in which he said it.

She went into her studio and sat on the stool before her easel. She had not come to work. She had not been working. Her smock was hanging on a chair arm, the sleeves along the floor. She had no purpose in coming there.

Suddenly she got up and went to the pine dough-trough in which she stored her sketches. She slid off the heavy top and left its weight to pass through her nervous hands to strike thunderously on the floor. She took up a chalk drawing she had made of her own head and quickly tore it into strips.

"I'll get him some ties or something before he comes back," she said, tears of frustration starting in her eyes so that the contents of colored sketches and drawings in the trough swam together in nauseating formless blobs like party ices. She both sued for Mr. Abbott's attention and rejected it when it was offered her. She surmised his struggle to put her off from him as she struggled to put him off from her. She recognized his embarrassment at the difference in their ages as she recognized her own embarrassment at it. She fought against his defenses as she prepared her own. She was angered at his voluntary residence outside Dunmeade and yet relieved that it was so. She invited him to repeat his bold gesture of the evening of the basketball game and still she rehearsed in her mind the savage blow she would strike if he made it. She anticipated that in some way, perhaps far in the future, whatever it was that was growing between them would be allowed and made all right. But she conspired with her own indignant heart daily to defeat such a possibility. And at this moment she was miserable that he was not to be in Dunmeade for Christmas, where he would be accessible to torment for her own solace!

When New Year's came, Fenton proposed that she join with him in sending a telegram to Mr. Abbott, still at the university.

"I will write out a greeting, dear," he said, "and if it seems quite nice to you, perhaps you'd care to put your signature with mine."

"I don't think so," declined August. She did not intend to give any attention to Mr. Abbott which would disclose that he was in her thoughts.

Fenton did not press her. There was an expression of stubborn withdrawal on her face and he had learned to honor her resistance on small issues.

"I have heard from Mr. Aaron Aitken, dear," he said, abruptly changing the subject. "He has confirmed that he is to join the faculty of Marion College on the special basis proposed, for the semester beginning in February."

August made no response. But she regarded Fenton with an undisguised air of suspicion of his motive in telling her that he had now succeeded in contracting for Mr. Aitken's unique services.

"I have not spoken to you before, dear," Fenton went on, "because I wished first to allow you to come forward with any suggestion you might have regarding further schooling after Newtown High." He paused then as if giving her a last physical opportunity to speak up. He was lying, of course. He had been careful never to inquire if she knew of a school which seemed attractive and to which she might like to go. He had meant to dangle Mr. Aitken before her at a moment when he was reasonably sure that she would not oppose his plan for her with an alternate choice – a choice which might be as worth her making as going to Marion College for special study in art.

"Is it necessary for me to be educated?" asked August.

"I'm afraid I don't understand you, dear," said Fenton. And then he argued, "You are educated now."

"I can read and write and I've memorized some historical facts and the usual lines from the well-known English and American poets," said August, dryly. "I'm not illiterate, if that's what you mean. But it isn't necessary for girls to know anything, really. Is it? And besides, I'm very rich."

Fenton looked away from her half-amused smile. He did not know what to answer her. He was not certain that she was serious. And yet, beneath what she had said so matter-of-factly, there seemed to be something she had not said – something which was the real thing, the serious thing with which she was challenging him. Fenton dodged with a generalization.

"Education consists in helping one to think, to employ one's past experience in combination with one's reason to the benefit of one's relationships in the world."

Suddenly August laughed outright and Fenton observed her with an odd new discomfort. "It would benefit our relationship if I said I wanted to study art with Mr. Aitken. Wouldn't it?" she asked him: "From past experience I know that you have decided for me and my reason tells me that since I like to paint and have no other ability, it is the only choice I have. I am really better off than Billy Pickett was. Aren't I?"

"I don't see the parallel," objected Fenton, shying instantly from guilt. "I have only tried to make it possible for you to become accomplished in something in which you enjoy an extraordinary natural ability. Am I to be blamed for thinking only of you?"

August did not answer his suit for understanding and approval. "When do you want me to start with Mr. Aitken?" she asked him. And then she answered for him, in nearly his own tone of neatly arranging his conclusions, "Since he's coming right away and for his first semester will not have many to instruct, I can have a great deal of personal attention. I would be foolish not to register at Marion College in February. Wouldn't I? So I shall do that."

Fenton only nodded and said, "Yes."

And so they came to the last bend in the stream of their relationship as father and child.

On the afternoon when August was admitted as a special student to Marion College, the front campus, or rather that stretch of ground before the main buildings, was covered in a stiff frosting of ice. It further emphasized the school's unmistakable bare look of an institution. And despite its recent precarious financial condition, it had the air of impregnability common to institutions.

She was registered by a senior student named Lizzie Whimper, a thin-bodied girl with an unexpected large pale muscular face and thick extremities. Miss Whimper worked as an assistant to the Registrar to earn a part of her tuition. She regarded August with a faintly superior smile and, in a flat twanging voice, dictated the answers which August was to write into the blanks on the registration form.

August took up a pen and said, "Thank you very much. I think I can state the facts of my biography correctly. They are very few to date." She was angry at the girl's dictatorial manner and, examining the face, she had perceived an interesting thing about Lizzie. Her face was beginning to fold along the cheeks and under the chin with the unconcealable lines of age. Lizzie was not a girl. She was a woman. And quickly into August's mind had come the memory of another face which had had just such a maturity to distinguish it from the faces of other students about it. Lizzie Whimper was the Ruby Boyle of Marion College. And like Ruby Boyle, she unconsciously demanded acknowledgment of her seniority without divulging the reason she felt it her due.

At August's undisguised reference to her own youth, Lizzie's eyes had seemed to pale into a watery stare and her edemic lids had slid half over the pallid green irises in an expression of pure and instant hatred. She left August to complete the form in her own words and remained silent until it was done. Then she said, "I am honored to have registered the daughter of our benefactor."

It was then that August detected the slight whistling lisp, and before Lizzie pulled her thick lips together August saw the rubber bands of braces on her upper teeth. She looks a mess with braces at her age, thought August. Then she replied to Lizzie, "Thank you for your help."

Lizzie turned away from her and went to a forward desk to file the completed form in a box on the top. She kept her back turned and, when she seemed to be going on with something else and to have finished with August, August asked her, "Do you know if Mr. Aitken has arrived and if I might see him in his office?"

"Mr. Aitken has not reported to this office," Lizzie obliged her in the flat cold twang, and continued her occupation with her back to August.

"Thank you," said August. She waited a moment longer and then asked, "Is there anything more for me to do?"

"No, Miss Chadley," replied Lizzie above the deliberate rustle of a sheaf of papers in her hands. "That is all we want of you."

August said no good-by. She went out of the Registrar's office and down the heat-stuffy hall to the building's entrance door. She had a little smile on her face and she was thinking: That's all that she or any of the rest will ever want of me. And then, outside, the little smile seemed to evaporate in the chill which struck her face as she went down the steps to the car where O'Smyre waited. What she doesn't know is that I neither want nor need anything of any of them, either. I'm quite used to being with stupid people.

"How did it go, Miss August?" asked O'Smyre kindly when he had helped her into the car.

"It was pretty cut-and-dried," she answered. "I'm not going to try for a degree so they didn't have to list all my sorry grades in High School." She laughed then and added, "It's not the prettiest place I've ever seen. You and mother ought to come out here and try to do something to this terrible yard."

"Yes ma'am," agreed O'Smyre. "Mrs. Chadley was just saying something about it herself the other day. I guess she's at least going to give these people out here some advice about the landscaping, even if we don't do anything on the place ourselves." He spoke along easily and proudly of his association with Mrs. Chadley and their common opinion of conditions at Marion.

But August's mind was drifting away from what O'Smyre was saying about possible shrubs and blooms with which to beautify the campus. She was staring at the back of his head and the strip of his skin above the gabardine collar of his chauffeur's jacket. Two of the questions on her admittance form had come slowly into her mind, and a curious feeling began to come over her as she realized her answers had not been the exact ones sought. Out of innocence and inexperience she had written, after the query COLOR?: *Olive complexion, blue-gray eyes and dark brown hair.* After the query CHURCH? she had filled in: *No special denomination.* She should have supplied in those blanks the two simple identifying words, *White* and *Christian.*

August did not begin her work with Mr. Aitken immediately after her registration that winter afternoon, for Mr. Aitken was a week late in arriving at Marion College. He had a painting to complete, he explained in a three-line letter to Dr. White, but would come immediately it was finished.

Dr. White was outraged. He threatened to write the artist that perhaps he should reconsider coming to Marion College at all, since a specific amount of his time and attention would be demanded by his students and his employers and therefore his painting might suffer.

Fenton, however, restrained this impulse in Dr. White. He pointed out that Mr. Aitken's rather vigorously expressed independence was a part of his artistic temperament and that they were engaging a man of unique abilities and would have to put up with his unconventional view of his obligations to them. Fenton, of course, was in Newtown and would not have to live with Mr. Aitken's artistic temperament close beside him.

Walter Abbott was delegated to meet the painter at the Newtown Station and escort him to the quiet of Marion College.

"What about this Chadley girl?" Mr. Aitken demanded immediately, as they went down the ramp. "I suppose I'm expected to make salaams before including her in an ordinary class assignment." He breathed belligerently and Walter could feel a lust for opposition and argument wave out from him like an animal odor. He was large and handsome with a carefully cultivated stubble of red beard.

He thinks rugged individualism is a physical condition, thought Walter, and he's going to show me that artists are not long-haired esthetes. He needs to grow up. Walter reflected carefully and then answered him, "I don't think Miss Chadley expects any special attention."

"Well, she isn't going to get any," Aitken insisted, disgruntled. "No one's going to be coddled in my classes. I'm not interested in teaching rich young ladies to paint sprigs of flowers on china plates!"

"I think you'll find that Miss Chadley is a long way from being the china-plate type," said Walter mildly.

"Oh ho!" Aitken snorted. "Lady tyrant, eh?"

Walter was becoming weary of Mr. Aitken's determination to justify an unjustifiable prejudice against August. But he gave another soft answer. "She's an unusual young woman in many ways," he said, "and it's entirely possible that she may have a worth-while talent."

Mr. Aitken looked at him sharply. "You're pretty sold on these Chadleys. Aren't you?" he challenged Walter with a mixture of scorn and suspicion in his tone.

"I know them, that's all. You'll get to in time."

"Not on your life," snorted Aitken. "They don't interest me."

"That's too bad," observed Walter. "They interest me a great deal. They have for a long time. Seriously."

"Okay, okay," Aitken sucked the words through his cold pipe; "they're nice people. With all that dough they can afford to be."

"They can afford not to be," Walter murmured. He directed the artist to the car.

Then they rode in complete silence the nine miles out to Marion College.

Mr. Aitken had apparently decided upon a plan to protect himself from possibly favoring August Chadley, for when his first class of twelve girls met, he did not call the roll or attempt to learn the names of his pupils. After making a few general remarks on what his course was *not* going to include, he set up a simple still-life, passed out the charcoal and sheets of brown wrapping paper, and instructed them to start on what he was sure would be a collection of literal uninteresting scratches. He walked about among them, beginning slowly to give a pointer to this one and that one until by the end of the period he had become unconsciously engrossed in lifting the feeble efforts of the timid and encouraging the demanding offerings of the bold. In particular, he was attracted to watch the work of two of the students. One was a small fair girl who drew rapidly and badly and had a pronounced impulse to shade and wipe on a weak structure. The other was a tall dark girl with an intensity of interest in the single forms of the still-life group and a marked disinterest in their correlation into a pleasing composition.

When the bell rang at the end of two hours, he dismissed them without giving any study assignment and retired instantly to a cloakroom at the far end of the large studio classroom. When he was certain that he was alone in the building which had been temporarily allotted him, he came out with the intention of studying the single messes which were left pinned on the newly supplied easels.

And then he saw that the tall dark girl had waited for him.

She was seated on one of the high stools with her feet drawn up on one of the rungs, her plaid skirt spread wide so that only the toes of her heavy Oxfords were showing. She wore a cotton shirt and a dark green cardigan sweater and she had put on her wool tam o'shanter. Her coat was hanging over the next stool beside her.

"Mr. Aitken," she said, directly, getting down from her perch but not coming any closer to him, "I am August Chadley. I thought I should tell you which one I am."

"Why, Miss Chadley?" he asked, standing where he was when he had first seen her.

"Because it isn't necessary for you not to know the names of the girls in order not to know which is me."

The answer surprised Mr. Aitken and an annoying embarrassment at her discernment stirred a harsh and revealing remark from him. "You are not so important to me that I will play silly games with myself, Miss Chadley. I am not interested in the names of my students. I am only interested in their work."

"I am very glad then, if that is so. It means that you will tell me the truth and not let me do whatever I like whether it's worth doing or not, just because of who I am. I won't learn anything or be any better than I am now if you just pass me along easily."

"Miss Chadley, I don't know quite what it is you want of me," said Mr. Aitken, beginning to smile. "I suspect that you really want particular attention, whether it's criticism or praise."

"Most people want to think they deserve particular attention, don't they, Mr. Aitken?" August said, returning his smile with a faintly cunning but rather inviting one of her own. "I want the criticism as well as the praise."

"And what made you think you wouldn't get criticism?" he asked her.

"Because it would be easier in your situation not to either criticize or praise me very much. If you didn't praise me very much you wouldn't be threatening your own integrity, and if you didn't criticize me very much you wouldn't be antagonizing my uncle. But I wouldn't learn anything that way."

Mr. Aitken regarded her in silence a moment after this and then he asked directly, "How much interest do you have in art, Miss Chadley?"

"I want to be a painter," she answered.

"Do you have any idea whether or not you can be?"

"I think I can be."

"Is that pride or judgment talking?"

"Both," she said, and laughed.

"Are you going to ask me every day when I'll be ready to tell you my opinion? Assuming that you want my opinion."

"I will never ask any questions except technical ones, Mr.

Aitken. And if my uncle, or anyone else, asks you how I'm getting along, I want you not to answer."

"That's agreed, Miss Chadley. The truth about your ability, insofar as I can ascertain it, will remain a secret with me."

"Thank you, Mr. Aitken," she said. Then she picked up her coat from the stool beside her and went to the door. There she paused a moment as if trying to decide whether or not to say something else which was in her mind. She decided to say it.

"Mr. Aitken, I know you had no choice but to teach me. However, I had no choice but to study with you."

Late on a Sunday afternoon when Fenton was driving Mr. Abbott back to Marion College, Fenton said to him, "I'm sorry we've never been able to get Mr. Aitken to come for a family meal at Dunmeade. I don't know quite what to make of it. Mrs. Chadley has invited him on three occasions and I don't think I can fairly ask her to risk another refusal." He was offended that his hospitality had been rejected so summarily by the artist. "I dare say," he went on, "that I would not have met Mr. Aitken at all, despite our relationship, had I not been present at the dinner which Dr. White gave to welcome the new faculty members."

"He hasn't any manners, Mr. Chadley," Walter said bluntly. "Just remind yourself that he's a first-rate artist and that to have him here it's worth bearing his social offenses."

"Yes," said Fenton. "That is no doubt good advice. You have a gift for keeping the important facts before one, Mr. Abbott."

"I hope so," replied Walter with an odd sobriety in his tone.

"However, August seems to find him very agreeable," Fenton said, apparently reluctant to give up the subject of Mr. Aitken's irritating ways.

"Does she?" Walter said. "I've been wondering how she was getting on. She hasn't much time for me these days. She must be quite busy." He was not being truthful and so put a slightly self-pitying earnestness in his voice.

"Yes, she is working quite faithfully on her assignments," said Fenton. "As a matter of fact, she hasn't shown me any of her finished studies either, now that I think of it. But I know she likes Mr. Aitken and I am very glad of that." And then his mind slipped from his hold over it and he said, quite without realizing the admission, "That is the important thing to keep before us – that Mr. Aitken is here to teach August. So you are entirely right that we should all ignore his little social breaches as long as August is happy studying with him."

At that moment, Fenton steered the big car into the grounds of the college and as no confirmation seemed necessary, Mr. Abbott remained silent.

But when he got out at the entrance to the Administration Building, Walter told Fenton that he would not be present as usual on the following Sunday for the midday family meal.

"I have asked Dr. White for Saturday off," he explained. "I need to consult with my supervisor at the university about submitting my thesis for publication. I don't think I'll get back to Newtown before evening on Sunday."

"I'm sorry you won't be with us," said Fenton, "but I'm delighted that you have got so far on your paper. I had no idea you were near the conclusion of your work. I think that's splendid, Mr. Abbott. It's been a long serious study for you, hasn't it? We shall all be most proud to see the results issued in print."

A look of near-fright came over Walter's features suddenly and he almost ignored Fenton's hand stretched out to him. Then he managed to say, "It's a little early for me to accept your congratulations, Mr. Chadley. But thank you for your blind faith." Then with an abrupt twist away from the car, he left Fenton and went around the path to Dr. White's modest private office and let himself in.

Fenton looked after him wonderingly a moment and then smiled. Mr. Abbott is really very modest, he thought; he has not yet learned to accept praise with the proper poise. But he will learn, once recognition is his. And it will be. Then he drove away from the building.

When he came to a full stop at the exit from the grounds and cautiously looked up and down the public road before he crossed it and turned the car toward home, he noticed the painted clapboard façade and strange flimsy portico of the grocery store directly in front of him. He thought instantly of Mr. Aitken. Mr. Aitken's rooms were above the store. He looked up, wondering if Mr. Aitken were in and if he would receive him. Fenton never intruded upon anyone's privacy, but, at that moment he was taken with a compelling impulse to visit this strange and independent man whom he had brought to Marion College and who steadfastly refused to come to Dunmeade.

"I shall withdraw immediately if I see that it is not a convenient time for me to call," he promised himself, as he carefully parked the car before the grocery store and got out to look for the way of getting to the upstairs apartment of Mr. Aitken.

He found some wooden steps hanging in a mysterious way of their own to the store side, and, with understandable apprehension, climbed them to the two-foot-square platform at the top. He knocked on the doorframe, as the door itself seemed to be off its hinges and was leaning against the plaster wall inside.

"Come in," Mr. Aitken's voice ordered from a room within.

Fenton entered and picked his way through a passage insulated against intrusion by a double line of crates and packing cases. It began to be understandable why the door had been taken down. Without choice of his own, Fenton tipped into the first room at the left; the passage to any other room beyond was blocked.

Mr. Aitken was before him, standing on a chair, tying knots in the cord by which a naked electric light bulb was suspended from a soiled fixture at the ceiling. He wished to raise the bulb higher. As the light was on and its unshaded glare was directly in his face, he was blinded.

"Well," he demanded, "who is it and what do you want?"

"It's Mr. Chadley, Mr. Aitken, I hope I'm not calling at an inconvenient time," answered Fenton. He was instantly sorry that he had come. He felt helpless with this unconventional person.

"You should be able to make up your own mind about that," commented Mr. Aitken. He tied still another knot in the cord and then got down from the chair. He closed his eyes and held his hand over them a few moments and then, blinking to clear the last bulb-spots from his vision, he began to examine Fenton.

"Making an unannounced campus check, are you, Mr. Chadley?" he asked.

Fenton felt a curious and disconcerting tremor pass through him.

"Oh, no, certainly not, Mr. Aitken," he protested with no real force. "I have just driven Mr. Abbott back to the college and I thought I would pay a brief call upon you. We have not had the pleasure of your company at Dunmeade and I have been sorry not to have known you all by this time."

"I have no time for social engagements," stated Mr. Aitken.

"Yes," said Fenton, instantly assuming guilt, "I'm afraid that organizing the department of art has been a draining task for you, Mr. Aitken. I have wanted to ask you if you wished me to engage a qualified assistant for you. Of course, there will be two art teachers under you when we open your department officially next term. But until then, you may have any help you require."

"The only help I require is a lack of interference," Mr. Aitken said.

"That is little to ask, and I shall see that you continue to have it," Fenton stiffly replied.

Mr. Aitken seemed to bow slightly and there was a smile on his face. Then he cocked his head to one side and listened intently a moment. Suddenly he bolted into what seemed to be a closet behind Fenton, close to the hallway door. A visible bubble of steam billowed out into the room and a strange and olfactorily assaulting odor was deposited in the atmosphere before the bubble was dissipated in a draft. Hard behind it came Mr. Aitken with a large, hot, stewpot and a long fork. The smoking victuals in the pot gave off a steam, the bouquet of which reinforced the sour or briny character of the original odor which had escaped when Mr. Aitken first opened the closet door.

"Pull that table under the light," Mr. Aitken ordered Fenton, "and find two chairs."

In a kind of daze, Fenton mutely did as he was bid. And as for the activity of the next few minutes, he was never able to remember in what order the following things were accomplished: two places were set at the table with crockery and utensils produced from a confusion of painter's equipment and some of Mr. Aitken's toilet articles; Mr. Aitken cut several slices of bread from a black-crusted loaf he kept wound in a damp pillowcase to preserve its freshness; Fenton unpeeled the foil from a ball of cheese with a nearly overpowering aroma of rotting plant life; Mr. Aitken ladled a mound of kraut and boiled spicy sausages on each of the plates; Fenton knocked the caps off two bottles of ale by striking them against a chair rung according to Mr. Aitken's instructions, and the two sat down together to the meal. Halfway through it, when Fenton had overcome the terror of his introduction to such delicacies (which it turned out were sent to Mr. Aitken regularly by friends in the North who were concerned for his health in the polite society of the chicken-and-biscuits South) he began to eat with relish. He was finishing the last of his ale when suddenly he got up and went to the front windows and primly pulled down the ragged shades. When he came back, he said, "My father once described to me a similar beverage he developed a taste for on the Continent. He always regretted that our laws here did not permit him to import it for his own cellar. Father had very broad tastes."

"You're doing all right, Mr. Chadley," conceded Mr. Aitken as he held up a sausage on his fork and peeled off the skin in a spiral action with his knife blade.

A strange happiness came over Fenton. All his life he had wanted to sit down in male company, throw off the yoke of his form-and-letter life and enjoy indulging one human weakness—the least reprehensible, of course. Now he was doing it. He was eating the most common of dishes and actually stuffing himself.

And Mr. Aitken seemed pleased to have him as his guest. He could not have been seated before a table more generously spread. A great relief passed through him and he rejoiced that Mr. Aitken himself had prevented him from exposing what seemed to him now the puerile character of his own board. He wondered if Mr. Aitken would like Southern barbecue. He would drive a hundred miles to the East and obtain it for him himself. He would have a small pig spit-roasted by special order, and see that the sauce in which it was basted was the true, chopped, red-pepper-pod sauce which the East knew best the secret of preparing.

"How is my daughter, August, getting along, Mr. Aitken?" he asked suddenly, inspired by the artist's coarse but compelling charm – the charm which, he was fast deciding, had won August to Mr. Aitken.

"All right," replied his host, who was getting up now to fetch the coffee which was boiling with characteristic guttural complaints on the hot plate in the closet. Mr. Aitken picked out two eggshells which were drying with a row of others on the sill of a side window. Then, when the grounds had been settled and the brew was of a strength and clarity to please him, he poured Fenton's coffee in the only cup he owned and drank his from a small fruit jar which he hastily cleaned of a ring of turpentine in the bottom.

"You can understand, of course, that I am anxious to know your opinion of my daughter's ability," Fenton pursued the subject.

"Yes, I can understand that," said Mr. Aitken, giving Fenton no answer. There was a ring of wet around his nose and mouth from the edge of the fruit jar and some drops of coffee were trickling slowly down his short beard. He shook his head and flung them off.

Fenton accepted his failure to draw out Mr. Aitken's estimate of August's talent. Then suddenly, with an intuition rare to him, Fenton said, "I should like very much to see some of your own work, Mr. Aitken."

The smile of an innocent child began to play over Mr. Aitken's forceful features and he went immediately and brought Fenton a painting which had been standing against the wall away from the windows and covered with a rag of grain sacking to protect it from dust. He pushed the table away and wheeled his easel to stand just under the light. Then he propped the painting on it and, with an actual shove, moved Fenton back to a distance of five feet from it. Then he moved from in front of Fenton and stood beside him to study it. He waited impatiently while Fenton changed his glasses.

"Now," he said, shortly, and waved Fenton's delayed attention to his work.

For what seemed in the silence an inexcusable length of time, Fenton peered at the carefully worked-out pattern of juxtaposed colors which combined to form a single unit impression. Then he moved back another step from the painting; and then, after some hesitation, still another step. Mr. Aitken moved with him, looking expectantly and a little challengingly at Fenton as he followed suit.

"Well?" he demanded.

But Fenton did not hear him. Fenton was not conscious of Mr. Aitken being beside him, urging him to comment, to disclose his reaction. Fenton's whole attention was suddenly pressed by the shock of recognition into considering only the image which had, at last, come into focus before him in the painting. At that moment he was lost to the artist, to the untidy room in which he stood, to the world of the college outside the windows, to every other impression. His mind and his heart had traveled from a visual trauma to a time long ago, when he had been a boy and in his father's house. For the painting before him, when the striking beauty of it had become understandable in subject, and his eyes had related its subtly arranged color-forms into their correct and identifiable image, bore a nerve-shattering likeness to that other painting which had hung once over the mantel in his father's little morning room at Dunmeade!

It was a study of August. But in her face was that same nearly affronting beauty, that same expression of a being driven counter to her needs, of a spirit struggling to repress its violent urgings – all the characteristics which so shockingly qualified the face of Fenton's unhappy mother, as it appeared in the portrait she had painted of herself.

Fenton turned helplessly to Mr. Aitken. He could say nothing. Frozen, he watched the artist's offended pride turn into anger. He knew that he must speak of the painting, that he must say something, that he must manage some praise.

Mr. Aitken stomped to the easel and threw the rag of sacking over the study and hid it from sight.

And then Fenton blurted, "I wish to own the painting, Mr. Aitken. I hope you will do me the honor of allowing me to buy it from you."

Mr. Aitken only wheeled away the easel and began to clear the table of the empty bottles and soiled plates. Fenton stood still and watched him make two trips to the sink in the closet. Then Fenton went to the table and began to roll the remaining cheese into its foil and wrap the quarter loaf of uneaten bread into its damp pillowcase again.

"I have overstayed, I'm afraid, Mr. Aitken," he said. "I am indebted to you for your hospitality."

Mr. Aitken seemed to have forgotten Fenton entirely.

At last, when Fenton stood in the door and said what courteous good-by he could manage, the artist came up to him, and, fixing his eyes upon Fenton's face to catch any change of expression, asked, "Why do you dislike the study of your daughter, Mr. Chadley?"

"I do not dislike it, Mr. Aitken," denied Fenton, "I would like to own it. I hope that you have been considering a price."

Mr. Aitken began to laugh. "True to form, aren't you, Mr. Chadley? When you cannot best your enemy, you take him in. Stratagem for survival."

He left Fenton and went to the covered picture and removed it from the easel. "The price is five hundred dollars, Mr. Chadley. Make your check payable to the Thomason Gallery. There was a prospective sale for the painting in New York and the price had been set. My agents are entitled to their commission."

"Thank you for selling it to me, Mr. Aitken," murmured Fenton. "I will send my check in payment immediately."

Mr. Aitken tore up a carton in which he had been keeping his towels and sheets and used the strips of corrugated paper to wind around the painting. Then he carried it down the quivering outside staircase to the car and laid it carefully on the rear floor.

Fenton preceded him down the steps and hurried, unconsciously, so that their combined weights would not tax the frail structure at the same time. As he stood under the tin portico of the country grocery store, waiting for Mr. Aitken to bed down the picture to his satisfaction, Fenton remarked, "I am surprised that you were able to get August to sit. She's rather shy." He wanted the answer to a question which had come into his mind. He wanted to know if August were in the habit of visiting Mr. Aitken in his rooms.

Mr. Aitken backed out of the rear door and closed it. Then he faced Fenton. He smiled knowingly. "She didn't sit for it," he said. "That wasn't necessary."

"You deserve more praise than I've given you," said Fenton promptly. At that moment he was willing to add fulsome compliments to the flattery of his having bought the painting, for he realized that there was a good possibility that August did not even know of the picture's existence! Good fortune indeed was with him!

"Good night, Mr. Chadley," Aaron Aitken said, and then with a certain slyness in it, he concluded: "Come again when I've time to give you a lesson on how to judge a painting. If you're going to have a serious artist in your family, you should know that."

"You are quite right," replied Fenton, gallantly, "and I shall be grateful for your instruction. Good night, Mr. Aitken."

As he drove carefully out into the public road, Fenton took one instant to look back, drawn by some urge to see if Mr. Aitken were still standing at the curb watching his departure. He was.

Mr. Aitken was leaning against one of the metal posts which supported the grocery store's tin portico. And he was laughing. Fenton caught the jerking of his shoulders in the light from the bald globe of the street lamp as it came on.

It was eight o'clock and Fenton was going to be late for dinner at Dunmeade. He did not know what excuse he was going to make to Gilberta for his tardiness and his lack of appetite. But surely some acceptable explanation would occur to him before he drove in the gates. Of much more concern to him at the moment was his problem of removing the painting from the car and carrying it, undetected, to his apartment.

It was not framed, of course, but even so, the stretcher upon which the canvas was secured must measure two feet by three, and there was, in addition, the casing of corrugated paper. Fenton anticipated that he might have to effect its removal late in the night, when the household was asleep. Accordingly, when he arrived, he locked his car and kept the keys in his possession, instead of hanging them, as was customary, on a designated hook in the foyer closet.

"I ran into Dr. White as I was leaving the college," he lied with embarrassment to Gilberta, who had finally sat down and dined without him, "and we became absorbed in going over some blueprints for the new buildings."

"On Sunday?" Gilberta queried.

"Well, yes," said Fenton. And then he added, in an assumed critical tone, "I was rather astonished myself at Dr. White's insistence that we confer."

"I will have Susie fix you a tray," said Gilberta, matter-of-factly.

"A glass of milk will do," Fenton protested. "Please don't trouble. I'm not hungry, really."

"You should take care not to tire yourself so that you cannot eat your meals," Gilberta remarked, looking at him steadily and a little disapprovingly. Since Gilberta employed herself regularly in the physical labor of gardening, she favored serving meals of a substantial character. It was something of a problem for

Fenton, with his stocky build, to keep himself at a healthful weight.

"You are entirely right, dear," he admitted placatingly. "I shall see that I don't fall into bad habits while I am so occupied with this project."

Gilberta then brought his milk to him herself.

When she was standing beside him, she sniffed suddenly. And then she sniffed again.

"I hope that you and Dr. White were not walking on the newly planted front lawn. Were you?" she asked, frowning.

"What do you mean, dear?" asked Fenton, pretending offense. "Have I ever tramped in your flower borders here? Like a stray dog?"

"There is a strong odor of fertilizer about you," Gilberta stated accusingly.

"I must have brushed against one of the shrubs at Dr. White's office entrance. Perhaps it had been sprayed recently," volunteered Fenton. Instantly his mind went to the ripe cheese and the ale he had enjoyed with Mr. Aitken.

"You had better change," advised Gilberta, "and let me examine your suit. Some sprays leave a stain which is permanent. If it hasn't dried, I may be able to weaken it with a sponging of cold water. Whatever it is, it has a really quite offensive odor."

"I'm very sorry, dear," murmured Fenton meekly, and, taking his glass of milk, he went quickly up the stair and into his apartment.

When he returned to the downstairs, he said to Gilberta, "I found the spots on my trousers' cuffs. I submerged them in cold water in my lavatory and then pressed out the moisture between two of my towels. Was that the correct procedure? I didn't want you to bother."

"That will probably help," said Gilberta. "I hope so."

"Thank you, dear," said Fenton.

They stood looking at one another awkwardly a moment and then Gilberta announced that she was going to retire early.

"Where is August this evening?" asked Fenton.

"She has gone with Billy Pickett to a little gathering at the York girl's. I think she said it was Jane's birthday."

"She doesn't expect to be out late, does she?"

Gilberta looked at the thin, diamond-encircled watch on her wrist. It had been a gift from Fenton on her own birthday last December.

"It's 9:30. She will be home by 10:30, I'm sure."

"Perhaps I'll wait up for her," Fenton said, "I would like to read awhile before retiring."

"Good night," said Gilberta, and started up to the gallery.

"Good night, dear," Fenton responded, and he went to the library.

He stood just inside the library door for nearly ten minutes to be certain Gilberta did not return to leave some newly-thought-of order on Susie's kitchen pad. Then, quietly, he went through the patio and back to the garage and opened the rear door of his car.

In the dark, he felt for the wrapped painting. He slid it out and leaned it against the running board while he relocked the car door. Then he got a firm hold upon it by working some of the cord through his fingers. He was surprised at its lightness. He carried it easily into the house and up the stair and into his bedroom. His bed had already been turned back for the night, so he feared no necessary intrusions from the servants.

Very methodically, he unwrapped the disturbing portrait of August. Then, without ever looking at it, he removed the corner wedges from the stretcher over which the canvas was pulled. He broke the pieces of wood into kindling size and put them into his fireplace grate. Then he loosely rolled up the painting and tied it with the cord with which Mr. Aitken had bound the protecting paper about it.

Behind the printed linen draperies, at the head of his tall-post bed, was a hidden closet. It was the place from which Marcus Chadley, years ago, had taken the little document box in which he kept his private papers, and sat down to go over his holdings with Fenton, who was, from that hour of his choosing, his trusted successor. To this closet, now, Fenton took the painting of August. Inside it, carefully wrapped in bundles of time-yellow paper, stood the sculptures which Lesley had left to Fenton. And lying with them, loosely rolled and tied, as Fenton had now prepared Mr. Aitken's work for hiding, was the portrait of his mother, Elizabeth Wortham Chadley – that portrait which had hung, with its mystery and its reproaching gaze, in the little morning room.

Among these troubling things, Fenton now concealed Mr. Aitken's study of August.

Throughout Fenton's long parenthood of August, submerged beneath his sense of duty and that tender love which had incited all the acts of his care, there had lain in his conscience an eradicable pit of guilt. It was like the concealed stone in a fruit. And Fenton had learned to guard himself against striking the tooth of his longing against it. That guilt could not be withdrawn and cast away. It was protected from his will by the thin tough membrane of Fenton's self-knowledge; for, although he had never doubted that his grief at Lesley's death had been true and pure, he knew also that he had experienced, with the very shock of his loss, another and condemning emotion – an almost overwhelming happiness in his inheritance of his brother's child!

As the years passed, and there was no child of his own marriage, the deep yearning within him for the continuation of his line into the future caused him to salve his pride with treacherous thinking. He began to reason that August was not removed from him by being his brother's daughter, for he and his brother were of the same parentage and the same mingling of blood. And Gilberta, the mother of August, was now his wife. Therefore August was his own, although she called him Uncle. August herself had once asked him why she did not call him Father, avowing that she considered him her parent. And he had answered, feeling instantly the stone in the fruit, and yielding before its resisting truth: "Because I am not really your father, and your mother, rightly, has never wished you to confuse the facts." But he had taken an unworthy joy in her asking, and, with the pit of guilt swelling in the flesh of his conscience, he had bound it down again to containable size with the old promise to himself: When she is older, I will tell her more of Lesley's artistic efforts, and I will give her his few works. I will provide her an image of him. I have never done that. But I will, when there's a proper time.

Now the proper time was upon him.

But it seemed to Fenton, with his conscience confronting his heart and pointing the way he must take to diminish his paternity in favor of Lesley's, that the future and the present and the past were locked together in an unyielding trap and that his sacrifice was not the key to release them. For his task was to stir in August a sense of descendency from Lesley, an emotion which was more than acceptance of the fact. And to do that, he must arouse in her a sympathetic identification of the unique tie which bound them, and excluded him. She must know of Lesley's hopes and frustrations. But how could he reveal the truth of his brother's life, trimmed to propriety and shaped to avoid a bruise to the memory of his father, and yet have it remain the truth and effective for the purpose? Already August accepted that Lesley had worked in clay in the hours he had to himself when his duties at the bank were performed and his attentions paid to her and to Gilberta. Yet her father remained to her as Fenton's mother remained to him – a figure about whom there was no reality except in the statement that such a life had been. What was needed to provide August an image of Lesley was the truth about him – that he was dedicated, against disapproval of his intentions and lack of sympathy for his talent, to the driving, actually life-sustaining creative task of becoming an artist. And this knowledge Fenton could not give her. However impelled, he could not.

It was here, before his final decision, that the specter of Lesley's pathetic legacies – those sculptures hid and awaiting whatever time of unveiling he appointed – rose before his mind and reproached him. And, in a strange trick of internal vision, he saw the separate heads not with the faces Lesley had fashioned, but with Lesley's own impassioned face repeated variously.

Surely there is another way! he cried out within him, struggling to find it. . . . It is to him as an artist that I owe her recognition, more than to him as a father. . . . And then, in a merciful twisting of the emphasis of his obligation, he found the lever to release his suffering and guilty spirit from its condition.

August continues his talent, consciously or not, he reasoned, and it can be her hand which brings his own gift to fruition.

Thus it came to him that the great auditorium which was to honor the war dead of Newtown should itself be the sanctum for a certain other memorial.

Fenton went at once to find August.

As the spring afternoons had lengthened and light had lasted to extend her working day, August had kept to her studio at her assignments and not joined Fenton for tea in the patio. For that reason, Fenton had seen her alone infrequently. And he wished now to meet her informally, and, in their conversation, come gradually to the proposal he was so urged to make.

On the few occasions in the recent past when he had reported his activities in connection with the erecting of the war memorial auditorium, she had listened with interest. And she had been pleased when he had brought the news that he had been delegated to petition the authorities for state and Federal funds.

When he had returned from his business trip to the state capital with the solicited support guaranteed, she had greeted him with an unexpected, and, in its way, touching gesture. She had found an old plume which had adorned one of Gilberta's hats of a now forgotten fashion, and, when she had put her arms about his neck to embrace him in her child's way, she had deftly fastened the plume in his thick hair with one of her barrettes.

"For the good knight of Newtown!" she had exclaimed, laughing, and drawn him to see himself in the looking glass in the foyer.

Embarrassed and confused, Fenton had gazed at his image, its ridiculous aspect emphasized by the outline of fine carved and gilded mirror frame, and then pawed clumsily to dislodge the decoration of honor, at the same time murmuring his thanks and struggling to keep his briefcase from slipping from his arms. But he had been pleased. And he had been grateful for her approval of his efforts.

He had remarked later to her that his interest – indeed, that her own and Gilberta's too – could not be less than great; for the memorial was to honor Lesley. Lesley's name, with the others of the war dead, would be engraved under a proper legend upon a bronze tablet which would be fastened at the entrance to the building.

August had made a reply which had seemed to Fenton to indicate a strange disregard concerning the facts of Lesley's death. August had said, "I thought he died of influenza."

Disturbed a little that she had implied impropriety in the listing of her father's name with those of men who had died in battle, Fenton had answered, "He did, dear; but what is important to remember is that he died in the army camp at Huntsville, and that he volunteered to fight for his country. He did not wait to be drafted."

"Oh," August had murmured. Then she had reflected and said, "I thought the auditorium was being built to relieve our unemployment in Newtown. And that is what everyone else thinks, too."

"There is no confusion of purpose, dear," Fenton had explained, conscious that he was holding his tone to softness. "How better can we honor these special dead than by helping the needy living among us? It was to preserve our right to freely help each other that our soldiers gave their lives – for that reason, together with certain others having to do with the privileges protected by our democratic form of government."

"It's the government that's paying the costs of putting up the building, isn't it?" she had contested. She had seemed unwilling to accord any generous motives to the citizenry and Fenton had felt a personal slight in her question.

He had inbreathed slowly and then protested gently, "You have forgotten that a body of private citizens initiated the project and guaranteed a third of the total costs in their application for an appropriation." He had waited for August to indicate that she understood and that her impression had been altered to one more compatible with the truth. But she had said nothing.

"The government is ourselves, too, dear," he had reminded her then, though that view was a fresh one with him. "The funds which it grants for such work-providing construction as this derive from the taxes we pay."

August nodded that she had heard and accepted his statement of the government's character. But Fenton had not been satisfied. He had come upon a thesis which challenged his own dearly held opinions on the functions proper to government.

"Sometimes, in private business," he had said, as much to himself as to her, "it is necessary to dip into one's reserves to meet a crisis. In this instance, the government, which is, after all, the custodian of the people's reserves, has approved a grant to enable us to meet a public emergency here. No precedent for the practice of underwriting private enterprise is being established." Then after a minute of silence, during which August moved restlessly and seemed anxious that he conclude his remarks, he had finished, reflectively, "One must only remember that the government is the servant of the people, and any collaboration between it and private interests must always be by the will of those interests."

When he thought of this conversation with August, he always smiled a little in self-approval. It was time that he gave her some general instruction which would help her toward a proper viewpoint of her relationship to the institutions of her world. It would prepare her against many superficial shocks which might otherwise seem to rock her true security if she had no formed convictions upon which to consciously rest. She must understand that it is sometimes expedient to compromise, or seem to compromise, one's principles for the sake of preserving or protecting one's investments. A man does not question the ownership of a weapon which he may need in sudden desperation to defend himself. He must teach her to think ahead but to take only one step at a time. But of course, he had long since taken most of her steps for her, so there would really be nothing for her to worry about when he was no longer alive to watch over her.

Now the step ahead, for him, was to lead her to accept the proposal he was fired to make for his own conscience's sake. And when he had had his tea and she did not come to the patio to join him and enjoy the spring afternoon sun, he went upstairs and along the gallery to her studio door and knocked.

But there was no answer from inside.

He knocked again and waited. Leaning forward, he put his head against the molded panel of the door beside the high lock and asked, "May I come in, dear?" Then he straightened and waited again.

But August did not invite him to enter.

He stood a minute longer, wondering if he had been mistaken and she had gone out. Then he looked at his watch. It was near seven o'clock. He decided she had gone to her room to change. He would have to hope for an opportunity to speak to her later, after dinner perhaps, if Gilberta left them early.

Then, as he moved away down the gallery, he heard a curious whishing sound coming from inside August's studio – a sound similar to the protest of flames under the pressure of a cold draught of air. He listened intently to the sound as it was repeated over and over. Then he went back to the door and rapped on it with a force unusual for him and called out, "Are you there, August?"

This time, she answered.

"I'm busy, Uncle Chad," she said. "I'd rather not be disturbed." And her voice came over the odd whishing sound and he heard her walking rapidly about.

"What are you doing, dear?" he insisted. There was something alarming in her tone. But he kept his fingers from the latch. He would not intrude.

August did not reply.

"Are you all right?" he asked. It was unlike August to close herself in her studio and refuse him – or anyoine else – admittance, even when she was working.

Suddenly, she opened the door.

"What do you want, Uncle Chad?" she said, wearily, clearly indicating that she felt her privacy invaded.

At that moment, Fenton was as unprepared to state his request as she was unprepared to receive it.

"I want to ask you to consider contributing a picture for the war memorial auditorium," he said. And the thing he wanted of her ran out between them like a drop of quicksilver on a plate.

August stood back, as if moving away from it. And beyond her, in the room, Fenton saw what she had been about.

Her newly completed drawings, which had been fastened along the walls, were lying now like giant popcorn balls in crumpled bunches on the floor. The old pine dough-trough, in which she had been used to store her gouaches and charcoal sketches as later work succeeded them in her interest, had been emptied of all it had held. Even her few oils and watercolors, which had been framed, had been taken from their places and were lying against the furniture awaiting destruction.

Fenton knew what the strange sound had been. It had been the ripping and crushing of all her work, from the time she had been a child and had been given this room in which to grow and develop the gift which was in her.

"What have you done, dear?" he whispered mournfully from the door.

Her only answer was to kick through a pile of ruined drawings and go to a laundry bag thrown over a chair back. Fenton followed her in and mutely watched her stuff the bag with scooped-up mounds of her work.

"Has something gone wrong, dear?" he finally asked, suffering at the sight of the spectacle before him. And then, timidly:

"Has Mr. Aitken made some criticism which has discouraged you?"

"I don't need Mr. Aitken to tell me what is good and what is bad," she said bluntly. Then, as an afterthought, she added, "No, you don't need to fire Mr. Aitken." And this bit deep into Fenton.

At that moment, he was incapable of containing her cruel insinuation with dignity. He left her abruptly and went to his apartment. Safe, he permitted the tears to rise, and fall, unrepressed. How could she have come to destroy her first accomplishments? And how had she come to so regard him! The face of Miss Applewhite, her teacher in childhood, rose before him. Its image defended him.

When she warned me that she might not, in good conscience, be able to promote August, I made no ugly bargain with her, he soothed his wound. I have never stooped to bribery. And I have never been urged to punish anyone for a critical opinion of August's talent.

Now he had come to an unexpected impasse in his relations with his child. More than that, in this impasse in his relations, he was learning that August was not any more a child, not even in part – and not his, nor anyone else's. She would be for herself the judge and the judged. She would not lean, nor invite. Even before she was formally free of him, with her coming of age, he knew she was already unconscious of any need for his guidance and decision in the thing which mattered most to her – her work. She was a woman. Now. And she was more. She was a being separated from him by a perceived but impenetrable guard, that of immersion in her own interests. And those interests, which he encouraged and protected from the intrusion of any rivals, had now provided her a world into which he had no pass to enter. He remembered Lesley, and his incorrigible disinterest in participating in the joined life of the family. He saw his father's face, lit in its strange cold way from the internal angry fire in which the pain of his rejection first by his wife and then by his son was never burned out.

Fenton shivered. The echo of that old and final summation he had made upon his father's tragedy whispered through him: *Not to be loved above the gift—that was what he could not endure.*

He prepared himself to go down to dinner. Abruptly, he cleared his mind of depressing memories. I will honor whatever place she gives me, he promised himself, dignity regained. And then he thought of what he would say to August, and how to promote her consent to execute a painting for the war memorial auditorium. It was more important to him than ever now. Helping her to plan the painting would be participating in her artistic life.

Supporting Fenton's determination to have August contribute a work of her own to the dedicated building was the undisturbed belief that she intended to go on with her studies with Mr. Aitken, despite her shocking, complete destruction of all her drawings and paintings to date.

August did intend to go on.

In its way, her otherwise frightening demonstration confirmed the seriousness of her aim. She had come to the place where she could stand away from her work and evaluate it without having her judgment conditioned by the emotion of possessiveness. Mr. Aitken, in a short time, had brought her a long way. He had led her to regard a finished drawing, sketch, or painting with an eye of fresh demand upon the artist. The work must not have been "editorialized" with tricks of pencil or brush and thus made a statement the artist did not envision in prospect. There was neither art nor promise in that. And for this tutoring, Mr. Aitken had had a self-instructed hand to rid of its cultivated technical faults, and an intelligence overly excited by its world to free of its yoke of unspent emotions. Very slowly, he had made the craft of the artist intelligible to her, as a means of illuminating the truth of an object or a place, and not merely a means of revealing the truth of her own feelings about that object or place. And very slowly, she was beginning to lose interest in embroidering her studies with the visual smudges and shadings of her emotional reactions and to employ instead the principle of economy of line to strengthen impressions.

In no way was Mr. Aitken's teaching academic. He helped her first to re-create, with means more restricted than nature's, the things which she saw before her, and to restrain her impulse to reproduce what she knew to be there. She began, without being conscious of it, to prove that to perceive is to know. As one discovery led to another, a strange joy in her progress began to take August. It was this joy, which, more than despair at seeing the failure of her past work, brought her to destroy her old drawings and paintings. Whatever fine frenzy had seemed to spur her to crush them, it was not a rage directed against herself. When she had finished the existence of all, she was lifted in heart. She was embarked. More than that, though she could not so early determine the precise outline of the shore toward which she made, she yet was certain of its broad and inviting aspect. She sensed that it was an island place and that there was a certain loneliness about it.

When she went down to dinner on the evening when Fenton had intruded and observed her special ruins, she had about her a gaiety peculiar to those who have realised not too late that they have been proceeding in a direction which will take them *beside* but not *to* their desired destination. Set straight, she was eager to run forward with renewed love of the race. The mood was a phase, but Fenton in his preoccupation had not the insight to know it. She seemed to him to be almost giddy in her manner. He questioned if she were feeling well.

"I should like to have a word with you privately, dear," he said then to her before Gilberta joined them.

"Yes, of course," August agreed, and there was an expression on her face as if she were inwardly laughing.

Fenton looked at her in wonder. It was possible that after the emotional strain of the afternoon, she had been left a little lightheaded.

Then dinner was announced and they went in to the conversation at table, which was, from old habit, usually concerned with interest in Gilberta's progress in her greenhouse, or the general news from the city.

After coffee, Gilberta excused herself to make her choice of flowers to be delivered in the morning to the hospitals. Besides keeping up Mr. Chadley's charitable practice she often arranged special small bouquets for the little girls in the wards for crippled children.

"I wanted to say to you, dear," Fenton began immediately to August, "that, upon reflection, I have come to see your motive in destroying your past art work."

August looked at him inquiringly. She made no comment.

"Of course, I was unprepared for your doing it," Fenton went on, "and so I must apologize for my abrupt departure from your studio this afternoon. I'm sure you can understand my astonishment at that moment when I saw your drawings strewn about the floor."

Still August made no comment. Nor did she nod or change her expression, which was one of mild question. She understood that he was getting to something beyond his apology and she was waiting to hear it.

"Though it didn't come to my mind, then," Fenton said, slowly, choosing his phrases with care, "I have since recalled a very wise opinion Professor Hanley once expressed to Father." He took in his breath and thought it through again to be certain he could quote it correctly. "Professor Hanley was defending a certain great figure sculptor against Father's assertion that there was a critical unevenness in the quality of his work. Father elaborated with specific examples, calling out admitted faults in conception and execution. He reminded Professor Hanley that there were few examples which could support the judgment that the sculptor worked out of superior creative powers."

Fenton paused then and fixed his eyes upon August's face. What he was about to quote was an opinion which had become for him a sustaining structure upon which to gather and rest his own anxieties over the incident of the afternoon. He hoped that it would turn out the statement of a right concerning all artists, which August would recognize as being the true motivation of her recent acts.

"Professor Hanley declared that it is the privilege and due of any painter or sculptor, or writer, or any craftsman even, to be judged solely upon the best of his work, and to have any inferior examples disregarded."

For what seemed to Fenton an almost unbearable length of time, August continued to sit before him in silence, with only a slow changing of her expression indicating her response to what he had said. Then when her reaction was apparently fixed in form in her mind and her face revealed it in an approving smile, she said, "I think it is also the privilege of an artist to be his own critic, if he is capable of being it. I think he has the right to select the work he is to be judged by."

"Yes, dear," agreed Fenton, with unconcealed joy, "I concur with you in that opinion. Surmising later that you must have acted out of some such conviction brought me to take an approving view of what you did this afternoon."

"I'm not a painter yet," said August, "but if I become one, it will be what I do from now on that makes me an artist. I really know very little and I'm not sure that I can accomplish anything original and good. It takes a long time. Mr. Aitken has been working for twenty years and he said himself that he has only been a real painter for the last ten."

She had an earnest, nearly humble tone in her voice as she said it and Fenton's sympathy for her and his pride in her unexpectedly discovered resolution made it impossible for him to speak. He wanted to cheer her and lift her up, but he knew no phrases to repeat which would not be trite and inadequate and his mind could not invent any new ones. Finally, when it seemed they had reached the end of their talk together and had sat silent for several minutes, August surprised him with the question, "What was it you wanted for the war memorial auditorium?"

"I hadn't an exact picture in mind, dear," Fenton said, "I

wanted to leave that to you. It struck me that perhaps you might want to make a special and personal contribution in memory of your father, and a painting of your own seemed to me particularly appropriate."

"By the time the building is finished, I'll have completed some new things," she said agreeably, "and you can look them over and see if there's one you think I could give." She smiled at him shyly and seemed embarrassed at the idea that anything of hers would be important enough to present.

Fenton came near telling her that he had not made his idea clear to her, that he had meant she was to paint something directly for the building, something of a commemorative nature. But the same intuition which had saved him from pressing her too hard when she was a child, rescued him now from committing that error. So instead he replied easily, "Yes, there's plenty of time ahead. I doubt if we'll be able to hold the dedication services much before next November. But it will do no harm for you to keep this matter in mind while you are at your summer work."

"I'll do that," she said.

Then she stood up suddenly.

"I'm very tired tonight," she said. "I should like to retire, if you'll excuse me."

"Of course," Fenton complied instantly and stood. August kissed his cheek and then, hesitantly, patted it.

Not ten days later, August went early to class, seated herself on the slab of granite which served as the art building's doorstep, rested one elbow lightly against the hatbox she had brought with care, and waited for Mr. Aitken.

However, on this morning, Mr. Aitken was late. He had worked until past midnight in his rooms on a night landscape he was doing in oils and after that had gone walking for an hour to exercise his legs. Four other pupils besides August were waiting when he arrived to open the door to the classroom studio.

August took the hatbox, which bore the name of a local milliner in orchid lettering across the top, and put it for safekeeping in Mr. Aitken's office.

"Do you mind if I leave it here until I can show you what is inside? Tomorrow morning?" she asked him. The contents seemed to be of a substantial weight for she lowered it to a cleared corner area as if she were letting down gymnasium weights.

Mr. Aitken looked on with interest. "Can't you show me now?" he asked her.

August shook her head. "There's quite a build-up to this unveiling," she said, and smiled mysteriously. "I would rather come early again tomorrow morning. And I'd rather no one else be here."

"Very well," agreed the artist, "I'll give you an hour. Is that what you want?"

"Yes, thank you," said August. Then she went into the classroom and began with the others to get out her materials and arrange her easel to go on with the figure study which was the present project.

When she had left him behind in his office, Mr. Aitken examined the cord wound around the hatbox and through the handle. It was simply knotted, he observed with satisfaction. Then he went out to meet his class.

Though it was often her custom to return to Dunmeade for luncheon and a short rest before resuming work for the afternoon, August on this day remained on the campus to go with two of the other art students to lunch in the college cafeteria. They waited for Mr. Aitken to close the studio and start to his rooms for his own midday meal. Then they walked along with him a little self-consciously, while one girl talked to him about impressionistic painting, mildly arguing in its defense against the sweeping slanders of supporters of representational art. She gave her views in an oddly artificial way as if she had planned for a long time to engage the artist in this one-sided conversation and were now repeating her opinion as one plays back a recording of one's own voice.

August was silent. She seemed caught in the contemplation of something quite puzzling to her, for alternately she frowned and smiled and then grimaced. Whatever was in her mind compelled her whole attention and she did not hear Mr. Aitken when he asked her, looking across the two attentive pupils walking between them, "And where do you stand on this vital issue? Do you say 'Down with the academicians!' also, Miss Chadley?"

But because August did not hear him, she did not answer.

Mr. Aitken laughed and said quickly to the other girls, while the one beside August pinched her, "Our Miss Chadley has other more vital issues to resolve, I think. She is probably trying to decide if it will help her to look older to put her hair up. She is more concerned with devising means to advance her years prematurely than she is in deciding whether or not she shall be an expressionist in art." He said it with a curious gruffness and his skin had reddened along the edges of his ears.

"I was wondering if one could inherit a talent for music or painting or writing. I have a particular reason for wondering about it just now. I'm sorry to have lost out on the conversation," said August. She seemed in no way offended at Mr. Aitken's remarks. She smiled at him, quite understanding his pique at her inattention and therefore forgiving his criticism. "You are quite right that I would like to advance my years prematurely, Mr. Aitken. And there's a particular reason for that, also." She had ignored the two girls with them and addressed Mr. Aitken in a tone which suggested that she enjoyed his teasing and wished their familiar discussion of her personal interests to continue.

They had arrived at a place where their ways diverged.

"If it doesn't rain this afternoon, I'm going to take the B class out sketching," said Mr. Aitken, abruptly changing the subject. "Will you mind working alone in the studio, Miss Chadley? I can't supervise you every hour, you know." He was complaining for the benefit of the other two students. Some of his old arbitrary hostility toward the Chadleys seeped into his tone and he let himself sound an objection to giving August special consideration merely because she was doing special work – work which lasted all day every day.

"I'm not afraid, if that's what you mean, Mr. Aitken," said August.

"That isn't what I mean," said the artist. "I want to know if you will mind working through the afternoon without my being there to help you."

The two girls looked at each other surreptitiously. Faint little smiles pinched the corners of their mouths into expressions of smug approval.

"I shall try to have a great deal done by your return," said August to Mr. Aitken.

With a quick dismissing movement of his hand, the artist then took leave of the three of them and each of the girls waved in return an imitation of his odd farewell gesture. In silence they proceeded to the college cafeteria.

Just after three o'clock, Mr. Aitken returned to the classroom studio from the site a mile and a half away where he had camped the B class to do its sketching. He had obviously returned for a purpose and he came to it without hesitation. Some of the vigor which was so attractive and inspiring in him was sparked by equal parts of curiosity and impatience.

He came up to August, working diligently in the quiet, and said, "Miss Chadley, I looked into your hatbox. I've spoiled your grand opening. Are you about to ask me to encourage you to be a sculptor?"

"Would you encourage me to be one?" countered August, wiping her brush, and not looking at him. "Basing your judgment of my ability on the evidence in the hatbox?"

"I'm not a prophet. And I'm not going to let you trick me into estimating your future upon the basis of work done far back in the past – probably in your precocious childhood," declared the artist.

August smiled. "I'm flattered that you were so interested that you came in from the field to tell me this, Mr. Aitken. I would have waited until tomorrow morning for the answer to the question I am going to put to you."

"State the question, then, since we've got this far," demanded Mr. Aitken, "and let me get back to the class." He was obviously nettled and picked at his short beard nervously.

"Will you risk making a prophecy for the immediate future? Based upon present performance, Mr. Aitken?" asked August, easily. She put down her palette and rubbed some viridian green from her left hand with a rag dampened in turpentine.

"That clay sculpture in the box, which you are offering as proof of your ability, was not executed in the recent past, much less the present," said the artist. "I have not observed you working in this medium and I will give you no answer."

"You have leaped to a wrong conclusion, Mr. Aitken," said August. "The clay head is not my work. It was done by my real father. I had never seen it until yesterday, when my uncle gave it to me with three others which my father left to him. My uncle made a present of them all to me. He placed them in my studio and I found them there just before dinner. Here is the letter which was leaned against the one I brought to show you."

She found it in the pocket of her dotted Swiss dress beneath her protecting linen smock.

She gave it to Mr. Aitken.

The artist looked down at it, incredulity opening his eyes in a stare at the neat writing on the thick single sheet. He read aloud:

My dear,

I planned on your eighteenth birthday to give you these few pieces which your dear father sculpt in his free time. But something quite important and complimentary to you happened today and I am now presenting them with a request which I have been authorized to make by the War Memorial Committee.

Would you paint a large picture directly for the entrance hall of the Memorial Auditorium? Mr. Jesse Oats, when I reported that you wished to contribute a painting in memory of your father, agreed that a mural of the type being executed for many public buildings at this time, would be most gratefully accepted. There is a suitable space between and over two of the center doors leading into the auditorium proper. Mr. York and Mr. Starburg ventured the suggestion that you might find inspiration in reading the *Newtown Guidebook* which is given out to visitors and persons contemplating removal of their business interests to our city. If you would depict the characteristic aspects of our life here, reminding us of those things for which our soldiers gave their lives, I know you would be making an impressive and unique contribution to this effort at a proper memorial to them.

I hope that you will accept this commission (without fee, of course) and that the possession of your father's artistic work will support and inspire you as you proceed in this ambitious and worthy task.

Your ever fond,

UNCLE CHAD

"Well," asked Mr. Aitken, "what was your answer?"

"I haven't given it yet," said August. "I told Uncle Chad that I wished to think it over."

"Would you like to paint a mural?"

"I would like to work on a big canvas. But whether or not I can paint something 'on commission,' I don't know."

"There's no trick to it," said the artist. "What's this *Newtown Guidebook?*"

"It tells a lot of facts about the city and there are photographs of the principal sites of interest. That's what bothers me. I don't think I can do what they want. Filling a wall space with painted scenes of places around Newtown doesn't interest me."

"I don't think that's what they're ordering either," said Mr. Aitken.

"Then what is it they're asking for?"

"They want you to illustrate the facts with scenes which suggest the spirit of life here – the spirit being what promoted the facts in the first place. Suppose, for example, you took the statistic that five hundred babies are born here every year. You wouldn't paint the maternity hospital. You'd paint a scene illustrating that people here love babies and that rearing children is regarded as an important part of life. You'd show happy children together in play areas or parks provided for them or something like that."

As he talked to her, August's face took on a quiet sobriety and she listened to him with her eyes directly on his, in an animal-like still gaze.

"Your family has played a conspicuous part in the building up of Newtown. Your family pride and your civic pride will help you respond to some of the otherwise dull statements in the *Guidebook*. You've probably never called it forth into your conscious eye, but I'm sure that you have a visual image of the city as a whole in your mind. That visual image is inspired by what you know about it, combined with its actual appearance. It's what comes into your mind when you're away from it and remember it. You can recite the layout of the streets and you know the façades of all the buildings in the downtown section, but you also know what life is going on behind those façades. It's this knowledge that makes you homesick. Actually Newtown doesn't look very different from a hundred other small cities, but it's what you know about it that gives it individuality for you. And that is what you will paint."

August looked away from him. Her eyes went toward the door at the rear of the great room, the door to the small office where she had left Lesley's clay sculpture. Then she wiped her hands slowly on her smock. They were perspiring.

"Mr. Aitken," she asked him, "do you think I can paint this mural?"

And the artist answered her, "Yes. I know you can."

For a moment, August's face moved as if in defense against the pressure of tears. Then she asked, "Will you help me? I don't know what to do first, even."

"You prepare your sketches first," said Mr. Aitken, matter-of-factly. "Rough out your general idea after you've got the dimensions of the space and have decided what information in the *Guidebook* you intend to use. Keep it simple and broad. The unifying idea, I mean."

"Will I have to paint directly on the plaster wall? Up on a scaffolding or something?" She was obviously terrified of this possibility.

Mr. Aitken laughed. "Certainly not. You'll make final drawings to scale after the committee passes on your sketches. Then we'll prepare a canvas right in here and rig it so that it can be pulled up and down by ropes from the ceiling. You'll do a tempera underpainting following the scaled drawings after you've worked out your colors. Then you'll isolate it with thin varnish and go over it in thinned oils."

"Oh, my goodness!" exclaimed August.

"It sounds like punishment, doesn't it?" Mr. Aitken said, smiling and cocking his eye at her. "You haven't committed yourself. You can say 'No' to Mr. Chadley tonight."

"It has to be ready by November, Mr. Aitken. Do you think there's enough time for me to have it finished by then?"

"I'll help you by preparing your canvas. You worry about keeping the idea simple. And get a rough general sketch out right away," he said. Then he added, "Of course, if you feel this effort will be too heroic for you and you can't sacrifice your other more frivolous summer activities to the cause, then don't try it. It will take time and strength and patience and most of your attention. You won't see much of your family – or any other special friends."

"I'm going to do it," she said. And then with a slight quaver in her voice, she asked, "You aren't planning to go away from here on a vacation or something this summer, are you?"

"I won't desert you, if that's what you mean," he said. Suddenly, a sentimentality quite strange to him softened his tone and he finished, "Even if I had planned to take off for a while, I'd stay and see you through the preparations for your public debut." And then, embarrassed, he made abruptly for his office, messed about noisily among the supplies, came bounding out, and left August again alone with, "You always manage to take more of my time than any one of the other students, Miss Chadley. It's four o'clock and the B class is still propped on a hill overlooking Farmer Rooters' cow pasture. I'd better get back and advance them beyond detailed drawings of horns or tails!"

When Mr. Aitken was gone, August went into his office and opened the hatbox and gently lifted out the clay sculpture. Layers and layers of tissue were twisted about it to guard it against chipping. She had prepared the box with cushions of paper. She handled the modeled head with an air of tender possession and carried it into the studio and placed it beneath the skylight on a high stool. Then she stood away from it to study it.

The clay had dried and hardened and along the smoothed-out areas of chin and forehead and cheek there were small cracks from shrinkage. It was a portrait of a sitter apparently unknown to Fenton, and her father had struck no name into the base when his clay was moist. It was a portrait of a man. And August had brought it to show to Mr. Aitken, rather than the recognizable head of Fenton, because in the crudeness and simplicity of its style it was quite different from the other pieces. The others had been modeled smoothly, with care taken to reproduce those details which gave a literal lifelikeness to the features. But this work seemed, in a way, to shape out in expression the nature of the sitter rather than to present a facsimile of his combined facial characteristics. Though there was a handsome boniness to the features and a certain nobility to the classic oval form of the head, yet it was not these visual attributes which the artist had exploited or which best qualified the portrait. It was something else – a strange and subtle, but unmistakable, cruelty in the face which had been gained by the coarse, nearly impressionistic execution.

She studied the head for a long time, noting the close fastening of the lips above the accentuated round muscle of the chin, and the arched orbital processes from out of which no really formed eyes looked. There was something about the face and its expression which was reminiscent of a face she could not bring clearly to memory. Her grandfather Chadley had had such a structure to his head, but he had had a feature of beauty not indicated in the hard clay before her – his hair had waved thickly to complete the pleasing contour of his head.

At last, when she heard the voices of the students in the returning B class, she took the sculpture back to its box in Mr. Aitken's office and carefully rewound the tissue paper about it and prepared to take it home again to Dunmeade. Someday, when he had time to examine it, she wanted to show Mr. Aitken all her father's work. Owning the sculptures had given her a key to a small knowledge of him, and with it she had released and let flow upon him in memory, that special filial love which, unknown to her, had lain in the heart unused, not called out by Fenton's foster parentage. For the first time in her life, she began to feel a descendancy from Lesley.

Suddenly the thought came to her, "It *is* of Grandfather! It's unfinished, that's all!"

After August began her sketches for the mural (her picture, as Fenton continued to call it) there could be observed in her a temper toward her work which had not been a characteristic during any previous efforts. She had always applied her talent with industry. There had been a special emotional excitement for each endeavor. And that excitement, which is in the artist as an irritant to his creative power, had always projected into her work the quality of life. But this new temper, which developed as she prepared her sketches for approval by the War Memorial Committee, was something quite different from any other attitude or impulse. August, with defined purpose, had become a professional.

She proceeded thoughtfully and critically, never moved to disregard her requirements. She presented to the Committee, through Fenton, a set of four carefully prepared sketches. One was the sketch of the whole, in which the city was represented as an architectural bright crown resting upon the supporting and sustaining heads of the citizenry. The other three were details of that whole, scenes within it depicting Education, Civic Government, and Industry – which jointly accomplished the life of Newtown. Each one illustrated a statement lifted from the *Newtown Guidebook.*

When she had first planned the mural, there had been a fourth scene within the whole, meant to describe the recreational life of the adult citizenry. She had wanted to give a visual account of the balance between work and restorative play. But except for statements that Newtown was the county seat and therefore the site of the yearly county fair, and that there were four motion picture theaters for the public and a country club with game privileges for members, there was no record that Newtown provided itself with any creative recreation. There were no centers for crafts, no singing societies, no amateur orchestral groups, no organizations interested in producing plays or even sponsoring pageants for charity benefits.

The sketches were passed on with unanimous approval and Mr. Lyndon even sent August a message by Fenton. Into Fenton's face he coughed one of his dusty sour laughs and said, "Tell Miss August that I'd almost be willing to pay her something. At least I can make out what I'm looking at, and that's saying a whole sight more than anybody can say about those Project pictures the taxpayers' good money is paying to get painted in public buildings where nobody is going to look up and see them anyway!"

When Fenton delivered the message, he said, "Mr. Lyndon felt, dear, that your painting had every possibility of turning out better than many of those which professional artists have executed for the walls of public buildings."

And to this, August answered, "Mr. Lyndon probably doesn't know a good painting from a bad. But it's nice of him to express confidence in me."

Then August began the transferring of the scaled drawings to the intimidating stretch of canvas which Mr. Aitken prepared for her with a surprising fussiness and exactitude.

"All right," he said one morning when he was at last satisfied with the apparatus for raising and lowering the canvas, "get at it. You haven't got a lifetime, you know." And he handed her a box of thin expensive charcoal sticks which he had ordered from his supply house in the North.

"Are these a good-luck present, Mr. Aitken?" August asked him.

"They're good sticks if you mean that. Don't throw them around," he said and went for the small stepladder he kept in his office. Carrying it to the canvas, he said, "You aren't going to faint if you climb up three steps. You've got to rule it off yourself. I'm not going to do everything for you. Here's the chalk line."

He left her then without helping her up the ladder or steadying it while she stood on the top step. However, when August looked along the top rim of the canvas she saw that he had taken the trouble to mark it off at twelve-inch intervals. She fastened the chalk line to the first marking and then climbed down and fastened it against the first marking along the base rim. She was smiling when she snapped the chalked cord against the canvas to make a vertical line. And she was still smiling when Mr. Aitken came and watched her snap the final line of the verticals and begin to mark off the horizontals.

"I'd be lost without you, Mr. Aitken," she said. But he pretended not to hear her. He began cracking up some gelatin sheets into a melting pot and examining the cord to the electric burner as if he were searching out the cause of a short circuit.

"If I manage to do this mural the way it ought to be done, I'll owe a great deal to you," August said.

"You will indeed, Miss Chadley," replied the artist, beginning to stir the melting gelatin.

After an interval of silence, during which time August completed the marking-off of the horizontal lines, Mr. Aitken asked,

"Do you have any idea how to begin with the charcoal, Miss Chadley?"

August began to laugh.

"I thought not," said the artist. He went on with his stirring. "Bring me your scaled drawings."

August handed him the drawings and took the stick with which he was moving the melting glue in the pot. There with the odious fumes steaming into their faces and the damp warping the paper of her sketches, August absorbed another lesson – illustrated, because Mr. Aitken at one point could not resist going to her canvas and striking one great sweeping charcoal curve upon it.

"It's ruled off to guide you on your proportions, but don't turn out a diagram, Miss Chadley. Give some sweep to your strokes. Just keep your eye on where you're going. Do you see?"

"Yes," said August. "Thank you."

"Well, don't look so frightened," protested Mr. Aitken. "Here, turn off that mess and come here."

He dragged a chair to her ladder and stood on it beside her when she had climbed up the three steps. He handed her the thin stick of charcoal he had used.

"Go ahead, now. Right across the top. Give us the sky line of Newtown."

On a June afternoon when August was advanced to working out the final background colors for the merging details of the mural, she took her water colors and pad to a place which overlooked the cluster of farmhouses just beyond the Art Building. She wanted to study the ripe midday light on the fields and catch some of the heat and brightness of summer in her colors. She placed her folding stool in the narrow rim of shade from a maple tree and sat a long time looking out across the immediate landscape to a farther basin of cultivated acres which dipped to the right of the largest of the farmhouses and its whitewashed sheds and unstained barn. She had begun to experiment with colors and was settling her bottle of water within a circle of supporting pebbles, when she heard someone whistling to her.

It was Mr. Abbott in the roadway below and he stood waiting for her to invite him to join her.

When she beckoned, he picked his way up the rise through some wild blackberry bushes and said when he was directly before her, "Do you know how long it's been since you let me watch you sketch from a hillside?"

"I'm not very sentimental," she replied, "I don't remember." She bent over and tipped some water from her bottle into a spot on her wiping rag. Then she cleaned a brush which was only faintly tinted with yellow.

"Then the memory will be sharper for being a private one with me," he said easily. "Do you object to my being here? I don't see much of you these days."

"You know the way to Dunmeade," she answered.

"Is that a reproach?" he asked, moving aside out of her vision.

"It was you who complained," she said. She concentrated upon placing a clear blue beside an alizarin red in repeated strokes. There was a silence. Then Walter asked, "Is it association with your Mr. Aitken that has given you that sharpness?"

"If you're referring to the change in my painting technique, the answer is 'yes,'" August answered. "There was a time not far back when I mixed all the colors on the palette because I didn't know how to place them so the eye would do it for me."

"Is that a quotation from Aitken's book?"

"I think all the good painters have it in their books."

She wet the rag again and wiped her brushes.

"You like studying with Mr. Aitken, don't you? You've changed quite a lot since he came."

"Yes," said August, "I suppose I have changed. I know a lot more, so I'm not so sure of myself."

"That's a slight contradiction, isn't it?"

"You know what I mean."

"I hope you're sure enough to go on with your work when he's gone. I don't think Mr. Aitken will be at Marion after the next semester. It may be he won't stay through that."

"Because he's a rolling stone and unreliable, like all artists?" August asked, with a mild soft sarcasm in her tone.

"Because I don't think Dr. White is really going to support Mr. Chadley long in these innovations in the curriculum."

"Dr. White will keep all the new courses in the curriculum as long as Uncle Chad wishes them there," said August.

"Yes," Walter admitted, dryly, "but there are ways of diminishing the attractiveness of the courses so that they lose student enrollment. It is not to the advantage of the college to carry a course when the enrollment does not justify the expense. Dr. White has a way of inhibiting a teacher from inspiring his students to meet the challenge of new knowledge. It isn't easy to explain. You probably don't understand what I'm saying and I suppose it's just as well. I shouldn't be saying it."

"No," said August, "I don't understand you. But I think it must be something I should understand, if you have bothered to bring up the subject. I should like to know why you think Mr. Aitken will not stay at Marion College."

She went on laying streaks of colors against each other in a mechanical way. "Tell me why?" she asked him.

"For the same reason I won't, August," he replied quietly.

And then August put down her brushes on her pad and turned to look into his face with her whole attention, for this was what he had come up the rise from the roadway to tell her.

"I think you have wanted to leave since you got here," she said. "Are you sure it's Dr. White who's driving you away? You moved out of Dunmeade when there was no one who wanted you to go."

There was a curious spasm of the muscle of his chin when she said this and he only gazed at her in silence a few minutes. And then, working his hands in his pockets in his old nervous habit, he said, "I will leave, and Aitken will leave, because there will not be any place for us at Marion College. The character of our regard for the students and for teaching is something with which Dr. White does not sympathize."

"I'm sorry," August said. "You aren't being very clear. I know Dr. White is old-fashioned and that he'll probably always be stubborn about putting in courses he doesn't think of himself. But he's come around to Uncle Chad's view on the importance of business training for women and he'll do anything to keep up Marion College. Besides, you don't have to teach — ever, if you don't want to. Uncle Chad thinks you're a good assistant administrator."

"Listen, August, because I'm very serious. There is an improvement needed here which it will be impossible for Dr. White to make. It will be impossible because of his point of view. And it is his point of view which makes it impossible for your Mr. Aitken and me and serious instructors to remain here long."

He came and stood looking down at her a moment and then he stooped suddenly to sit on his heels and took one of her hands in his and held it tightly. "August," he said, "Dr. White speaks to the faculty often and at great length about inspiring 'these dear girls' spirits to work their benevolent womanly influence in the world today.' He never speaks of opening their minds to knowledge of the world about them. He never speaks of inspiring their intelligences to inquire into the facts and conditions of their world. He never speaks of challenging them to find their individual positions within the particular society which surrounds them. He wants them to have no opinions except the traditional one of their domestic place. He thinks that any other opinion on any other subject will cause them to forfeit that one. Inspiration is not meant to be a substitute for knowledge, it best serves when it is a result of it. Can you understand what I am trying to tell you?"

"Yes," she said. A deep color came into her face and she looked at her hand in his and added, with her eyes averted from his, so closely watching her: "I know what you're talking about in a way. It's like Mother. She thinks that if I really learn to paint—*really* learn—not a soul will want to marry me! That will be a disgrace, and I will be a failure as a woman."

Because he could not help it, Walter smiled. The idea of August's rare appeal losing its power behind a paint-daubed smock was so ridiculous!

"There will be many who will want to marry you, August," he said, "but if they don't ask you, it will not be because you are a lady artist."

Then suddenly his smile was gone and he had leaned forward to pull her head toward him and kiss her. He did not wait for the relaxing of her face in his hands as he drew his mouth away from hers. He escaped her response with a sound of anger in his throat, stood up, looked with desperation toward the road below them, and then, without a word, made for it.

August sat staring after him, a kind of terror beginning to sicken her. She could not move her eyes away from following his figure, half running to put distance quickly between them as he scrambled through the wild blackberry bushes and leaped the ditch to the road.

"He isn't going to get away," she uttered in the deep and soundless area of her heart. "He isn't going to get away!"

Then, with a shudder as the resolution passed into her will and rooted there, she turned back to her work, and, in an agony of determination, set about once more violently placing vibrant colors against vibrant colors in unordered streaks across her pad.

She kept her gaze above the roadway down which he had vanished—and observed, with eyes suddenly more quickened to their beauty, the changes of light upon the far fields until it was sundown.

Then she cleaned her brushes in the bottle of water and returned to the Art Building.

O'Smyre was waiting to drive her home.

"I'll only be a minute," she said to him as she passed the car and went inside.

She walked rapidly down the length of the studio, not stopping to put down her watercolors or pad.

"Mr. Aitken," she said, peeping around the door of the artist's cloakroom office, "I want to ask you something. May I?"

Aaron Aitken looked out from under the arch of his left arm to where she waited. He was leaning over a crate, withdrawing the nails from the slats at one side.

"What is it?" he replied.

August went to him and grasped the flimsy pine crate to steady it while he dug out the nailheads with a chisel too large for the purpose.

"What does Dr. White think you should do to inspire the students' spirits?"

The artist slowly splintered a crosspiece of wood and swore. Then he snatched at the resisting nail with his fingers.

"I don't attend the faculty meetings, Miss Chadley. I am summoned but I do not answer the call. I do not consider myself to be on the faculty. I am only something that has happened to Dr. White."

"Then how do you know what I'm talking about, Mr. Aitken?"

"Your friend Mr. Abbott brings me the news from the throneroom. It eases him to repeat the dicta to someone who never intended to obey them and therefore never goes to receive them."

"You know the answer to what I am asking, Mr. Aitken," pleaded August. "What is it?" She stared down at his muscular back, bent stubbornly in his search for restraining tacks and nails.

"I suppose, Miss Chadley, that Dr. White is afraid to inform the minds of what he calls his 'spiritually unprepared young ladies.' And a good teacher will always rebel against serving up comforting platitudes about the nobility of the soul and the virtue of humility in place of leading his students to discover these truths for themselves out of knowledge. I'm not an academician and these problems are not mine. But I don't savor supporting a rule of intellectual deceit any more than does your Mr. Abbott or any of the others. Have I answered you now, Miss Chadley?"

"Thank you, Mr. Aitken," said August, "you have. Good night."

"Good night," responded the artist, straightening up and looking at her thoughtfully. "Leave your work where I can look it over, please."

"I will," she said, taking it from the floor where she had left it hastily when she went to help him hold the crate steady. After a slight hesitation she confessed, "I didn't do too well this afternoon."

The artist turned back to prizing up the slats.

"Keep your mind on your work, Miss Chadley," he said; "the only happiness for an artist lies in accomplishment. Don't go looking for it anywhere else. You'll break your heart. The only union possible between one of us and another person is in the single moment of yearning itself for union. You have a tyrant living inside you, Miss Chadley. And I have lately been helping him to grow stronger. He does not permit rivals. Don't let it shock you when you realize one day that you cannot respond in kind to the love of a person who is free of such a tyrant. Marry a man who cannot love you too much either, Miss Chadley. Life will be easier for you both. Now, go home."

August made no reply. She stood watching him methodically going on with his task while a curious feeling quite foreign to any she had ever experienced began to come over her. She wanted to go to Mr. Aitken and put her arms about his neck and let the weight of her body and spirit together hang against his certainty and his strength for just one relieving moment. But she could not move, not even to leave as he had ordered her.

He glanced at her, as if to say, "Well?" And then she spoke.

"Mr. Aitken," she said, "you have never been as hard on me as you pretend you are trying to be. I don't want you ever to leave Newtown. I think I love you very much."

"You love what you recognize of yourself in me, Miss Chadley," said the artist; "now, go home."

And August turned and ran down the length of the studio, flinging down her afternoon's work beside her easel as she passed it, and fleeing to the confines of the limousine outside. There, in the rear seat, she let the shame of having exhibited such emotion dissipate slowly as she stared out the window at the landscape of long rolling lands which suddenly were ended at the limits of Newtown by a row of machine shops and filling stations.

She got out of the car in the drive and was about to go directly into the house. Then she saw her mother coming from the greenhouse removing her gardening gloves as she walked. August stopped on the flags of the patio and waited. The sun was behind Gilberta and from where August stood watching her it seemed that Gilberta had no features until she was quite close, but was instead a concentrated shadow disengaging itself from the sun as it moved forward. In her state of confused feelings, such an image of her mother gave her a startling instant realization of the loneliness in which each of them lived in Dunmeade. It caused her to conclude in her mind a never completed thought which had for a long time been present in it.

Mother doesn't even live in the house with the rest of us. She lives out here with the flowers. Flowers do not talk and there aren't any ugly ones, she thought.

There had been times lately, when, watching her mother with Fenton, she had wondered if Gilberta had always been so mysteriously remote, if she had been so with August's real father. She had wondered if her mother had ever loved anyone in the world, or even liked them enough to seek their company.

Suddenly, when Gilberta reached her, she impulsively put her arm about her mother's waist and drew herself close to her mother. She had never done such a thing before.

"Mother," she said, in what was almost a cry, "do you think you could help me to look as beautiful as you?"

Gilberta moved forward with August into the house, with no gesture or response of her body acknowledging her daughter's embrace. She answered seriously, "You have begun to carry yourself badly of late. That detracts from your appearance."

"Thank you for telling me, Mother," August replied, "I'll be mindful of my posture hereafter."

She let Gilberta step forward out of the circle of her arm. A little smile, almost of agedness, was on her mouth as she watched her mother escape what had been an embarrassing as well as unexpected demonstration of August's filial regard.

When she reached the top of the stair on her way to her room, August stopped and looked into the guest chamber which Walter Abbott occupied when he was in Dunmeade. She did not enter. She only stood looking into it. Then she suddenly closed its door.

Halfway home to his room in the farmhouse, Walter Abbott stopped in his flight from August. From there on, he tried by the controlled measuring of his steps and a naïve attempt at calm breathing to master in himself what had been a deep stirring of denied emotion, emotion which was the churned and breaking skim which floated above a still deeper yearning and necessity.

There is no answer, he repeated to himself, as he had practiced saying it from the time, long ago, when she was even more a child. There is no answer, and I must not allow the question. And all the sharpness of his instinct for self-preservation was pressed into his mind, demanding resistance to his heart. Doggedly, he reiterated the facts, the facts which, more times than August would ever know, had prohibited the gesture he might have made, silenced the invitation and the plea he might have uttered.

She is one person and I am another, and however far she may advance toward me out of her traditional position, and however far I may advance toward her out of mine, from which I am already more emancipated – still we may never meet on that bed of union upon which we must base and anchor a marriage! With this already, the years which divide us will slowly stretch between us a recognizable but insoluble growth of disparity. I could not endure watching for the day when I might detect her efforts to enter my world because she realizes that I cannot go backward into hers, and she is frightened that it will be another father and not a husband who travels with her in her middle years!

And here, as always, his mind stopped – content at numbing for another time, perhaps finally, the faulty heart which persisted in expanding and contracting to the needle of hope which August's strange ashamed desire for him had always shot into it.

He entered the farmer's house and spoke to one of the children, pulling his disobedient hound from the parlor to the back porch with grunts and chuckles in sympathetic discernment and half-approval of the dog's waywardness.

Then he went to his room and took up his work on the revisions to be made in the supplement to the college catalogue. The supplement had been a suggestion of Fenton's. He had argued that sending it out in the autumn to a selected list of young women expecting to be graduated from High School at midyear, might bring a number of applications to the new department of business training. As they would not be able to enter a college until the next fall term, they might be interested in using the spring to learn stenography and typing.

Fenton often surprised Walter with such suggestions. And he was often embarrassed afterwards when he realized the reason for his surprise. He was foolishly thinking of practicality as the child of necessity. True, it was the natural child, but it could be born also from such characteristics as he knew to be Mr. Chadley's – the instinct for arranging means to beget ends and the simple love of doing business, any business at all. Sometimes it was very troublesome to keep Fenton Chadley distant from him for the sake of his observations upon him as a symbol. And Fenton was most necessary to him as a symbol, for the structure of points in his thesis would be weakened if he could not keep Fenton supporting them as his prime illustration. He was beginning to admire Fenton, not just to pity him or be curious. He opened the drawer to his table and took out his manuscript and looked at the title page. He remembered that day in the hospital when Fenton had asked him the subject of his thesis and the bewildered expression which had come on Fenton's face when he had answered. The title now was not exactly the one which he had given Fenton. It now read: Class and Caste Ideologies in

Southern Society, with Special Reference to Patterns of Paternalism. This was the title and statement of theme which he had taken that summer when he had lived in Dunmeade and tutored Ralph.

That summer he had had more conflicting and yet more clearly defined reactions to the man Fenton Chadley, with whom he lived closely and yet put apart from him to study. Now, with all his thoughts about Fenton and the Chadley family strained through the dependable mesh of his broad critical ability and set down in a record nearly completed, he was beginning to slip into that bog of merging responses which lay between and joined the two parts of his carefully preserved ambivalent attitude. No longer could he feel the firm sustaining edge of distrust which is the academician's invisible cloak against the suffocating embrace of such men as Fenton Chadley. Instead he was looking more and more often into Fenton's goodness of heart and suffering at the sight of the trap which tradition and circumstance had sprung upon it. He was being pressed toward a reconsideration of Fenton by Dr. White, the identifiable enemy both to his own ideals and to Fenton's schemes for practical improvement. He had written his paper with care and wrenching detachment, as, toward his conclusion, he had begun to recognize in himself the signs of corrosion in the armor of integrity which the scholarly mind must learn to wear like a natural membrane upon it. He was beginning in the last pages to want to editorialize upon his observations — and his motive was not to explain but to excuse.

He put the thesis back into the table drawer, roughly, as if he saw it suddenly as a thing out of himself quite hostile to his own well-being and quite capable of destroying him if he tried to hold it to him longer. "I am done with it," he said to himself, "and I must send it now to Professor Elwige at the university."

He took a sheet of typing paper and wrote a short note to the man who had been his teacher, and, through the years of his labor toward obtaining his doctorate, had become his close friend and intellectual supporter.

"Here it is," he wrote, "and the study is over, however I may be delaying sending it in the hope of there being one last certain dramatic incident to record and tie up the Chadley dossier with a fast knot."

He knew, of course, that, editorially, it was not a finished work which he was now sending to Professor Elwige. But the unexpected and shaking encounter with August, pricking his awareness of his changing attitude toward Fenton, had stimulated a desperation to put the manuscript quickly out of his hands. His need to commit his work to judgment, just as it was, outweighed his pride and he was willing to suffer his supervisor's reading it with all its rough transitions and sometimes inadequately prepared-for summations. He needed a certain reassurance. He needed to know that he had not compromised his scholar's mandatory distance from his subject with his unanticipated emotional responses to August and to Fenton.

That first summer in Dunmeade, when he realized his unique advantage in observing intimately a classic example of a paternalistic family, he had, with Professor Elwige's permission, changed from the original theme of his thesis to write what now was primarily an historical-sociological study, essentially an analysis of ideologies. He had been aware that with his research limited to one family group – the Chadleys of Newtown – the error of probability would be great because of the restricted sampling. But he had believed that his conclusions did not depend for validity upon his sampling a number of cases, for his intention was to use his material on the Chadleys to illustrate key points in analysis.

But when his supervisor had submitted his dissertation subject to the department head, he had been warned that his finished work might turn out to be literary rather than scientific, a record of subjective impressions rather than the acceptable and proper compilation of scientific data required. Although the head had approved his subject, Walter had never lost the anxiety which that sober warning had put into his mind.

His study of the Chadleys was done now. His paper ended with Fenton's participation in the raising of the war memorial auditorium. He would have liked having one last example of the influence of the pattern of paternalism upon August, one concluding instance reflecting the conflict which it engendered in her – such as had been exposed in her reaction to Ralph's tragic accident.

But August was deeply absorbed in her painting of the Newtown mural. And though there were changes going on within the depths of her unusual personality and Walter could observe, to his excitement, her often surprising expressions of those changes, there was nothing more to report upon August in his thesis.

And then, one morning, a week after he had sent his manuscript to Professor Elwige and was awaiting a reply and the setting of a conference date, he ran into Aaron Aitken in the roadway beyond the Art Building. The artist was off for an hour's sketching before his first class.

"Look here, Abbott," he greeted Walter, "I've been trying to waylay you for days. Come with me. I've something to show you." He thumped Walter's arm with his knuckles, jumped the shallow roadside ditch, and headed for his office across a stretch of field grass parched to an even brown mat.

"Sorry," declined Walter, "not this morning. I've an early appointment. I'll drop around another time." And he continued walking down the middle of the road.

"Nonsense," bellowed the artist from the field, "I know your habits. I see you loping to the post every morning. You've time for this. Come on."

Irritated, Walter still delayed, as if working out in his mind the exact fraction of his time he could afford to give Aitken. Then he crossed the ditch. But the artist did not wait to walk along with him. He swung on ahead singing out snatches of "O Paradiso" from *L'Africano* and popping his sketch pad against his right thigh on high notes that he hit.

Walter followed him to the building and then took a stance in the doorway. The artist had thrown down his pad and had gone to the wall and started loosening the ropes by which a large canvas had been drawn to the ceiling out of the way.

"You can't see it out there, you know," Aitken said. "You'll have to come in. I'm a peace-loving man. You've nothing to fear." He laughed and turned his back to Walter as he carefully lowered the painting. There was a curious tenderness in the care he took which surprised Walter.

Overhead, a skylight had been let into half the roof and the early cold light was clear and even over the studio. Walter walked to where he could see the canvas, took off his glasses, puffed a vapor over each lens and cleaned it carefully.

There was a protecting sheet of muslin over the whole picture and this Mr. Aitken methodically rolled up from the bottom and swung into an improvised cradle of brackets along the top of the stretcher.

"This is the tempera underpainting," he said, "and it draws dust like a chalk bin. Now, step over here." He pulled Walter by the arm to a position slightly to the left front of the canvas. "This should interest you very much, Abbott. It interests me. In fact, it fascinates me. And let me tell you, it's going to knock a whole crowd of people we know right off their feet. Take a look. It's beautiful to see!"

And Walter stood in astonishment and stared at August's great free portrait of the world about her – the likeness of the city of Newtown!

For the first few moments no conclusive single impression of the whole lit upon his consciousness so that if he had walked away from it then, he would have carried only the memory of swarming colors and harsh purple-black outlinings of forms and figures. He studied it with an attention which began with a quivering recognition of the strange and unexpected condemnation in it and ended with the slow examination of its combining parts. It followed the exact drawing August had made for submission to the committee.

It was the world of the doer.

But it was August's reaction to that world which was so clear and startling to the beholder of her painting!

The figures stood separated from each other, even in the children's group, and implied in their physical attitudes the selfish direction of each to his own goal. Nowhere was there a feeling of bondage together in humanity, nowhere a hint of that transcendent love which reaches beyond aim and material achievement and declares the interdependent relationship of humans to each other. Although they faced the continuing accomplishment of their city and were the symbolic support of it, absent from their faces was any joy in either it or themselves. Nowhere were spiritual values illustrated by their acts. And that absence was undeniable and reproaching. August had painted Newtown's particular richness and allure, but she had also, in an unconsciousness of what she did, painted, in the human figures who symbolically sponsored its bright and worldly aspect, the visual impression of spirits driven in pursuits for which there was no reward in the end.

The painting was eloquent, condemning, and ugly. It was the world as August saw it, particularized by Newtown. Walter Abbott stared at it in silence and with a desperate grief for her.

"Look at this figure!" said Aaron Aitken at his side. He pointed toward a farm boy dropping his plow in his unfinished row, his body tensed for the moment of escape, and his eyes enlarged with and reflecting the image of the city beyond him. "It illustrates the statement that Newtown's great mills draw their labor from Newtown's environs and that preference is given local job-applicants."

Walter gazed at the striking pose of the boy, the only one of the figures upon which August had begun her thin over-painting in oils.

"I've always been curious about this detail of the mural," went on the artist. "Miss Chadley works on it with such a feverish interest. Technically, she has developed such feeling in it, in contrast to the others, that it threatens the whole's unity of impression. I ought to have restrained her. But I didn't. Do you know who this is? This farm boy?"

"Why should it be anyone?" countered Walter. He was disturbed and moved by the mural, and he wanted to get free from Aitken to think about it alone.

The artist smiled at him slyly. "Never mind," he said. Then, as he began to cover the canvas and prepared to draw it again to its rack above their heads, he added, "I won't ask you to comment, Mr. Abbott. You and I will not be the ones to make the important remarks – either now or later."

"I don't know what you mean by that," said Walter. But he was not really challenging Aitken to explain. He was moving to the vestibule toward the front door. What he said was only murmured.

Aaron Aitken laughed. "Don't scare yourself to death over it," he said, jerking his head toward the painting. "You can put ideas into an artist's head but you can't make him paint them, Abbott – if that's any relief to know. The Newtown mural is all Miss Chadley's, lock, stock and barrel."

Walter did not reply. He was beginning to tremble in a purely private rage of realization. With all the confusion the sight of it had stirred in his emotions, the mural and its meaning was sinking fast into its real significance in his mind. It was the unexpected climactic end he had needed for his thesis. It was the real finish to the Chadley story. It was the revelation of August's unconscious revolt against the pattern by which her life had been traced, but not yet cut. It was the declaration of her freedom!

Walter walked out of the building into the warmth of the summer morning.

"Don't let pride tie your tongue too long, Abbott," he heard Aitken call after him. And he began to run along the path to the campus, away from the artist's laughter. He could feel the strange temper of the mural pushing him on.

"I know who that farm boy is," he thought. "It's Pedro de Ventura. And all her scorn of his desertion of the land is in the glittering city's image with which she has blinded his eyes!"

Then he stopped short on the path and began to laugh. He stood staring vacantly ahead of him at the sprawl of college buildings and the broad dip of fresh morning sky between the black smokestack of the laundry and the purposeless classic cupola crowning a dormitory. His laughter broke in spasms as if jerking itself from the giddying realization in his mind which had released it.

"I'm lying to myself," he said out loud. "I'm lying to myself! What's important to me is that August is *free* – not one of *them!* She's free and she's a woman, not a girl – and we are not apart, not really!"

He moved on toward the post office without any consciousness of his feet propelling him or his legs supporting him. He saw his face reflected in the glass of the delivery entrance door. At that single moment it was fixed in a curious grimace, still of laughter but tightening into a strange sobriety. He shook his head to clear it and then opened the door with shaking fingers.

He collected Dr. White's mail first and fastened it with an elastic band. Then he went to his own box and withdrew the one letter in it. It was from Professor Elwige.

Dear Abbott:

I'm afraid I have some rather disappointing news. You have done a first-rate job – absolutely first-rate; but the Head, who has the utmost respect for your choice of subject and the greatest sympathy with your whole approach, makes the point that one does not use one's own mother for generalizing on the habits of women. The Chadleys are recognizable, Abbott. It seems to the Head a matter of bad taste that your illustrative material should be drawn from a family the head of which is a benefactor of this university and who has just accepted the invitation of the Board of Trustees to become one of its members. He agrees that portions of your study can stand, of course, but he feels it mandatory that you support your points with additional samplings and alter the form of your presentation to remove from it its present personal, literary tone.

I regret this setback, Abbott. I did not anticipate it. Come down as soon as you can for a conference.

As always,

ELWIGE

Without rereading it, Walter tore the letter into tiny pieces, let the bits flutter from his opened hand onto the floor and walked away from them. At noon, before he went to the cafeteria for his lunch, he telephoned Dunmeade.

"Mr. Chadley," he said to Fenton, "I should like to come into Newtown this afternoon to see you. I can be there at two o'clock if that time is convenient for you."

"Is there something wrong, Mr. Abbott?" Fenton asked. "Your voice sounds rather strained."

"Yes," Walter admitted. "There is something wrong."

There was a momentary silence before Fenton then consented soberly, "I will be waiting for you in my study at two o'clock, Mr. Abbott."

Walter did not take the chair which Fenton proffered. He strode instead to the narrow wall between the open windows taking a stance instantly made dramatic by the erratic blowing of the silk gauze curtains against his legs.

"Mr. Chadley," he said directly to Fenton's solicitous and obviously anxious face, "a scholar has no life if he hasn't the right to freely inquire and freely report. I am fighting for my life this afternoon."

Fenton stared at him, incredulity rapidly replacing his previous expression of concern. He too had remained standing, but with Walter's unbelievable statement, he sank into his old wing chair, feeling for it beneath him while he kept his eyes upon Walter's face.

"Against what or against whom are you fighting, Mr. Abbott?" he asked in a low voice.

"I am fighting against you, Mr. Chadley. You are both the 'what' and the 'whom,'" Walter answered. He was holding his elbows close to his sides, pushing his hands deep into his pockets. His suffering was plain upon his face. The curtains writhed about his ankles from the hot gusts of summer wind and there was a long silence before Fenton spoke.

"I do not understand what you are trying to tell me, Mr.

Abbott," he said at last, his breath so stoppered by emotion that his voice was faint. "I can see that you are quite distressed. Be patient with me and try again, Mr. Abbott. Tell me why you feel I am your enemy when I have never been anything but your most respectful admirer and friend."

At this response to his accusation, Walter whipped around to the window at his right to stand with his back to Fenton, his face hidden.

"Do you remember once asking me the subject of my thesis, Mr. Chadley?"

"Yes, I remember. It was when I was ill in the Doughtry Memorial Hospital."

"Do you remember the title I quoted you?"

"I cannot quote the title, no. But I remember that you were beginning a study of those changes which take place when a community progresses from an agricultural to an industrial center."

"You have a good memory, Mr. Chadley. That is what I began to write as my doctor's thesis. But after I had been in Dunmeade a short while tutoring Ralph, I obtained permission from my supervisor at the university to change the subject of my study to 'Class and Caste Ideologies in Southern Society, with Special Reference to Patterns of Paternalism.' I began to record in detail the life at Dunmeade, particularly your attitudes and opinions and actions. Last week I submitted my finished paper for acceptance for publication, without which I cannot obtain my degree. This morning, Mr. Chadley, I learned something which has motivated this final and unanticipated example of paternalism in which you and I are the principals. This is the climaxing point of my study, Mr. Chadley. I am forced to ask your permission to allow my paper to be published!"

"Why, Mr. Abbott?"

"Because you are a benefactor and trustee of the university, and because my sponsor and the authorities and my fellow scholars do not dare to risk offending you even to advance truth."

"What you have written is a criticism of what I am, Mr. Abbott. Is that correct?"

"I have only observed and recorded, Mr. Chadley. I have not judged you."

"Please turn around, Mr. Abbott, so that I may see your face," Fenton requested softly. As he did so he stood. Looking directly into Walter's eyes he asked, "What would your judgment of me have been if you *had* written it, Mr. Abbott?"

And Walter replied without hesitation, "The one which is implied in the study, Mr. Chadley."

"Thank you for your honesty," said Fenton. He turned and walked to the door. Standing against the frame so that Walter might pass before him, he said, "At this moment, I cannot answer your request, Mr. Abbott. When I am able to, I will communicate with you."

It seemed to Fenton that his next hour was the hour of his greatest aging. He wondered if ever there were any learning which prepared the spirit for its trials. Surely his heart stood naked before the future, its stings in evidence and the fingers of his mind powerless with sorrow and shock and unable to withdraw them. So he had been robbed of anger and its healing.

I must remind myself of my blessings, he thought in desperation. My blessings refute critical judgments of me. If my life has not been good, then why have I been so rewarded? . . . And clearest in his mind, to support him in his struggle for reassurance, was the vision of August. He was impelled to seek her out; for in her independent manner and unrestrained expressiveness he could view the superficial aspect of the deepest and widest measure of his generous impulses. This he needed to do.

He spoke to O'Smyre in the greenhouse.

"Did Miss August take out a car today? Or were you to fetch her home from the college?" he asked. Gilberta was away from Dunmeade also that afternoon and he did not know whether she or August had the small car.

"I was to fetch her at five o'clock, Mr. Chadley," O'Smyre answered.

"Go on with whatever Mrs. Chadley has left for you to do here," Fenton instructed him, "I'm going out to Marion myself and I'll drive Miss August in with me."

"Yes, sir, Mr. Chadley," O'Smyre said. He stood respectfully holding his trowel in one hand at his side until Fenton had finished with him and was gone. Then he went back to his work.

As Fenton backed his car into the drive, he glanced toward the greenhouse. The midafternoon sun penetrating the glass panes illumined the interior of boxes and sprinklers and rows of pots into a clear and ordered form before the eye. Fenton saw O'Smyre bent at his particular occupation amongst the blooms and foliage.

At that moment he remembered something which had long ago ceased to have any importance for him, although it had been the reason for his engaging O'Smyre. O'Smyre was an educated man with a college degree, and, at the time he had persuaded O'Smyre to come to Dunmeade, a teacher in the college to which Fenton had wanted to send Ralph. O'Smyre had taught horticulture and aspired to become a full professor.

. . . I shall never know, of course, if he has ever regretted coming to Dunmeade. It is not in my power to confer a higher degree upon him for his years of work and practical research here. But I have rewarded him as I could, and he has brought up a family in greater comfort than a teacher's salary would have permitted. He enjoys our confidence and respect for his ability with the flowers, and Mrs. Chadley very generously admits her dependence upon him. Could he have spent his years and used his education to any better advantage? . . . These thoughts were themselves answers; the question which had preceded them had been in his conscience and he had not let it shape into the blunt query: Is it the salary of a horticulturist that I pay him, or is it the wages of a servant who is my gardener and chauffeur?

Fenton accelerated the speed of the car as he passed out of the gates and drove with a kind of doggedness away from the memory of Walter Abbott's earnest face and the quiet voice which returned in his ear: "You will find no criticism, Mr. Chadley. I have only observed and recorded."

On the road to Marion College he leaned forward, away from the upholstery of the seat, and let what breeze was fanned by the motion of the car pass across his shoulders and head. It was the dry heat of late July and the sun was even and harsh across the fields of slowly yellowing cornstalks. But Fenton looked only forward at the road slipping away beneath the wheels as in a strange and exaggerated way he devoured the distance between him and August and the surety he sought.

He did not have to drive in to the entrance of the college to reach the building which was temporarily Mr. Aitken's headquarters and the studio in which his classes met. It was gained by a dirt road which ran along beside the front campus for approximately six hundred feet. The road continued past the stained frame building, winding and narrowing into only a country lane two miles farther on. The farmer with whom Mr. Abbott lived owned the first house beyond the college. Fenton could see the glitter of the sun on the lightning rods along its roof and the snout of the red silo against the smooth blue heaven above.

He wiped the dust from his glasses and put them in their case. Then he cleaned his other pair for close-range sight and put them on and patted at his hair and went up the short walk to the door.

There was a small vestibule, for the building had once been used as a chapel and also as a meeting place for the students' organizations. Here Fenton paused, taken suddenly with a kind of timidity at intruding during Mr. Aitken's teaching hours. He listened for the sound of a voice giving instructions or perhaps one of the girls' voices asking a question. But it was quiet inside the studio. Perhaps they were all busy at their easels, he thought. He recalled the morning he had gone with August to her school to invite her class to the Christmas party at Dunmeade. The children's heads had been bent in last-minute reviews of their lessons before the starting bell and he had been touched by the sight of their absorption and industry. He expected to see such a scene now when he entered the room before him.

But he was disappointed.

There was no one at all in the studio. The high vaulted ceiling allowed a coolness to the room and he stood alone in it looking about at the drawings and sketches tacked to improvised panels of beaverboard along the walls. The unenclosed beams above had been rigged with pulleys to enable a very large canvas on its frame to be lowered and raised. Fenton looked up at it and then unconsciously moved out from under it. He went farther forward and looked in the open door of Mr. Aitken's office which had been a kind of cloakroom in the days when visiting speakers had come to address an assembly of students there. Mr. Aitken was not there but a stained smock hung on one of the hooks and the floor had been stacked with rolls of drawing paper and other teaching equipment. At the far end was a table supporting a typewriter and before it a stool.

Unlike the disorder which had characterized Mr. Aitken's rooms over the grocery store, this place had a neatness which surprised Fenton. It bespoke Mr. Aitken's efficient approach to his teaching responsibilities. Fenton was pleased. He turned away and started back across the long studio, stopping once or twice to examine some of the pupils' work tacked to the beaverboard panels.

He did not see any sketches bearing August's signature until he came upon a small panel braced like an easel and standing in front of the others. It was movable. He leaned to examine the drawings fastened to it and recognized the preliminary work August had done to submit to the committee. She had now added notations here and there in pencil describing the colors she had worked out for the various sections of the picture and the dimensions of the figures and other forms. A warming emotion began to grow in Fenton as he looked at her plans before him. It was as if he were looking at a map of a journey she proposed taking. A tremendous pride swelled in him. He gazed down at her copy of the *Newtown Guidebook* which she had fastened to the panel alongside her drawings. She had pinned back one of the pages. Apparently it had on it a statement which she intended to illustrate among the merging scenes in the full picture. Her conscientiousness and system were very evident.

He moved on and then looked among the large easels to see if August's painting itself were set up. But he did not find it. He had not asked to see it and she had never invited him out to the college to inspect her progress at any stage. There had been a few times when he had noticed that she seemed depressed over her work. But she had made no complaints about the magnitude of the task and he had been relieved to see the moods pass as they had come – apparently without any real reason provoking them. He had never questioned her for fear of suggesting to her mind that he had some anxiety concerning her ability to accomplish such an ambitious picture.

He began to wonder if perhaps Mr. Aitken had not taken the class on a sketching trip in the neighborhood and if it would not be better to return to Dunmeade and let O'Smyre call for August as previously arranged.

He had been greatly restored in spirit by his view of the work going on under Mr. Aitken's tutelage. Pulling Marion College out of its dilemma had been a truly worthy effort, and if, after all the combined effort put upon making it a forward institution, he lost his investment – there would certainly have been other rewards.

He walked to the entrance and there in the vestibule came face to face with Mr. Aitken entering the door.

"Good afternoon, Mr. Chadley," the artist greeted him with a smile. "I have been expecting you."

"Have you indeed, Mr. Aitken?" replied Fenton, puzzled and a little thrown off. "Why, may I ask?"

"To ask me again how your daughter is getting along," said Mr. Aitken. "The question has more pertinence, now. Don't you think?" He waved Fenton back into the studio and followed just behind him.

"I don't see that it has," protested Fenton. "My daughter's happiness and prospects in her chosen career have always concerned me deeply. No doubt the fact that you are a bachelor makes it hard for you to understand parental feelings in these matters." Fenton felt that Mr. Aitken had been unnecessarily contesting and rude.

"I am not a bachelor, Mr. Chadley," the artist answered with a certain softening of his tone and no humor. "I am a widower. I have a grown son who works for the Municipal Transit System of a large city in the West. I have two small grandchildren." He did not allow Fenton to interrupt with the apology which had come instantly to Fenton's lips. He wiped his hand across the stubble of his beard and concluded with his strange alive eyes on Fenton's face, "I never earned enough to pay my son's way through a college. But with what I did give him, and what he earned himself at different jobs, he got through in five years with fair grades. He's safe today in civil service."

"None of this information was given in our correspondence before you came here, Mr. Aitken, and I had no way of knowing these facts of your private life," Fenton defended himself. "I'm very sorry to have made the remark I did. You seemed to challenge my affection for my daughter and I retorted without thinking." He hesitated then, but came with effort to confess, "August is not my own child. She is my deceased brother's child and my stepdaughter. I have no children of my own." He could feel a quivering inside him as he exposed his inferior position to that of the true parent before him. He wanted earnestly to make amends for his mistake.

"I know that, Mr. Chadley," said Mr. Aitken, matter-of-factly. He was moving to the side wall at the right toward what seemed to be a sort of winch or windlass apparatus affixed to a beam support. He began to turn the crank to release the length of rope wound upon it and Fenton followed his gaze to the large canvas drawn up near the ceiling in the center of the room. The canvas was being slowly and carefully lowered to eye level.

"Miss Chadley showed me the clay heads her father executed.

She brought them out here one at a time. We discussed them very seriously and at great length. She has never made up her mind about them and I will not help her," Aaron Aitken said.

This intelligence startled Fenton. He continued to watch the giant canvas being lowered before him.

He wondered what had made August seek Mr. Aitken's judgment of her father's work. It seemed to him that she had invited an unnecessary invasion of family privacy when she solicited the criticism of a man who had known nothing of Lesley. And then he realized in the instant of his resentment that Lesley would not have wanted to have his work considered for his intentions, but only for his accomplishment in it. At the moment Fenton was turning in the spin of confusing and overlapping reactions to all that had happened to him from the hour when Mr. Abbott had made his stunning and, as yet, unanswered appeal.

He stood silent, observing the thickly colored painting come to rest at eye level before him.

"This is what you came to see, isn't it, Mr. Chadley?" the artist asked him, dryly, as, with a mechanical twisting of the ropes, he secured the canvas to stand taut.

Fenton did not understand. He backed away from it. It was a blur of coarse patches of color caught and divided by labyrinthine black lines. He moved back and back from it until he stood under the lintel of the door and distance had shrunk the masses and outlines into a breathtaking scene. Then he knew what it was.

It was August's painting for the war memorial auditorium. It was *Newtown!*

Fenton felt as if the building had disappeared from about him and no floor supported him, and suddenly he were there alone confronting the picture with a cold and motionless space between, a space which gave a terrible clarity to the image of the city and the figures drawn to it and supporting it. It was *ugly*. His heart pounded so that it seemed in some unconscious way to be beating against any encroachment of the painting upon his already shocked vision. He stood there nearly ill with disappointment and offense at what he could not deny, even in his bewilderment as to how it came to be — August's view of her city, the view which stemmed in a terrible projection from the life he had given her. His gaze, drawn to it in sorrow, could not be broken and he could not turn away. He perceived more than he understood. He understood more than he could ever seek from her in an answer. This was the answer. And never asked would be the question.

He heard Mr. Aitken say to him, "It is incomplete, of course, Mr. Chadley." But he could not indicate that he had heard. A pervious bitterness which he had never known entered and surfeited and so, finally, in its excess dulled his mind. His sight stayed upon the most striking single figure, glistening and bold — the figure of the farm boy with his dream leading him to the city. He examined the painted gross insensitive hands dropping the plow, the strange blind eyes, seeming at once to be opaque and yet transparent, as if their reflection of the city beckoning before him were also the exposure of an internal unworthy design of desire, a startling and repelling decoration seen through glass.

Suddenly Fenton covered his face with his hands, shutting out the avid smile of the blind farm boy. Through his fingers he heard himself gasp, "Is it a good painting? Mr. Aitken, I must know!"

And the artist answered, "Yes, Mr. Chadley, it is a good painting. But you do not have to hang it, of course."

The wrenching protest *No!* screamed inside him, but he could not utter it. He could not defend himself against such a suggestion — that the power was his to prohibit the hanging of the picture.

When he removed his hands from his face, he saw that Mr. Aitken, perhaps out of some strange mercy, had begun to wind the painting back to safety above their heads. His back was to Fenton.

"Will my daughter be returning here for dismissal, Mr. Aitken?" Fenton asked him. The ordinary question smarted like an acid in his throat. He felt so estranged from August that to call her his daughter seemed an uncontainable affront to his heart. She could not possibly feel any true kinship existing between them. Her impression of the life which surrounded them, and of which she was as much a part as he, was an impression so foreign to his own that he was set apart from her by his new and shaking knowledge of it. In him was a dread of meeting her now, of suspecting her affection, of searching her eyes for the deceit he feared behind them.

"Miss Chadley escorted a group of summer school students on a field trip," Mr. Aitken replied to his question. "I don't expect her here again. It will be too late for her to work inside." He had finished hoisting the canvas up and was now knotting the ropes to fasten it, still with his back to Fenton.

"I shall wait for her before the Administration Building," said Fenton. "If, by chance, she should come back for some of her pencils or something, would you tell her where I am?"

"Yes, Mr. Chadley," said the artist. "I will tell her."

Fenton took the one step remaining to enter the vestibule from where he stood under the door lintel. He murmured, "Thank you." Then he walked out of the building and to his car and, with a certain slowness and precision, started the motor. He was turning in the roadway, backing awkwardly and uncertainly toward a dry ditch at the side, when he saw August coming toward him. She waved the silk scarf which she snatched from her head. The three girls with her, and a little child in overalls who had apparently taken up with them, left her and stepped onto a footpath leading to the dormitories.

"Hey!" she called out to him. "Wait a minute. I'll direct you." Then she ran the few yards left between them and, taking a position at the roadside, she began to guide him as he backed the big car still closer to the shallow ditch. Then, following her instructions, he brought it forward, twisting the steering wheel sharply to make a short turn. She directed him to reverse again, and then when it was certain that he could cut straight forward and be headed down the center of the road to the highway, she waved him to stop and then she got in beside him.

"This is a surprise," she said. "Did you have business with Dr. White?"

"Well," he evaded, "there is always some business or other

about the school." He was conscious of her eyes upon him and the innocence of her simple inquiry. He wanted not to talk but to drive on without thinking of anything. He wanted to go home, to Dunmeade. There in its seclusion he would be most private and safe to reflect upon the strange and unbelievable gussets of knowledge which had been so rudely and unexpectedly let into the garment of his experience this day. But he could not move toward the sanctuary he longed for, numb and insensitive. His life was changing in that hour. And despite his longing, he was urged from peace to final battle.

"I have been wondering, dear," he said, "if I might not have imposed too great an obligation upon you when I persuaded you to paint a commemorative picture to present in your father's memory. I'm afraid I might have put it into your mind that you had some duty to complete a work of art to which could be affixed our family name. That is not true, of course. And if you are straining to accomplish this ambitious painting, you are not to go on with it to the detriment of your health and nerves."

"I won't say it isn't a strain," replied August. "But I like it, in a way. There isn't much more to do. Only the finishing of the over-painting in oils." She said it with no expression of excitement or happiness in her voice. They were statements she made.

"There are other things which are important if you are to live a good life, dear. I have been troubled that perhaps in our concentration upon helping you to forge ahead in your art work we might have neglected to give the proper attention to those things."

"What things do you mean?" August asked bluntly. "All this sounds as if Mother has been at you. Mother got it into her head years ago that if I became an artist I would end up an old maid. That is a fate worse than death in Mother's opinion."

Fenton did not answer at once. He pretended to have sniffed a dust particle into his nostril and at the first stop light on the outskirts of the city he drew alongside the curb and, with apology to August, blew his nose.

"Well, dear, as a matter of fact, I have been thinking recently on the subject of marriage," he said. "In a few days, you will come of age. Your mother and I are going to have a small reception for you when cool weather sets in. The real meaning of presenting you to the adult world is that we acknowledge you to have attained sufficient years to belong among us. Marriage is the next and correct step from there."

"I intend to get married," said August. "Please don't worry about it. I am going to get married and I am going to get somewhere as an artist, too."

"Of course, dear," Fenton said. He could feel the never-outgrown belligerence coming into her tone. He did not want to quarrel. All the skill he could muster was needed now to sway her from the very course he had pressed her to pursue.

They rode in silence until they were near the old Barron house where noisy and deceitful Earl had lived. August looked up at it as they passed and a strange little smile came on her mouth. Then, as if the memory of that old child's heartbreak provoked her to confess suddenly now to Fenton, she said, "I am going to marry Mr. Abbott."

"Are you, dear?" Fenton heard himself say, not believing that he could speak.

"Yes." She confirmed it with a curious emphasis as if she were struggling against her voice or her courage or her will crumbling beneath suspected impossibility despite her resolution. "You will have to help me."

"Should I have to, dear?" he asked. He held the steering wheel firmly and turned the car into Dunmeade's gates. Within him a shameful sickness was beginning and he prayed to reach the garage quickly and stop the machine and escape her.

"No," she answered, "you shouldn't have to help me. But he'll never ask me to marry him, and I must find a way to make him see that it doesn't matter if I ask him. One day, he can be the president of Marion College; Dr. White is an old man. Marion College will belong to all of us then. That will make a difference. And the college will be different, too. It can be a wonderful college."

"Does Mr. Abbott want you to be his wife, dear?" Fenton asked. "You must be sure." They were in the garage and Fenton had turned off the ignition and he spoke softly in the sudden quiet of that strange rude place for such a conversation.

"I'm sure," she said. "And I'm sure about me, too. You've got to tell him that he can succeed Dr. White when Dr. White retires. You've got to help me — at least that much. That really isn't much."

Fenton did not answer.

"I'll tell you when to speak to him," August said. She had not waited for his promise. She had been as certain of it as she had been of wheedling filberts or fudge or nickels from him when she had begged behind her mother's back.

She opened the door on her side and did not wait for him to leave his side and help her. Very quickly, as if she were suddenly embarrassed, she leaned and kissed his cheek. Then she left him to follow.

Fenton put his head down against the hard rubber rim of the steering wheel. His glasses were pressed into his face, the edges of the lenses cutting into his flesh. He did not move. There, between his two pains, he came to wisdom.

Love cannot be earned by love. It is not grateful. It is not reciprocal. It draws indiscriminately its own persecutor or a like responsive heart. It is, for some, a thing of hopeless mystery full of dark turnings. It is, for others, a thing to contemplate with bitterness and come at last to squeeze from a wounded heart like a nettle. But for him, love was a live necessity and he had come to see that lack of reciprocity in kind could not be condemned. To condemn the object of his own excessive devotion was to indulge in himself what had become in its extreme no longer a blessing he bestowed but a curse.

Serving, bearing, and loving — these were not means to an end, a reward. They were each an end and a reward. Out of such ultimate learning came the power to contain the true statement of human relationships. He knew now the answer he would give

Walter Abbott. He knew the barbs of anger and offense he would bear with August when her great ugly painting was hung. He knew the shape of his own life – as it had been, and as it would be until he died. And he honored what he was with his acceptance of it.